HERE COMES
the
RIDE

**Center Point
Large Print**

**This Large Print Book carries the
Seal of Approval of N.A.V.H.**

HERE COMES
the
RIDE

The Andi McConnell Mysteries

Lorena McCourtney

CENTER POINT PUBLISHING
THORNDIKE, MAINE

This Center Point Large Print edition is published in
the year 2011 by arrangement with the author.
Contact the author through the website:
www.lorenamccourtney.com

The text of this Large Print edition is unabridged.
In other aspects, this book may vary
from the original edition.
Printed in the United States of America
on permanent paper.
Set in 16-point Times New Roman type.

ISBN: 978-1-61173-051-7

Library of Congress Cataloging-in-Publication Data

McCourtney, Lorena.
 Here comes the ride : the Andi McConnell mysteries / Lorena McCourtney. —
Center point large print ed.
 p. cm.
 ISBN 978-1-61173-051-7 (library binding : alk. paper)
 1. Limousine services—Fiction. 2. Washington (State)—Fiction.
 3. Large type books. I. Title.
PS3563.C3449H47 2011
813′.54—dc22

2010052651

Chapter One

"Oh, no. It's *black*."

The woman in the doorway didn't even look at me. Towel poised at her throat, she stared past my shoulder at my limousine parked in her circular drive, as if it were a junker with crumpled fenders and a bumper sticker advertising mud wrestling.

"Pammi will not be pleased."

This was a first. No other client of my new limousine service had objected to black. "What color did Pammi have in mind?"

"White, of course. White is the *only* color for a wedding."

"Pammi is the bride?"

"Yes. Pamela Gibson. My stepdaughter. This is a joyous occasion, and black is much too, oh, you know, *funereal*."

I'm not sure what hackles are, but I immediately felt mine rise defensively. The freshly washed limo, sleek and elegant as a black jewel, gleamed in the August sunshine. I felt like rushing out and draping myself protectively over its long hood. *There, there. What do we care what picky Pammi thinks?*

"Perhaps it would be best if Pammi engaged

some other limousine service then," I said stiffly.

I didn't want to lose a customer, but this wasn't a big job. My friend Keegan "Fitz" Fitzgerald had said that all it involved was driving the bride from the house to the wedding, then ferrying the newlyweds to the Vigland marina, where they would board Fitz's son's charter sailboat for their honeymoon.

The woman shook her head. A blue headband held back an impressive tousle of blond hair. She'd apparently come to the door from a workout session, because she was still in Spandex shorts and a skimpy top exposing a midsection taut enough to bounce chocolate chips. Which is probably as close as she ever came to a relationship with chocolate chips. Unlike some of us.

"No, we can't do that," she said. "There have already been two limo services from Olympia that didn't work out."

The license plate her unlucky numbers? Upholstery the wrong material? Or perhaps Pammi the Picky Princess's demands made them simply decide, no way.

The woman tilted her head, and her expression brightened. "But by the time we decorate with flowers and streamers, I think we can make it do."

It would "do"? My hackles were still stiff as porcupine quills. I was ready to say that as far as

I was concerned Pammi could ride to her wedding in a wheelbarrow, when the stepmother said the magic words that made me swallow my retort.

"We have numerous guests flying in who'll need to be met at Sea-Tac and driven back later for their flights home. Plus various local trips. So what I need is to engage you full-time for at least five days. I assume you have an hourly or daily rate?"

A five-day job? Whoo-ee! My limousine service hadn't been up and running long, but I'd never had any gig like this.

"In fact, I'm thinking it would be best if you stayed here at the house so you'd be available whenever you're needed. There's a room next to our cook/housekeeper's room. Would that be possible?"

For a five-day job, I'd sleep in the backyard in a pup tent. With a pup in residence. But I controlled any crude display of eagerness and said, "Yes, I could arrange that."

"Good." She gave me a warm smile and held out a hand with short but shimmery nails. "Forgive my manners. I'm afraid this wedding has me to the point where I don't know if I'm coming or going. I'm Michelle Gibson. As I said, Pammi's stepmother."

"Andi McConnell. Andi's Limouzeen Service."

The firmness of her handshake belied the delicate appearance of the slim hand.

7

"What Pammi has in mind is the wedding of the century, you know. I just wish she'd given me more than a few weeks to plan it." She rolled spectacular blue eyes. "Sometimes I get a bit overwrought, I'm afraid."

I could understand that. Big weddings often take months of preparation. Another woman has already reserved limo time with me for her daughter's wedding six months off.

"Come inside and we'll discuss the details. Can you give me a minute to go shower and throw on some different clothes?"

"Certainly."

"You can wait in the Africa Room."

She led me through a wide entry hall, where windows looked out on a lush expanse of grass sweeping down to the long inlet that connected Vigland Bay with Puget Sound, and past a staircase winding to the second floor.

The Africa Room had all the office necessities: computer, printer, fax, copier, a couple of file cabinets, and a small leather sofa, but African masks and spears flanked a leopard skin on the wall. The skin had the head attached, open mouth showing a lot of teeth. Beautiful, but a little jungle-creepy for my taste.

"Would you like iced tea or a soft drink?"

"Thanks, no, I'm fine."

"I'll be back in a minute then. Make yourself comfortable."

I'd been inside this house before, long ago, when my former husband and I sold new and antique furniture. It had been occupied then by eccentric sisters who needed to dispose of several rooms of old furniture. The exterior was still vintage, with a wide front porch, two huge dormer windows above, and a gothic-type tower on one corner, which was where this Africa Room was located. The interior had been considerably remodeled. The dark rooms I remembered were now lightened by big windows and white walls and woodwork. Nice, but a certain old-fashioned warmth and charm had vanished with the remodeling, replaced by a chilly, lightbulb-in-the-refrigerator feeling.

Was the office hers or her husband's? I resisted an urge to peek at the contents of the papers scattered across the desk. I was no longer in detective mode, I reminded myself sternly, as I had been when I first acquired the limo and found myself tracking down a murderer. Although peeking was still tempting. Reading upside down, I deciphered a letterhead that read *Steffan Productions*, with a Los Angeles address.

Good thing I hadn't gone further than that minuscule peek, however, because Michelle was already returning. She was in dark blue sweats now, barefoot, damp hair tied back in a swingy ponytail, accompanied by a whiff of some heady perfume. Thirties had been my original guess on

9

her age, but now I noted some lines around her eyes and decided that determined exercise and a diet regimen had probably preserved her nicely. Fortyish, then.

"Now, about the dates." She sat down at the desk and put on glasses, small, no frames, and flipped pages on a calendar. "The wedding is Friday evening, the twenty-fourth. So you should be here on the twenty-first and stay until at least the day after the wedding. I'll arrange for someone from the florist's shop to decorate the limo on Friday."

"Where will the wedding be held?"

"Right here. They'll set up the tent the day before. One end will be arranged with seating for the ceremony, the other will be set up for the reception and dinner. Sit-down, of course. Prime rib and lobster, catered by a company from Tacoma. With live music and dancing afterwards."

Prime rib and lobster. Too bad I'd be relegated to waiting outside in the limo.

"You won't actually be needing the limo for transportation to the wedding then."

"Oh, yes indeed! Pammi and I can't walk from the house over to the tent in our gowns."

Michelle shuffled through a drawer with a familiarity that said this was her desk, not the husband's. She brought out a thick file. "Then there's the ice sculpture. . . . But they'll be delivering that in a refrigerated van, of course."

I pictured a swan floating in a punch bowl, a graceful image dispelled by Michelle's next words.

"It's a life-sized bride and groom. A sculptor is creating it especially for Pammi's wedding."

I've heard about some extravagant weddings, but none that included a life-sized ice sculpture. That would leave some puddle, wouldn't it? I wondered how the husband/father was feeling about the cost of Pammi's wedding of the century.

Michelle went through more plans, checking off items. The wedding gown, which was being flown in from a designer down in LA. The cake, six tiers, with bridges to side cakes and a sterling silver ornament of bride and groom on top. Hair and makeup people. Photographer. The fog machine, which would deliver an ethereal mist around the bride as she walked down the aisle.

I wondered why she was telling me all this, then decided she wanted to make sure I realized this was the Wedding of the Century. "Her father will be escorting Pammi down the aisle?"

"Unfortunately her father passed away several years ago. I'll be giving the bride away."

Unusual but nice, I decided. So Michelle herself must be footing the bill. Very generous of a stepmother, especially with a stepdaughter making demands on the scale of a Hollywood production number.

"There are a few other details, but that's it for

the moment." She removed the glasses and rubbed her temples. "I can count on you for nine o'clock on the morning of the twenty-first?"

"You certainly can." I realized we hadn't discussed price yet. I had a daily rate, although so far I'd never had a job lengthy enough to use it. I calculated a reasonable amount for overnight and named a five-day figure, although I was prepared to negotiate.

She didn't bother. "Yes, that'll be fine. I'll give you a deposit now."

She wrote out a check for a fourth of the amount while I did another silent *Whoo-ee!* My daughter, Sarah, and granddaughter, Rachel, were both starting at the University of Florida. Now I'd be able to send them something to help out. *Hey, God, thank You!*

Check firmly in hand, I started toward the door.

"Oh, and if this works out," she called, "I'll need you again in September. I think arrival by limo would be appropriate for the grand opening of my new health club. Maybe you've seen the sign? The Change Your World Fitness Center."

"That's where they've been remodeling the old Penny's building?"

"Right. The new sign just went up yesterday."

An impressive sign it was, the name written in glittery silver, with an icon of a lightning bolt branding a symbol of the earth, the whole thing dwarfing any other business sign in Vigland.

"I can reserve the date for you now, if you'd like."

"Yes, let's do that." She handed me a sheet from a memo pad with a date in September scribbled on it. "So far I haven't been able to devote as much time to the grand opening as I should, what with all the wedding details to take care of. But things should calm down after Pammi and Sterling are on their honeymoon."

Outside, I congratulated myself on my good fortune. The bride might be a charter member of Bridezillas, Inc., but a five-day job—!

I was halfway down the wide steps when I spotted a figure leaning over the back of the limo. My first instinct was to yell, *Hey, get away from there!* But then I realized this couldn't be someone just wandering by, not with that security gate at the end of the driveway.

So I held my yell and approached with a more cooperative attitude. Until I saw what she was doing.

Chapter Two

Whoever she was, she'd instantly found the lone flaw in my glossy limo. She'd loosened the circles of painted duct tape with which I'd covered the bullet holes in the trunk and now had a finger stuck in each of them. My start-up business had been doing nicely, but not nicely enough that I could afford a whole new lid for the limo's trunk. Especially after the expense of getting all the other damage repaired.

"Are you looking for something?" I inquired with as much politeness as I could muster.

She was perhaps fifteen, a little shorter than my five-foot-six, with an unruly mass of dark hair, eyebrows to make Groucho Marx envious, and a figure on the pudgy side. A skinned-up knee was probably the result of the skateboard overturned on the grass.

I looked at the skateboard with a certain envy. I've long had this secret desire to fly down a hill on a skateboard, a desire unfortunately not compatible with aging bones and joints.

"How'd the bullet holes get here?" she asked.

"What makes you think they're bullet holes?"

"Limousines don't get termites."

Smart-alecky, but true. "A couple of thugs shot at it."

She removed a finger and put an eye to the hole. The nail looked chewed on. "Don't the holes leak when it rains?"

I started to point out that that was what the circles of duct tape she'd removed were for, but decided to ignore the question. "Are you Pammi's little sister?"

"Are you one of Michelle's cronies?"

14

Crony. Not necessarily an insult, but not something I could remember being called before.

"I'm the chauffeur for Pammi's wedding. Andi's Limouzeen Service." I pulled a card out of the pocket of my black uniform and handed it to her.

"Why the misspelling?"

"Long story." I wasn't about to explain right now. "Will Pammi object to that along with her objection to the color of the limo?"

She hesitated, then said, "She doesn't like being called Pammi. Especially with an *i*."

"That's what Michelle calls her."

"That's because Michelle thinks it sounds all fuzzy-wuzzy cute and cozy. What Michelle would really like to call her is This Pest of a Stepdaughter I Got Stuck With."

Definite hostility here. Protective of the older sister?

"Michelle is going to an incredible amount of effort and expense to make Pammi's wedding a success. Perhaps Pammi should be more appreciative."

"Yeah, right."

The girl's cynical tone made me look closer, and I realized she could be older than I first thought. The hazel eyes had a definite fifteen-going-on-forty flintiness.

"And I told you," she added, "she doesn't like to be called Pammi."

"What does she like to be called?"

"Pam. Pamela." Pause. "Her dad used to call her Pixie."

"Should I call her Pixie?"

"No. She's not a Pixie now. The people she went to school with thought she was one of those quiet types who might any day blast into a post office or school and shoot everyone in sight."

I felt a dawning realization. Baggy khaki shorts, oversized yellow T-shirt with So What? written across it, no makeup. Not what I expected of a Picky Princess who demanded everything from a life-sized ice sculpture to a wedding gown from LA. But . . .

"You're Pammi . . . Pamela, aren't you?"

She shrugged, then, with undisguised belligerence, added, "So?"

Now I noticed what I hadn't earlier, that she was wearing a ring on her left hand, a small diamond in an old-fashioned white gold setting.

"Is any of what you said true?"

"That people thought I might attack a school or post office? Or that I might actually do it?"

"Either one."

"I think some of them thought I might really do it."

"What about the ones who didn't think that?"

"They just thought I was a nerdy, geeky, fat slob."

"So, would you ever really do it?"

"I guess not. The only people I murder are in my stories."

She sounded regretful, disappointed with herself; but perhaps, as proof of her inability to do harm, a cat appeared out of the nearby woods and twined itself around her legs. He had crystal-blue eyes and some Siamese markings, but a few misplaced splotches of gray suggested his genetic pool was a little swampy. She swooped up the cat and snuggled him under her chin. "This is Phreddie. With a Ph, not Freddie with an F."

She'd asked why I misspelled *limousine,* so I figured I could challenge her. "That's an unusual spelling. How come?"

She almost smiled. "He's an unusual cat. He likes broccoli. And he's a very good judge of character. I found him wandering around the post office all skinny and hungry."

We were getting off track here, and I jumped back on it. "Why didn't you tell me right off who you are?"

She hadn't outright lied, but neither had she corrected my errors about age and identity.

"What difference does it make? People always think I'm younger than I am." With a sly smirkiness, she added, "That should come in handy when I'm your age, shouldn't it?"

Her tone suggested my age rivaled that of the ground she was standing on. *Five-day job,* I reminded myself. "So, how old are you?"

"Why?"

"Why not?" I challenged.

That seemed to satisfy logic for her. "I'm nineteen. How old are you?"

I felt like reminding her that polite young ladies don't ask that of their elders, but instead I said, "I had a sixtieth birthday earlier this year." Prime time, Fitz calls it, though I sometimes have to grit my teeth to remind myself of that.

"Does the limo have a name?"

"You mean like Belinda or Black Beauty or Cleopatra? No, it's a working limo, not a pet with wheels."

"Good. I think naming a car or a computer or anything like that is ridiculous." She abruptly changed the subject. "Were you in the limo when it was shot at?"

"Yes. I was driving."

"You must have been running away, if only the trunk got hit."

Definite disparagement in that observation. Apparently I was supposed to have stood my ground and returned fire. I was annoyed with myself, but I rose to the bait anyway.

"The windshield right in front of me was hit several times. Also the passenger's side window. One headlight was shot out, along with a tire. Then they shot a couple more times and hit the trunk when I was getting away."

"How come you didn't get killed?" she asked

in a tone skeptical of my story. Probably disappointed too.

"The glass was bulletproof. Bullets don't bounce off like ping-pong balls, but they don't get through. They do ruin the glass."

"Is it still bulletproof?" Looking interested, cat tucked securely under one arm, she swiped a section of glass with her elbow.

"It is. The limo was custom built to accommodate the thickness of bulletproof glass, so changing to an ordinary windshield would have meant expensive alterations."

Besides, even though I had no intention of getting involved with any more killers, I rather liked the make-my-day feeling of bulletproof glass.

"So what was all the shooting about?"

"A man hired a couple of guys to kill a friend of mine. After which the killer decided I knew too much and wanted me dead too. Then Fitz and I captured him in my backyard."

I could tell that this boosted me a notch in her estimation. I frowned. As a budding Christian, I'm not sure I want to be admired for the bullet holes in my limo or my criminal-capturing escapade.

"Maybe you've met Fitz?" I added. "He works with his son on the *Miss Nora*—the charter boat you'll be taking your honeymoon on."

Her scrunched eyebrows relaxed, and she

actually smiled. "I met Fitz. I like him. I'm looking forward to the sailboat trip."

I noted she said she was looking forward to the "sailboat trip," not the honeymoon. Meaningful? Or just a slip of words? Where was the groom anyway? So far I hadn't heard anything about him beyond his name. Sterling.

"So you and Fitz solved the murder?"

"It was actually in kind of an accidental way," I had to admit. "But Fitz knows a lot about crime. He was in a detective show on TV called *Ed Montrose, P.I.E.*—that's Private Investigator Extraordinaire—before your time."

"I'm interested in detective work. *Real* detective work, not TV stuff. I'm writing a mystery novel. Do you know anything about cold cases?"

Her tone was casual, but I had the feeling the question was not. "Not really. Cold case means one from a long time back that's never been solved, doesn't it?"

She nodded and looked me over with a gaze that was definitely speculative, although I had no idea what she could be speculating about.

"Maybe—"

She broke off as a red BMW whizzed down to the circular driveway from the three-car garage to the east side of the house. Michelle braked by the limo. Pamela struggled to keep Phreddie from squirming out of her arms.

"I'm glad to see you two have met. Pammi,

I'm going to the florist's to discuss suitable decorations for the limo. Want to come along?"

"No, thanks."

"I'll probably run over to the health club also and make certain Cindy isn't ordering the wrong treadmills behind my back. Don't let that cat in where he can scratch the furniture."

We both watched the security gate at the far end of the long driveway open to let the red car exit, then close behind it. The cat was still squirming.

"Everything's okay." Pamela rubbed her cheek against its wiggling body. To me she added, "Michelle makes Phreddie nervous."

One of his character judgments? I was, oddly, beginning to feel a bit nervous about this whole job myself. There were peculiar undercurrents here. Has a bride ever barged into her own wedding brandishing a machine gun?

"I would think you'd want to go along to choose the flowers and streamers for decorating the limo," I suggested.

"Why?"

I was taken back by the lack of interest in her tone. "Michelle said you'd objected to the color of the limo—too funereal."

"Funereal." She sounded thoughtful. "What an interesting concept."

And what an odd comment. "She said you preferred white."

"Ms. McConnell—"

"Andi," I said impulsively. I couldn't say I *liked* this rather strange young woman, but I sensed a vulnerability that she determinedly tried to keep hidden.

"Andi, I wouldn't care if your 'limouzeen' was purple with pea green polka dots. And as far as I'm concerned, Michelle can take that life-sized ice sculpture and pulverize it into snow cones."

The cat squirmed out of her arms and Pamela took after it, leaving me to wonder about this wedding. And "cold cases."

Chapter Three

Fitz had wanted me to call him after I met with Michelle Gibson. I stopped outside the gate and punched in his number on my speed dial. He'd given Michelle my name when she and Pamela came to inspect the *Miss Nora* for the honeymoon and she'd mentioned needing a limo.

"Fitz here. Cruising the spectacular waters of Puget Sound on the glorious *Miss Nora*. Don't you wish you were here? I do."

"I trust you aren't issuing invitations to any stray lady who calls. Where are you exactly?"

"Wonderful thing, caller ID. We're just sailing

by Whidby Island. How did it go with the Gibson woman?"

I told him about my conversation with Michelle, including some of the more extravagant details of the wedding, and my rather odd meeting with the stepdaughter-bride.

"Five days. Wow! That's terrific."

"I have you to thank for it, of course."

"Did she tell you how she was a movie star back in her Michelle DeShea days? I got the impression she usually manages to work that into a conversation. She said she gave it all up for love."

"The husband is dead now, and she didn't mention a movie career. Actually, she seemed pretty well stressed-out about the wedding. Michelle DeShea," I repeated. "Sounds vaguely familiar. Did you know her back in your Ed Montrose days?"

"I never met her personally back then, but she made quite a splash in some prehistoric thing where she wore skimpy skins and threw spears and fought with dinosaurs."

"She's still very attractive. Although Pamela, that's the bride, doesn't seem to appreciate all the effort her stepmother is making on the wedding."

"Hey, I've gotta go. One of our guests just hooked a fish!"

"Okay. See you when you get back to Vigland."

"I miss you."

"I miss you too."

• • •

That afternoon I had a limo job gathering up a herd of kids for a birthday party, and that evening I went to the weekly Bible study at church. We were into an intensive study of the Sermon on the Mount, and I was still thinking about not storing up treasures on earth when I turned my old Toyota onto Secret View Lane.

It was eight o'clock by then, with a light rain falling, and I was surprised to see an ancient yellow Volkswagen bug parked in front of my duplex. I blinked. I'd never seen that egg-yolk color on a vehicle before.

Oddly, my nosy neighbor Tom Bolton didn't appear to have it under surveillance. Was the man ill? He rarely missed spying on anything happening in the neighborhood. I parked my car out on the street because I'd need to back the limo out of the driveway in a few minutes.

A second surprise came when Pamela Gibson got out of the garishly-colored bug. The old car didn't look like something a girl demanding a Hollywood extravaganza of a wedding would choose.

"Hi." She was in a translucent rain jacket and jeans that rivaled the shapeless sag of the shorts she'd been wearing earlier. She'd tamed her hair slightly with a couple of those clampy things, but nothing less than a tweezer-ectomy would help those eyebrows. "I tried to call, but all I got was an answering machine. And no answer on the cell number."

"I've been to Bible study at my church. I had the cell turned off."

"Bible study? You believe all that God stuff?" The term was not exactly doctrinally correct, but she sounded more curious than disparaging.

I thought for a moment before I answered. "I'm still confused on some points, but one thing I've figured out is that you have to go beyond just believing God exists and find a personal relationship with Him."

"I guess I never got past the confused part."

"How did you know where I live?" I asked, suddenly wary of this surprise visit. The business card I'd given her had my phone numbers, but the only address was a Vigland post office box.

"Internet. You put in a phone number and it gives you a name and address."

Which reminded me that privacy in the age of the Internet is a joke. But, on the old theory *If you can't beat 'em, join 'em,* I've been thinking it's time I got a computer and Internet service. E-mail would make keeping in touch with Sarah and Rachel down in Florida easier, and I could run background checks on new customers too. Sometimes it can be scary letting strangers ride with you, even well-paying ones. And I definitely needed a website for the limousine business.

"Did you want to discuss the wedding plans?" I asked, puzzled why she was here, especially considering how hostile she'd seemed earlier. I glanced at my watch.

"Am I interrupting something?"

"I have to make a limo trip over to Olympia yet tonight."

I hesitated a moment. This trip was a twice-a-month thing in which I ferried a little girl named Lisa from her mother's place in Vigland to her father's place in Olympia for the weekend, a custody and visitation rights arrangement set up in their divorce.

"You could come along, if you'd like," I added. I doubted either parent would notice an extra person in the front seat.

"Is that the only way I can talk to you?"

Obviously not a girl impressed with the idea of riding around in a limo.

"That's the only way." I didn't feel like putting myself out for this girl by making other arrangements.

"Okay then."

I changed into my black chauffeur's uniform, and we were on our way. I started to ask her about the wedding, then decided to keep my mouth shut. During our sleuthing adventure with a murderer, I'd learned from Fitz that silence can sometimes be more effective than questions for gleaning information.

After several minutes of quiet while I drove across town, she finally said, "I'm wondering about 'Andi's Limouzeen Service.' With a z."

I doubted this was why she'd come, but I told her about inheriting the limo from my rich but eccentric Uncle Ned in Texas, who had spelled the word that way in his handwritten will. "Using that spelling is just kind of a, you know, nod to him."

"I like it. It's in your face. Anti-glamorous."

Pam looked as if she could give lessons in anti-glamour.

"But you didn't come to see me just to talk about my 'limouzeen.' "

"Maybe I did."

She sounded defensive, and I sensed she was still undecided about cluing me in on her real purpose. I turned onto the street in which the apartment complex of my client was located, and switched subjects.

"Does the man you're marrying live in Vigland?"

"No."

"I think Michelle said his name was Sterling?"

"Yes."

"Sterling what?" This felt like trying to pry information out of an ice cube.

"Sterling Forsythe."

"Are you in love with him?" I asked impulsively. That aura of anticipation and excitement usually hovering around a bride seemed more like a halo of gloom around her.

"Of course I'm in love with him! Although I really think love is . . . overrated. A successful marriage takes more than love."

In one way that sounded so mature. No reckless infatuation here. But in another way, putting such a low value on love also sounded sad.

"I was in love once, for all the good it did me," she muttered.

"In love with someone other than Sterling?"

"Sterling is a great guy," she snapped as if I'd attacked his character. "We're going to be very happy."

I had the uneasy feeling this was a mantra she repeated daily.

"Will you and Sterling be living here in Vigland?" I asked as I pulled into the parking lot behind the apartment complex.

"No." She finally relented and offered a smidgen of information. "Sterling works for a big biochemical research company in California. We'll live down there."

"What does he research?"

"Genetics and cloning. It's very hush-hush. He's kind of, ummm, nerdy. Like me. A loner too. But he's much smarter than I am. He graduated from Harvard when he was nineteen, and he has his doctorate. Scholarships for everything."

"How old is he now?"

"Twenty-nine. He's the youngest head of a department they've ever had at this research facility."

"How did you get together?"

"His mother is a cousin or something of Michelle's. Michelle invited them all up for a visit last summer. Later the guy I thought I was in love with and I broke up, and Sterling and I got together."

"Got together how?"

"E-mail mostly. I've been going to Dartmouth."

Dartmouth. Not a university for dummies.

"You're going to attend Dartmouth along with being married to Sterling in California?"

"I don't plan to go back. Maybe I'll go to UCLA or somewhere. Or maybe I'll just start publishing my novels. Sterling and I are going to be very happy." She touched the ring on her finger. "This was his grandmother's ring."

Two nerdy loners united. Maybe an ideal relationship. At least they weren't jumping into marriage on a few weeks' acquaintance. They'd known each other a year. And the grandmother's ring was a nice touch. But I wasn't convinced this was a happily-ever-after situation.

"You know, Pam," I said in another burst of carefully-worded impulsiveness, "nineteen is awfully young to get married. Maybe you should go back to Dartmouth and wait for another year or two and see how things look then."

"How old were you when you got married?" she challenged.

"Nineteen. Which is how I know it's way too young."

"A big wedding?"

"No, we drove to Reno for a quickie ceremony."

Followed by a $3.98 buffet special at a casino. Although anything more would have been a lousy investment anyway. The marriage ended when Richard traded me and life in Vigland for a woman named Tamara and a future dedicated to saving the flora and fauna in some South American jungle. Admirable, I suppose, by environmental standards. Less admirable from the discarded wife's point of view.

"So you're saying I should back out and ruin Michelle's big production number? She'd kill me." She paused. "Although . . ."

I didn't have a chance to ask what the *although* was about, because little Lisa knocked on the limo door. She must have been watching out the window for my arrival. Her mother, tall, slim, and hostile, as if this custody arrangement were somehow my fault, stood behind her with a plastic bag of weekend supplies.

I got out and gave the little girl a hug. Not standard limo operating procedure, but I always felt she needed it. I opened the rear door for her,

30

giving it my best flourish and my standard line, "Your chariot awaits, ma'am."

Lisa giggled, but the mother did not. She stuffed the sack inside with the girl. "Maybe one of these days that cheapskate will buy her some decent luggage."

Once inside, the little girl immediately knelt on the curved seat behind the opening in the partition between the driver's and passengers' areas. "Who're you?" she inquired of Pam.

"I'm Pamela. Bride-to-be."

Little-girl-like, Lisa didn't question this unusual form of self-identification. "I had a bride doll. Stephanie gave her to me. But I dropped her, and her head broke off."

"How far did you have to drop her to do that?" Pam asked, as if this were an interesting bridal possibility.

They carried on a lively conversation all the way to the father's house in Olympia, where stepmother Stephanie gave me a check and accepted the plastic bag as if it contained dog poo.

"You'd think with all the child support that woman gets, she could come up with something more than a bag lady outfit."

"'Bye, Lisa," I said. "See you in a couple weeks." The father took her back to the mother himself on Sunday evenings.

Back on the street, I took a turn that in a few

blocks put us into a lineup of fast-food places. "Would you mind if we drove through Taco Bell? I haven't had anything to eat since lunch."

"You're going to the drive-up window in a limo?"

"Sure."

She straightened in the seat. "I could use a burrito." Just riding in a limo hadn't impressed her, but apparently going through the drive-up window at Taco Bell in a limo generated some interest.

Ordering a chalupa for me and a burrito for her, plus soft drinks, brought a double take from the teenager at the window when he saw the limo. Before I could get to my purse, Pam leaned across me and paid the bill.

She laughed delightedly as I pulled around the building. "Did you see the look on that guy's face?"

I angled the limo across two spaces out in the shopping center parking lot. I put a lone packet of taco sauce on my chalupa. Pam doused her burrito with four.

"Your wedding sounds nice," I offered as an opening gambit.

She momentarily stopped eating. "Which part? The ice sculpture? Those expensive hair and makeup people from Seattle? My Barbie-doll wedding gown? That sterling silver bride-and-groom ornament on top of the cake? The fog machine? The sit-down dinner? Enough roses to stage our own personal Rose Bowl parade?" She went through the list as if she were naming rip-off charities soliciting donations, then gave me a glance. "Plus five days' worth of limousine service."

I was startled. Hadn't she demanded all this for her "wedding of the century"?

"What's all that costing?" I asked, since we didn't seem to be into tact here.

"I don't know. Maybe 250 thou? Maybe three, by the time you add on airfare and hotel bills for half of Hollywood. It's ridiculous."

My thought exactly. It also made me wonder how eager these guests were to come, if they had to be bribed with expense-paid trips. And, much as I appreciated the biggest limo job I'd ever had, five days of limo service might also classify as "ridiculous."

"What happened to the limo services that didn't work out?" I asked.

"One couldn't do the five days. Michelle got in an argument with the other people about the driver being too fat. She said it would detract from the 'ambiance' of the wedding."

I supposed I was fortunate Michelle didn't disqualify a limo on the basis of the driver's age too. "Who's performing the ceremony?"

"Michelle picked some guy for his good looks. Heaven forbid we should have someone with a

Donald Trump toupee or too much nose hair."

I tried to think of something to say that wouldn't fuel Pam's obvious hostility toward her stepmother. Michelle's priorities might be a bit skewed, but . . . "You have to admit Michelle is being very generous to do all this for you."

"Generous?" Pam snorted. "She's not spending her money. She's spending *mine*."

"Your money?"

"My dad had all this complicated money stuff set up. Michelle has control of my trust fund until I'm twenty-three or graduate college or get married. She can only spend the money for my benefit, and she has to account to some legal firm for what she does with it, but I guess she's convinced them that anything goes for the wedding. I know Dad thought he was looking out for me, but . . ." There was a shrug in her voice as it trailed off.

"Are you getting married just so *you* can get hold of the money?"

I figured she'd tell me to mind my own business, but all she said was, "It's a thought."

I thought about that beat-up VW bug back at the duplex. "Michelle apparently didn't spend much of your money on a car for you."

"I saved up my allowance at school and bought it. Michelle was horrified, of course." Pam's smile held malicious satisfaction. "She hates it."

I decided now that she had come to me because she needed someone to vent to. I seemed an unlikely choice, but maybe she didn't have anyone else. But surely a wedding like this had attendants. . . .

"How many bridesmaids do you have?"

"Four, I think. I wanted to have a friend from college as maid of honor, but she's in Europe for a year. So Michelle got people. Bridesmaids and groomsmen too. She's also getting all these hotshot guests up from Hollywood so she can show them how well she's doing by throwing an overpriced wedding for her stepdaughter. And at the same time butter up some producer-director guy so she can get a part in his new movie."

"That's what she said?"

"Of course not. She acts like it's all for *me,* but I know what she's thinking."

Steffan Productions. I remembered seeing the name on that letterhead on Michelle's desk. Was that the guy Pam was talking about?

"But why would she want a part in a movie when she's opening this fancy new fitness center here in Vigland?"

"Because she figures she's Superwoman, I suppose. Who knows? What I do know is that Michelle looks out for herself all the way."

"Aren't you being a little harsh on her? Maybe she is going overboard on some of the details, if all these extravagances are her idea, not yours. And maybe you and she aren't exactly best buddies . . . But she did introduce you to the man you love."

"I think she killed my father."

Chapter Four

I choked over my Pepsi and stared at her in astonishment. It was dark now, but I could see her dimly-lit face by the parking-lot lights. She looked up and met my shocked gaze.

"This is why you asked if I knew anything about cold cases. This is why you came to see me."

"I figured with bullet holes in the limo, and the fact that you'd been involved with a murder before—"

"Pam, if you know anything," I interrupted, "go to the police!"

"I did, when Dad died. I yelled my head off. They thought I was just an overwrought teenager making nasty accusations because I had a freaky imagination and didn't like my stepmother."

That sounded plausible to me too. "So what makes you think she killed him?" I asked warily. I wiped spilled Pepsi off the steering wheel.

"Motive, of course. Plus means and

opportunity. Those are the biggies when you're considering murder. I've done a lot of research for the book I'm working on."

I remembered Fitz mentioning those factors too. "Okay, go on."

"Dad had asthma. Mom rushed him to the emergency room several times when I was a kid. He was also very allergic to bee stings and had to carry one of those Epi-Pen things so he could have an injection immediately to keep him from going into anaphylactic shock if he got stung. He also had a bad hip, left over from a bicycle accident in high school. It bothered him more as he got older, I guess. He had some blood pressure and heart problems too."

So far what this sounded like was a man whose health was on the iffy side, someone whose death probably shouldn't have come as any big surprise.

Pam set the burrito on the console between the seats and took a deep breath. "Dad had had a bad night with the hip and hadn't slept much—" She broke off sharply. "You understand what I'm telling you now is Michelle's version, okay?"

"Okay."

"Anyway, he'd taken some pain pills in the night, but they hadn't helped much. So about six A.M. he took sleeping pills."

"Sleeping pills at six in the morning? Isn't that a little unusual?"

"Not for Dad." She sounded reluctant, as if she'd rather not admit that. "Sometimes he'd even take them in the middle of the day and then get up about midnight to work on something in his office."

Okay, so Pam's father lived on a strange schedule.

"He was still asleep when Michelle left to go to her health club over in Olympia around nine. This was before she had the Superwoman Room built in the basement at the house."

"The Superwoman Room?" I repeated doubtfully.

"Every room in the house has a name. Michelle calls that one the Fitness Room, but it's the Superwoman Room to me. Which she paid for with my money because she convinced the legal people I needed to exercise and lose weight. Anyway, after the health club she went to lunch, then did some shopping. When she got home about four, Dad was dead."

"Dead from what?"

"At the emergency room the doctors determined he'd been stung on the arm several times. Because of the sleeping pills, he didn't wake up when it happened. Which meant he didn't get the shot of epinephrine he needed. And he . . . died."

"Pam, how *awful*. Where were you?"

"Back east at school. Michelle had convinced

Dad that the schools here were 'inadequate,' as she put it, so they sent me back there. Where I fit in like a big ugly cockroach in a bouquet of orchids. She called to tell me he was dead, and I flew out the next morning."

"How old were you then?"

"Fifteen. Dad was forty-nine."

"And Michelle?"

"Who knows? She hasn't had a birthday since Dad died. She had to have them before that, of course, so she could get some big gift. But I never heard any numbers mentioned."

"There wasn't an investigation into his death?"

"When I went to the police, because I was right away suspicious of her, they told me there was nothing to investigate. Dad was extremely allergic to bee stings, he'd been stung, hadn't had proper treatment, and died. That was it. There was one officer who seemed interested that Dad took sleeping pills at six in the morning, but then I had to tell him Dad often did stuff like that, and he lost interest."

"How did your dad get stung right there in his bed?"

"It was May, and the window was open. Michelle said they always slept with it open. There were a lot of yellow jackets around. Several got in and stung him. *Her* version, of course."

I considered this scenario of her father's death.

If she'd said he'd died of a fall down the stairs, a drug overdose, or even an overdose of exercise in an effort to keep up with Michelle, I'd have seen possibilities for murder, but . . . bee stings?

"But, Pam, if the bees just wandered in and stung him, I don't see—"

"I don't think they were accidental stings. I think they were deliberate. And she left him to die."

"How could stings be deliberate? You can't hire a herd of yellow jackets to fly in and sting on command." I was immediately sorry I'd said that. It sounded facetious, and this was her father's death we were discussing.

"I've never been able to figure out that part," she admitted reluctantly. She leaned back and sloshed the ice in her Sprite. "I can't really see her chasing around with a net trying to catch bees. But I'm sure she did it somehow."

I crumpled the paper that had come around my chalupa and remembered something from long ago. "Back when I was a kid, when we went camping or picnicking, my dad always put a chunk of raw meat outside the campsite area to draw the yellow jackets away." I paused, thinking, considering a scenario. "I suppose, if you put the meat in a jar and then, when several yellow jackets were inside, put the lid on . . ."

"And then you took the jar of angry yellow

jackets up to a sleeping person, a *drugged* sleeping person, and opened it up right against the skin . . .”

“I doubt it would be that simple—”

“That’s how she did it, Andi. You figured it out, just like that!” She reached across the console and squeezed my arm with fierce appreciation. “I knew you could do it!”

“No. Wait! I didn’t mean I think it really happened that way.” I’d just been musing. Speculating. The last thing I wanted was to encourage this girl in what still struck me as a wildly implausible accusation. “I really can’t see Michelle out trapping yellow jackets.”

“I can. It’s . . . sneaky. And that’s exactly what Michelle is. Sneaky. I can see exactly how she did it now. She always dished out Dad’s pills. He took stuff for high blood pressure and cholesterol, and she was always giving him vitamins and herbal stuff too. He just took whatever she handed him.”

“That sounds as if she cared about his health, not as if she was planning to murder him.”

Pam ignored that. “She gave him the sleeping pills that morning and deliberately gave him more than usual so not even a bomb would wake him up. Then she got these yellow jackets she’d already captured and deliberately let them sting him several times. Sliding the jar around, because all the stings in one place wouldn’t look natural. Then she just walked off and left him to die."

I swallowed. That would work, wouldn't it? But surely that wasn't what really happened. I had to remember I was dealing with a girl who was still overwrought about losing her father, a girl who was perhaps a little shaky mentally or emotionally. And wildly imaginative.

"Pam, I think that's rather . . . farfetched. Why would she do it?"

"For a couple million dollars of insurance money, that's why! Dad made a lot of money in real estate down in California. Michelle's so-called movie career was tanking, and she figured she'd better latch onto some rich guy while she could. So she glommed onto Dad. But not long after he and Michelle were married, he lost a bundle when something went wrong with a land development deal. Maybe he didn't even have as much money to begin with as she thought, and after the development deal went sour he sure didn't. That was when we moved up here."

"Why here?"

"Dad thought the area was ripe for development, as he put it. I guess he figured he could get in on it with less of an investment than it would take in southern California. Michelle also said I'd be better off in the schools here."

"But they sent you back east to school."

"Yeah. Little glitch in logic there, right? But

Michelle always could convince Dad of almost anything."

Like maybe taking way more than the proper number of sleeping pills? Reluctantly I considered those three biggies of murder: motive, means, and opportunity. A check mark on each one for Michelle.

"I think she had another reason for wanting to get out of LA too."

"Like what?"

"Later. Right now what we need to do is go see that officer who seemed interested at the time and tell him everything." She spoke as if we were already a team on this. "I think he might listen. His name was Molino. Deputy Molino."

"Molino?" I repeated with a certain dismay. "Detective Sergeant Molino?"

DDS Molino, as I'd started thinking of him, for Dear Detective Sergeant Molino, back at the time I was dealing with him when the body of my former boyfriend turned up in the trunk of the limo. When Pam's father died four years ago, DDS Molino had probably been a regular deputy rather than a detective.

"You know him?" she asked eagerly.

"We've met." And he'd certainly let me know, even if Fitz and I had helped capture the murderer, that civilians had no business muddling around in criminal matters.

I jumped backward in the conversation. "Your

father and Michelle must not have been hard up for money when they moved up here, because they obviously spent a lot of it on remodeling the house. She shouldn't have been desperate enough to commit murder."

"With Michelle, 'hard up' is a relative term. Down to your last couple million, maybe. And Michelle always hated this house. She wanted something big and contemporary, lots of angles and sharp rooflines. Probably stainless steel furniture. But Dad put his foot down for once and said they were getting this place. He liked the ten wooded acres around it, and the inlet frontage. Although he also told her she could remodel the interior however she wanted."

"She must like it now. She hasn't sold it since your father died."

Pam held up a forefinger. "One of the interesting stipulations in Dad's will. It requires that if he died she has to 'provide a home' for me there until I'm twenty-three, graduated from college, or married, whichever comes first. Then it's hers. If she *doesn't* do her duty and provide me with a home until then, it goes to me."

Her father must have had a flock of lawyers working overtime to get all these tricky details into the will and trust fund. I suspected Michelle had checked to see if they were enforceable.

"Interesting stipulations," I murmured. And

possibly a strong reason for Michelle to push Pam's marriage to Sterling. She'd lose control of Pam's trust fund, but she couldn't spend that money on herself anyway, and she'd be able to sell the house.

"Like I said, I know Dad was trying to do his best for me and protect me, but . . ."

But sometimes micromanagement from the grave causes more problems than it solves. I shook my head. "But *murder* . . ."

"Yes, murder. And so far she's gotten away with it. She had him cremated faster than Burger King grilling a double cheeseburger, probably so if someone got suspicious later they couldn't do tests and find out he had a big overdose of sleeping pills in his system. But now, since you've figured out how she did it, we can do something."

We. "You're saying you want me to go to Detective Sergeant Molino with this?"

She scooted toward me on the seat. "It's probably too late tonight, but we can do it first thing in the morning."

"Pam, I haven't 'figured out' anything! I was just . . . speculating." Out loud, unfortunately. "I hate to disappoint you, but I'm not a hotshot sleuth who can pull some heretofore unnoticed clue out of the woodwork and convict someone with it. This is an extremely serious accusation, and Detective Sergeant Molino is going to want

45

a lot more than wild speculation about how it *might* have happened."

I squashed everything into the litterbag hanging from a knob on the dashboard and started the engine. I pulled from the parking lot onto the street and headed back toward Vigland. Pam folded her arms and sat in rigid silence, obviously disappointed that I didn't intend to pound on Detective Sergeant Molino's door first thing in the morning.

"Thank you for the ride," she said stiffly when I turned into the driveway at the duplex.

I turned off the engine. "Pam, you have some interesting arguments here, and the idea that your father was deliberately stung isn't totally out of the realm of possibility. But the whole idea is just too—" I broke off. I'd started to say *preposterous* but amended it to a softer "—is just so unlikely."

"So you won't even talk to Detective Molino about it?"

"I don't think there's enough to go on."

Sure, a couple million dollars' worth of insurance money made for a strong motive. Murder had been done for a lot less. The scenario of how Michelle could have accomplished a murder was remotely possible. But it was also more like a plot line in one of Fitz's old Ed Montrose episodes on TV than a real-life situation.

"I'm sorry, Pam. What I really think you should do is reconsider this wedding. I don't think you're ready for it."

"I guess I figured you wouldn't believe me. So it's a sure thing you won't believe something else about Michelle."

"What's that?"

"I think she's going to try to kill me at the wedding."

Chapter Five

"You think she wants to kill you?"

"Yes."

"For heaven's sake, Pam, how do you think she could do it? Strangle you with your veil as you walk down the aisle? Plant a poisonous worm in your wedding bouquet? Douse your lobster tail with arsenic?"

"You can make fun of me all you want, but I think she's going to try. And just maybe succeed. She succeeded with Dad."

"But why? Marrying you off gets you out of her hair. She doesn't collect on some big insurance policy on your life, does she?"

"No, but—"

"She doesn't have to kill you to get the house. And a murder at the wedding probably wouldn't endear her to that producer or director you say she wants to impress. So why—"

"Maybe a murder *would* endear her to the producer. That's the kind of stuff Hollywood loves! Read it in the tabloids: *Star of new Steffan Productions drama confronts tragedy in personal life! Beloved stepdaughter murdered at her own wedding! Michelle heartbroken!*" Pam gave one of her scornful snorts. "The house is peanuts. With me dead before I'm actually married or turn twenty-three, she gets everything. The whole trust fund goes to her. So look for it to happen before the guy says 'I now pronounce you husband and wife,' so Sterling can't have some claim on it."

"That's how your father set it up?" I asked, dismayed.

"He did it right after he and Michelle were married, before he lost all that money on the land deal. He was trying to be fair and protect both of us, I guess."

And practically drawing a diagram for murder to anyone so inclined. Which, if Pam was right, Michelle definitely was.

"But she's spending all this trust fund money on the wedding. She wouldn't do that if she intended to grab it for herself."

"That's *why* she's doing it. Don't you see? Because whoever investigates the murder . . . *my* murder . . . will look at it exactly like you're doing. But it's really just a big fat smokescreen."

Uneasily I realized there was a certain sinister logic to that.

"There'll be plenty left in the trust fund, even after everything she's spending on the wedding?"

"I don't know how much, but I'm sure it will supplement her lifestyle nicely."

"Pam, if you really do believe you're in danger, then you have to stop the wedding immediately."

"Then you think she could try to do it at the wedding?"

"No, I don't mean that—"

"Then you think I'm perfectly safe."

"Well . . . ummm . . ." Not necessarily that either.

She crossed her arms again and regarded me like a judge waiting for the defendant to plead one way or the other. I wavered on a needle point of indecision. Michelle was obviously ambitious, given the new fitness center she had going and her hope of reviving a movie career. She had a definite flair for the expensive and ostentatious. If Pam were right, Michelle had married for money, not love—money enhanced with a big insurance payoff when her husband died. But that didn't mean she'd murder for more money. Or even that she'd murdered her husband.

Those bees probably had just flown in through the window. Bees do things like that. Michelle surely couldn't now hope to pull off a murder with a tent full of wedding guests as witnesses.

Although, if she *could* somehow figure a devious enough way to do it, all those guests would provide a fantastic alibi . . .

"You'd better be thinking about yourself too," Pam warned. "I doubt she'd object to an extra victim who happens to get in the way. Maybe she's planning to booby-trap the limo with a bomb that'll blow us both up right before the ceremony."

That pushed me off the needle of indecision and into the camp of this-is-ridiculous. "But Michelle is going to be in the limo *with* us. Remember? You're supposed to arrive at the tent together so she can walk down the aisle with you to give you away."

Pam scowled as if she'd forgotten that detail, but she was not deterred. "She'll think of something."

I threw up my hands. "Why not go whole-hog and plant a bomb to blow up everyone in the tent? If extra deaths don't matter, why not spew poison gas out of the fog machine? Do a mass poisoning at the dinner?"

"You won't be laughing when you're lying there dead," she warned in an ominous tone.

Which would have been more effective if I hadn't had this vision of myself sprawled on the grass clutching a purloined lobster tail seasoned with arsenic, and thinking, as I ricocheted off into eternity, *How about that? Pam was right after all.*

"If you're so worried about all this, why don't you just hire a couple of muscular bodyguards for protection?"

The question was more facetious than serious, but Pam pounced on it. "Michelle isn't going to do some dumb thing like a shooting or stabbing that a bodyguard could protect me from. It'll be more subtle. Sneaky."

Subtle and sneaky would be the way to go, all right. But what was more likely was that this girl was seriously paranoid.

"What would work best is if we can get the police on to her *before* the wedding. Look, I have an idea."

An idea. Just what we needed. Hadn't someone's great idea started everything from Silly Putty to the atom bomb?

"We don't go to the detective empty-handed. There are yellow jackets around now. I'll go out in the morning and trap some, just like you said. I'll even open the jar on my arm when we're with him and let them sting me, so he can see how it was done. I'm not allergic," she added.

"That sounds a little melodramatic." To say nothing of painful. "Kind of Perry Mason-ish."

"The dramatic courtroom crisis works for him on all those old reruns. I'd like a dramatic crisis *before* I'm dead and Michelle's on trial for murdering me."

"Pam, I'm sorry, but this is all just too . . . far out. Thinking Michelle killed your father, and now she's going to kill you too. . . ." I shook my head.

"So you definitely won't go to the detective?"

"I'm not saying I absolutely wouldn't ever do it, but the evidence would have to be a lot more convincing than it is now."

"Like me dead in my $24,000 wedding gown?"

Shock over the price momentarily derailed me. "Your gown cost twenty-four-*thousand?*"

"I think that includes the veil, but probably not the tiara with diamond chips. No overpriced wedding is complete without a diamond tiara."

I dropped the subject of the wedding gown and went back to what was more important here. "Pam, this isn't even a cold case about your father's death. It's a never-was case. As for Michelle trying to kill you . . . Has she ever said or done anything threatening?"

"She sent me clear across the country to school. I was really scared."

I didn't respond, and she tried again.

"She got me to take horseback riding lessons down in California. The horse spooked, and I fell off and broke a toe. And I almost choked on chips loaded with some strange spice that she gave me once."

I still didn't say anything, but I suppose my expression was comment enough.

"Basically what you think is that I'm a certifiable nut case, right? Paranoid. Delusional. Yada, yada."

"I think you're stressed and maybe having subconscious doubts about the wedding, but—"

"Okay, then, just to make certain you have no doubts about my being a gen-u-ine, brand-name nut case, try this on for size: I think Michelle may have killed my mother too."

"Your mother! Oh, Pam, come on. You're saying she has some murderous vendetta against your entire family?"

"No, not a vendetta. It's just that one by one we've stood in the way of something she wants, so she . . . gets us out of the way."

"Why would she want to get rid of your mother?"

"So she could grab Dad, of course. All the while pretending she was Mom's good friend."

I couldn't help a melodramatic sigh. "So how did she do it?"

"Mom was killed in a hit-and-run accident when she was crossing a street in LA. They never figured out who did it."

I didn't know what to say. It was all wildly *possible,* but as fantastic as some superspy movie. A James Bond terrorist working the Mom-and-Dad circuit.

"Never mind. I knew you wouldn't believe me." She opened the door and slid out of the limo.

I leaned across the center console to peer at her, concerned about her leaving in this agitated condition. "Where are you going?"

"I think I'll just dash on home and demand something really outrageous for the wedding. I haven't been doing my share. Release of a thousand doves, maybe? No, that's too mundane. I know—a thousand vultures!"

"Pam—"

"And maybe I should arrive in some more unique way. A limousine is so yesterday." She lifted her head to look down her nose, as if the limo were an oversized cockroach. "How about a hot-air balloon, or parachuting out of a plane? Michelle can arrange to have it shot down or blown up, and then I'll really go out with a bang."

Pam dashed to the Bug. She couldn't do an effective burn of rubber with the old vehicle, but she did determinedly *chug-chug* away.

I went inside shaking my head. Overwrought was putting it mildly. Pam was an explosion waiting to detonate, with imagination enough for a dozen episodes of *Ed Montrose, P.I.E.* I'd call her in the morning, I decided. Or maybe I should call Michelle. Not that I'd list all Pam's wild accusations, but maybe I could say enough to convince Michelle that it would be in Pam's best interests to postpone the wedding.

I wished I could talk to Fitz, but it was almost eleven thirty now. Not that he'd mind my calling at a late hour, but he and his son shared a cabin on the *Miss Nora*, and the ringing of the cell phone might disturb Matt. Who, ever since Fitz and I solved that murder together, seems to look on me as an overage Mata Hari leading his father astray.

By morning, I figured Pam would complain to Michelle and I'd be getting a call telling me I was off the job. No call came, so just before noon I called the house and asked for Pam and then Michelle, but neither was available. The housekeeper wouldn't give out private cell phone numbers for either of them.

I called to chat with Sarah in Florida, but didn't mention my five-day gig in case it still fell through. She was excited about the upcoming start of classes, and granddaughter Rachel had gotten over her snit about her mother enrolling in the same university.

The *Miss Nora* returned to the Vigland marina Monday afternoon. That evening Fitz brought over leftover clam chowder he'd made for guests on the boat, and I filled him in on what Pam had told me.

I figured he'd pass it off as paranoid or weird, but he seemed thoughtful, and the following evening when we went out to dinner he produced printouts of Gerald Gibson's obituary and a short article from *The Vigland Tides* about the death. Fitz had been to the library and located both in their records system.

The article was bare-bones, saying basically what Pam had said, that an ambulance had been called to 2217 Hornsby Drive and Gerald Gibson was dead on arrival at Vigland Hospital from an allergic reaction to bee stings. The sleeping pills were not mentioned. The obituary listed no survivors other than Pam and Michelle.

The printouts lay on the table between us. We were at a restaurant called The Log Cabin eating crab cakes with a divine shrimp sauce. Fitz had started to regrow the mustache he'd had back in his Ed Montrose days and looked particularly dashing. I felt a bit dashing myself, with a fresh dose of Cinnamon Sunrise on my hair. With the addition of flattering candlelight it was an evening ripe for romance. The fact that we were more concerned with murder perhaps said something about our relationship. I picked up the two pieces of paper and studied them again.

"If it was murder, it was a successful murder," Fitz commented. "As the daughter told you, there was no investigation."

"Maybe, if what Pam says is true, *two* successful murders. And another one in the works."

Fitz toyed with his coffee cup. "It's frustrating, but at this point I don't see any way we can investigate the mother's death."

I nodded. Too far distant in both miles and years. "Would there be any point in looking back at the medical examiner's records on Gerald Gibson's death? Or is that even possible?"

"I'm on good terms with a couple of police officers who were fans of my show. Hornsby Drive is outside the city limits, and they're Vigland city police, but if it's possible to look at those old records, one of them can probably do it. I'll check on it."

"More important at the moment is whether there's anything to Pam's suspicions that Michelle has murderous ideas about her."

I'd vowed to give up sleuthing after we caught my old boyfriend's murderer, and I wasn't eager to jump in again. Not only had my limo been shot up in that adventure, my nerves hadn't fared too well either. Also, catching one murderer does not make one an expert in the arena of criminal detection.

"For your own safety, you could just back out of the limo deal with Michelle," Fitz suggested. He smiled wryly. "But we both know that isn't going to happen."

Right. Pam and I weren't exactly good buddies here, but I didn't want anything happening to her. She seemed so vulnerably alone.

After dinner we took a stroll along the city park walkway bordering Vigland Bay. A nearly full moon lit the smooth water with a pathway of silver that looked solid enough to dance on, and in the distance Mt. Rainier floated dreamily on a layer of clouds. Even an old TV detective and an amateur sleuth couldn't concentrate on murder in such circumstances. Romance interrupted, including a kiss under the shadows of an old maple.

A very satisfactory interruption.

But back at my duplex, Fitz was in detective mode again.

"Keep your eyes and ears open while you're at the house. Snoop. Ask questions. And be careful. If there is anything to this, the stepmother may not mind some collateral damage. Which could be *you*."

A couple days later, hoping to convince her to at least postpone the wedding, I finally reached Pam on the phone.

"I was just wondering if you're . . . umm . . . okay," I said.

"Mentally stable, you mean? Not standing on street corners shouting out crazed accusations? Not dashing around the park waving a jar of raw meat at any passing yellow jacket?"

"Pam, I—"

"Never mind. I'm fine. You'll have to pardon

58

my outburst the other night. As you said, I'm nervous and stressed out."

But she sounded cool and calm now, nerveless as a brick.

"You're planning to go ahead with it, then."

"The wedding? Of course."

I wondered about doves . . . or vultures . . . but I decided not to ask. "I really think you should reconsider it. You could go back to Dartmouth for another year or two—"

"Don't be ridiculous. Sterling and I are going to be very happy. My mystery novel is coming along nicely. And, as I said, if I decide I need further education, I can go to UCLA or somewhere."

Levelheaded plans, mature and sensible. But . . . "You're not worried about the wedding now?"

"I have a few concerns, of course. Getting married is a major step in anyone's life. But Sterling and I are going to be very happy."

Did she think if she said it often enough, she could make it come true?

She hung up without saying good-bye. I debated calling Michelle, but even if I could persuade her to postpone the wedding, I was sure Pam would insist on going through with it. She had a stubborn streak, and it had definitely been activated. I wondered if she'd ever confided her suspicions about Michelle to the groom-to-be.

The next couple of weeks were busy. The limousine business perked along nicely. A couple of weddings . . . nice, ordinary ones. An anniversary party for an older couple, several trips to the Sea-Tac airport, one trip to the Seattle dock to pick up a family returning from an Alaskan cruise, a three-couple on-the-road pizza party, and several businessmen trips into Olympia and Seattle. I was accustomed to male clients who took advantage of travel time in the limo to use an electric shaver or laptop, but one of these guys actually took off his shoes and trimmed his toenails. You meet all kinds in the limo business.

The young couple who'd been renting the other side of my duplex gave their thirty days' notice. I was sorry to see them go. They'd been in the duplex only since my good friend Joella moved out to take a job as a live-in nanny. But they'd found a house they wanted to buy, and I was glad for them even though I dreaded the whole process of finding another reliable tenant. I figured I'd wait until after Pam's wedding to advertise.

Fitz and Matt went out on several more charter trips. In between, while they were docked at the marina, Fitz fixed a leak on my garage roof. We went to a local theater production of *Pride and Prejudice* and cooked together at my place or went out to dinner. I even got him to go to church with me one Sunday. His new mustache was coming along nicely. I was beginning to think I might need something more potent than Cinnamon Sunrise on my hair.

I was still hoping Pam would decide to call the wedding off, but when I hadn't heard anything by a couple days before I was supposed to show up, I called Michelle. I didn't want to turn down other business and then find there'd been a change of plans. She confirmed that she still wanted the limo for five days.

So on the morning of Tuesday the twenty-first, chauffeur's uniforms freshly dry-cleaned, suitcase tucked into the trunk of the limo, gas tank filled, and newly cut and painted circles of duct tape pasted over the bullet holes, I showed up for duty.

Chapter Six

Michelle met me on the front steps with cell phone clamped to her ear, blue eyes sparking with fury.

"What do you mean you can't make it? You're a *groomsman!*" A few more angry words and then she punched the disconnect button without a good-bye. "Can you believe this? Three days before the wedding, and he backs out. Now I'm going to have one bridesmaid dangling along behind alone, like a dead fish on a line."

A problem, perhaps, but I was guiltily relieved that it apparently took Michelle's mind off the blackness of the limo. She supplied me with a remote control to open the gate, and we dashed out to the casino complex south of town. She'd booked a block of rooms at their elegant Tschimikan Inn, where I found myself drafted as notetaker while she inspected each room. After a couple of picky-point complaints to the management, we were off to the florist's to pick out fresh flowers for each room. No expense spared, of course. Pam's money.

Still before noon, I drove over to Sea-Tac to pick up the first of the wedding-guest arrivals, five people. None of whom, I gathered, would know Pam without an *I Am the Bride* sticker plastered on her forehead. These guests were assigned to the inn, but the afternoon arrivals got a room at the house. In between those trips, because housekeeper Shirley was admiring the limo with such a yearning look, I gave her a quick ride to Safeway to pick up some extra supplies for dinner. Later I had to rush back to the inn to take a bridesmaid's mother into Vigland for a massage.

"She says her back is killing her after the plane trip." Michelle rolled her eyes after giving me instructions where to take the woman. "If she'd lose fifty pounds, she might actually fit into a plane seat, and her back wouldn't hurt so much."

When I went to pick up the woman, she grumbled about how inconvenient it was being stuck so far out of town. No comment on the nice accommodations or flowers. After the massage, on the way back to the inn, she suddenly got cozy and tried to pry information out of me about the houseguests, whom she apparently figured ranked above her on some invisible guest scale. I played dumb. No see, no hear, no speak.

Back at the house, Michelle was in the hallway listening to an irate mother complain about the bridesmaids' shoes. "Maybe the girls with feet like sausages can wear those things, but my Mackenzie's feet are much too slender and shapely. She's in much demand as a foot model, you know."

A jolly gathering this was shaping up to be.

I was so busy all day that I didn't see my own room until after dark. Housekeeper and cook Shirley—Shirley Berkhoff, I found out now— took me to it. She was sixtyish, short and wiry, inconspicuous as a dust mote.

The room was small, the only furniture a single bed, a nightstand and lamp, a small swivel rocker, and a skinny chest of drawers. A door opened onto a bathroom that was shared with

Shirley's room. Not luxurious, but the bed bounced comfortably, and I liked the nice scent of lavender.

I didn't realize until I set down my suitcase how my giving Shirley the limo ride had so favorably impressed her. Did I need a larger or softer pillow? She'd be happy to get me one. Would I like to watch TV? Come on over to her room anytime. A considerate gesture was apparently rare as food stamps here in the Gibson household.

Interesting.

I unpacked, and Shirley dished me up a late dinner in the kitchen, the same veal scaloppini she'd served to Michelle and guests. It was an impressive kitchen, stainless-steel refrigerator/freezer the size of a fortress, granite countertops, a six-burner stove, double ovens, a rack of expensive-looking knives, a cappuccino machine, microwave with enough controls to launch a rocket, a rotisserie, and a few more gadgets I didn't recognize and undoubtedly couldn't afford. A door led off to a separate pantry.

What I hadn't seen anywhere was a security system. I asked Shirley about that.

"There's the electronically controlled gate, of course, and the perimeter fence is electrified. I guess Michelle figures that's enough security."

"Vigland isn't a high crime area anyway."

"Michelle also keeps a handgun in her room.

64

How about a glass of wine? It's the pinot noir they had with dinner. Although I like tomorrow night's Riesling better myself."

She held up two bottles, and it was then I noted that in that inconspicuous face a pair of button-brown eyes gleamed with a hint of mischief.

I opted for tea, but Shirley helped herself to a tumbler of Riesling and sat down at the table with me. I still doubted there could be anything to Pam's suspicions about Michelle, but this seemed an opportune moment for some behind-the-scenes snooping.

After complimenting the veal, which was indeed excellent, I tested the waters by asking, "Do you like working here?"

She nodded vigorously. "It's a good job. Pay always right on time. No wild, messy parties, and meals are simple when they're here alone. Michelle hires special window- and carpet-cleaning people when we need them. A good job," she repeated enthusiastically.

An enthusiasm that made me suspicious. Perhaps something along the lines of, the lady doth protest too much?

"Sounds ideal."

She straightened the saltshaker on the table, meticulously lining it up with the pepper. "I doubt any job is totally ideal."

"Any advice for a newcomer? Just to be on the safe side?"

"Michelle can be a bit picky. But that's no doubt natural in a perfectionist." A cautious flip of criticism into compliment. Shirley, not knowing where I stood, wasn't taking any chances.

"Perfectionists can be hard to work for," I suggested to lead the way. "She didn't like the color of my limo. And she said my lipstick should be brighter so I wouldn't look so pale in this black uniform."

That comment had come from Michelle just after I delivered the second round of guests, and now it opened an indignant flood-burst from Shirley.

"Your lipstick is just fine! Not all of us can afford the seventeen different shades she has in *her* cosmetics drawer. She jumped on me tonight about the size of the croutons in the Caesar salad." She rolled her eyes. "Can you imagine? Too large, she said! And heaven help me if there's ever an extra gram of fat in her meals. And, by all means, avoid any hint of illness. She doesn't care that someone a bit older might need time off to see a doctor once in a while."

Resentment simmering like stew about to boil over. I felt guilty taking advantage of it, but the possibility of murder, both past and present, took precedence.

"I thought I felt a little tension between Michelle and Pam," I suggested.

Shirley's snort was not inconspicuous. "*Tense* is a hostage situation in a bank. Michelle and Pammi are a nuclear disaster just waiting for someone to push the button. They went at it this morning about what happens with the cat while Pammi is on her honeymoon. Michelle hates cats. That one better have extra lives in reserve. It may need them."

"How about Pam?" I noted that Shirley used Michelle's version of the name, so the girl apparently hadn't made her preference known to the housekeeper. Or perhaps Shirley figured she'd better conform to the preferences of the person who signed her paycheck. "What's she like?"

"She seems nice enough, in a standoffish kind of way. She's only been here since her college classes let out last spring. She spends most of her time up in her room pounding on that computer. She doesn't mind some extra grams of fat in *her* meals. Michelle is always nagging at her to lose weight and do something about her hair."

"I heard they're bringing in hair and makeup people for the wedding."

"I hope Pammi lets them work on her. From what I've seen, she hasn't been particularly cooperative with the wedding arrangements so far. Of course who can blame her, the way Michelle gives orders like a five-star general?"

"I gather some of the more extravagant aspects

of the wedding are Michelle's ideas, not Pam's."

Shirley got up and refilled her wine glass. "Extravagant . . . wow-ee! If I had the money they're spending on this shindig I could retire and sit under a palm tree on Tahiti. But Pammi doesn't seem excited about any of it."

"I don't think she knows many of the guests. Including her bridesmaids."

"She didn't even eat with the guests tonight. She asked for a hamburger and fries in her room. Which made Michelle furious, of course. She stormed up there and started yelling that if Pammi didn't stop eating like a fast-food junkie, she'd be splitting the seams on her wedding gown."

"What does Pam do when Michelle yells?"

"Yells right back. Said she hated the 'stupid wedding gown' anyway. And then she yelled at me that the fries were too soggy." Shirley shook her head. "Oh, they're a pair all right. But maybe with Pammi it's just bridal nerves."

I nodded, but what I was thinking was that bridal nerves didn't usually include a fear of being murdered at your own wedding. Did Pam stay away from dinner because she was afraid Michelle might make an early attempt? A little rat poison in her pinot noir or a spice of strychnine in her veal?

"Were you here when Mr. Gibson died?"

"No, that was several housekeepers ago. I've

only been here six months. Michelle goes through hired help like Pam goes through fries. Even soggy ones. I'm lucky I've lasted as long as I have."

"Why was the last one fired?"

"Michelle didn't say, but the woman was so mad she called up to warn me. She said Michelle had accused her of stealing a ring, and she might do the same thing to me."

I couldn't do anything to right some wrong that may have been done to the former housekeeper, but if I could locate her she might tell me who'd worked for Michelle before her, and I could then work my way back to the name of the housekeeper at the time of Gerald Gibson's death. Who knew what interesting tidbits might turn up with a bit of tactful questioning from moi?

"Do you know the woman's name, the one who was fired?"

"Mildred something-ordinary. Smith or Jones or something like that."

A disappointment, but then a shortcut occurred to me. A brilliant shortcut, if I did say so myself. I didn't need Mildred. Efficient and organized Michelle would surely have pay records going back to the time of her husband's death. All I need do was get into her office when no one was around and dig up the name.

"Oh, one more thing." Shirley leaned forward,

as if what she had to say was confidential. "There's a hot tub in the Fitness Room in the basement. I like to slip down there late at night and soak away the aches and pains."

"Michelle doesn't mind if employees use it?"

The button-brown eyes danced with surprising glee. "She'd probably say it was fine, but I figure it's easier not to give her a chance to say no. Anyway, slip on down there any night you want to try it."

"Thanks, I will."

But not tonight. Tonight I was so tired that after Shirley and I enjoyed slices of melt-in-your-mouth chocolate-swirl cheesecake, I went to bed and never stirred until morning.

The next day more guests arrived, including one couple who flew by private plane into the tiny Vigland airport, where I picked them up. Most guests were lodged at the inn, but this couple got a room at the house.

Because this was Mr. and Mrs. Stan Steffan, the big Hollywood producer-director. They got what I now knew was called the Lilac Room, the largest bedroom on the second floor. I expected a trophy-type wife, but Mrs. Steffan's face and shape were decidedly matronly and her tinted hair a little too goldy. An explosion of pink flowers sprigged her dress.

I carried in their luggage, and she opened one

bag immediately, kicked off her shoes, grabbed a pair of shapeless slippers, and flopped into a chair with a sigh of relief. Big bunions bulged on both feet.

"I do believe fashionable shoes were invented by the same person who invented the thumbscrew," she declared.

"Along with thong panties and skintight jeans."

She looked surprised, then smiled with a hint of conspiracy. "And false eyelashes. I glued my entire eye shut one time. And another time we were at one of those boring A-list parties, and when I leaned over to say something to a young man, an eyelash fell off in his drink."

"What happened?"

"I think he wanted to yell something about what a stupid, clumsy old broad I was. But he couldn't, of course, not to Stan Steffan's wife. So he just pretended nothing had happened and drank around the eyelash."

Her satisfied giggle was infectious. I liked her. She seemed quite down-to-earth, unlike some of the other Hollywood guests.

Mr. Steffan was a different story. I took up a second load of luggage, and he came in as I was going out. A beefy guy with mirror sunglasses, an oversized diamond ring, a paunch, a sour expression, and a cell phone at his ear. He looked straight out of central casting: *Send us a guy who looks like a big Hollywood producer. The kind*

71

who'll sic the Mafia on you if you give his movie a bad review.

He brushed by me as if I were a potted plant and slammed the door behind me. "If that woman thinks—" he stormed.

I was tempted to linger a moment, ear to door, but another guest was passing by so I had to move on.

Pam pointedly ignored me. She never asked for limousine service. I did manage to tell her, when I ran into her in the hallway, that I'd be happy to cat-sit Phreddie at my house while she was on her honeymoon. She paused momentarily, as if considering the offer, then said, "I think I'll take him along."

A cat on a honeymoon. Well, no more peculiar than some of the other oddities of this wedding, I decided.

But if Pam didn't want limo service, everyone else did. Shopping runs, manicure trips, sightseeing jaunts. Another run to the Sea-Tac airport. I was beginning to wonder if there would be any locals at this wedding.

I became increasingly aware of a tension, even an overall hostility, churning around the entire scene. Not an aura of doom-and-gloom; something more high-powered than that, more like a pressure cooker about to blow. Perhaps with applause from some of the participants if it were someone else who got blown.

The House People and Inn People didn't mingle, I noticed. House bridesmaids shopped at a mall in Olympia. Inn bridesmaids had their nails done at Vigland's best beauty shop. I didn't overhear as much conversation as I'd like, because people usually kept that partition in the limo slammed tight.

But not always. Snide remarks flew like rice at a wedding. *Sela Malloy must have put on ten pounds, have you seen her? Right, and did you watch Jody Simon's sitcom pilot? I was simply cringing.*

Plus jabs at Michelle and Pam. Of Pam an inn bridesmaid giggled, "Have you ever seen eyebrows like that? Like caterpillars trying to mate!" Answered by, "Caterpillars on steroids!"

A MOB (as I'd begun thinking of the mothers of bridesmaids) said you'd think Michelle would at least provide decent maid service there at the house. Which went along with my impression that most of these people thought they were up here slumming.

MOB #1 added, "I'm wondering if she thinks Stan Steffan is going to give her a part in *Any Day Now*." With the response from MOB #2, "At her age? She'd better think again. After that last flop he had, I hear he's having trouble raising money for the new one, and putting her in it would be a death blow." And then I heard MOB #2 say to someone else about MOB #1,

"Did you go to that awful party she had? The one where the caterer served the pasta that tasted like glue?"

Oh, lovely people, these. Like members of some reality show, all eager to vote someone else off the planet.

On the second evening Shirley waited to eat a late dinner with me.

"So, how's it going?" I inquired over the wonderfully tender rack of lamb.

"With all the catty stuff I'm hearing, maybe I shouldn't bother with good meals. I could just serve platters of Friskies."

"Why did all these people come, I wonder? They certainly don't seem to have much fondness for Michelle. Or each other."

"I think Michelle persuaded the Steffans to come first and then used that to lure everyone else. They're all Hollywood people, and you know what a herd mentality they have."

Being unfamiliar with Hollywood people, I didn't know, but I laughed and encouraged her. "I imagine you hear a lot of interesting tidbits."

"Do I! You can't help overhearing things sometimes, when you're dusting around doors. Especially if you dust v-e-r-r-y slowly." Shirley smiled slyly. "Like today."

I was happy to accept her obvious invitation. "What happened today?"

"Mr. Steffan . . . you know, Steffan Productions? The one everyone kowtows to?"

I nodded.

"He and Michelle were holed up in the Africa Room, and I just happened to have some dusting to do in that vicinity—"

"I do admire your conscientious dedication to dusting."

Another of her trademark sly smiles. "I couldn't hear much of anything at first. Then it sounded as if someone jumped up and knocked a chair over, and Michelle started yelling something about that being practically blackmail. Said she wasn't about to pay any million dollars to be in his lousy movie, but if that was the game he wanted to play, she could play it too."

"What did that mean?"

"I don't know. I was so startled when she yelled that I fell off my stepstool and crashed like an elephant walking a tightrope." She rubbed her knee.

"I suppose they heard you fall?"

"There was more yelling, both of them this time. Then Mr. Steffan yanked the door open, but I don't think he even saw me when he stomped out. Although you can't tell where that man is looking, with those sunglasses he wears 24/7. I keep wondering, does he wear them when he's brushing his teeth?"

"Or trimming his nose hair?"

"Anyway, Michelle came to the door then, and she knew I'd been listening, all right. I think she'd have fired me on the spot, but with a houseful of guests, she didn't dare. But I figure that after the wedding—" She sliced a finger across her throat. "You can just bet she won't give me a decent recommendation."

That was Wednesday evening, and I was surprised at how much I missed what had become my usual midweek activity of Bible study at church. But I'd brought a New Testament, along with the printed guidelines for our study this month, and I read in bed for a while.

On Thursday, the day before the wedding, the level of activity revved up. The tent people arrived and erected a giant green-and-white striped tent, with a divider between ceremony and reception areas. I had to limo a seamstress out to the inn to do last-minute alterations on a bridesmaid's dress. The casino, connected to the inn by a glass walkway, served a fantastic buffet, and apparently Pam wasn't the only one not watching her diet.

Right after lunch UPS brought a package for Pam. It was small but heavy. *Books,* I thought, as I hefted it. I took it up to her room on the attic floor. I knocked, but she didn't answer, so I opened the door to set the parcel inside. I suppose I could have left it in the hallway, but, hey, it was my duty to see it safely inside, wasn't it?

I realized when I cracked the door open that this part of the house had escaped Michelle's relentless modernizing. The ceiling sloped steeply to old knotty pine walls that Pam had decorated with posters of book covers. A zoo of stuffed animals occupied the bed. I didn't realize one of them was live until Phreddie gave a drowsy, "Mrrr?" The one window looked out on the backyard, and an array of computer equipment lined the opposite wall, a Mickey Mouse clock above the monitor. In spite of the high-tech equipment, the room felt old-fashioned and cozy.

I stroked Phreddie's head. He purred and turned on his back to encourage tummy rubbing. A sweet kitty. I looked around as I rubbed.

I hesitated for a moment, but curiosity triumphed over conscience, and I sneaked over for a peek. It was Pam's book manuscript, the title *The Sting of Death*. I flipped through the pages, skimming a line or two here and there. The victim had been killed by bee stings.

Except that this victim was female. A female *stepmother*.

A noise startled me. I hastily straightened the papers and rushed to the hallway, sure I was going to meet an angry Pam at the door. No, just

Phreddie, making an inspection tour. Apparently he didn't usually get out of the room. I didn't want him to run downstairs and arouse Michelle's ire, so I scooped him up and plopped him back on the bed.

I wanted to go back and read more. I'd like to say an attack of conscience deterred me, but it was really the thought that only luck had kept me from getting caught so far, and I'd better not push it.

I was safely downstairs before a thought occurred to me about what wasn't in the room. No wedding gown, no veil, no shoes, no fancy lingerie, no bridal frippery, nothing at all to suggest this was the abode of an excited bride. Not even a photo of the husband-to-be.

It wouldn't totally surprise me, I realized, that even if Pam didn't call off the wedding she might simply skip out on it. Where was she now, in fact? If she didn't show up she'd accomplish the proverbial killing of two birds . . . maybe even three . . . with one stone.

She'd avoid the risk of being murdered at the ceremony.

She'd satisfactorily humiliate and embarrass Michelle in front of her Hollywood guests.

And she wouldn't have to go through with a marriage that I was beginning to think was concocted of little more than desperation and a hopeful mantra.

I stopped in the kitchen to grab a glass of iced tea and asked Shirley about the wedding gown.

"Oh, it's here. It's in Michelle's bedroom. All $24,000 worth. After the ceremony it will be put on a mannequin and stored in some kind of hermetically sealed bubble that's supposed to preserve it for at least five generations. Can you imagine the poor girl in generation five with that monstrosity taking up space in her living room?"

"It's a little . . . creepy. Kind of like preserving a mummy."

"Really. By the time fifth-generation girl gets it, she'll probably be wondering if that is her dead great-great grandmother in there. The bridal bouquet is going to be freeze-dried for preservation too."

In spite of the creepiness of preserving the gown like a dead body, I also found it unexpectedly reassuring. If Michelle was thinking beyond the wedding, surely she wasn't planning Pam's demise during it. Unless this was more of what Pam called the "big, fat smokescreen."

"When is the groom arriving?" I asked. "Isn't there a three-day waiting period between getting the license and having the ceremony?"

"He flew up a couple weeks ago, and they did everything then. Though he was in such a hurry he didn't even stay overnight. If I were Pam, I'd be wondering how much time he's going to have to devote to a marriage. He hasn't seemed to have much time for the engagement."

One doesn't usually hope the groom doesn't show up for the wedding, but I found myself starting to wish for exactly that. I figured it would solve any number of problems.

Michelle doused that hope. When everyone gathered outside the tent for the wedding rehearsal late that afternoon, she announced that Sterling had been delayed because of a complication in his research work . . . his *globally important* research work, as she phrased it. But he and his parents would arrive tomorrow, in plenty of time for the real ceremony.

I was surprised that Michelle took his tardiness so calmly, because she did not take it well when she discovered there were two more no-shows for the rehearsal.

No minister.

No bride.

I was standing around watching because I'd just brought a full limo-load of people in from the inn. Michelle dispatched me to Pam's room to get her. When I returned to report that I couldn't find her, Michelle smiled and murmured something about bridal nerves, but I could see she was furious enough to chew holes in the tent.

Shirley then came out to say the service supplying the minister had just called. He'd been involved in a fender-bender en route and was in the emergency room. Michelle's dark scowl suggested that if he wasn't already in the emergency room, she'd have put him there. But again she gritted a smile and said, "I hope he isn't seriously injured."

I thought the absence of all the major players effectively squashed the rehearsal, but not Michelle. She grabbed a man from the inn contingent to play groom, another to play minister, and, to my astonishment, drafted me as bride. Then she lined everyone up outside the tent.

"Hey, this isn't right," one of the bridesmaids protested. "The bridesmaids and groomsmen are supposed to go in before the bride, not follow her."

Good thing there wasn't a gangplank handy, because Michelle's look would surely have sent the girl marching off into the deep blue sea. She didn't bother to justify her system, simply stated, "This is the way we're doing it at *this* wedding."

She then announced that since one of the groomsmen was going to be "unavailable," one of the bridesmaids would have to go in order to maintain balance in the wedding procession.

At this point, even though none of the girls had shown any enthusiasm for this event, apparently no one wanted to sacrifice herself for Michelle's Great Plan. There was uneasy shuffling in the ranks, then the MOBs got into the argument. And there's nothing more dangerous than a MOB who thinks her daughter is being slighted or insulted.

I'm not sure how it started. Maybe one MOB gave another a little shove? Maybe one MOB accidentally bumped into someone else? Maybe a bridesmaid whirled on shapely feet. But suddenly everyone was yelling and shoving. Pulled hair. Ripped blouse. A MOB went down. Her husband . . . who up until then had been my bridegroom . . . jammed a stiff arm into the belly of the man who had bumped her. Belly-rammed man retaliated with a fist to the chin. Bridesmaids shrieked. A groomsman yelled, rather inappropriately I thought, "Yee-haw!"

Mrs. Steffan had been just standing on the sidelines watching, matronly in her flowered dress and sensible shoes, umbrella in hand to protect her leathery skin from the afternoon sun. But suddenly she dived into the chaos, gleefully jabbing anyone within reach of her umbrella. *Poke,* and a MOB grabbed her injured derrière. *Jab,* and an astonished Michelle whirled. *Prod,* and she hit a buff groomsman in what was apparently her favorite anatomical target.

And then me. I'd been standing there unmoving, a flabbergasted non-participant, so I thought the undignified jab in the rump was totally uncalled for.

"Hey!" I yelled. I grabbed for the umbrella, but

just then the automatic sprinklers turned on, great sprays of water instantly soaking everyone. I was standing right over one and got a faceful. People yelped and dashed to the concrete driveway to escape the downpour.

Bridesmaids squealed. Hair squished and flattened. Wet clothes clung where they shouldn't. Mrs. Steffan got wet too, but she opened her umbrella and just stood there with a pleased, I've-always-wanted-to-do-that expression.

What could anyone say? This was the wife of Stan Steffan, powerful head of Steffan Productions, poking unwary bridal participants. I suspected every Hollywood bridesmaid here, and maybe some of their mothers too, had movie ambitions. No one moved.

I figured that if I were in Michelle's position, I'd burst into tears on the spot. But Michelle was made of sterner stuff.

She broke the wet tableau and rushed over to Mrs. Steffan. "Are you all right?" she asked as if the woman were an injured party rather than an eager umbrella-jabber. Water streamed down Michelle's face and flattened her blond hair.

"A lovely wedding," Mrs. Steffan announced, and proceeded leisurely toward the house while the sprinklers sprinkled on.

Michelle dumped water out of a shoe, swiped wet hair out of her eyes, and decreed that a rehearsal wasn't necessary. "You all know how it's done," she muttered. "Just follow the bride and me."

That wasn't exactly how it was done, ordinarily, but I figured it would work.

Then she squish-stalked off to find and probably behead the yard maintenance man who had charge of the sprinklers.

I went to my room and changed to a dry uniform. I figured there might soon be a demand for my services. But I kept thinking about this departure from the usual wedding processional. Pam had said Michelle would find a way to commit murder at the ceremony. Was this the first step in her plan?

Chapter Seven

Wedding Day!

Shirley and I caught up on current events over a quick breakfast. We'd missed doing this the night before because she was already in bed by the time I got everyone hauled back to the inn.

She reported that the rehearsal dinner had gone off okay, although I think by then we both figured any event that didn't end in a riot was "okay." Having a rehearsal dinner was a bit strange, she said, since there had been no actual rehearsal, and the main players were still missing, but those present seemed to enjoy the Steak Diane and chocolate mousse.

After dinner, Shirley said, Mr. Steffan got a poker game going. Which I already knew, since that was why I was so late getting people back to the inn. From the disgruntled remarks I heard, I gathered Mr. Steffan was the big winner. Apparently the sunglasses didn't keep him from seeing his cards.

It was a beautiful, cloudless day, with a tang of sea coming off the saltwaters of the inlet. And a tang of hysteria coming off Michelle. Out at the tent, she sounded as if she had a bullhorn in hand, even though she didn't.

Chair people, don't put the chairs so close together! This isn't a lap-sitting event!

Carpet people, we don't need speed bumps! This is a processional, not a parking lot! Smooth it out!

At least the sprinklers weren't making so much as a dribble this morning. I suspected they wouldn't dare, or Michelle would rip them out with her bare hands.

I wasn't present most of the time, of course. What I heard came between hairdo runs to the beauty shop, a golf-course trip for Mr. Steffan and buddies, and an emergency run to a drugstore for foot-fungus powder.

Foot-fungus powder?

Don't ask, Michelle said with a roll of eyes. Just be sure it's a big can.

About one o'clock, the flower people arrived to decorate the limo. Sterling and his parents still hadn't showed, but Michelle rushed over to tell me they'd be arriving at Sea-Tac at two fifteen, so I'd have to hurry. I couldn't take the limo, so she tossed me the keys to her BMW.

I hadn't seen Pam all morning, so I didn't know if she'd overslept or decided to take Phreddie and head for the wilds of Siberia. I was pulling for Siberia.

I got my first look at Sterling at the airport. Tall, skinny, heavy glasses, short hair, prominent ears and Adam's apple, strangely rumpled shirt. An experiment in cloning an Armani that had gone awry? As Pam had said, your basic nerd.

In spite of my doubts about Sterling, and his and Pam's relationship in general, she apparently *was* going to marry him, and I'd determined to like him. Nerdy is good! Dedication to work is admirable. Rumpled is endearingly non-pretentious. The kind of guy who'll age into an absentminded-professor type, good to his wife and kids, forever faithful.

Sterling had, after all, made the sweetly sentimental gesture of giving Pam his grandmother's ring. Big point in his favor.

After a few minutes, however, I came to the unhappy conclusion that liking Sterling Forsythe

86

was right up there with trying to like a toothache. His folks seemed okay, uncomfortable in what they obviously considered an over-their-heads situation, but nice. Good in-law types.

Medium-height Joe Forsythe wore an outdated sports jacket and slacks. His brown hair was thinning, but what was left had an expectedly boyish curl. Petite Phyllis's dishwater-blond hair was short, neat, and limp. She kept fingering the neckline of a new-looking blue dress as if it made her neck itch. Both seemed anxious to please, and treated me as if I were some all-knowing, all-powerful guru.

Mt. Rainier, in snowy dress even in summer, dazzled Joe and Phyllis; Sterling didn't even glance at it. Joe expressed an interest in seeing the state capital building in Olympia, and I told him we could take a brief detour and see it up close.

Sterling was on his cell phone, as he had been ever since we left Sea-Tac, but he took time to snap, "C'mon, Dad, we can't waste time on stuff like that."

"I guess we'd better not, then," Joe said apologetically.

"Thanks anyway," Phyllis added. She had a whispery voice that made everything sound tentative and uncertain.

"Does this place where we're staying have wi-fi?" Sterling demanded.

I had a vague idea that wi-fi had to do with computers and the Internet, but I didn't know what, much less whether the Tschimikan Inn had it. Since Sterling appeared to have that cell phone permanently implanted in his ear, my first inclination was to snap, "Why don't you call up Bill Gates and find out?" But I restrained myself and simply said, "I'm sorry, I don't know."

"Figures," Sterling muttered, although I couldn't tell if his disgust was with my ignorance or with the probability of primitive, non wi-fi accommodations.

He stayed on his phone for the remainder of the trip. Without a divider in the BMW, and without any attempt on his part to keep his voice down, I could hear most of what he said. Enough to tell the conversation was about something back at the lab, but it was mostly technical talk beyond my comprehension. Not beyond my comprehension was his arrogant, impatient tone and general rudeness both on the phone and to his folks. By now I suspected that giving Grandma's ring to Pam had been their nice idea, not his.

One sentence was the final death blow to my determination to like him. "I may be able to cut this boat trip short and get back a couple days early," he announced into the phone.

The guy wanted to downsize his own honeymoon.

Oh, Pam. Even if you aren't afraid of being murdered at the wedding ceremony now, run, run, run!

I took them directly to the inn. I usually carried passengers' luggage in, but Mr. Forsythe insisted on carrying theirs himself. Sterling carried his cell phone. Pam and Sterling weren't supposed to see each other until the ceremony that evening. A romantic nicety I thought was wasted on Sterling. I had the impression he'd just as soon skip the ceremony and call in his vows by cell phone.

The limo was parked in front of the house, fully decorated, by the time I got back. I stared in amazement: the decorators hadn't managed to conceal the black completely, but they'd made a good try at it. White and peach colored roses were ingeniously attached everywhere, across the top, fenders, trunk, and hood, around the rearview mirrors, even on the hubcaps. Greenery trailed down the sides, and the windows sported glitter-flecked stars. White, peach, and gold streamers drifted from the back bumper. It was a teensy bit overdone in my estimation . . . like a grand lady loaded down with too many gold chains and pendants . . . but definitely impressive. It practically screamed *Can you imagine how much it cost to do this?*

At this point, with the limo unmovable without risk of damaging the decorations, I hadn't much to do. I wandered around watching Michelle supervise every detail . . . and wondering about murder.

I'd been too busy to think much about it today, but now, as I strolled among banks of flowers sufficient to house stray wildlife and homeless persons, I found myself uneasily expanding on my earlier concerns about how Michelle had changed the processional.

If, as Pam claimed, the murder had to occur before the minister said, "I now pronounce you husband and wife," how was Michelle planning to pull it off?

I could see no way. She couldn't use the tried and true techniques of gunshot or stabbing, not in front of the crowd. A bomb set to detonate as they walked up the aisle might work, but it would surely catch Michelle in the blast too. Besides, where would it be set? Under the carpet?

I felt foolish, but I walked the length of the carpet anyway, looking for unnatural bumps, even getting down on my knees and feeling in a couple of places. Which produced a stray screwdriver and a carton of snuff, both possessing certain intrinsic dangers, but neither of which appeared potentially explosive.

An accomplice, perhaps? But what could that person do? Shoot a poison dart from a slit cut in the tent? Make a sly jab with a hypodermic needle as the procession passed by?

Of course there was still the possibility Michelle might pull off a murder before the start of the ceremony, somewhere behind the scenes. The bomb-in-the-limo thing.

Feeling even more foolish, but too uneasy to ignore that feeling, I checked the underside of the limo as thoroughly as I could. Nothing. Although I had to admit I probably wouldn't recognize a bomb unless it had a red-lettered THIS IS A BOMB, DO NOT REMOVE sign attached.

The fog machine arrived, and the man concealed it behind a bank of flowers, aiming it so fog would gently envelop Pam and Michelle as they walked down the aisle. Except that when Michelle demanded a test of the equipment, what spouted from the foliage was more volcanic eruption than gentle mist.

"No, no, no!" Michelle yelled. "Not so much fog! We want an ethereal mist, not a blast that's going to shut down every airport within fifty miles!"

The next emission of fog was suitably ethereal, and Michelle moved on to examining the huge candelabra set up behind the flower arbor and the rows of candles marching off in both directions. One candle didn't meet her approval, and it met quick candle termination, of course. Then on to the reception area on the other side of the dividing flap. I followed, curious.

In the reception area she physically shoved tables aside as she stormed through. "I told you, there has to be space in the center for the ice sculpture. Move these tables back!"

By this time I didn't see how she'd possibly have the time or energy to orchestrate some sinister murder plot.

Activity increased as show time neared. The ice sculpture arrived in a refrigerated van and was duly transported by forklift to its spot as centerpiece in the reception area. I stared at it in astonishment. I couldn't see any specific resemblance to Pam and Sterling, but it was definitely a bride and groom. Sculpted in ice and set on a low pedestal, the joined figures seemed even larger and more formidable than real life. And . . . menacing. Like ice monsters, ready to burst into malignant life and do some ghastly ice-monster thing. A more practical danger, I decided, was that if the sculpture tipped over it might take out live bride and groom and a few wedding guests to boot.

I was careful to stay well back.

The cake arrived. Eight tiers topped with that oversized silver ornament, each tier separated by garlands of peach and white roses, with bridges to side tiers. Had a bride ever been done in by a falling cake, choked in layers of frosting?

Creative possibilities, but, as I pointed out to

myself, too late. The demise had to come before the vows.

Except that the whole idea of a "demise" was surely right up there with danger of a sea creature rushing up from the inlet and wrapping giant tentacles around the entire wedding tent.

Caterers spread white tablecloths, with centerpieces of more peach and white roses. Rose gardens across half the state must now be denuded. Place cards, names delicately scrolled in silver, went by the place settings. The three-piece band for music during dinner and dancing afterward arrived. A small dance floor had been set up in front of them. I'd expected some stuffy group playing stuffy music, but these guys warmed up with Steppenwolf's "Born to be Wild."

An unforeseen glitch turned up, something that Michelle, in spite of all her planning, had forgotten, and something she couldn't correct by yelling louder. With the limo decorated, I couldn't drive out to the inn to pick up guests and members of the wedding party. Michelle looked panicky for a moment, but she quickly regained her cool and phoned for a fleet of taxis.

The minister showed up early, having been given the wrong time. He was tall, blond, and photogenic, though a bit uncomfortable looking with a heavy brace holding his neck stiffly in place. Michelle planted him near the flower arbor to wait. The harpists who were to play for the processional arrived, looking appropriately angelic in floaty white gowns. I'd never heard of harpists for a wedding processional, but what did I know about a wedding of this financial caliber?

Michelle finally disappeared to get dressed. I had to admire her for allowing less than an hour for this. Especially when at this point her hair looked like blond seaweed washed up on the shore.

I sat in the limo at the foot of the front steps, ready to make the 300-foot drive from house to the white carpet leading to the flower arbor inside the tent. Cars arrived, and I realized there would be no shortage of local guests after all. Two tuxedoed guys showed drivers where to park on the grass. Taxis arrived and disgorged their occupants. Groomsmen in tuxedos showed people to their seats and issued beribboned programs. A lovely evening star came out from behind a drift of clouds. The harpists played sweet angel music. The video cameraman planted himself at the walkway to catch Pam and Michelle's exit from the limo. Bridesmaids in dark peach dresses waited outside the tent, ready to fall in behind Pam and Michelle in the procession.

Three bridesmaids, three groomsmen, I counted. Which meant that Michelle had efficiently eliminated the dangling-fish one.

It only now occurred to me that there was

neither best man nor maid of honor in this lineup. Perhaps because neither Pam nor Sterling had anyone close enough to play that role?

The harpists played on, but in spite of the angel music and lovely setting, what I heard in my head was a movie score building to a crashing crescendo as the moment of disaster approaches. Lurid imagination, I scoffed. Everything was going to go off exactly as it was supposed to.

Except I didn't know what *supposed to* meant in Michelle's plans. . . .

I made a quick call to Fitz, who with Matt was on the *Miss Nora* awaiting arrival of the newlyweds. He reported the flower people had been there too, and the sailboat could double as Cleopatra's barge.

"Matt is grumbling about what we're going to do with all these flowers when they start to wilt. He's afraid some Coast Guard boat is going to roar up and ticket us for contaminating Puget Sound."

Fitz's son Matt has his good points, definitely, but he's also the kind of guy who'd grumble if he won the lottery. *All those taxes,* he'd complain.

"We're just about to get going here," I said.

"You okay? You sound a little breathless."

"I feel more as if I'm . . . holding my breath."

"Waiting for something to happen?"

I told him about Michelle's unusual arrangement for the processional, having the bridesmaids and groomsmen follow her and the bride down the aisle. "It kind of worries me."

"It would probably be a good idea to keep an eye on her, but it sounds more like a star-of-the-show thing to me. Michelle doesn't want to be upstaged by a bunch of beautiful bridesmaids coming in ahead of her."

"You're probably right," I agreed, feeling a smidgen of relief. "Everything is really quite beautiful. The harpists sound as if they're on loan from heaven. The cake and ice sculpture are magnificent."

"You want an ice sculpture when you get married?"

"I don't have any plans to get married."

"Plans change. Maybe you should be thinking ahead."

I jerked the phone from my ear and looked at it in astonishment. What was Fitz saying?

I didn't have time to consider the subtleties of this conversation, because Shirley suddenly ran out of the house.

"Gotta go," I said hurriedly.

"Call me when you're on your way with the newlyweds, okay? We have some old Don Ho wedding music we're going to play to welcome them."

The limo windows don't open because of the bulletproof glass, so I shoved the door open to find out what Shirley's problem was.

"Michelle wants you to come around to the back door."

My nerves jumped. This was outside the schedule of events. Not good. "Why?"

"She doesn't want the guests to see Pammi or her before their big exit from the limo."

Milking every bit of drama from the occasion was Michelle's style, so the change to the back door made a certain sense. No one could preview them coming out of the house and entering the limo. And yet . . .

Was this it? Was this how Michelle intended to arrange it so only Pam and I were in the limo?

"Hurry!" Shirley said. "Pam's about to melt into a nervous puddle."

Much as I was tempted to squeal out in a tempest of flying flowers, I couldn't leave Pam back there alone with Michelle. Who knew what Michelle might pull, out of sight of everyone? A deadly shove down the stairs. A gunshot out of nowhere, with some claim of a bushy-haired stranger . . .

No, no skipping out now.

I backed up and carefully pulled into the narrow gravel driveway that led between house and garage. A few blossoms fell along the way, but I doubted the loss would be noticeable. The limo carried more flowers than a casket. A comparison I wished hadn't occurred to me.

The backyard lights were on, throwing

shadows into the woods. Michelle and Pam stood on the small concrete patio at the back steps, Pam clutching her bouquet as if it were a lifeline.

I got out and opened the passenger door, but I was too nervous to give it my usual your-chariot-awaits flourish.

Pam looked beautiful. The laced bodice on the strapless white gown cinched her waist into almost willowy proportions, and a full tiered skirt flounced gently over her hips. Tiny beads edged each tier of the skirt and glittered in the white embroidery decorating the bodice. A filmy lace stole did lovely things for her shoulders, and the train lent a royal grandeur. A full veil flowed from the tiara planted on the smooth, upswept coil of her hair. And there was space, glorious space between a magnificent arch of eyebrows!

"Pam, you look gorgeous! So glamorous! And sophisticated!"

Pam pressed her lips together as if my honest compliment touched her, and she might even cry. "Glamorous?" she whispered doubtfully.

"Oh, yes. Cinderella glamorous," I assured her.

But then the usual Pam poked through the new glamour. "Amazing what an expert can do with a comb and a little hairspray, huh?" She spread her fingers, which were still the old Pam: stubby and unpolished.

"They wanted to put those fake fingernails on

me, but I said no. . . ." Her voice trailed off as if she didn't understand that reasoning herself.

But I thought I did. She'd let herself be made over into something she wasn't for this wedding, and she half-liked, half-hated the results. But she'd had to draw the line somewhere, and she'd drawn it at the fingernails.

Now she stuck out a foot clad in a silvery high-heeled sandal. "And if I don't fall flat on my face in these, it'll be a miracle."

"You're not going to fall. You'll do just fine." It wasn't my place to say anything, and yet . . . "Doesn't the veil usually cover the bride's face until it's thrown back for the big kiss?"

"Cover that $500 hair and makeup job with a veil? No way!" Michelle cut in.

Pam smiled self-consciously but didn't argue, and, for a change, it looked as if they agreed on something. The new Pam was worth displaying. *A good omen,* I thought gladly.

Pam gathered her train, and I helped scoop it all into the limo with her.

Then came a tense moment. Good omen or not, this was Michelle's opportunity to back out and . . . do what?

Michelle, belying my suspicions, immediately gathered her own skirt and stepped in behind Pam.

"You look gorgeous too," I said a little lamely. The Seattle experts had worked a hair-and-makeup miracle on her in that hour. But Michelle usually looked at least semi-gorgeous, so the change was not so startling with her as it was with Pam. Her gown was pale peach, also strapless, her hair upswept into a froth of blond curls with flirty tendrils escaping near her diamond-clad ears. Her trademark perfume scented the limo with a fragrance identifiable even over the scent of the engulfing flowers. But her expression was definitely dour as she settled into the rear seat.

"Did you see the minister? I picked a Mr. Gorgeous, and what do I have now? A guy with a neck brace big enough to hold up the tent. It's going to ruin the photos."

"We'll tell the photographer to just take him out of the photos if necessary," Pam soothed. "They can do that with the computer."

"Okay, everyone ready now?" I asked as I started to close the door.

"Would you like to come inside the tent for the ceremony?" Pam asked me. "There'll be extra seats in back. Shirley's going to be there." Almost shyly she added, "I'd really like it if you would."

I looked doubtfully at Michelle. A chauffeur in black uniform cluttering up her color scheme?

"Sure, why not?" she said. She lifted her hands airily. "We're all just one big, happy family, aren't we?"

I blinked, but she was smiling, and I didn't hear even a trace of sarcasm in her voice. A mellow Michelle? I went around to my driver's seat wondering if I should search the sky. Maybe pigs were flying tonight too.

I steered the limo back down to the concrete driveway and, trailing streamers and flowers, inched majestically toward the white carpet. I opened the door, and Michelle slid out first. The video camera whirred.

The groomsmen rushed forward to help. The one who gave Pam his hand actually did a double take when he saw her. The procession lined up on the carpet, and one of the bridesmaids spread Pam's train to its full length. Someone must have given the harpists a signal, because the ethereal music suddenly revved up to a more processional level. The lights in the tent dimmed until only flickering candlelight remained.

The procession started, Pam and Michelle in the lead. I surreptitiously circled the lineup of couples and stood near the tent opening, ready to slip in behind the last bridesmaid and groomsman and grab a seat next to Shirley. Sterling and the minister, looking acceptably gorgeous in spite of the neck brace, rose from wherever they were sitting and stood at the flower arbor waiting. I spotted Phyllis Forsythe's limp blond hair in the front row. And there were the Steffans sitting along the aisle, he in those sunglasses, she in another of her flowered creations that made her look like a walking bouquet. There were MOBs and husbands too, plus a lot of people I didn't recognize.

The procession moved majestically down the aisle. The crowd stood. An ethereal drift of mist wafted from the fog machine.

And then it wasn't just a mist. It was a blast, an eruption, an avalanche of fog, enough fog to inundate the Space Needle! The wedding procession and the crowd disappeared into it. It filled the inside of the tent like a storm cloud and boiled out the opening. Screams erupted.

And stink! Stink like I'd never smelled before. Garbage dump, pig sty, rotten eggs, outhouse!

I backed away, but not quickly enough. The foul-smelling fog engulfed me too. My eyes watered and blinded me. My throat spasmed and closed. Inside the tent, no harp music now, just coughs and shrieks. Someone rushed by me, hit my shoulder, and practically bowled me over. And then masses of people boiled out the opening along with the fog. Pushing and shoving, holding their noses, choking, stumbling, eyes streaming with tears.

And everywhere the stink, that incredible smell-from-the-Black-Lagoon stink.

My eyes were still watering, but through the tears I spotted Mrs. Steffan, her ample figure doubled over in a seizure of coughing. A bridesmaid stumbled and crashed to the grass. Another bridesmaid clutched her throat. The minister yanked at his neck brace as if he were choking. Two women barfed like something out of a horror movie.

And there was Sterling. He was a good hundred feet from the tent, blowing his nose and wiping his eyes. He must have bolted down the aisle and escaped first. Was he the one who'd almost flattened me? A real hero. But where was Pam? Apparently Sterling hadn't bothered to make sure she was okay, and I couldn't see her anywhere. Caterer people streamed out of the other side of the tent now too, the smell apparently flooding under and around the tent divider.

The fog was slowly dissipating into waves of mist, but the stench remained. People milled around, getting as far from the tent as they could. I winced when a harpist found a rip in her gown, her reaction a distinctly non-angelic outburst.

I shoved my way toward the tent through the crowd, an awful premonition suddenly giving me strength. This was it. This was how Michelle had figured a way to do it right in front of the wedding guests! Hide a murder behind a shroud of fog.

I was in better shape than the wedding people, because I hadn't been inside with the full force of the blast, but I had to blink and hold a tissue over my nose as I worked my way through the lingering fog inside.

The tent was empty now, dim. Only a lone candle had escaped the fog, and it burned with a ghostly flicker. Chairs were overturned, bows and drapery tangled. Banks of flowers awry where people had stumbled into them, flower arbor leaning at an angle. And stink, oh, the stink!

I stopped short halfway down the aisle. By the light of the flickering candle, I spotted something in the aisle up ahead, something that turned me as cold as the ice sculpture.

Because the tent wasn't quite empty after all. . . .

A body lay crumpled in the aisle. A knife buried to the hilt in its back.

Chapter Eight

No . . . oh, no . . . please, no . . .

I ran to her and felt for a pulse at her wrist, then her throat. Nothing. She lay on her stomach, arms spread, one leg pulled up, airbrushed makeup still intact, hair still elegantly upswept, scent of perfume still lingering. The diamonds at her ears and throat glittered in the candlelight. But the gown tangled around her legs, as if she'd tried to run and been brought down before she could escape. Running from the putrid fog like everyone else . . . or running from her killer? A faint trickle of blood darkened the corner of her mouth. The brass handle of the knife stuck out of her back like some bizarre accessory.

I felt peculiarly detached, horrified but numbed, my mind stalled. *Not possible,* one part of my mind insisted. But another part shivered in horror.

A man in a dark suit ran toward me through the dissipating mist. He knelt by Michelle's body and touched her bare shoulder.

"Is she dead?"

"I-I think so. I can't feel a pulse."

He checked her throat too. He seemed to know what he was doing. I couldn't think straight. Michelle dead. Not Pam, but *Michelle.*

The guy was already pulling out a cell phone as he stood up. "I'll call 911." He spoke with a bit of an accent, but I was too distressed to identify it.

I didn't recognize him. He hadn't been part of the wedding party, but he acted with a certain authority and familiarity. I appreciated the way he took charge. Yet . . .

Michelle was lying here on the wedding carpet dead. Murdered by someone among this crowd of "friends." And he'd showed up suspiciously quickly, coming out of nowhere.

I was still kneeling by Michelle's body. I felt

oddly protective of her. I'd been suspicious and distrustful of her, but here she was . . . not predator, but victim. And this guy, big and muscular, who was he? I looked up at him warily. Distinguished silver hair and mustache said he might be near my age, but a youthful face put him much younger. Forty-five-ish, maybe.

Suddenly a woman was beside him, her expression horrified as she looked down at Michelle. She put an arm around the guy's waist, a hand against his midsection. She was petite, slender in ivory pants and jacket, her dark hair short and curly.

"Uri . . . what . . ."

"She's dead." He tucked the phone back into a pocket inside the jacket of his suit. He blinked hard a couple of times, and I had the feeling he was working hard to keep his emotions under control. "They'll have deputies here within a few minutes. We've got to keep the crowd back so they don't disturb evidence. And where are the lights?" He suddenly yelled it out, as if he had to release a held-back fury somewhere. "We've got to have light in here!"

So far, keeping people back didn't appear to be a problem. No one but the three of us seemed interested in venturing back inside the still-foggy, stench-infested tent.

"Who are you?" I asked bluntly.

"I'm Uri Hubbard, and this is my wife, Cindy.

We're Michelle's partners in the new health club."

That fit. They both looked tan and toned and athletic, though she was considerably younger than her husband.

"I can't believe this." The tremor in Cindy's voice echoed her disbelief. "She was my best friend. Who could have . . . and *why?*"

The name Cindy rang a faint bell now. This must be the person Michelle had been going to see about something . . . treadmills, yes, that was it . . . treadmills at the health club the first day I was here.

"Did either of you see anything?" I asked.

Uri Hubbard shook his head. "No. The fog practically blinded me. I was just holding my breath and stumbling around trying to get back there to the machine and get it turned off. Everybody else was going the other way."

"Including me," Cindy said. "I've never smelled anything so awful. What was it? How did it get in the fog?"

Uri must have been successful with the machine, because the remnants of the fog were motionless now and nothing more was spewing out of the flower bank. The fog felt peculiar on the skin, dampish but in an oily kind of way.

I wondered how hard it was going to be to get the smell out of my uniform. Then I was ashamed of myself for even thinking such a self-centered thought. A few minutes ago Michelle was alive, maybe even mellowing, and now she was *dead*.

"Wasn't someone running the machine?" Cindy demanded. "Where is he?"

"There wasn't anyone back there. I finally got it shut down."

"You know how to run the machine?" I asked, still suspicious. I'd learned in my only other encounter with murder that you have to be suspicious of everyone. As Fitz said, it went with the territory.

The tidal wave of fog could possibly have been an accident or malfunction of the machinery. But that stink was no accident. There'd been no smell when Michelle demanded the fog test earlier. Someone had sabotaged the system. And if this guy knew how to run the machine . . .

Then Pam, skirt lifted, veil flying, came running down the aisle. She stumbled in her high heels when she reached me, almost crashing into the body before she scrambled to her knees, unmindful of the sound of a rip when a heel caught the expensive wedding gown. Another rip already separated skirt and bodice of the gown, probably from when someone stepped on the train. The long train had enough dirty footprints on it to double as a welcome mat. Her tiara tilted to one side, veil half covering her face, and the lacy wrap lay like a wisp of angel lace where she'd dropped it ten feet down the aisle.

She made a noise, more strangled choke than scream, but a bridesmaid who'd followed her inside had no problem producing a full-blown scream. Her shriek rose to horror-movie howl that people on the far side of the inlet and maybe all the way to Olympia could probably hear. Under different conditions I'd have been impressed with her lung power . . . *You take special vitamins or something?* . . . but now I just wanted to join her in a howl of horror. Murder.

Shirley came running. She dropped to the carpet beside Pam and me. "Michelle?" she asked, and I couldn't tell if she was asking a question or hoping for a reply from the crumpled body. "I ran out. . . . I just ran out. . . ." Her wiry shoulders slumped, as if she'd failed in some duty.

I squeezed her arm. "Everybody did. It's okay."

The shrieking girl brought more people running. They crowded around, shoving and trying to see over and around each other. More chairs tumbled, and I realized Uri was right. We had to keep these people back before they destroyed evidence.

I stood up, my knees already going stiff from kneeling. I spread my arms wide. "Okay, everybody, keep back. The police are on their way."

Pam stood up too, but she didn't try to guard the body. She stumbled toward the tilted flower arbor. She was still holding her bouquet. Suddenly, as if it had caught fire in her hands, she gave a little cry and threw it at the arbor. No freeze-dried eternity for that bouquet. Then she just stood there staring at the foliage from which the fog had erupted. When she turned back to where the rest of us were still standing around the body, she looked, as the old saying goes, as if she'd seen a ghost. Face pale, the artfully applied blush now standing out like skateboard burns on her bloodless skin.

"Pam?" I said. "Are you okay? Did you see something?"

I searched the bank of flowers where she'd been staring. I couldn't see anything except flowers, and, when I peered more closely in the dim light, the hole that had been made in them to let the fog through.

Pam walked back to the body, her steps stiff as some science-fiction robot. "I thought . . . but now . . . she's *dead*. Somebody *killed* her. Who would want to kill her?"

She looked straight at me, her eyes dark pockets in the flicker of candlelight, and I couldn't say anything because the first thought that slammed into my head was *You?*

A do-unto-Michelle, before Michelle did unto her?

Pam's gaze held mine, and I could see she knew what I was thinking.

"I didn't do it. I don't know what happened. One minute we were walking down the aisle . . . and then I couldn't see anything in the fog. I couldn't even keep my eyes open. But . . . *I didn't do it!*"

No, not Pam, I agreed. Surely not Pam. Just because she'd been the person closest to Michelle in the procession didn't mean she'd done it. In the chaos, anyone could have jumped in and jammed that knife in Michelle's back, then joined the panicky crowd in escape. Yes, Pam may have had a motive. And yes, she had been closest in the procession. But other people undoubtedly had motives too.

Then shouts and questions started shooting out of the crowd, and a shock wave rolled back through it as information spread. A MOB elbowed to the front and put her arms around the girl who'd stopped shrieking for a moment, but only to take a breath and start again. A man followed and less kindly grabbed the girl's shoulders from behind and told her to *shut up.*

Joe Forsythe pushed his way through the gawkers, pulling his wife with him. Sterling dragged along behind them. They all stared down at Michelle's crumpled body. The gold-colored knife handle gleamed in the light of the lone candle.

111

Tears straggled down Phyllis's stricken face, and she kept blinking. Joe wrapped his arms around her in a gesture that struck me as a desperate but helpless effort to comfort. Joe was not a take-charge kind of guy. Tall Sterling peered out over the crowd as if he'd like to fly over their heads and escape. No emotion from him.

The strings of overhead lights suddenly flared on as someone hit a switch somewhere. They were soft, non-glare bulbs, but under them the whole scene looked unreal, almost staged. As if actress Michelle might jump up any moment, pleased with her performance. Maybe looking to see if Stan Steffan had caught it.

The minister appeared. He touched Pam's arm lightly. "Can—" He broke off when Pam jumped as if he'd hit her with an electric shock. "I'm sorry. I didn't mean to startle you. Can I do anything? Make an announcement to the crowd perhaps?"

Michelle may have chosen him for his good looks, but he also seemed like a nice guy. I appreciated the fact that he wanted to do something other than pray right now.

"Should the ceremony go on?" he inquired. He sounded as if the idea appalled him, but he wanted to be helpful.

My own inclination was to yell, *No, there never should have been any ceremony to begin with!* But what I did was touch Pam's other arm gently and say, "What about the ceremony?"

She just gave me a horrified look and shoved through the crowd, discarding the veil and tiara and losing a silver sandal as she stumbled away with her stepped-on train straggling behind her. I grabbed the tiara, but I didn't know whether to follow or stay with the body.

Fitz, I thought frantically. I yanked the phone out of my pocket and punched the speed dial for his number.

"Cleopatra's barge awaits. Are you on your way?"

"No! Fitz, something's happened. Michelle is dead! I-I'm looking at her body right now. Someone killed her!"

"You're sure?" He sounded doubtful, as if he thought I might be pulling some strange prank.

"There's a knife in her back!"

"A *knife?* When did it happen?"

"Right during the processional! Something went wrong with the fog machine. It put out this incredible blast of fog . . . and *stink.* No one could see anything. And someone stabbed her while everyone was trying to escape!"

"You've called 911? Or the sheriff's office?"

"Someone did. I-I think I can hear a siren now."

"Good. I'll be there in a few minutes."

A sheriff's car screamed up the driveway, and

the crowd that had closed behind Pam parted as two officers charged through.

"Okay, everybody stand back now."

Both officers were coughing by the time they reached the body.

"What is that *smell?*" one of them gasped as he wiped his eyes.

Uri stepped up to talk to the officers. I was glad to relinquish my position as stiff-kneed guard dog beside the body. My head pounded now, though whether from nerves or aftermath of the reeking fog I didn't know. Another car arrived with two more officers, then a third car. I recognized one of the men in plainclothes when he jumped out of the third car. Detective Sergeant Molino, the detective I'd encountered after my old boyfriend's murder, the one who'd warned me civilians had no business muddling around in solving crime. I was glad he didn't spot me.

I stumbled toward the limo. The flowers engulfing it looked macabre now . . . an oversized coffin . . . but still it was a safe haven. I slid inside, grateful for the familiar refuge, like the comforting presence of an old friend.

I watched the officers herd everyone out of the tent. "But nobody leave," one of them yelled. With the crowd moved back, I could see Detective Sergeant Molino and the deputies clustered around the body. Molino was on his cell phone.

Fitz arrived in record time. He parked in front of the limo. I got out to meet him. He wrapped his arms around me and just held me for a long minute.

"You okay?"

"I'm . . . not sure. I can't believe it. Someone murdered her, right there in front of everyone."

"Get back in the limo and tell me about it."

So I did. How Michelle had seemed almost mellow out behind the house. How beautiful Pam looked. The harps. The processional. Then that incredible outpouring of stinking fog. "I've never smelled anything like it."

"It's not gone yet." Fitz wrinkled his nose, although I couldn't smell it now.

Outside the limo, the scene had a garish, nightmare quality. Everyone in dress clothes, as if they'd all dressed up for murder. Flashing lights circling atop the police cars. The three guys from the band clustered off to one side, one of them carrying a guitar. Caterer people in white clothes. Inside the tent, the officers were using heavy-duty flashlights to probe in and under and around things.

"Was the fog really so thick no one could see anything?" Fitz asked.

"It just swallowed up the processional, the crowd, everything. Though the stink was the worst part. Like something out of a horror movie. And people were shoving and pushing and trying to get out. Anyone could have done it in that frenzy."

"What about Pam?"

"I didn't see her outside the tent. But when she ran back in, she acted . . . strange. Then she just ran off." I'd told her she looked Cinderella glamorous, and like Cinderella she'd left a silver sandal behind. But I doubted Sterling was any prince to the rescue.

"Did you see the knife?" Fitz asked.

"Just the part that was sticking out of her back." I couldn't recall looking closely at the knife, yet when I squinched my eyes I could see it clearly, as if the image were branded on my brain. "It was goldy colored, brass I guess."

"Not a kitchen-type knife, then. Maybe a hunting knife?"

"I don't know. It had kind of an odd double handle, as if it were split down the middle. And scrolling on it, swirled lines, maybe leaves and flowers." I squinched again, straining to see the picture buried in my mind. "Or maybe dragons. And a jewel! No, two jewels! Red, one on each section of the handle."

I grabbed a napkin, memento of my last drive-through at Burger King, and sketched what I'd seen of the knife before it faded from my mind. Fitz studied the odd double handle and flowers and dragons I'd drawn. I reached over and shaded the small circles I'd drawn as jewels.

"It looks as if it could be what's called a butterfly knife."

"A butterfly knife," I echoed. I shivered. Such a delicate, lovely name for the deadly weapon now lodged in Michelle's back.

"There are two handles, with the blade concealed between them. You squeeze the handles, which releases the catch holding the handles together." He added a little oblong catch to the end of the handles in my sketch. "Then you give it a spin and the blade flips out. Not quite as fast as a switchblade with a button, but almost."

"It doesn't sound like something the average person would carry around. Are they rare?"

"They're illegal in some states, but they're not rare. You often see cheap, imported models displayed along with pocketknives at flea markets. Although what you've described with the scrolling and jewels sounds more like a collector's knife, probably a valuable one."

A couple of officers moved into the crowd now, moving people around and sorting them into groups, probably for questioning. Then I saw a familiar figure headed toward the limo.

Apparently they intended to start the questioning with me.

Chapter Nine

I got out of the limo before Detective Molino could start hammering on the window. Fitz stepped out too.

The detective stopped short when he saw me. It took him a moment, but that steel-trap mind clicked on my name. "Mrs. McConnell."

"Yes. Andi McConnell. You remember my friend too, I'm sure. Keegan Fitzpatrick." I grabbed Fitz's arm, though it was more for support than identification.

"Fitz," Fitz said, shortening his name to the one everyone knew him by. "Nice to see you again." He sounded as if he meant it.

I didn't share that feeling, but Fitz has a genial personality and can be friendly with anyone. Hey, you space aliens with fourteen tentacles and three unidentifiable extra appendages . . . c'mon over and meet Fitz. He'll give you a welcoming hand-to-tentacle shake.

Detective Molino nodded to acknowledge the acquaintance. I was relieved that he apparently didn't intend to pounce on the oddity of Fitz's presence here. He eyed the flower-bedecked limo. "You were part of the wedding?"

"Michelle hired me to take care of the guests'

transportation needs for several days. Some were staying here at the house, some out at Tschimikan Inn. I was also supposed to take the bride and groom to the marina after the ceremony. They were going to honeymoon on Fitz's son's sailboat."

"So you were parked here waiting for them?"

"Yes, but I also drove Michelle and Pam, the bride, from the house to the tent. Michelle is . . . was . . . Pam's stepmother, and she was giving Pam away in the ceremony. Pam's father is dead," I added, in case Uri Hubbard hadn't already filled him in on all these details.

Detective Molino glanced toward the house, but made no comment on the rather extravagant use of the limo for such a short trip.

"Too bad your limo seems to be a . . . ah . . . magnet for murder," he suggested.

Magnet for murder. A catchy phrase, but not one I'd latch onto for my business cards. And wasn't it just a little unfair? It wasn't as if this murder had happened in my limo. But I just swallowed and kept my comments to myself.

"I trust you'll both let the proper authorities investigate this situation?" Detective Molino asked. "We don't want anything, ah, unpleasant happening. Like the last time you got involved."

Which was when my limo . . . and I . . . had turned into the target du jour. No, I didn't want that happening again.

"I don't know anything about what happened here," I assured him. "I was still outside the tent when the fog machine went wild and started spewing that awful smell and everyone panicked."

With those statements I had sidestepped any promise of not doing any personal investigating, but hopefully Detective Molino wouldn't notice that. I had the uneasy feeling Pam's name would soon top their list of suspects. So even though I'd vowed some time back that my sleuthing days were over, I couldn't just stand by and let her be ensnared in something she hadn't done.

At least something I was fairly certain she hadn't done . . .

"Someone said the chauffeur was the first person to reach the body. I should have realized right away that would be you." He turned to Fitz. "You were there too?"

"No, I just arrived."

"I called him," I said. "For, uh, moral support."

Detective Molino's eyebrows twitched in a scowl, but he made no comment except to tell another officer to get someone on the gate. Michelle had arranged for it to stay open as guests were arriving.

"Uri Hubbard got there just a minute after I did," I said to get the detective's attention off Fitz's presence. "He's also the person who turned the fog machine off. I guess he probably told you that."

I was wondering again how Uri knew how to do that. But it wasn't necessarily a relevant point, I had to admit. Not everyone is as mechanically challenged as I am. Fitz too, for that matter. Between us, we'd probably starve to death on the typical desert island if all we had were canned goods and an unfamiliar can opener. Maybe the fog machine simply had a big valve labeled *Off.*

"You know Mr. Hubbard?" Detective Molino asked.

"I've never seen him before tonight. I understand he and his wife are—were—partners with Michelle in that new health club opening up downtown. You've probably seen the sign. The Change Your World Fitness Center."

"Okay. Follow me," Detective Molino ordered. "I'll take your statement now, although we may need more information later."

At least he didn't seem to have me lined up as a possible suspect, as he had when old boyfriend Jerry was murdered. He turned and started back to the tent without looking to see if I followed.

Fitz's presence wasn't requested, but he followed too. At the tent opening, Detective Molino stopped and turned to face the milling crowd. He raised his voice and said, "We'll start interviewing you individually now. No one is to leave the premises until you've been interviewed and released. Is that clear? No one leaves. For those of you from out of town, it may be necessary to detain you for a longer period of time while the investigation continues."

"What kind of 'period of time'?" Stan Steffan demanded. His dark glasses gleamed like big insect eyes in the light from the tent.

I didn't see Mrs. Steffan. She'd looked sick in that fog.

"I have an important meeting in LA tomorrow night. We have a flight to catch in the morning."

"So do we," someone from the crowd yelled.

Detective Molino held up a hand. He wore a badge pinned to a plain khaki shirt. He'd been in uniform the first time I met him a few months ago, but apparently he'd gone plainclothes now. Those *gotcha* blue eyes hadn't changed, however. "I'm sorry for the inconvenience, but you may be required to stay in the area while the investigation proceeds."

"Actually, they can't do that," Fitz whispered. "They may try to make you think they can make you stay, but unless you're actually under arrest, they can't."

Fitz knows lots of interesting facts about murder and criminal investigation, and, considering our conversation in the limo, knives as well. He'd done considerable research to be sure the facts were right on his TV show.

"I'm not going to tell anyone," I whispered back, although I suspected Stan Steffan had a herd of lawyers back in LA who would clue him in quickly enough on what he could do. "Someone here did it. I want that person caught."

"You have any suspects?" Fitz asked.

"Wasn't it you who told me everyone's a suspect?"

The deputies had blocked off the entrance to the tent with yellow crime-scene tape, and Detective Molino led me to the other section of tent that had been set up for the reception. His upheld hand told Fitz not to follow. Other officers were bringing people in to interview also, spacing us out at tables around the tent. He gave the ice sculpture a passing shot with his flashlight, and I was careful to give it space. The thing still looked like a menace, an iceberg waiting for the Titanic to float by.

I knew the questioning routine from past experience. Name, address, phone number, relationship to the victim, etc. This time, however, Detective Molino had upgraded to a laptop for his notes. Then came the first question actually relating to the murder: Why had I come back into the tent before anyone else?

"Because Pam had fears about her own safety during the ceremony, and I was afraid that in the fog someone might have . . . harmed her. So I went looking for her."

"And Pam is?"

"Pamela Gibson, the bride."

"Yes, of course. Stepdaughter of the victim. Would she be the next of kin?"

"I don't know." Technically, with Pam's father dead, were she and Michelle kin of any kind? "I think the groom's mother is a distant cousin of Michelle's."

"Did you find Ms. Gibson when you went looking for her?"

"No, she must have run out with everyone else. It was total chaos, with everyone yelling and shoving."

"Why did she have fears about her safety?"

"It's kind of complicated, but it had to do with her father's death several years ago." For the first time a startling possibility occurred to me. "Maybe the person really intended to kill Pam, but made a mistake in the fog and killed Michelle instead!"

His fingers paused on the keys. "Mistake?" he repeated. He tapped out something, enough keystrokes to spell the word. Then two more taps. Skeptical question marks after the word?

On second thought, *mistake* didn't seem likely even to me. If someone was close enough to stick a knife in Michelle's back, he could surely see, even in the fog, that his victim was wearing peach, not a white wedding gown.

"You didn't see anyone around the body?"

"No. The tent was empty." I paused. "Well,

124

maybe Uri Hubbard was in there and I just didn't see him. He showed up a minute later."

Detective Molino asked a few more questions, but the interview was actually quite brief. Understandably so, with so many people to interview. I suspected the crowd was already getting restless. A kind of buzz, and once a shrill laugh, came from people milling around outside the tent. I asked Detective Molino a question before I left.

"Did you locate the fog machine operator?"

To which I received the not-unexpected chiding. "Now, Ms. McConnell, you know I can't discuss such matters."

Fitz and I headed back to the limo. I had a peculiar urge to start yanking flowers off it. It looked so foolishly frivolous in the midst of death. I'd have to get them off before long anyway. There were people who'd need transportation back to the inn.

Behind us, a ruckus started just outside the interview area, and I looked back to see meek little Phyllis Forsythe standing in front of her son, arms protectively outspread as she yelled, "No, you can't do that. We want a lawyer!"

I watched, astonished, as she actually advanced on the deputy who was trying to talk to Sterling. She looked ready to pounce if the deputy made a wrong move. He took a step backward, but he also had a hand on the gun at his belt.

For a moment I thought this was going to turn into a strange mom vs. cop showdown, but Joe Forsythe suddenly appeared and grabbed his wife around the shoulders.

I couldn't hear what he said to the officer, although I presumed it was something apologetic, but Phyllis was yelling back over her shoulder even as her husband led her away, and I could hear her plain enough.

"You lay a hand on my son, and I'll have every lawyer in the state after you!"

Shirley the housekeeper suddenly ducked out of the crowd and rushed up to me. "Do you know where Pam is?"

"No, she ran off before the police arrived. Are they looking for her?" I was still watching Joe and Phyllis.

"I don't know. They haven't talked to me yet. What I'm thinking is, the caterers have all that food, and I don't suppose any of these people have eaten, since they were expecting dinner at the reception. I'm wondering if we could just go ahead and feed everyone. They could do it buffet style. But Pam would have to tell them, I think, not me."

Leave it to sensible cook Shirley to think of such a practical matter. In my world, people must be transported. In hers, people must be fed. Food might also serve to keep the crowd's restlessness from escalating into full mutiny at being detained.

"But I don't know," she said, hesitating now, with a glance toward the tent. "Serving a meal, with the body still lying right there . . ."

"The medical examiner will probably be here soon and remove it."

"Good."

"And I think feeding these people is an excellent idea. I'll see if I can find Pam. What in the world was going on with Sterling's mother?"

"They were going to question him alone, like they're doing everyone else, and she had a fit."

The mouse turned tiger when she thought her cub . . . her oversized cub . . . was threatened? But why would she see his questioning as a threat?

Unless she thought he had something to do with the murder.

Oh, surely not. Pam might have a motive, but what motive could Sterling have? Besides, he'd dashed out of the tent so fast he hadn't even had time to connect his cell phone to his ear, no doubt a first for him. No time to commit a murder.

Yet his mother surely knew him better than anyone else. . . .

There were no chairs outside the tent, but Joe had helped Phyllis to a place on the grass well away from the light. He crouched beside her, obviously trying to soothe her. I thought briefly of going over to see if I could do something, but Shirley was saying something more about finding Pam.

I didn't know what had happened to Sterling, but he was nowhere in sight now. The right kind of almost-a-groom would be with Pam, but I doubted that Sterling was.

Phyllis Forsythe's outburst was odd, but it didn't necessarily mean anything, I reasoned. I knew Phyllis was uncomfortable here, and maybe the murder had simply pushed her over the edge. But if she was as protective of her son as this appeared, perhaps she wasn't such great mother-in-law material after all.

Fitz stayed at the limo, Shirley went off to check further into the food situation, and I ran up to the house. The lights were out. Michelle hadn't wanted a blaze of house lights distracting the audience from the candlelit ceremony, but I felt a need for all light possible now. I flicked on every switch I passed on my way up to the attic floor. I knocked on the door, but there was no answer. I tentatively pushed it open. I realized that I was still clutching the tiara. I tossed it onto a chair.

Pam was sitting cross-legged on the bed, torn wedding gown tangled around her as carelessly as if it were a Goodwill reject. The rip in the skirt was bigger now. Fuzzy wisps had escaped the sleek coil the hairdresser had created for her hair. She was holding Phreddie in her lap as if he were all in this world she had to cling to.

No Sterling.

I went to the bed and put an arm around her. "You okay?"

"I'm alive. Michelle's dead." She still sounded as if she couldn't quite comprehend that.

"The police will figure out who did it. They know how to handle these things."

"They're going to think I did it."

I couldn't think of any soothing remark to contradict that statement, because I thought it too. Detective Molino would poke around in the money and house situation, that was for sure. He'd see motive in neon. And Pam's wild accusations about Michelle back when her father died would surely surface too. Due in part, at least, to me.

"Sweetie, I know it's difficult, but I think you should come back down to the tent. Officers from the sheriff's department are here to help now. They'll need to talk to you."

"I don't know anything! I didn't see anything! I don't want to talk to anyone."

"You'll have to talk to them sooner or later. You need to help them find out who did this awful thing. And you need to talk to Sterling too. His mother seems quite upset."

"Sterling." She repeated the name in a strangely scornful tone and made no move to act on my plea to go back outside.

I tried a different tactic. "The officers said no one could leave. Shirley suggested the caterers might as well offer all that food to the guests."

"By all means. What's the line? Let them eat cake! Or in this case, prime rib, lobster, *and* cake."

Phreddie stood up in mild alarm at Pam's outburst, and her moment of giddiness collapsed.

She clutched him again and gave me a wan look. "I'm sorry. That was uncalled for, wasn't it? I just feel so . . . strange."

"It's a strange situation."

"Okay." She seemed to gather herself together. "It isn't the guests' fault this happened, and someone may as well get some good out of that food. I'll change my clothes, and we'll go see that they get fed."

I wasn't quite in agreement with her no-fault statement about the guests. So far as I could see, the killer had to be one of the guests. I was firmly stuffing any possibility of Pam's guilt off in a dead-end corner of my mind.

"You'll have to help me undress. Michelle cinched me into this thing, and I don't think I can get out of it by myself."

She placed Phreddie on a pillow, and I struggled with the laces at the back of the bodice. Pam took a deep breath when the torn gown finally puddled around her feet. Actually, by then, I was wondering how she'd been able to breathe at all in it. Wedding gown as murder weapon? But that was irrelevant now. Pam hadn't died. Michelle had.

Pam stepped out of the gown and abandoned it there on the floor, but I gathered the frothy tiers and folded them at the foot of the bed. Phreddie came over to investigate, then made himself at home. I started to remove him, then shrugged. Maybe, at this point, the highest and best use for the $24,000 gown was as a cat bed. I strongly doubted it was ever going to see another wedding.

I don't know what I expected Pam to change into, but what she chose were a pair of baggy old cargo pants and an equally baggy gray sweatshirt with *Geeks Rule!* emblazoned on it.

When we got to the front door, she stopped me with an almost fierce clutch on my arm.

"Will you stay with me, Andi?"

"I don't think they'll let me be with you when you're questioned."

"I don't mean that. I mean, will you stay . . . for a while? I'll see that you get paid."

I'd agreed with Michelle to stay through tomorrow and transport the guests to their flights as needed. Beyond that I had a couple of short limo reservations, but I could cancel them. So staying was possible, but I couldn't think what help I could be beyond transporting people. And I was certain Pam needed more than that.

"Please, Andi?" she added when I hesitated. "I need you. I-I feel as if I'm still wandering around in that fog. You're the only one I trust."

"Me? Why would you trust me?"

"I know you didn't kill Michelle, but I'm not so sure about anyone else. I don't have any relatives or anyone to call on. You're honest and dependable and you do what's right and you don't want anything."

"There's Sterling and his parents—"

She didn't say anything, and I filled in my own thoughts. Which were that she didn't know any of them all that well, either.

"Of course, Pam." I patted her hand reassuringly in spite of another doubtful thought of my own: I wasn't totally sure about Pam herself. "I'll stay as long as you need me."

Chapter Ten

Outside, another sheriff's department car had arrived, plus a van from the medical examiner's office. Inside the tent, one officer was videotaping the body and interior of the tent from all angles; another was doing the same thing with a regular camera. Another was taking measurements and marking them on a clipboard. A man I assumed was the medical examiner knelt by the body, but I couldn't see what he was doing. Flashlight beams, disembodied in the darkness, probed outside the tent now. A few cars were leaving, occupants apparently questioned and released.

I figured we'd better ask Detective Molino about feeding the crowd, but he was conferring with the medical examiner. Pam clung to me while we waited, as if she were afraid I might vanish into the night. A few people glanced at us, but I had the odd feeling most of them didn't even recognize Pam out of her wedding finery. In her baggy old clothes, with about $498 of her $500 hair and makeup job gone, she looked about the fifteen I'd thought she was the day I met her.

I spotted Fitz several times as he circulated through the crowd, being his usual friendly and helpful self, once disappearing and then returning with a glass of water for an elderly woman. But if I knew Fitz, he was also shrewdly gathering bits of information.

Pam stared in dismay when Michelle's body was loaded onto a stretcher, covered, and carried past where we stood by the entrance.

"What are they doing?" Her voice rose on a note of panic.

"In a homicide, the medical examiner takes charge of the body. They have to determine cause of death—"

"But they don't need to do that. There's a knife in her back!"

Which now made a spiky hump in the sheet. They'd loaded her on her stomach, apparently to keep from disturbing the knife. I knew from what Fitz had told me about a case on his TV show that entry angle of a knife could be important. I'd already concluded that anyone who could shove that knife to the hilt in Michelle's back was no weakling.

Pam looked as if she might be going to interrupt the procession to the van, and I put a restraining hand on her arm. "Pam, you know about things like this. You did research for your book, remember?"

She hesitated but finally nodded and stepped back.

Detective Molino had followed the body to the van, and we intercepted him on the way back to the tent. He hesitated for a minute, as if the question I asked had never arisen before, but he finally agreed that it would be okay to feed the crowd.

Shirley showed up again, and she and Pam went off to talk to the caterers. The other deputies consolidated their interview areas into one corner of the tent so guests could eat while the questioning went on. I noted that catering people, harpists, and anyone else who'd had any connection with the wedding were being interviewed along with guests. My contribution was to go around and gather place cards from the tables, so people could sit wherever it was convenient to eat. I saw a couple of guys from the crime-scene crew carrying out what I assumed was the fog machine. I wondered if they'd located the machine's operator, who definitely had some explaining to do.

It certainly wasn't a party-time atmosphere as the guests ate. Most people still seemed to be in shock, so even though there wasn't exactly a reverential silence, the voices were generally subdued. Appetites did not appear to be unduly affected, however. For no particular reason, I thought about the biblical account of Jesus feeding a crowd with just a few loaves and fishes. And he'd done it without a caterer from Tacoma.

When the line finally thinned, Fitz and I filled plates too. I was a bit ashamed, but I hadn't eaten much today and, in spite of murder, I was hungry. Michelle hadn't skimped on the quality of food. The lobster tails were generous sized, the prime rib superb. I didn't see anyone drinking the expensive champagne she had bought for the reception. The cake was also left untouched, although I didn't know whether this was by Pam's orders or some sensitivity of the caterer. In any case, I was relieved. Prime rib and lobster might be rationalized as necessities of life, but wedding cake and champagne under the circumstances would have been . . . macabre.

Michelle had wanted this to be the wedding of

the century. And it was. Though definitely not in the way she'd intended. That thought too felt a bit macabre.

Afterward Fitz got a couple of oversized garbage bags from the caterer, and we started un-decorating the limo. The questioning of the guests continued. Detective Molino kept Pam at his table longer than anyone else, and her steps were unsteady when she finally stumbled out of the tent. I ran over to her.

"Pam, can I do anything? Maybe—"

She brushed by me. "I'm going up to bed."

"Good idea. We'll talk in the morning, okay?"

Three taxis had come and gone by the time Fitz and I finished with the limo, although I didn't see who left in them. About that time, media people arrived, the only surprise about that being the time it had taken them to get wind of this newsworthy event.

Deputy Molino talked to them for a minute, but I was fairly certain he blew them off. A video cameraman targeted me, and a hyperactive lady I recognized from a TV news show shoved a microphone in my face.

"I understand you were the first person to find the body!" She said it with the same breathless enthusiasm she might have used if I'd been gold-starred as Limousine Driver of the Year.

I started to mutter, "No comment," which

probably wouldn't have deterred her. Fitz had a better solution.

"She has a problem with English," he said helpfully. Not exactly an untruth. Who doesn't have a problem with the English language?

"Then would you translate the question for her?" the woman snapped impatiently.

Fitz smiled amiably. "Sorry, I don't speak Litzomenian."

The woman frowned.

I offered her a rose and said, "*Mika ur ubra*?" in my best Litzomenian, whatever that might be.

She turned away and sought more productive pastures. Fitz and I exchanged conspiratorial glances.

"The Daisy Detectives score again," he whispered.

That was what his son Matt had labeled us once, because of our mutual appreciation of those unpretentious flowers . . . and his frustration with our sleuthing activities.

What would I do without Fitz? A woman could fall in love with a man like this. "*Siko umo eaknit yum*," I said to him earnestly.

"Huh?"

"It's Litzomenian. You figure it out."

By now a limo-load of released people had gathered for transport to the inn. Joe and Phyllis Forsythe were there, but when I inquired about Sterling, Joe said he'd left earlier in a taxi.

On a sinking ship, I figured Sterling Forsythe

would beat the rats to the escape hatch.

I made two trips to the inn. Fitz came along, riding in the passenger's seat beside me, welcome company and support. My nerves were beginning to tell on me by the time I finally parked the limo in the graveled driveway by the garage, where it would be out of the way. Police cars still littered the driveway. In spite of my weariness, Fitz and I walked back to the tent to see what was going on. Most of the guests appeared to be gone now. The tent entrance was still blocked with yellow tape. Inside, I saw that the section of carpet where Michelle's body had lain had been cut out and removed. Which would no doubt come as an unpleasant surprise to the carpet people. I wondered if Pam was now responsible for paying for a new carpet.

"Did you learn anything interesting from people you talked to tonight?" I asked Fitz.

"Oh, this and that. We can talk about it tomorrow. You're too tired tonight."

True.

He walked me back to the house, planted a kiss on my cheek, and said to call him as soon as I felt like it in the morning.

Inside, I found Shirley gathering cups from the living room. She'd provided late coffee and snacks for everyone, of course. I doubted earthquake, flood, or invasion by ice monsters would stop Shirley from providing coffee.

"So, did they figure out who did it?" I asked, since it looked as if the House People had spent some time sitting around rehashing the situation.

"It's a toss-up between two theories. Number One: some unknown stranger sneaked in, purposely sabotaged the fog machine in order to commit the murder, and then escaped unseen. Number Two: the fog thing was a weird accident, and someone already on scene impulsively took advantage of that to commit murder."

Someone who just happened to be carrying a butterfly knife?

"Were they naming names?" I asked.

"No, but they were watching each other like chickens suspecting a hawk. One sharp noise and they'd all have hit the ceiling."

"So what do you think?"

"I think . . . I'll just have to think about it some more."

Me too.

I trundled wearily down the hallway and opened the door to my room. And stopped short when I saw the faint outline of a body on my bed.

Chapter Eleven

Okay, not a *body,* just a prone figure, I realized with relief when she sat up.

"I'm sorry, I didn't mean to scare you," Pam said.

"I thought you were going to bed."

"I couldn't sleep."

She'd brought Phreddie along, I saw when I turned on the overhead light. He was curled up on my pillow. Sleeplessness isn't a problem for cats. I closed the door behind me. Even tired as I was, I realized I probably couldn't sleep either.

"Did you want to talk about what happened?"

For a moment that peculiar haunted look I'd seen out in the tent when she'd stared into the flowers passed across her face. She swallowed convulsively, and her lips parted as if she were about to make some startling revelation. But all she said was, "I just didn't want to be alone."

Flattering that she'd chosen me, perhaps, but under the circumstances, there probably wasn't a wide choice. "Did you talk to Sterling?"

"By phone. He's leaving tomorrow, but his folks are staying for a few days. I think I told you Phyllis is Michelle's cousin. Though it's second or third cousin, or some cousin once removed, however that stuff works."

Good ol' Sterling. High-tailing it out of town as if a hanging posse were after him. Which birthed a thought. *Should* a hanging posse be after him? I couldn't think why Sterling would want to murder Michelle, but everyone's a suspect.

Pam hauled her feet up on the bed to sit cross-legged. I envied her bendability. If I tried it, I'd hear a snap-crackle-pop that had nothing to do with breakfast cereal.

"That's good Joe and Phyllis are staying, don't you think?" I took off my black jacket and hung it in the closet. It had had a long, hard, and smelly day and needed a trip to the dry-cleaners. "Maybe they can help you with arrangements for the funeral."

"A funeral?" she repeated, her tone aghast, as if this thought had never occurred to her.

"A funeral, plus all the legalities that will have to be taken care of." I wondered if Michelle had a will, and, if so, who her executor and heirs were, but I wasn't going to bring that up now. "But we don't have to worry about that tonight."

"Okay." She sounded willing to put these complications off indefinitely. She peered around the tiny room. "As soon as the guests leave, you can move to one of the bigger bedrooms upstairs if you'd like. The Nautical Room is nice. Michelle did it with seashells and netting and some old steering wheels off boats."

"Maybe you should invite Sterling's parents to stay here."

"Here?"

"I think the reservations at the inn were only through tonight. And the cost of rooms at the casino may be prohibitive for them. Phyllis seems to be the closest thing Michelle had to a relative."

"I guess it would be the polite thing to do, wouldn't it?"

"Have you and Sterling decided to postpone the wedding?"

She twisted the ring that was still on her finger. "Only if *postpone* means not in this lifetime."

Which would make Joe and Phyllis's staying here awkward to say the least. Which also meant they'd probably decline. Good. Pam didn't need any more stress.

"Do you want to talk about you and Sterling?"

"Not really."

I switched on the lamp, turned off the glary overhead light, and plopped down in the swivel chair. My feet gave a big sigh of relief when I kicked off my shoes.

"I guess what I'm thinking about tonight is . . . other things."

Murder, I presumed. So what she said next startled me.

"Death kind of makes you think about . . . God and stuff. It's scary, you know, *dying*. And

142

afterward." She sounded uncomfortable but determined, back to that fifteenish streak that sometimes surfaced in her on-again off-again maturity.

"I don't think even believers relish going through the process of dying, but they don't have to be afraid of afterward."

"Why not?"

Hey, wait a minute, God. What's going on? I'm just an amateur here. I don't understand a lot of things myself. And You expect me to jump right in and spout words of wisdom to some other lost soul? Not fair!

But she was sitting there looking at me expectantly, so, even though I felt as if I were trying to lead the way with a head of cauliflower instead of a spotlight, I took a deep breath and said, "I think it all comes down to God loving the world so much that He sent Jesus. And the Bible says if we believe in Him we'll live forever with God."

"That doesn't sound too complicated."

Hey, how about that? I was amazed. Maybe God had lit up my cauliflower! Though I hoped she wouldn't ask what "living forever" would be like. I sometimes have these misgivings when it comes down to the specifics. Endless hymn singing? Strolling through fields of flowers? Crocheting angel robes? I had to admit that sometimes it seems a little, well . . . unreal.

"How'd you get started on the God stuff?"

The God stuff. A phrase she'd used before. Well, if that's what we had to work with, so be it.

"With me it wasn't a death situation. It was a *life* thing. I had a young friend who was pregnant, and, through an unlikely set of circumstances, her baby was born in my limousine."

Pam sat up straighter. "Really?"

"Really. Right by the side of the road. A doctor was on the phone with me, but he wasn't there. I was the first one to hold the baby in my hands, and it just hit me. Here was this miracle, this new life, God's miracle of creation, and it happened right there in front of me. It made me think I wanted to know more about this . . . God stuff. So I've been trying to learn. And what I see now is that the start of life and the end of it are connected, both part of God's plan."

"What happened to the girl and her baby?"

"The family she works for moved down to Portland, and she went with them." And how I did miss both Joella and baby Tricia A.!

"Does God talk to you? I read some of the Old Testament after Dad died, because the guy Michelle had do the funeral quoted some verses. I never could find the ones he mentioned, but from what I read it looked as if back then God was more talkative than an infomercial."

"Sometimes I think He's communicating with

me, but I don't hear a big voice booming out of my mashed potatoes, if that's what you mean. Though I've sometimes thought it would be easier if I did."

"Yeah." She smiled slightly and played with one of Phreddie's ears. Kind of a beat-up ear, I noticed now. "An e-mail would be nice. Or maybe a text message on my cell phone."

"Looking back, I see that God used the birth of Joella's baby to talk to me." To give me the kind of "shove into faith" that Joella had said she'd received when she was feeling lost and confused. "I never heard any actual voice or words, but He was communicating. I think, even if we think we want to hear God talking to us, we don't pay attention when He does. We're too busy worrying and fussing and trying to do everything on our own."

"Christian people don't seem to have life easier than anyone else."

A troubling observation I'd made myself. But I had a little different perspective on it now. "God isn't a vending machine, where you deposit your faith or your good works and He spews out a great job or fantastic abs or a Ferrari. Although some people come to Him thinking like that. Then they're disappointed when that isn't the way it works."

"So how does it work?"

I heard a challenge in her voice, and again I

145

wondered what God was doing here. Surely He could have assigned someone more experienced and competent than I am to talk to Pam. But I didn't see any volunteers standing in line, so apparently I was elected.

"When you make a commitment of belief and ask for forgiveness of your sins—"

"That's such a old-fashioned word. *Sins*."

"You can call them something more politically correct if you want, I suppose, but a sin's a sin. Anyway, God then gives you the promise of eternal life. And He also promises to help you cope with this here-and-now life. He's promised that He'll never leave you or abandon you. But that doesn't mean He's going to give you an angelic boost over all the potholes and rough spots. You have to slog through them like everyone else. But the difference is, you have God beside you, and you can lean on Him."

She gave this some thoughtful consideration, then asked skeptically, "And you really do believe all this?"

Leave it to Pam to get right down to the nitty-gritty. I sighed. Sometimes my beliefs and doubts get as tangled as spaghetti leftovers at an Italian greasy spoon.

"I think I do. Mostly I do. But I don't understand a lot of things, and I have to admit that doubts creep in on little pitter-patter paws." Or sometimes clomp in on big clown feet.

"Like about Noah and his ark? Jonah and his fish?"

"You did read your Old Testament, didn't you?"

"Some in the New, too. Some of that stuff in Revelation is pretty wild."

I smiled reluctantly. "Yeah, it is, isn't it? But some things you just have to take on faith. Unlike, say, gravity, which is also God's doing, but it's more self-evident. And there's also the mystery of how two ounces of chocolate can add two pounds to your thighs."

Pam smiled again. "I've wondered about that too." Phreddie rolled over on his back, and Pam absentmindedly rubbed his tummy.

"I'm sure what I'm saying is overly simplistic, but I have to go with simplistic until I understand things better myself. But one thing I do know is that God puts a very high value on faith. On believing and trusting even when we don't understand everything."

"Simplistic is okay. I think I can come closer to believing about God when you admit you have doubts and aren't just swallowing it all like some gullible groupie. Though I have a little trouble taking things on faith. I like things solid. Like a mathematical equation."

Pam stood up. She wrapped Phreddie around her neck like a big fur collar, two feet and head on one side, two feet and tail on the other. He purred contented agreement with the arrangement.

But if I thought she was going to jump into a big "God stuff" commitment, and earn me brownie points in some heavenly rating scheme, I should have known better.

"I'll think about all this," she said.

"Me too." *Odd,* I thought. I still felt in way over my head here, but maybe helping Pam find her way was how God would help clarify things in *my* head.

"Thanks for talking to me."

I opened the door for her. I still felt she was holding something back, but apparently she wasn't going to reveal it tonight.

"See you in the morning," I said. "Although if you decide you want to talk to someone in the middle of the night or anything, I'm here."

"Like if I want to confess to murdering Michelle?"

There it was, out in the open. But all I said was, "Whatever."

"And you're going to pray for me." Her tone was gently mocking, but she smiled.

"I am," I admitted. "You could also pray for yourself. And me too, for that matter. And anyone else who needs it."

"I could?"

"You don't have to know a special password or anything. God's always listening. Actually, I find that kind of—" I broke off, searching for the right word, and came up with one that isn't a usual part of my vocabulary, but seemed to fit. "Kind of breathtaking. Here's God, with a whole universe to run, and yet He's still willing to listen to me at any time."

"That is kind of . . . breathtaking."

She started to step into the hallway, but impulsively I put a hand on her arm. "Pam, do you know something about Michelle's murder that you aren't telling me?"

"You're hoping for that confession?"

"Not necessarily. But if you did it, confessing would be the best thing to do."

"I'm sorry if it disappoints you, but I didn't do it. I didn't have kindly feelings toward Michelle, you know that. But I could never stick a knife in anyone's back, not even hers."

"Could someone else have the same suspicions you've had about your father's death, or perhaps even know something for certain, and have killed her because of that?"

"I can't think of anyone except me who cared that much about his death. Maybe it was something else entirely." A hint of that haunted look crossed her tired face again.

"What kind of 'something else'?"

"I'm going to bed."

Chapter Twelve

I made two fast trips to Sea-Tac the following morning, doubling up on passengers. That emptied the house, except for the Steffans, and got rid of the MOBs and bridesmaids from the inn as well. The sky opened up with a downpour that settled into a steady drizzle, and complaints about the weather were a bigger topic than murder. Which suggested to me that priorities among some of these people had all the depth of a smear of mascara.

Apparently the authorities hadn't requested that any of them stay. I wondered if that meant they were cleared of all suspicion, or if Detective Molino had decided he couldn't get away with some en masse detainment order. Or if he already had the killer in his sights.

There were still police cars and crime-scene people working the area, and yellow crime-scene tape encircled the entire tent now. Joe and Phyllis Forsythe had quickly accepted Pam's invitation to stay at the house, and after lunch I helped them move from the inn. I was rather curious about why they were staying on. Was Michelle's funeral really that important to them?

I'd decided I preferred to stay where I was, so

they got the Nautical Room, which Shirley speed-cleaned when the guests cleared out. Although not without some unflattering commentary.

"That girl shed worse than a St. Bernard. I've never seen so much stray hair. And how could anyone leave fingernail polish blobs on the *ceiling?*"

The shapely-footed bridesmaid had occupied the room. Maybe she had some secret ceiling exercise to keep her feet photogenic. Or maybe it was just that Hollywood people are big-time different from you and me.

I talked to Fitz by phone a couple of times, and we planned to meet at the CyberClam Café that evening and use their Internet to see what we could dig up on both Michelle and guests. But late that afternoon, while I was returning from one last run to Sea-Tac, he called to say they'd picked up a last-minute overnight cruise with the *Miss Nora*, so he couldn't make it.

"What about all those flowers?" I asked.

"I made up a bunch of bouquets and spread them around some nursing and assisted living homes."

Leave it to Fitz to think of something like that. Yes indeed, even a semi-disillusioned-about-men, sixty-year-old limousine driver might fall in love with such a guy. Although I wasn't making ice-sculpture plans yet.

Fitz said he'd call the next day when they got back to the marina.

Shirley, in the midst of making baked salmon and potatoes au gratin for dinner, offered a glass of raspberry iced tea when I got back to the house. I guess by then I looked as if I needed a boost.

I hadn't seen Pam all day, but now, I was surprised to hear from Shirley, she was in the living room with her not-to-be in-laws and the Steffans, apparently being politely social. Or could she be doing a bit of sleuthing on her own? Was she wondering, as I was, why both the Forsythes and the Steffans were still here? I couldn't think, even if the police had told Stan Steffan and his wife that they had to stay, that he'd knuckle under so easily. Didn't he have some big meeting in LA scheduled for this evening?

"What's the deal with the Steffans?" I asked Shirley as I added a smidgen of sugar to the tea.

"Mrs. Steffan came to tell me they'd be staying on for a few days, so I'd know how many to expect for meals. She said they'd decided if there was anything they could do to help with the investigation, they owed it to Michelle to do so. Michelle starred in one of their first big hits, and they were very fond of her."

Hmmm. That didn't jibe with the hostility of the conference between Michelle and Mr. Steffan in the Africa Room that Shirley had overheard.

"Do you believe that?"

"Mrs. Steffan said Stan was very upset, and I think she'd been crying."

So Stan Steffan was now going all sentimental and bighearted about Michelle, and didn't mind losing out on his important meeting? Pardon my cynicism, but I couldn't buy that. And just what kind of "help" did they plan to offer?

Phreddie wandered into the kitchen, which apparently meant he was no longer confined to the attic. He stopped short when he spotted Shirley, however, and the fur on his back stiffened into a ridge, as if perhaps they'd had unfriendly confrontations before.

She flapped her hands at him. "Scat, cat."

Phreddie scatted, and Shirley sat down at the kitchen table with me. "The Stan Man, as I heard someone call him, is about as sensitive as a turnip, but she seems nice. She made a point of telling me how much she's enjoyed the meals here, especially my breakfast biscuits and rack of lamb."

"She seems like a friendly, down-to-earth sort."

"I'd guess she's put up with a lot over the years. Offhand, I suspect the ol' Stan Man is a skirt chaser big-time. Though I didn't actually see anything to confirm that." Shirley sounded disappointed with the admission. "He just seems the type."

"Doesn't she have a first name? I never hear anyone call her anything but Mrs. Steffan."

"She seemed so friendly that I asked her about that. But she didn't even tell me her first name— just said she preferred to be called Mrs. Steffan."

"Well, okay. Mrs. Steffan it is, then."

When Shirley went in to announce dinner, I went to my room to change out of my chauffeur's uniform. It was almost dark by then, but the sky had cleared to a soft blue, and I decided there was still time to wash the limo. Roadspray thrown up by too many eighteen-wheelers on all those trips to Sea-Tac, plus a few too many visits by local seagulls here on the inlet, had dimmed its sleek elegance.

I didn't have the supplies and long-handled brush I use at home, but I looked in the garage and found car-wash detergent, a bucket, soft rags, and a stepstool to stand on. These were storebought "rags," however, not the tattered remnants of old sheets and towels that I'm accustomed to. I drove around back of the house, turned on the yard lights, found a hose, and got started.

Pam came out when I was about halfway done, by which time I had as much water on me as on the limo.

"Hey, I'll pay for a car wash," she called. "You don't have to do this."

I paused in scrubbing a hubcap. "Actually, I

154

enjoy it. It's kind of like playing in the sprinkler when I was a kid."

"Really? I never did that. We always had a pool. Can I help?"

I started to say, no, never mind, but then I changed my mind. The physical activity might do her good. She hadn't dressed for dinner and was in shorts and T-shirt. "Sure. Grab a rag."

So we companionably sloshed and scrubbed and rinsed, and I got a fresh supply of rags from the garage for drying. After the limo was back to its black-jewel gleam, I asked if she'd like to wash her bug. It was sitting over behind the garage, a hidden spot to which Michelle must have banished it.

"Sure! Let's do it."

So we scrubbed and polished the bug. It was a bit like trying to beautify a wart, but maybe cleanliness is next to godliness, even for a VW beetle.

Somewhere along the way Pam stood back and said, "It's really an awful color, isn't it?"

Under the yard lights, the yellow gleamed more egg-yolky than ever.

"Any more awful, and you'd be pulled over for littering on the highway."

Pam rubbed the rusty edge of a fender. "I guess the only reason I never had it repainted, or got a different car, was because Michelle hated it so much."

For a moment I thought I heard guilt or regret in her voice, but then she shot a harsh blast of water at the windshield, as if she were determinedly rejecting regret.

"You still think Michelle killed your father?" I asked bluntly.

"I'm sorry I never told her I liked what she did with the Nautical Room. I'm sorry I did some other kind of . . . mean things. And I know it's not nice to say bad things about the dead. But I still think she did it. Although I guess it doesn't matter now, does it?"

"Probably not." Someone else had already given Michelle a death sentence. But who? And why? I still felt there was something Pam wasn't telling me. An unexpected thought occurred to me.

"Do you really want to know who killed her, Pam?"

She lowered the hose and looked at me. "What a peculiar thing to say!" She managed to sound aghast.

"Which you've just avoided answering."

"Of course I want the guilty person caught. A murderer can't just get away with it. In fact, I've been thinking, maybe you and I should get together and make up a list of suspects for Detective Molino."

From past experience, I figured the detective would greet presentation of any such list with the

Pentagon's enthusiasm for a to-do list from a housewife in New Jersey. But putting our heads together couldn't hurt. Fitz and I figured on doing that anyway.

"I think we need to consider all the guests, and I didn't even know most of them. Though Michelle must have had a guest list somewhere." After a moment's hesitation, as if she was uneasy about snooping, Pam added, "I guess we could look in her office."

I remembered then what I hadn't thought about since I'd done it. "I picked up the place cards that were set up for dinner at the reception. They must still be in the pocket of the uniform I was wearing. We can get all the names there."

She looked surprised. "Why did you pick up the place cards?"

"I was just trying to be helpful, so people would feel free to sit and eat anywhere and not have to go around looking for an assigned place." I'd planned to give the cards to Detective Molino, but I'd forgotten. Or maybe my sneaky subconscious had something like this in mind all along.

But now, thinking of Theory #1 that had been espoused by some of the wedding guests, that a stranger could have come in and committed the murder, I added, "Maybe you can come up with names of people who weren't necessarily guests—outside people, anyone with whom she'd had a problem or conflict."

"But someone like that wouldn't have been at the wedding," Pam said, in what, oddly, sounded to me like a sidestep. But what could she be sidestepping?

We finished washing the bug and agreed that I'd come up to her attic room after I changed into dry clothes, but Stan Steffan met us in the hallway.

"Could I talk to you for a minute, Pam?" He actually pulled off the dark glasses when he spoke, something that immediately put me on guard. It's the kind of gesture someone makes if trying to appear all open and accessible. Not the Stan Man's usual demeanor, which tended more toward a disdainful *You're in the way. Get off my planet.*

Pam held her hands out from her sides and turned up her palms. "I'm kind of wet—"

"That's okay. I don't mind."

No thought that Pam's wet condition might be uncomfortable for *her*.

Pam didn't miss that either. "Well, if you don't mind, then I'm sure it will be fine. Let's go to Michelle's office."

The sarcasm passed right over his head, and he motioned for her to lead the way to the Africa Room.

I wished I had a reason to dust around the doorway so I could listen in, but since I didn't, I went to my room, showered, and changed to dry jeans and sweatshirt. I found the place cards where I'd stuffed them in the pocket of the uniform that I'd wrapped in a plastic bag to contain the smell.

Shirley wasn't in the kitchen, but I ate a plate of leftover salmon and salad and then climbed the stairs to the attic room.

Pam, in cotton pajamas definitely not of the honeymoon variety, opened the door. Phreddie was curled up on his $24,000 cat bed. I saw that the space beside the computer where Pam's manuscript had been stacked was now empty, and I dumped the place cards there. Curious as I was about Pam's meeting with Stan Steffan, I didn't feel I had any business questioning her about it, but she jumped right in without my asking.

"Mr. Steffan had a business proposition for me."

"What kind of business proposition?"

"He said Michelle had wanted to invest in his new movie, and he'd agreed to let her do it. Then he said, under the circumstances, he thought it would be only fair to give me the same opportunity."

Pardon my continuing cynicism, but I doubted that "letting" Michelle or Pam invest was some big favor. Other guests had known he was having trouble raising money, and the term "blackmail" in regard to the money he wanted from Michelle had been tossed around in that conversation Shirley overheard.

"He said he was going to let her invest a million dollars. An even million."

If I could whistle, I would have, but I've been whistle-challenged all my life. Though another thought occurred to me. "A million strikes me as a lot of money, but I don't think it would go far toward actually making a movie."

"You know that old politician's saying. A million here and a million there, and pretty soon you're into real money. Maybe he needed it for seed money, something he could use to raise more or get a big loan."

"Did Michelle have that kind of money?"

"Probably. She seemed to be throwing a lot of it around on the new fitness center, though I heard the three of them arguing one time about what that big sign was costing."

"Are you interested in Mr. Steffan's offer?"

"I don't have a clear idea of what my financial situation is. I'll have to contact the legal firm over in Olympia that handles the trust fund. But offhand . . . I doubt it. I don't think I'd be comfortable investing money that way."

Good thinking. Investing in a movie struck me as about as sound an investment as buying real estate on Mars. "I overheard one of the MOBs say—"

"MOBs?" she interrupted.

160

Oh dear, I hadn't meant to reveal that unlovely little acronym. "Mothers of bridesmaids. I'm sorry. It just seemed easier than trying to keep their names straight."

"Never mind. I started thinking of the bridesmaids as the Four Stooges because I never could remember their names."

MOBs. Four Stooges. We smiled at each other in rueful conspiracy.

"But then there turned out to be only the usual Three Stooges at the ceremony," she added. "I never did know how I lost one."

I explained about Michelle's efficient re-balancing of the procession when one groomsman went AWOL. "Could the ousted one have been peeved enough for murder?" I wondered.

"I wouldn't think so, but who knows? Do you know who she was?" She fanned through the scattered place cards.

"If I do, I can't think of her name at the moment. What I overheard was a MOB saying that Stan Steffan was having trouble raising money for his new project. Which makes his 'offer' look like something less than the investment of the year."

"And I overheard a couple of bridesmaids saying you had to watch out for him. That he had roving hands."

Which went along with Shirley's observation

about skirt-chasing. No rave reviews for Stan Steffan here.

"Are you thinking there may have been something going on between him and Michelle?" I asked.

"Maybe way back sometime," Pam said. "But not now."

"Not even if she was trying to get into his current movie?"

"I don't think so."

Pam suddenly stalked across the room and swept the place cards to the floor. "I wish I'd never even thought about getting married! I wish I'd spent the summer backpacking in Italy. Or living in my VW and being a bag lady for the summer. Then none of this would have happened."

"You don't think there was some sort of cosmic justice in what happened to Michelle? That maybe she got what was coming to her?"

"I'd rather she were alive so there'd be a chance I could find out if she killed my father! This way I'll probably never know."

Not the most noble of reasons for regretting Michelle's death, but I was relieved that she wasn't taking some ugly satisfaction in it.

"Are you sorry your relationship with Sterling seems to be—" I broke off, trying to pick a suitable word. "Stalled?" I suggested finally.

Unexpectedly, she smiled at my choice. "My

bug *stalls*. Airplanes *stall*. Sterling and I are roadkill. But I don't think you'll find either of us shedding buckets of tears."

"I have to admit I've been curious about your relationship. It didn't really look like a, oh, fairy-tale romance."

"Sterling definitely isn't into fairy tales. Or anything else you can't put under a microscope and examine. He's twenty-nine. He has a lot of responsibility with his work, and he's very busy. I know he often stays at the lab until ten o'clock at night. He's also efficient and practical. I think he figured it was time to get married and start a family, but he didn't want to bother with dinners and movies and romantic walks on the beach. I was acceptable and available without all those bothersome details."

"Why were you so 'available'?"

"I wanted to get control of my trust fund. I wasn't happy at Dartmouth. I was supposed to be working toward a degree in mathematics—"

"Michelle's plan?" I guessed.

"Oh, yes. And she had control of the trust fund, of course."

"You don't like mathematics?"

"Well, yeah, I do." She sounded as if she made the admission reluctantly, as if she'd have preferred to say she hated the subject. "I was taking advanced college level courses even in high school. Numbers are solid. They don't change on you. Two plus two equals four is going to come out the same tomorrow as it does today."

"Unlike people?" I guessed.

"And God."

"God doesn't change!"

"I've been thinking about it, and I really do have trouble just taking things on faith. It would be a lot easier if I could come up with a mathematical equation that proves God exists."

"But can you come up with a mathematical equation that proves He *doesn't?*"

She blinked. "I guess not."

"Okay, so if you like math, why were you unhappy at Dartmouth studying it?"

"Mostly I didn't want Michelle telling me what to do," Pam admitted. "I decided I'd rather go off somewhere and write mysteries. Which infuriated her, of course. She put anything to do with creative writing on a level with Tattooing 101."

"So you're writing a mystery in which you kill off the stepmother."

She whirled as if I'd jabbed her with a tattooing needle. "How did you know that?"

"I'm nosy. I snooped."

I expected chastisement, maybe even a heave-ho down the stairs, but she just smiled wryly. She didn't even ask when or how.

"Well, you're honest about it. Which is why I trust you."

"I'd suggest you not let the authorities get hold of that manuscript. Given that it concerns murdering a stepmother, it might give them suspicious ideas."

"You didn't mention the manuscript to them?"

"No."

"See? That's why I can trust you. Anyway, I thought of that already."

I wondered what she'd done with the manuscript, but she didn't elaborate.

"Anyway, married to Sterling, I figured I'd have plenty of time to write or do whatever I wanted."

Right. Sterling would probably never notice what she was doing unless she smashed his cell phone with an overweight manuscript.

"And after losing Dad, and then Mike, I guess I wanted to . . . belong to someone." She sounded wistful.

Don't we all? For a moment I felt a echoing wistfulness in myself. Mostly life on my own is fine, but sometimes . . . But hey, who was Mike?

"Mike and I had broken up, and I felt as if I were just blowing in the wind."

So, Mike was another man. "It's better to blow in the wind than be weighed down with the wrong anchor."

Pam lifted her neatly shorn eyebrows. "Words of wisdom and experience from the older generation? Or a bumper sticker?"

"Whatever."

She blinked hard for a few seconds, but she wasn't one to give in to emotions. With a wry smile she finally added, "The only point against Sterling was that Michelle thought he was catch of the year. But I decided there were enough advantages to marrying him that I could ignore her approval."

"What about his grandmother's ring?"

"I'll give it back to his folks. I'm sure it was their idea for him to give it to me. He'd never think of anything so sweet and sentimental himself."

She dismissed Sterling with a brisk gathering of scattered place cards, then picked up the top one on the stack. "Okay, let's get started. Who's Rosamund Blanchard?"

Chapter Thirteen

"I think she's a MOB. The one whose daughter is the foot model. She was unhappy about the bridesmaids' shoes."

"Murderously unhappy?" Pam asked.

"I wouldn't think anyone could be *murderously* unhappy about shoes. But I'm a tennies person, and maybe it's a different world when you're into Manolo Blahniks or Ferragamos."

Pam pulled a manila envelope from a box on top of her file cabinet. She labeled it *Probably Not* and dropped the place card inside. "For now anyway. No one's a definite no at this point." She picked up another card. "So here's Kristin Deacon."

We looked at each other blankly for a minute until Pam finally said, "I kind of remember her. Red hair. Supersized boob job. Maybe she was the bridesmaid Michelle eliminated?"

"No, I think that was a tall blond."

Pam added Kristin to the *Probably Not* folder, and we worked our way on through the cards. Groomsmen, husbands of MOBs, miscellaneous Hollywood people, plus a number of names that left us both blank, possibly locals. At Stan Steffan's card, we looked at each other again.

"Maybe?" Pam said.

Nothing truly solid to go on with the Stan Man, except that hostile confrontation Shirley had overheard. But murdering Michelle, if he was trying to pry money out of her for his new movie, didn't sound logical. Still, Stan Steffan struck me as a streetwise guy who'd know about such things as butterfly knives, and he was big and beefy enough to use one. And call me judgmental, but I was just suspicious of him.

"A *Maybe*," I agreed. Pam labeled a new envelope and stuffed his card inside.

We came to Mrs. Steffan's name farther down

in the jumbled pile. Pam tapped the card reflectively.

"Even if there was something between Michelle and Mr. Steffan a long time ago, I wouldn't think Mrs. Steffan would do anything about it at this late date. I can't really imagine her jumping up in her flowered dress and attacking Michelle. She's not exactly your all-around athlete."

I agreed. Although if the murder weapon had been an umbrella, I might have considered it. Then another thought. "Unless she was afraid Michelle would get a part in the new movie, and she and Stan might revive an old relationship?"

"I hadn't thought of that." Pam wavered a moment, then dropped Mrs. Steffan's card in the *Maybe* file.

My own thought was that Mrs. Steffan might be of greater value as a source of information than as a suspect. She might know something about Michelle's past relationships with Hollywood people, some old grudge bitter enough to carry over to the present. She might even know something about Michelle's early relationship with Pam's father and birth mother.

I started to mention this to Pam, then backed off. Not knowing about her father's death was frustrating for Pam, yes, but frustration might be preferable to entangling herself in that past. Better she let go and move on. Which didn't

168

mean I wouldn't try a bit of probing with Mrs. Steffan myself.

"What makes you so certain there wasn't anything going on between Michelle and Stan Steffan now?" I asked.

I thought she was ignoring my question, because she riffled through the remaining cards and pulled out two, and it was another minute before I realized this *was* an answer when I saw the cards. *Uri Hubbard. Cindy Hubbard.*

"Michelle's partners in the new fitness center?"

"Cindy started out as Michelle's personal trainer. She came here to the house several days a week. They were really good friends, the BFF type."

"Best Friends Forever?"

Pam nodded. "I think Uri was working at a health club over in Olympia. Then they all got together on starting a new fitness center here in Vigland, and Uri and Cindy have been living in a cottage in the woods over on the east side of the property. But I think Michelle's and Cindy's BFF relationship may have been under some strain lately. They were arguing a lot about the center."

"I don't think I've ever seen them coming and going to a cottage."

"There's a separate gate over there. I think Michelle was putting up most of the money for the health club, but the big drawing card was some new exercise machine Uri invented. It's supposed to take off weight and build muscles and probably raise your IQ too. There's one down in Michelle's Fitness Room, but they were planning a big public unveiling at the grand opening of the club."

"But what would this have to do with a relationship between Michelle and Stan Steffan?"

Pam hesitated. Finally she said, "I think Michelle and Uri had something going, which may have been another strain on the BFF relationship." Wryly she added, "If you had your choice between Uri and Mr. Steffan, which would you choose?"

Stan Steffan, sixty-five-ish, paunchy, heavy-jowled, and arrogant.

Uri Hubbard, tall, muscled, and buff, with distinguished good looks and that handsome silver mustache.

Like choosing between Pam's egg-yolk beetle and my glossy limo.

Then Pam shook her head as if angry with herself. "It isn't right, is it? Saying ugly things about Michelle when she's dead. And I don't know for sure about her and Uri. I'm just guessing."

"But it's a strong guess?"

"I saw him kiss her one time. It didn't look like a business-partners kind of kiss. And I ran into him in the upstairs hallway just outside Michelle's bedroom one night."

170

"A business meeting, perhaps?"

"At two A.M.?"

"The truth can be ugly. But it may have to be brought out if it will help pinpoint who killed her."

But just whom would this kind of truth pinpoint? Stan Steffan was the one who had the power to put her in a movie, and power can trump good looks and muscles.

"Maybe Uri thought she did have something going with Mr. Steffan and got jealous, with or without good reason, and took action?" I suggested.

"In that case wouldn't he have put the knife in Mr. Steffan, not Michelle?"

True, which tended to drop Uri out of the *Maybe* category. Yet I couldn't get past the uneasiness I felt with how quickly he'd appeared at the body.

Pam tilted her head thoughtfully. "I'd be more inclined to think Cindy was afraid she was going to lose Uri to Michelle, and she could be the one who 'took action.' Since they were also arguing about the health club so much, maybe Cindy figured she'd just as soon Michelle was out of the picture. Two birds with one stone and all that."

I thought back to the only time I'd seen Cindy, there beside Michelle's dead body. A petite woman, smaller than Michelle, but trim and fit.

With the qualifications to be a personal trainer, she probably had sufficient strength to wield a knife. This was where that angle of the knife in the body might be important. It would definitely be different if petite Cindy rather than someone taller had done it.

"What do you know about Uri and Cindy?"

"Not a lot. Except Uri is an unusual name, and he talks with a bit of an accent. Although I'm not sure what kind of accent."

The possibility that Cindy might have decided to do away with her rival, and/or her adversary in the business, definitely put her in the *Maybe* file. Yet wouldn't the new business collapse without Michelle's money? I was still thinking about that when I saw Pam slip both cards into the *Maybe* folder.

"Why Uri?" I asked. "You're thinking maybe Cindy didn't know about his relationship with Michelle, and Michelle threatened to tell Cindy so Uri killed her?"

Pam looked surprised. "I hadn't even thought of that, but it's possible, I suppose." She thoughtfully jiggled the envelope between her fingertips. "Basically, I was just thinking, if he's cheating on his wife, I don't think he falls into the good-guy category."

Possibly a bit judgmental, but it worked for me. Could Uri have been hiding some if-I-can't-have-her-no-one-else-can rage? Or could there have been some murder-deep conflict over the health club, and Uri and Cindy were knife-deep in it together?

On with the names. Two more went in the *Maybe* file, one of them the blond ousted as a bridesmaid, another the guy I thought had lost the most money to Stan Steffan in the poker game. Neither struck me as really viable suspects, and I thought Pam was grabbing at straws to include them, but she insisted. We were almost through the stack of cards when the phone on the nightstand by Pam's bed rang. There was a private, unlisted line to Michelle's office, but the main phone system was set up to ring downstairs where Shirley could screen out unwanted calls or transfer the call on to Michelle or Pam.

"We can finish this up tomorrow," I said, not wanting to intrude. Maybe it was Sterling calling.

"No, that's okay. It's probably just a guest who forgot something." She crossed the room and picked up the phone.

I studied the remaining names. Sterling's parents. Would they have any reason to want Michelle out of the way? I couldn't think of any, and neither could I imagine either of them having the level of nerve or rage it took for murder. Although Phyllis had turned tigerish when she thought Sterling was threatened. . . .

But Michelle was no threat to Sterling; she'd given a big thumbs-up to his marrying Pam.

Sterling himself? Certainly no obvious motive. Which might only mean we hadn't yet discovered an *un*obvious one. Which could be true of any number of people.

I considered people whose names were not on place cards. All the people hired to make this wedding work, from harpists to caterers to parking-lot guys. Doubtful on any of them. Except for one, who stood out like the stink he'd made. The fog machine operator.

In fact, I now wondered why Pam hadn't started with him rather than all these guests. Without the bizarre performance of the fog machine, there'd have been no opportunity for murder. So did that mean he could be the murderer? Or a murderer's accomplice?

Although it was possible, of course, that the fog machine simply malfunctioned, and the killer took advantage of the situation. Yet if that was true, what kind of person just *happened* to be carrying a fancy, collector's-type butterfly knife?

Which brought me full circle to the thought that no way could the incredible *stink* have been an accidental malfunction.

Sometimes, when I'm tired or nervous, I have a tedious dream in which I walk round and round on what seems to be a giant cookie. I felt as if I were cookie-walking now.

But it shouldn't be difficult to find out who supplied the fog machine for the ceremony. Efficient Michelle had surely kept records about everything.

I hadn't been paying attention to Pam's telephone conversation, but now I realized it was mostly a one-sided dialogue. Her lips were parted and her eyes wide, but she wasn't saying anything, and she'd gone peculiarly pale.

"I-I'll have to think about it," she said finally. The person on the other end said something more, and she scribbled on the scratch pad by the phone. "But I'll have to think about it," she repeated with an edge of stubbornness.

She put the phone down and slumped on the bed.

"Is something wrong?"

She picked up the pad and looked at what she'd scribbled. Reading upside down . . . a skill I'd cultivated because Fitz's TV detective used it so effectively, and it was kind of fun . . . I could see that it was a phone number.

"That was Mike."

Mike . . . Mike. I ran the name through my mental directory of guests and came up blank. Then a dawning. "Mike, the old boyfriend?"

"He wants me to meet him. He says he has to talk to me."

"Do you want to see him?" I asked, puzzled why his call had jittered her so badly. Until the obvious thought hit me. "Are you still in love with him?"

"No!" The answer was almost too quick. She paused. "I was so young when we were together, what did I know about real love?"

As if she were so old and jaded now! But I know that young love can sometimes be very deep. And last a lifetime, even if mine didn't.

"Does he know about Michelle's murder? And that you didn't marry Sterling after all? Or did he even know you were getting married?"

"He didn't mention any of that, but the murder has been all over the news. They made a big deal about it ending the wedding."

I hadn't seen either newspapers or TV, but I knew Shirley had turned away many phone calls from reporters, and there'd been a few of them hanging around the gate, even taking photos through the bars. I'd squelched an urge to stick my thumbs in my ears and wave fingertips at them.

"He just said he had to see me."

If he still had feelings for her, which seemed an obvious reason for the call, calling the day after the collapse of her wedding struck me as short on sensitivity. But then, the early bird gets the worm and all that.

"Are you going to see him?"

She looked down at the scratch pad still in her hand, then up at me. "Will you come with me?"

"Me! Why would you want me along when you meet an old boyfriend?"

"Last night, at the wedding—" She broke off as if checking her mental time frame.

I had to agree. The wedding seemed much longer ago than last night. A veil of unreality hung over the whole evening, like a lingering shroud of that fog.

"Yes, last night at the wedding," I encouraged, because she seemed to have stalled.

"I-I thought I saw him."

"You mean he . . . what? Gate crashed?"

"I don't know. But just after the fog started, I thought I saw him looking at me over that bank of flowers."

"The flowers where the fog machine was concealed?"

She nodded. "Except I'm not sure I really saw him. Maybe I was imagining it. Maybe I just *wanted* to see him. Maybe some foolish part of me hoped he was going to swoop in like a knight on a white horse and rescue me, and so I imagined him. But then after Michelle was murdered I was afraid I *hadn't* imagined him. . . ."

"Are you thinking he could have had something to do with the fog machine?"

"Back in college he played drums with a band. They used a fog machine with some of their performances."

"So what you're saying is—?"

"I-I think maybe . . . he killed Michelle. If he was there, at the fog machine, and the terrible smelly fog was what made the murder possible . . ."

"But why would he want to kill her? You haven't even seen him since . . . when?"

"Over a year ago. You think I'm a total flake, don't you?" she demanded suddenly. "First I think Michelle killed my father. Maybe my mother too. Then I think she's going to murder me. Now I think the guy I was in love with may have killed Michelle. What other weird ideas do I have bouncing around in my head? Maybe Phreddie is really a space-alien from the Planet of the Cats, with plans to turn the world into a catnip farm?"

"I don't know what to think." Except maybe I should take a closer look at Phreddie. But now I understood her haunted expression when she stared into the bank of flowers after the murder. She thought she'd seen the man with whom . . . if my guess was correct . . . she could still be in love. Was this why she was trying so hard to come up with suspects for Detective Molino—someone other than Mike?

"Maybe you should just add Mike's name to the list of suspects for Detective Molino, and let him handle it," I suggested.

"I think I owe it to Mike to talk to him first. Maybe he has some explanation about being there. Will you come with me, Andi?" she repeated.

"I don't see why—" And then another thought occurred to me. "Are you afraid of him?"

"No, of course not!"

"Maybe you should be. If he did kill Michelle and realizes you saw him there, maybe he figures you're a danger to him. Maybe he has in mind getting rid of you too."

"Mike isn't like that!"

"But you think he could have murdered Michelle."

That was enough to make her throat move in a convulsive swallow. "I have to talk to him." She grabbed the scratch pad with the scribbled numbers and reached for the phone.

I figured she'd set up the meeting for tomorrow. Bright daylight, public place. But she no more than put the phone down than she was slipping into shoes.

"Hey, what're you doing?"

She peered at herself in the mirror and flicked a comb through her hair. She didn't look as beautiful as she had after the $500 hair-and-makeup job, but she looked more *alive* than I'd ever seen her. "I'm going to meet Mike."

I glanced at the Mickey Mouse clock on the wall. "You can't go now. It's after ten o'clock."

In answer she grabbed a jacket from the back of a chair.

I put a hand on her arm. "Pam, I don't think this is a good idea." In fact, I thought it was a really lousy idea, right up there with meeting your friendly neighborhood terrorist in a dark alley. "Even if you don't think Mike could be dangerous, you don't know. Maybe he's changed, different from when you knew him. You never have told me why you broke up."

She hesitated. The jacket dropped back to the chair. "Actually, considering what he did, I'm not sure I knew him all that well even back then." The *alive* glow dimmed as her flash of eagerness faded. As common sense took over, I hoped.

"Call him back and tell him you'd rather just talk over the phone," I urged.

"No, I want to see him face to face." She picked up the jacket again and grabbed her car keys from a hook by the door. At this point she seemed to have forgotten all about wanting me to come along.

Well, too bad, young lady, I thought as I shouldered ahead of her at the door.

Because I'm coming.

Chapter Fourteen

One *thing about this,* I thought as I raced to catch up with Pam after detouring through my room to grab a denim jacket, in that egg-yolk bug, *wherever we were going we wouldn't be inconspicuous.*

Which brought up the next point as the electronically-controlled gate opened to let us out. "Where *are* we going?"

"The marina."

"The *marina?*"

I've been to the marina numerous times when the *Miss Nora* is docked, and it's a lovely place, especially on a moonlit night like tonight. Gently lapping water, friendly sounds of boats creaking and rubbing, people on deck companionably enjoying the evening, scent of steak on a barbecue grill.

But the dock would probably be deserted at this late hour, and all this Mike person had to do to get rid of whatever danger Pam posed to him was knock her in the head, shove her off into deep water, and make sure she didn't climb out.

Except that now I'd be there too. Would I be protection . . . or just another splash?

"Why the marina?" I repeated.

"Mike and I used to go there and watch the boats and sit and talk."

Okay, point in Mike's favor. I couldn't imagine Sterling ever doing something at that waste-of-time level. But a lone point in Mike's favor wasn't enough to cancel my suspicion this could be a dangerous trap. Was he shrewdly playing a sweet-nostalgia card to entice Pam to that particular spot?

"Look, before we get to the marina, at least fill me in on some background. Mike who, by the way?"

"Mike Andreson. We met a couple years ago when I was here for the summer. He'd attended the University of Washington for a year and a half, but his dad had a heart attack and he dropped out to keep his dad's business from going under. He thought it would be temporary, but I don't think his father was ever able to go back to work."

"What kind of business?"

"Landscaping and yard care. I met him when he came to the house to do some mowing and pruning." She smiled reminiscently, and for a moment that glow surfaced again. "I crashed my skateboard, and he picked me up as if I were some petite princess instead of a chunky geek. It took me about five minutes to fall in love. It lasted over a year, although I was away at school most of the time."

I didn't say anything, but I could imagine what Michelle thought of her stepdaughter taking up with hired yard help. No wonder she'd pushed Sterling Forsythe. *Dr.* Sterling Forsythe, actually.

Yet there was certainly something admirable about Mike Andreson sacrificing his own education to keep the business going for his father. Also something rather white-knightish about rescuing a skateboard-dumped damsel. Which, for no particular reason, reminded me of that urge I'd long had to try skateboarding. "So what caused the breakup?"

"I'd just gone back to school last year when Mike's sister called me. She said—" Pam broke off and clutched the steering wheel as if it were trying to escape.

We were going by the site of the new fitness center now, the lightning bolt across the emblem of the world garishly lit. I fleetingly wondered how Michelle's murder would affect the planned grand opening.

"She said Mike had been seeing another girl all the time he was going with me, and now she was pregnant. So they were getting married."

Gaping hole in the white-knight armor.

"Did you talk to Mike about this?"

"Kathleen said Mike asked her to call because he didn't want to talk to me. So I didn't try to talk to him either. There really wasn't anything to say. I didn't feel like congratulating him on his upcoming nuptials."

"What about this summer? Did you ever check up on him?"

"No. I was concentrating on marrying Sterling." She hesitated, then, sounding guilty, added, "I did look in the Yellow Pages once. The business is called Andreson and Son Landscaping and Maintenance now. I guess Mike is into it permanently."

Not surprising, with a wife and baby to support.

We were zipping through town now, varying between kissing the speed limit and crawling, as if the speed of the vehicle echoed Pam's mixed feelings about this meeting. Going past the CyberClam Café, where Fitz and I occasionally surfed the Internet, we were down to snail-with-arthritis mode. I fervently wished Fitz and the *Miss Nora* were in port.

"You've never heard anything about Mike and the wife, then?"

"Vigland is a small town, but there are still separate worlds here. Offhand, I don't even know anyone who knows him."

"Maybe you should have inquired into his marital status before rushing into this meeting."

"I don't think it's the kind of meeting that has anything to do with marital status."

"No? What kind of meeting it is, then?"

"I think it must have to do with his being at the wedding. Because I did see him. I wasn't imagining it. And he knows I saw him. I'm thinking he may ask me not to tell the police he was there. He sounded . . . edgy."

My thought was that he might intend to take it beyond a request and make sure she couldn't tell anything. In which case he had definite reason to be edgy. Though I doubted he could be any more edgy than I was. I felt as if my nerves could cut a laser swath through solid steel.

"Pam, I really think we should back out on this and let Detective Molino handle it." A sensible statement which Detective Molino would heartily approve, I'm sure.

"I'll let you out at the corner. You can wait in Bay Burgers, and I'll pick you up afterward."

So much for sensibility pitted against a nineteen-year-old's reckless stubbornness. "If there is an afterward," I muttered ominously.

She reached over and patted my leg. "If there isn't, you can say, 'I told you so.'"

Like being *right* would be much comfort when we're both gurgling to the bottom of the bay, because no way was I letting her go into this alone.

A tardy thought occurred to me. "We should have brought a tape recorder so we could have a record of whatever he says."

I expected Pam to scoff at such an amateur-detective ploy, but instead, after thinking for a minute, she said, "How about if, just before we meet him, I call Michelle's private number on my cell phone. I'll leave the phone on, and the machine at home will record the conversation."

"This is something you learned at Dartmouth?"

"No, I read it in a murder mystery," she admitted. "One in which the murder weapon was a frozen pineapple."

My first thought was that freezing pineapple ruins it, but that probably isn't relevant when you're using it as a murder weapon. "But won't the answering machine cut off after a minute or two and lose most of the conversation?"

"Michelle was paranoid about that. Someone once left her a message about a movie part, but it was cut off before the person left a number and he never called back. So she got a machine that just keeps recording until the person stops talking."

I wasn't sure I wanted to stake my life on the intricacies of Michelle's answering machine and the thought processes of a murder-by-pineapple mystery writer. The phone might not pick up enough of the conversation to be helpful. And even if it did, we could be dead before anyone heard it. But I supposed it was marginally better than nothing.

"Let's do it with my phone. Mike will be paying attention to you, not me, and maybe I can sneak the cell phone in closer so it will pick up more."

She gave me the number to Michelle's private line, and I punched it in so all I'd have to do at the marina was hit the call button. I tucked the phone in the shirt pocket of my jacket, the best place I could think to pick up a conversation.

Then I repeated my earlier, unanswered question. I had big suspicions of Mike Andreson, but I didn't have a *why* for them. "So what reason could Mike have for killing Michelle?"

"She never liked him. Although she could never see beyond his doing yard work to know what he was really like, of course. I was still going with him when she invited Sterling and his folks up to visit. She was trying to get Sterling and me together then, though I didn't realize it until after Mike and I broke up."

"But it wasn't anything Michelle said or did that broke you up. You didn't end the relationship with Mike in order to jump to Sterling. Mike ended it himself. So why kill Michelle?"

"Yeah," Pam agreed, but it was a tentative kind of agreement. As if it were something with which logic required her to agree, but she wasn't sold on it.

"So why do you think he could have killed her?" I persisted as she braked for a red light.

"I can't think of any reason. But he was right

back there where all the fog and stink came from. Why would he have been there—and then vanished—unless it was connected with Michelle's murder?"

True. These were not the actions of an innocent man.

Pam pulled into the parking lot at the marina. About a dozen cars were parked at the far end, which was where people who lived on their boats, or who had gone out on the water for a few days, usually parked. I spotted Fitz's car and his son's SUV.

A motorcycle stood off by itself. It was newer looking, but not a high-powered biker-type model. A blue-and-white helmet hung on the handlebars. My daughter, Sarah, had briefly dated a motorcycle guy back in high school. Perhaps I was prejudiced, but after he squirreled through my big daisy flower bed, I acquired a dim view of motorcycle boyfriends.

"Mike's?" I asked with a nod at the bike.

"I don't know. He drove an old pickup when I knew him."

As I'd warned her, maybe he'd changed. Or as she'd acknowledged to me, maybe she'd never really known him.

We got out of the bug and walked down the steep steps to the dock. A night breeze jingled the lines of the sailboats. Water lapped against the wooden dock, and boats squeaked and creaked and scraped. A seal that had slipped up to spend the night on the dock grunted. The moon danced a silvery trail across the water, and snow-covered Mt. Rainier shimmered softly in the distance.

All very serene and lovely, but the whole place felt different from when I was meeting Fitz here, when the *Miss Nora*'s lights blazed and good scents came from something he was cooking in the galley.

Now I was more conscious of the depth and faintly murky scent of the dark water on either side of the dock, an oily iridescence in spots on the water, and lumpy shadows lurking around the boats. Plus the memory of some creepy TV movie I'd seen in which a hand rose out of the water and gripped an unsuspecting ankle. I carefully walked a straight line down the middle of the dock, primly keeping my ankles so close together that my socks swished. Would anyone even hear a couple of stray splashes if Mike dumped us?

A guy appeared out of the shadow of a boat and walked toward us.

I don't know what we could have brought as a weapon, but I suddenly wished we had something. The Baby Ruth in my pocket felt a little short on firepower.

Chapter Fifteen

"Mike?" I whispered to Pam.

She nodded, her expression wary, and I punched the call button on the phone. I heard the machine pick up and shivered at the tinny sound of Michelle's voice on the answering machine. A voice from the dead. Were we about to meet her killer?

He was alone, although I hadn't really expected him to show up with a baby stroller in tow. Medium-height, with a husky build and dark hair. An angular face, not hunk-handsome but definitely no need for a paper bag over his head. His hands were stuffed in the pockets of a worn leather jacket, and his heavy motorcycle boots clomped on the wooden dock. At least he wasn't trying to sneak up on us.

"Thanks for coming," he said. "I was afraid you'd change your mind."

I thought both he and Pam might be so caught up in seeing each other again that they'd forget my presence, but Pam had a firmer grip on the situation than that. She grabbed my arm.

"I'd like you to meet my friend, Andi McConnell," Pam said, her voice a little louder than normal. "Andi, Mike Andreson."

Mike looked at me uncertainly, as if wondering what I was doing here. But I realized what was going on. Pam was getting our identification down on the answering machine back at the house.

Also speaking a bit louder than normal, I said, "Thank you, Pam," coming down heavy on the name to add to the identification. I whipped out a business card and handed it to Mike. "Andi's Limouzeen Service. Available for all occasions." I made my professional dip. "Your chariot awaits."

Mike looked at the card, then at Pam. "You came in a limousine?" He sounded dumb-founded.

"No. We're in my bug. I asked Andi to come along. She's been staying at the house to provide limo service for the guests."

"The wedding guests."

"Yes."

"Oh." He looked at the card again, as if he couldn't figure out what to do with it. I doubted Mike Andreson would become a regular client, but he finally stuffed the card into a hip pocket.

"There's still a bench out that way." He pointed to the far end of the dock, out where the *Miss Nora* always tied up. Also, I was uncomfortably aware, where the water around the dock was deepest. I didn't know about Pam's swimming ability, but mine rivals that of a stale bagel.

Pam briskly led the way. At the bench, she maneuvered so I was sitting between her and Mike. I couldn't exactly stick my chest up in Mike's face, but I wiggled my shoulders trying to get the cell phone into a more prominent position.

"You said you had to talk to me, so here I am," Pam said. No alive glow now, just stiff challenge. The moonlight emphasized the hard set of her expression. "Talk."

"I hardly know where to start."

My tart thought was that he might tell us how the wife and baby were doing, but Pam chose to skip the sarcasm so I remained silent too.

"My sister called you at school and told you I'd gotten a girlfriend pregnant, and we were getting married."

"Sorry if I didn't send a proper wedding or baby gift. I guess it just slipped my mind."

Ooooh, an avalanche of sarcasm there.

"What Kathleen told *me* was that you called her and told her you'd met someone, and you asked her to tell me that you were sorry, but it would never work out between us. What with my being a yard-care worker and all. And please not to contact you because it would just cause problems."

Pam's mouth dropped open. "But that's not true! I never, never said anything like that! I never *thought* anything like that. I never even talked to Kathleen except the one time she called me."

Mike leaned forward, his voice low and intense. "And I never had another girlfriend, and I never got anyone pregnant, and I never wanted to marry anyone but you."

His statement hung in the air like a suspended hammer.

"But your *sister*—?" I finally cut in doubtfully.

"Yes, my dear sister. Who heard through some friend that Michelle was throwing a fancy wedding for her stepdaughter there at the house, and mentioned it to me. And then, when she saw how hard it hit me, had an attack of conscience . . . a very tardy attack . . . and told me the truth."

"The truth," Pam repeated, sounding dazed.

"It seems Michelle decided she had to do something about your totally unsuitable relationship with me. So she made my sister an offer she couldn't refuse."

"What kind of offer?"

"I don't know the exact amount, but not long after Kathleen told me you were breaking off our relationship she suddenly had money enough for a down payment on one of those fancy new houses on Randolph Hill, and a new Lexus to boot. At the time she said the money came from her ex-husband, who finally paid up what he owed her."

Pam just sat there looking as if that suspended hammer had smacked her between the eyes.

"Michelle paid Kathleen . . . *paid* her . . . to break us up."

We were all silent for the moment, thinking of the enormity of that deception and betrayal. Betrayal from two sides.

"But your *sister*," Pam finally protested, as I had. "I can't believe she'd do something like that. I always thought she liked me."

I noted she didn't say anything about doubting Michelle could pull such a heartbreaker stunt. Though my question was *Why?* Why was breaking up Pam and Mike's relationship important enough for Michelle to spend a bundle of money on it?

"Liking you didn't matter, not when Kathleen had a chance at all that money. Anyway, when she told me all this a couple days ago, she said that at the time she didn't think it was any big deal. You and I were just kids. We'd break up sooner or later anyway. So she might as well have the money."

"For a house and a Lexus. She sold us out for *a house and a Lexus*." The furious sparks in Pam's voice could have set that house ablaze.

"As you might guess, my relationship with Kathleen is a little strained right now. She has the house up for sale, by the way. The payments are way more than she can keep up. Come to think of it, maybe I'm giving her too much credit saying conscience was what made her tell me about the lies. Maybe it was the fact that Michelle had never paid her all the money she'd promised. It's not exactly something you can take to small claims court."

"Now wait a minute," I cut in. "How do we know you aren't just telling us some wild story? Why would it have been worth a lot of money to Michelle to keep Pam from marrying you?"

"A yard-care guy with dirt under his fingernails in the family?" He held out his hand as if to show me, although I didn't see any dirt there. "She'd have been humiliated."

Okay, maybe Pam's marrying Mike wouldn't have enhanced Michelle's social prestige, but could it really have been *that* important? Couldn't she have just cut Pam out of her life and let it go at that?

"Or I suppose it's possible Michelle really did think Pam would be better off without me."

An unladylike snort from Pam. "Yeah. Right. Like my welfare kept her awake nights."

"Anyway, if you don't believe me, you can check with my folks about whether I've ever had any wife and baby. My mother anyway. I'd rather you didn't talk to my dad unless you have to. Finding out the sneaky deal Kathleen pulled might be hard on his heart. He always liked you."

"I-I don't think that will be necessary. I believe you."

I was inclined that way too, but I still thought there must be more to this than what we were hearing here. Although, setting aside exactly why Michelle was willing to invest some large amount of money in breaking up the relationship, she'd shrewdly picked the perfect person to carry out her scheme. Neither Pam nor Mike would have believed these stories coming direct from Michelle, but Mike's sister made them gold-standard solid.

"But what were you doing at the wedding?" Pam demanded.

"That's what I want to explain before I go to the police. I didn't want you to see something on TV or in the newspaper before I had a chance to tell you myself."

Pam's voice dropped to a whisper. "Tell me . . . you killed Michelle?"

I leaned in closer to Mike with the cell phone. Because we had it now, the motive for murder that we hadn't been able to come up with earlier. Revenge. Payback. Fury. Greedy sister Kathleen may have sold out to sabotage Pam and Mike's relationship, but Michelle was the buyer.

"No! Yes, I was there." He groaned. "I was there with the dumbest, strangest, most idiotic scheme ever concocted this side of a Keystone Cops plot. But it was the only way I could think to stop the wedding at the last minute, and it had nothing to do with murder."

He got up, paced to the edge of the dock, then came back to stand in front of Pam, hands jammed in his jacket pockets again. I stood up, jockeying to get the cell phone in better position and also keep from making some ignominious splash over the side of the dock. These undercover spy techniques aren't as easy to pull off as they look on TV.

"I tried to call you at the house as soon as Kathleen told me. I thought, hoped, that knowing we'd both been lied to would make a difference in your marrying that guy. But I never could get through. Some woman always answered the phone, and I couldn't give my name because I knew you wouldn't talk if you knew it was me, and she wouldn't put me through without a name." He sounded frustrated. "I came out to the house, too, but I couldn't get past the gate. I think the same woman had control of it."

"Shirley, the housekeeper," Pam said. "With the wedding so close, Michelle gave her strict instructions about letting anyone in or calls through."

"She'd make a good prison guard. Don't let her get her hands on an AK-47."

"So how'd you get through on the phone tonight?" I challenged.

"I lied," he said flatly. "I told the woman I was

from the sheriff's department and had to talk to Miss Gibson. Maybe I should have tried an outright lie earlier. It would have made more sense than what I did instead."

He paused and kicked at a clamshell lodged in a crack between boards on the dock, though I had the feeling where he really wanted to kick wasn't anatomically possible.

"Drastic measures with the fog machine, Mike?" I asked. I maneuvered closer and spoke into my chest, trying to get it all on the answering machine. Under normal circumstances talking to one's chest would probably make someone suspicious, but Mike was too agitated to notice.

"Remember Simon? Simon Edelson?" He spoke to Pam.

"He played guitar in that band you were with."

"Right. And usually operated our fog machine, although we all worked it at various times. He's a plumber now, but he does some part-time fog machine work for an outfit over in Olympia. I see him fairly often, and I knew he had a wedding scheduled for Friday night. After Kathleen dropped her bomb on me about your wedding, it occurred to me that Simon's gig could be your wedding. Which it was. He did the set-up, but I talked him into taking his wife out to dinner that night and letting me handle the fog machine at the wedding."

Oh yeah, he'd handled it.

"At first I just planned an overdose of fog to disrupt the wedding, so I could get a chance to talk to you. But then I was afraid fog alone wouldn't be enough." He paused and looked as if he'd like to step off the end of the dock rather than go on. "Okay, I'm not proud of this. But I was desperate. I went to a place in Olympia that sells gag supplies and got some stuff to dump in with the liquid in the fog machine. They didn't know what I had planned, of course, but they said the stink would be strong enough to break up a riot."

"I don't know about breaking up a riot, but it almost caused one," I said.

He groaned again, put his hands over his ears, and closed his eyes as if trying to shut out the voices that were apparently shouting to him about what an idiot he'd been.

I added mine. "That was an idiotic thing to do."

"Yes. And just after I did it, after I sent enough fog and stink into the tent to practically asphyxiate everyone, I crawled out and looked over the flowers. And just for a second before everything disappeared in the fog I saw Pam there in her wedding gown. Holding her flowers. Looking scared and beautiful and . . . angelic, as if she were standing on a cloud." He blinked and swallowed. "Then it finally got through to me. Pam probably loved this guy. This should be the happiest day of her life. And I was wrecking it."

He dropped to the bench, head down, hands between his knees.

"So why didn't you turn the machine off instead of letting it just keep spewing?" I asked.

"I did. Though by then the fog was so thick and smelly that I was coughing, and my eyes were watering so bad I could hardly see. It took me a little while to crawl back under the flowers and feel around to find the machine and then the controls."

But Uri Hubbard had said *he* turned the machine off. Making himself look like a hero? Or was he doing something considerably less heroic, like trying to account for a few moments of time when he was stabbing Michelle in the back?

"You didn't see the murder, then?"

"No, I just got out of there. Another of my bad decisions. I should have stayed around to apologize and make amends. Instead I ran back to where I'd parked my pickup outside the gate. I figured that after the fog and smell cleared out, you'd all decide it was just some terrible malfunction and go on with the ceremony. A little later I heard sirens, but I didn't know anything about the murder until the next day when it was all over the news."

He took a choked breath, as if it was hard to get air into his lungs. "Pam, I can't tell you how sorry I am. And I know that my being sorry

200

doesn't begin to make up for all the hurt and damage I've done to you. And even worse to Michelle. Because it was the fog and the smell that made it possible for someone to murder her." He pounded his thigh with a clenched fist. "It was my fault. *My fault.*"

Pam was studying her feet as if she'd never seen them before. She didn't say anything, so I did. "Now what?"

"Now I go to the police and tell them everything."

Pam looked up. "They may think you killed Michelle!"

Yes indeed. Plenty of motive and opportunity for murder for Mike Andreson. But means?

"What about your butterfly knife?" One side of me leaned toward his innocence, but the everybody's-a-suspect side was still taking potshots at that innocence.

"Butterfly knife?" He looked at me so blankly I knew he must be thinking I had a few butterflies loose in my belfry. Pam also gave me a baffled look. I shrugged and didn't explain.

Mike went back to Pam's comment about the police. "I'll just have to take that chance. I can't *not* tell them. What I did was probably a crime—"

He paused as if considering what that crime might be. *Assault with a dangerous fog? Stink stalking? Bridal mayhem?*

"But you're not a killer," Pam filled in.

"No. Just stupid, foolish, ridiculous, weird, over-the-top, unbalanced . . . and whatever other derogatory adjectives you want to pile on."

That list seemed sufficient. Though I wondered about temporary insanity. Or maybe it was lovesick insanity.

"I never doubted what your sister said. Never once." Pam shook her head in self-recrimination. "How could I have just *believed* her?"

"I believed her too."

Which was the beauty of Michelle's scheme, of course. Who'd doubt what Mike's very own sister said?

Mike knelt in front of her and took her hand. "I love you, Pam. I always have. But love doesn't justify what I did. I can't say it enough times, how sorry I am. On the news they said the wedding had been postponed, but I hope somehow it all works out for you."

"The wedding isn't postponed, it's off. Permanently. I'm not sorry about that." Pam flicked her fingers in a small gesture of dismissal. Then her fingers clenched into a fist. "But *Michelle* . . ."

Yes, Michelle. Whose death lay like an anchor on Mike's shoulders.

"You didn't see anyone who wasn't running to escape the fog?" I asked. "Someone who could have murdered her?"

"I didn't see anything, except that momentary glimpse of Pam. Then the fog covered everything. But it's my fault Michelle is dead. If it weren't for what I did, she'd still be alive."

Make that two anchors on his shoulders.

Chapter Sixteen

"Why did you ask Mike about—what did you call it—a butterfly knife?" Pam asked on our way home.

I hesitated. The authorities were apparently being very tight-lipped about what kind of weapon had been used on Michelle. Yet surely they must be checking into its ownership.

"Did you see the knife?" I asked.

"I-I realized there was a knife in Michelle's back. But I didn't really look at it."

"I described it to Fitz. He said it sounded like what's called a butterfly knife." I described it to Pam, including the jewels and scrollwork.

"Dragons?"

"I think so. Dragons and flowers. The scrolling was very intricate. A valuable, collector's-type knife probably. Does that mean anything to you?"

"My dad was never a hunter. His allergies kept him from doing a lot of things. But he liked to let people think he was more of a rough-and-tough outdoorsman than he was." She made the admission with a shrug, as if it was just a quirk she accepted about the father she loved. "He was a great father."

"But that leopard skin in the office—"

"He bought it. Along with several high-powered hunting rifles. They used to hang in the office too, but Michelle took them down. I don't know what she did with them. I kind of remember something about a knife collection he bought from an estate."

"Where would that be now?"

"I have no idea."

Fitz called before I left for church the following morning. He said he'd tried to call my cell the previous evening, but couldn't get me. I told him about the meeting with Mike Andreson and how we'd recorded it. We agreed to meet at the CyberClam that evening.

At church the limo drew some second looks. I usually drive my old Toyota on Sundays, but by now most people knew the limo service was my occupation. I'd intended to invite Pam to come along, but she didn't show up at breakfast, nor did she answer my tap on her attic door. I wondered if she was already meeting Mike somewhere. He hadn't pressed to see her again, and she hadn't said much when we came home last night, but I knew she was into some deep thinking.

It was a drizzly day, though much too early in the season to mark the start of the fall rains. A scent of wet grass and trees blended with the sea scent, the feeling in the air almost more springy than fall. The tide was rushing up the inlet when I drove back to the house after the service, bringing with it a stray log and some floating branches. I punched the remote control, and the gate opened to let me in. I was curious about the ice sculpture, but the crime-scene tape still circled the tent even though there were no sheriff's cars in the driveway now. It seemed a shame to waste all that ice, but a bride and groom in Popsicle form probably wasn't a donation the homeless could use. I wondered if it was time for me to go on home. I couldn't see what I could do for Pam here now.

Well, there was one thing I could do, I realized as I drove up the sloping driveway and saw Pam sprawled on the curb.

The girl's stepmother has been murdered, and Pam herself is probably on the suspect list. Her wedding is down the drain, and she's just learned the guy she was once in love with pulled one of the strangest capers outside an Animal House movie. She has lawyers and legal entanglements and a funeral to face. So what is she doing in the midst of all that turmoil? Skateboarding, of course.

I stopped the limo, got out, and helped her to her feet. "Are we having fun yet?" I inquired as I turned her arm to look at her skinned elbow.

She shook off her helmet, and her hair sprang out to its pre-wedding halo of frizz. "I don't *always* crash. Yeah, I know, both times you've seen me I'm crashing, but I made a half dozen good runs before this one. It helps me think. I just shouldn't have tried a kickflip when I haven't been practicing."

"Crashing helps you think?" I asked doubtfully.

"No, I don't think *while* I'm skateboarding. But it clears my head. On a good day, you feel as if you're *one* with the skateboard, as if it's an extension of you. It flushes out the cobwebs so I think better afterward."

A thinking aid. Every generation to its own, I decided. And skateboarding was probably as good a response as any to the troubles she had looming over her. It also occurred to me that a skateboard crash was how she'd met Mike, so maybe there was some emotional connection there.

"Okay, I know what you're thinking," she muttered. "That I shouldn't rush back into something with Mike."

"Probably a good idea," I agreed. "But actually, I was thinking maybe you could teach me to skateboard. I've always wanted to try it."

"*You* want to skateboard?" She looked at me as if I were Phreddie expressing a sudden interest in quantum physics.

"There's an age limit? No cellulite or wrinkles allowed?"

She ignored my grumpy challenge and raised a different point. "You can't do it in those clothes. Did you go out to breakfast or something? You look very nice."

"I went to church. I didn't have anything here to wear, so I stopped by my place and changed." To burgundy skirt and black, high-heeled boots, which I had to agree were not suitable skateboarding attire. "I was going to ask if you'd like to come along, but you didn't answer when I knocked."

"I got up early and went for a long walk on the beach." She gave me a speculative glance. "So what was church all about today?"

What was it all about? I looked at her in dismay. Was I supposed to have taken notes? I hadn't realized there was going to be a test.

You're doing it again, aren't You, Lord? Making me pull stuff deep down inside and think about it, not let it just sit up there on the surface like an imitation tattoo.

"Well, umm, basically the sermon was about GIGO."

"GIGO?" she repeated doubtfully. "GIGO is in the Bible?"

207

"Not in that exact wording. But the pastor used it in his sermon."

"Garbage In, Garbage Out," she reflected. "The greatest computer in the world will spew out garbage results if you put garbage data into it."

"Right. And if you put garbage into your life in the form of wrong beliefs, wrong values and standards, then garbage is what will come out of your life. It's a reflection of what we're 'eating' spiritually. So a different interpretation of GIGO might be Good In, Good Out."

She picked up the skateboard and tucked it under her arm. "It's a nice theory. But there are people who are living good lives and doing good things who aren't going to church or reading the Bible or praying or any of that stuff. And I knew a girl back at school who never missed a Sunday at church and who could whip out a Bible verse for any occasion, from flunking a test to a bad hair day. Her take on the 'do not steal' commandment was that it was okay if you shoplifted from big stores because they calculated that into their profit margins. It was stealing only if you took it from an individual."

"Thou shalt not steal . . . unless it's from Wal-Mart?" I asked in dismay.

"No Wal-Mart for her. She liked the high-end stuff. Neiman Marcus was her favorite, especially for cosmetics."

So, Lord, how about that? The Good-In system had apparently hit some speed bumps with that girl. I wished I could whip out a verse to fit the situation, but as usual I was frustratingly blank. For two reasons. One, I'm reading and trying, but I'm still woefully ignorant about Scripture. Two, I apparently lost the ability to memorize about the time cellulite started homesteading on my thighs. Now my brain seems to have a Teflon coating; everything slides right on through it. The only quotation that surfaced at this moment was, "Blessed are those who run around in circles for they shall be called big wheels," which didn't seem particularly relevant. And was definitely more bumper sticker than biblical.

"I'd say that somewhere along the line the girl at school had some garbage input that booby-trapped the good input. And it's kind of a surprising fact, but as I understand it, piling up a mountain of good deeds still isn't going to get you into an eternal life with Jesus. It's faith and belief that does that."

"If you have faith and belief you can go ahead and sin all you want?"

Leave it to Pam to vault right into what looked like a loophole.

"No, if you really have faith and belief, you're going to *want* to do the things God considers right and good. If what you want is to keep on with the sins, it puts a big question mark on whether you're really committed to the faith. Although people who are faithful and committed sometimes slip, so I suppose that kind of muddies the waters," I admitted.

"The waters are pretty muddy about the whole 'eternal life' thing, as far as I'm concerned."

No, they're not, I realized suddenly. I may not understand many things yet. I may be puzzled about whether we'll be in robes or jeans. Whether we'll eat manna or stuffed zucchini. Or if we'll eat at all. And what everyone will be doing in all that timeless eternity. But this I understood as surely as I knew the tides were going to keep rushing in and out: there is an eternal life.

Pam turned a palm up to the sky, abruptly dismissing this discussion. Which, I thought with a regretful sigh, had probably benefited me more than it had her.

"Okay, if you're going to skateboard, let's get going before it really starts raining."

"I'll go change. What should I wear?"

"Something padded. Skateboarding is a contact sport."

"Contact?"

"Contact with the pavement." She waved a hand as if to dismiss that small detail. "Some skateboarders wear special shoes, but you can just use whatever you have handy. Just remember that skateboarding is rough on shoes. And various parts of the anatomy."

Okay, I heard her. She disapproved. But I'd long wanted to do this, and I felt ridiculously elated as I started back to the limo. Me . . . skateboarding! Then I remembered something I wanted to ask. "Did you listen to Michelle's answering machine to see what it picked up last night?"

"It got quite a lot of the conversation, actually." She hesitated and then added, "I erased it."

"What? Why?"

"I didn't see any point in saving it."

I was mildly dismayed that she hadn't preserved the conversation, which was evidence, of sorts, in case Mike backed out on going to the police. I wondered if she'd tell them what he'd done if he didn't, or if she'd protectively try to keep him out of it. Which probably didn't matter, of course. Detective Molino most likely already knew all about Mike, up to and including his shoe size and whether he flossed his teeth daily.

As if reading my mind, Pam added, "Mike is going to the police. He's no criminal."

Though his stop-the-wedding technique could use some fine-tuning.

In any case, the recording was now gone and there wasn't much point in arguing with her about it. "I'll be back in a few minutes."

I drove on up to the house. Inside I changed to

211

jeans, long-sleeved sweatshirt, and the heavy tennies I use for chores like limo washing. Coming out of my room, I ran into Phyllis Forsythe in a pink terrycloth robe and fuzzy slippers, hair tied up with a pink scarf.

"I thought I'd take a soak in the hot tub. My nerves have been rather tense, and it's very relaxing," she said in her whispery little voice.

"That sounds like a good idea."

"Would you like to join me? If you don't have a swimsuit, there are extras down there, and dressing rooms to change in. I just prefer the privacy of my room for changing." She gave the robe a tightening twitch.

The hot tub, which was in a corner of Michelle's basement Fitness Room, struck me as a good place to pick Phyllis's brain. As an employee, I'd never used the tub, but no one had ever said I couldn't, and Shirley had said she used it. "Pam's going to show me how to skateboard, but I'll join you as soon as we're through."

"Skateboard? Oh, isn't that dangerous?" Her whispery voice took on a note of alarm, with an undercurrent of disapproval.

Skateboarding, I knew without asking, was not one of Sterling's chosen activities.

"I won't be long. I'll quit when the first bone breaks."

I meant that as a little joke, but Phyllis just

looked appalled and said, "Do be careful." Sense of humor, I was fairly certain, was not one of her strong points.

Outside, Pam was headed down the hill again. As I watched, she and the skateboard lifted off the pavement and separated. I thought she was crashing again, but this time she reconnected with the board and swirled to a graceful stop.

"Was that a kickflip?" I called.

"No, that was just an easy little ollie. It's a good move for jumping over something." She picked up the board and motioned me to join her down on the flat part of the driveway. "Are you right-footed or left-footed?"

Not a question that had ever arisen before. I tested my feet. They didn't offer an opinion. "I don't know."

"Okay, you can start out doing it the regular way. Left foot up front on the board, right foot pushing. If that doesn't feel comfortable, you can switch. Or there's mongo style, pushing with a front foot. But not many people do that."

The first thing I learned when she set the skateboard in front of me was that skateboards aren't flat, as I'd always assumed. There's a slight concave dip in the board.

She fastened the helmet on my head, showed me where to place my foot and how to push. She ran along beside me as I pushed, a balancing hand on my lower back. We did that for several trips back and forth to the gate. I wobbled, but her steadying hand kept me upright.

Finally she said, "Now just give a good push, then pick up your foot and put it on the board. And keep your eyes to the front. Always watch where you're going."

I tentatively placed my pushing foot on the board. She let go. I sailed forward.

"See, you're doing it!"

Hey, I was! I was skateboarding! Although that lasted all of thirty seconds before the board scooted out from under me, and I hit the concrete and skated on my derrière. But if I thought Pam was going to give me the kid-glove treatment because of my age or inexperience, I was mistaken. Tough love all the way.

"Get up and try it again," she yelled.

So I did. After another half hour or so I wasn't doing ollies, but I was scooting along the flat concrete by myself. Although gravity seemed to take a much sterner attitude with me than it did with all those young kids you see blithely defying it with twists and turns and flips. But when I was upright, skateboarding was every bit as exhilarating as I'd imagined. Wheee!

I figured this was probably my once-in-a-lifetime go, and I didn't want it to end, but when Pam said, "I think that's enough for today," I regretfully agreed. Partly because I had sore spots where I didn't know spots existed, partly because I wanted to get to the hot tub before Phyllis left it. Partly because, although I hadn't noticed until then, the drizzle had turned to a steady rain and my back was soaked.

So I was surprised when, as we were walking up to the house, Pam said, "Tomorrow, same time, same place?"

"It's probably time I headed on home. I don't think there's anything I can do to help you here now."

Pam stopped short, the scrunch of her eyebrows dismayed. "Mr. Steffan wants to go out to the casino this evening, so he'll need the limo for that."

"Calling a cab for him would be cheaper than my staying on." And I had plans with Fitz for this evening.

"I'm not positive, but I don't think I have to worry about money. And I need you to stay on, Andi. Please? I feel as if I'm wandering through a swamp full of hungry alligators. Lawyers, the funeral, that autopsy thing . . ."

She sounded so momentarily little-girl-lost that I quickly assured her I didn't have to leave yet. "I'll do whatever I can."

"You can figure out who killed Michelle."

"That's Detective Molino's job."

"Detective Molino isn't here at the house."

And maybe the killer was? Though after talking to Mike last night, Uri Hubbard was edging up to top place on my suspect list. And he wasn't here at the house.

"Would you mind if I poked around in Michelle's office?"

"I've been thinking I'll have to do it sooner or later, but if you want to do it, poke away," she said. "We'll do the skateboard thing again tomorrow?"

"When do I get to try it on the slope, where I can pick up some speed?"

I thought I heard *in your dreams,* but her out-loud answer was more diplomatic. "Not for a while yet. Be patient."

I went directly to the Fitness Room. The water in the hot tub churned energetically, but it looked empty. No, something was floating in it.

I rushed over, an awful possibility flashing like a murder mystery title across my mind. Murder in the Hot Tub . . .

Chapter Seventeen

I peered closer. Blue things floated in the churning water, like tiny, multi-headed creatures flung up from the bottom of the sea.

Then, on the other side of the tub, a human head broke through the bubbling water.

"Mrs. Steffan! Are you okay?"

She let out a huge held breath, then reached over and turned the control knob down to something below storm-surge level. "I'm fine. I just like to go all the way under occasionally."

Which struck me as about as appealing as washing your hair in a dishwasher, but everyone to her own taste.

She leaned back against the side of the tub, and the blue things rose again. Not strange sea creatures after all. Just Mrs. Steffan's feet with toenails pedicured blue.

"C'mon in," she urged. "I turned the heat up, and it's just right."

"I'll have to find a swimsuit."

"Skinny dipping's more fun."

I stopped, momentarily dismayed at the sight of Mrs. Steffan's bare shoulders. Was she really—? Then she rose higher out of the water and I saw the exotic flowers twined across her strapless suit.

She gave me a mischievous smile, as if she'd caught me at something. "You didn't think I'd actually go skinny dipping here, did you?"

I found a burgundy, one-piece suit and changed in the dressing room. It fit surprisingly well, and the halter-type neckline was quite flattering. Though, like every swimsuit in existence, it did nothing to conceal my jiggly thighs.

Mrs. Steffan pointed to a corner spot in the tub when I returned. "That jet is good for sore shoulders. Or if you want your lower back massaged, the center one is best."

I picked the lower-back area and slid into the just-right water, not too hot, not too cool. The life of luxury. I could get accustomed to this.

"Do you come for a soak every day?" I asked.

"I've been doing what I do at home, working out on the machines for a while and then relaxing in the hot tub. I like that one the German guy invented." She pointed to a machine with curved bands that looked as if it might take off like a rocket ship if all those bands went sproing at once. "They were planning to unveil it to the public at the opening of the fitness center, but I haven't heard what's going to happen now."

I wouldn't have guessed Mrs. Steffan knew one exercise machine from another, let alone used them regularly. Although her body, revealed by the swimsuit, was not as dumpy as I'd assumed from those shapeless flowered dresses she always wore.

"Was Phyllis here earlier? I met her when she was coming down."

"She left just a few minutes ago. Said she hasn't been sleeping well and was going to take a nap. I think she's afraid someone is going to creep in and murder her in the night."

"Surely people aren't afraid there could be more murders!"

"I don't see any reason to think there's some

serial killer on the loose here. I think someone just had it in for Michelle. Although one does start to wonder, considering the other unfortunate deaths in the family."

"Pam's father's death, you mean? And her mother too."

"Mother, father, stepmother. If I were Pam, I think I'd be afraid I might be next in line. But I don't see any reason for Phyllis to worry. Who'd benefit if she were dead?"

"You're suggesting someone benefited from the other deaths?" Which was certainly a reasonable line of thinking from my point of view.

"Oh, my, no. Just tragic coincidences, I'm sure." Mrs. Steffan lifted a leg out of the water and examined it critically. "I need a wax job, but I think I'll wait until I get home."

I wasn't about to be sidetracked. "Michelle and Phyllis were distant cousins, as you probably know. I suppose there's a possibility she may benefit from Michelle's death."

"Surely Pam will benefit considerably."

"Only in that she'll now have control of her trust fund herself."

"Ummm." Examination of the other leg.

"This must be a very difficult time for Phyllis. I wonder how she feels about Sterling and Pam's breakup?"

"She didn't say." Mrs. Steffan let her legs drift back into the water.

Now the toes were ten blue eyes, all staring at me. I tried not to stare back.

"I imagine she's disappointed," Mrs. Steffan continued. "There's considerable prestige connected with their son's position, I'm sure, but I don't think research pays particularly well. And even if the son comes up with some discovery or invention worth a bundle, it'll belong to the company. That's the way those things work. I'd feel awfully awkward if I were them, staying here and taking advantage of their son's ex-fiancée's hospitality."

"There's probably satisfaction in what he does even if the money isn't outstanding."

"True. Although Pam's money would surely have made the marriage more comfortable. Which has nothing to do with Michelle's murder, of course."

Also true. Yet the scent of a money-murder connection lingered like a whiff of that smelly fog.

"So, who do you think did it?" I asked conversationally. I shifted a bit to let the thrust of jetting water hit my hip, which had taken a beating in the skateboard lesson.

"I've been wracking my brain. Stan and I don't have children, so Michelle was almost like the daughter we never had. We were very close to her at one time. She even lived with us for a while. I always appreciated the fact that, unlike most of the attractive women Stan works with, she never had an affair with him. Her death hits us very hard."

Well, there was a level of openness I hadn't expected and didn't know what to do with. How do you deal with a woman who speaks of her husband's affairs as if only the woman involved were to blame? I had some indignant thoughts on this subject, but taking potshots at the Stan Man probably wouldn't aid my information-gathering project. "Did Michelle have enemies in Hollywood?"

"Everyone has enemies in Hollywood. It's a jungle of rivalries and jealousies and backstabbings—" She broke off and touched her fingers to her lips. "Oh dear, that didn't come out right. I didn't mean literally, not like what happened to Michelle." She frowned. "Although you never know how far some people will carry a grudge, do you?"

"Are you saying someone she knew from a long time back could have murdered her? Because of something she'd done to that person in the past?"

"It's possible. When Michelle wanted something, she went after it. Fond as I was of her, I have to say she didn't care who she had to crawl over to get it. But she wasn't alone in that, of course. *Get yours* is the general Hollywood ethic."

"You have anyone specific in mind?"

"Well, she didn't invite those with whom her past relationships were the most, ummm, disagreeable. Although she and Rosamund Blanchard had their differences."

"The woman whose daughter was the foot model?"

"She was Rose Beaumont back then. They had a vicious little rivalry going. Once Michelle tricked Rose into going to the wrong place for an audition, took her place, and got the part. But I think they were laughing about that now, as if it were just a mischievous girlhood prank."

"Sometimes even murderers laugh."

"True. But a recent conflict would more likely be behind such a vicious murder, wouldn't you think?"

"All murder is vicious."

"I suppose so. But a knife in the back . . ." Mrs. Steffan's bare shoulders shivered in spite of the warmth of the hot tub. "As for recent conflicts in her life, I really don't know. We haven't been close in recent years. Not since she took up with Gerald Gibson."

"You mean because they moved away from Hollywood?"

"That too." She rubbed a little finger over a damp eyebrow as if trying to erase the frown clinging there. "But I couldn't approve of her relationship with him, and we had a serious falling out over that."

"You didn't like him?"

"I didn't like her being involved with a married man. And I didn't like him for cheating on that lovely wife of his."

But she was willing to tolerate the Stan Man cheating on her. An interesting double standard. In any case, Pam's suspicion about Michelle and her father was apparently not unwarranted. The relationship had started before her mother's fatal accident. If it was an accident.

I tried to think of some clever way to waltz into that subject, but finally I decided time was short, and I'd just charge into it. "Do you think Michelle could have been involved in Pam's mother's death?"

"The police investigated the death. The hit-and-run driver was never located."

An interesting answer. It didn't accuse Michelle, but neither did it exonerate her. And I saw no indication of indignation or shock at my asking.

"There was a slight suspicion Michelle could have been involved in her husband's death right here in this house," I said.

"Really? I hadn't heard that."

Mrs. Steffan's underwater dunk had left her goldy hair plastered to her head and emphasized her blue eye shadow. Matching toes and eyelids. Some fashion trend I didn't know about?

"Was there an investigation?"

"Apparently it wasn't deemed necessary."

"Then why do you say there was a suspicion Michelle could have been involved in the death?" Mrs. Steffan asked.

"Pam's suspicion."

Mrs. Steffan nodded as if that confirmed something for her. "Michelle confided something rather odd to me. It was . . . let's see, the day after we arrived, and she and I were sitting here in the hot tub, just like you and I are now. She said something . . . *unsettling* was going on her life, and she was very much afraid."

I sat up straighter in the water. "Afraid of what?"

"At the time I thought she meant a health problem. She'd always had this strange paranoia about getting a brain tumor. Her grandmother or someone had one."

"But now?"

"Well, now I think she may have meant she was afraid of some*one*. I tried to find out more at the time. I thought perhaps I could help, suggest a good doctor or something, but then she turned . . . I don't know, *hostile,* I guess you'd call it. As if she regretted confiding that much to me. So I just backed off, and we never discussed it again. But it seems significant now."

Yes indeed, very significant. And could that sudden hostility be because the someone Michelle was afraid of was Mrs. Steffan's own husband?

"Did you tell all this to the detectives?"

224

"Oh, yes. That Detective Molino asked both Stan and me all kinds of questions." She paused reflectively. "A lot of them about Pam."

"They're suspicious of Pam?" I tried to sound shocked, but I knew there was no way Detective Molino could not be suspicious of Pam. "Surely Michelle wasn't afraid of her."

"You wouldn't think so. She's nice, of course, so quiet and polite. But I sensed considerable resentment toward Michelle."

"Pam and Michelle weren't close, but Pam seems much too gentle a person for murder."

Mrs. Steffan unexpectedly chuckled. She hitched the strapless suit up a notch. "I think that detective's suspicious of everyone. He even asked a couple of questions about you."

"Me!"

"He asked if we knew of any conflict or arguments between you and Michelle."

"No! We got along fine."

"I think the authorities should zero in on that fog machine operator. Either as perpetrator, or at least as an accomplice. Because the murder couldn't have happened without that incredible smelly fog."

I switched to another subject, and to the other hip underwater. "Given what you say was a rather cool relationship in recent years, I guess I'm a little surprised that Michelle invited you to the wedding."

"Actually, the cool relationship was with me, not Stan, and she had an ulterior motive for getting him up here. She wanted a part in his new production, *Any Day Now*, that everyone's talking about. But I wanted to come. I thought it was time to let bygones be bygones, and we could be friends again."

"And did that happen?"

"I'm afraid not. Michelle was furious when Stan couldn't give her the part she wanted. And then . . . well, I was afraid she was doing it again."

"Doing what?"

"Another married man."

A name instantly came to mind, but I fished with a noncommittal "Oh?"

"That couple she was in partnership with on the health club thing? A very attractive man. But the wife was in the way, as wives so often are."

"But nothing happened to the wife. It was Michelle who was murdered."

"What's that old saying? Do unto others before they do unto you?"

It was phrased rather differently in my Bible, but could Mrs. Steffan's cynical version be Cindy Hubbard's philosophy? Was Cindy the "someone" Michelle had feared?

"It was rather sad about Michelle wanting a part in Stan's new production. Like too many mature actresses, she thought she could still play the kind of sexy romance and adventure roles she did when she was younger. She kept herself in marvelous shape, of course, but let's face it. It would have been ludicrous for a woman of forty-eight to try to play a twenty-five-year-old."

"Forty-eight?" I repeated, surprised.

"Michelle was older than she looked. Older than she admitted to being as well."

"But she was going to invest in the new movie?"

"Stan offered to let her do that, yes. He was trying to do her a favor. He felt bad when he couldn't give her a part, and it would have been a marvelous investment for her."

Which didn't go along with the rumors of his problems financing the movie. Or with what Shirley had overheard, when Michelle called Stan's wanting her to invest in the movie blackmail.

"Would he have given her a part if she invested enough money?" I asked.

I suspected the blunt question might get me a blue-toed whack in the ribs, but all Mrs. Steffan did was sound a little huffy when she said, "Of course not! Stan doesn't do business that way. The artistic merit of his productions is vital to him."

I made a mental note, when Fitz and I got together at the CyberClam, to check on the "artistic merit" of the Stan Man's films.

Chapter Eighteen

Getting together with Fitz turned out to be complicated. First I had to run Stan Steffan out to the casino. He expected me to sit around and wait for him, but I ignored his arrogant attitude, gave him my cell phone number, and told him to call when he wanted to go back to the house.

I parked off to the side at the CyberClam, where the limo stood out among the handful of pickups and compact cars like a tuxedo at a clam dig. Fitz wasn't there when I arrived, but he called just as I was logging onto the Internet on one of the rental computers. He said the *Miss Nora* was late getting in, but they'd just docked and he'd be up as soon as he got the guests taken care of.

Pam had disappeared before dinner, but I'd retrieved the place cards from her room anyway. Before starting on them I Googled Steffan Productions, which brought up more hits than I could look up in the entire evening. The first few were enough to tell me what I wanted to know about the "artistic merit" of Stan Steffan's movies. His earlier productions had been big commercial successes and received some praise for their story value, but later ones were R rated, with an artistic merit only slightly above dumpster level, though still fairly good moneymakers. The last one, however, had also tanked commercially, which perhaps explained why he was having to hustle for investors now. Although, given the attitude of the wedding guests, he still appeared to have considerable status in Hollywood.

I also learned some other gossipy tidbits about his recent relationship with a younger Italian actress, Mrs. Steffan's work with a South American orphanage organization, and a party at their home that featured an unscheduled catfight between two young actresses.

Oh yes, the Hollywood rich are different from you and me. The closest thing to a catfight at any party I ever gave was when a neighbor's tomcat and a skunk tangled, an altercation that did not make it into the fan magazines but did bring out a lot of neighbors.

Then, on a site that had some "at home" photos of the couple, something more interesting turned up. A photo showed Stan Steffan in his den, in the background a wall-mounted array of weapons that the accompanying description called "his collection of antique Japanese swords, one of which was reputedly used in the beheading of an important shogun." No butterfly knives, but the collection certainly showed an interest in sharp and deadly weapons.

I was jotting down the URL so I could find it again to show Fitz when something touched the back of my neck. At first I froze. Then the touch tingled all the way to my toes.

"Is that you, Fitz?" I asked without turning.

"If it isn't, how come you're letting some strange guy kiss you on the neck?"

"I'd recognize the touch of your lips anywhere. Atop the highest mountain, across the hottest desert, under the deepest sea—"

He snorted, gave me another kiss on the nape, and swiveled my chair around to face him. We grinned at each other. His mustache was coming along nicely. The man exuded fun and masculine vitality and a breezy elegance, living proof that some men do indeed age like fine wine.

"I've missed you," he said.

"You've only been gone overnight."

He put his hand over his heart. "One day without you is like a winter of a thousand years." Fitz could be melodramatic too.

We grinned at each other again.

"Okay, now that we have the formalities out of the way, shall we get down to work?" I suggested.

Fitz dropped another kiss on my forehead, and I showed him the website page of Stan Steffan and the head-chopping swords.

"Try to work it into a conversation with Mrs. Steffan and find out if he has any other interesting collections," Fitz suggested.

We split the place cards and worked on two computers so we could get through them faster.

"Do you remember a Tiffany Hartline?" Fitz asked after a few minutes.

"I think that was the tall blond who was scrubbed from the bridesmaids' lineup."

"There's some stuff here about her being arrested on a cocaine charge. After she got out, she blogged an account of the terrible five days she spent in jail. Very traumatic. She had no eyeliner or nail file, and the menu was overloaded with high-glycemic carbohydrates."

"Poor thing. But would she murder over Michelle's menu?"

"Not if it meant risking a broken fingernail, I'd guess."

I finished my half of the cards first. A couple of the starlet types had a number of hits, and most others a mention or two, but nothing popped out to arouse suspicion.

On impulse I Googled my own name. Nothing. In this day and age, do you really exist if Google has never heard of you? I must see about setting up a website for Andi's Limouzeen Service.

Next I did Pam's old boyfriend's name, which brought up only a site for the landscape design and maintenance business. Very professional looking, both the site and the business.

"Well, none of my place-card names showed

up on a Murderers-R-Us site," Fitz said finally. "I'm going to try Gerald Gibson."

"I'll do Michelle's business partners, the Hubbards."

Which yielded a website devoted to both the new fitness center and the mysterious exercise machine, the Uri-Blaster Extreme Body Builder. The site offered glitzy praise of the machine but no photos. Viewers were invited to the upcoming opening of the Change Your World Fitness Center to witness the unveiling and try it out.

"Listen to this on a biography page about the Hubbards. They met when Cindy's army unit was stationed in Germany, where Uri was an instructor in an athletic club and winner of numerous body-building contests. They married in Germany, and then he came back to the States with her and became a citizen. And here's a photo of her in uniform showing off her sharpshooter's medal!"

"Michelle wasn't shot."

"No, but maybe they were trained with knives too."

"Does the site mention Michelle?"

"Her page, as one of the 'creators' of this 'revolutionary new weight and fitness center,' has a long list of her acting credits. There are photos from the movies and a couple of her in workout gear, and she attributes her body to the

Uri-Blaster. There's a photo of the three of them together."

Fitz got up to look over my shoulder at my computer screen. The photo showed Uri in the center, silver-haired and handsome, muscles bulging in his form-fitting T-shirt. Michelle and Cindy book-ended him on either side, everyone smiling, as if the miracle machine might include teeth whitening as one of its side benefits.

"One big happy family," Fitz said.

"According to this, the opening date is still on schedule."

"The murder isn't mentioned?"

"Ignored completely. Although I can't tell when the site was last updated."

In spite of the fact that Pam's father had been dead for several years, his name as a prominent southern California developer brought up quite a few hits. Most of the references concerned environmental problems with his subdivisions, including numerous complaints from purchasers about houses built on unstable fill dirt.

"Sounds as if a number of people were mad enough to turn a few bees loose on him," Fitz suggested.

My surfing turned up a number of hits on Michelle before she married Gerald Gibson, but very little since then.

We gave up about nine-thirty, ordered decaf cappuccinos, and carried them out to the limo to talk. Fitz said he'd talked to his friend on the town police force, who'd looked into the autopsy report on Gerald Gibson and found it to be quite straightforward, nothing suspicious about the death.

"Which may only mean Michelle pulled off a successful murder," he added.

Michelle's death was a county sheriff's department matter, not city police, but the officer friend knew the knife used to kill Michelle was indeed what Fitz had named it, a butterfly knife.

"And it is a collector's type, quite fancy. I'm sure they were going to check and see if any local dealers remember it. But it could have been bought out of the area or off the Internet."

"In any case, it isn't the kind of knife the average person would be carrying around."

"Right."

"Were there fingerprints?" I asked.

"He wouldn't discuss that, although I don't know if it was because he didn't feel he could tell me or because he didn't know."

Personally I doubted they'd find any prints. The killer wasn't going to make it that simple. I couldn't remember seeing anyone wearing gloves, but the killer could have covered his or her hand with a handkerchief before plunging the knife into Michelle's back. Or it wouldn't have taken more than a couple of seconds to wipe the handle clean after the deed was done.

I passed along what Mrs. Steffan had told me about Michelle saying she was afraid of something. "Did anyone mention that when you were circulating the night of the murder?"

"Not a word. But it's probably not something Michelle would have spread around. The impression I got was that she liked to present herself as the epitome of health, both mentally and physically. Most of the talk was about the fog machine operator, who he was and why he wasn't around afterward."

My cell phone rang. Stan Steffan, of course. I said I'd be at the casino within fifteen minutes. Fitz got out and stuffed our cappucino cups into a trash container.

"I feel as if we just chased down empty rabbit holes tonight," I said with a bit of frustration when he came back. "We didn't really accomplish much of anything, did we?"

"We learned that Stan Steffan collects swords and Cindy Hubbard has a sharpshooter's medal. But the most interesting bit of information is what you got out of Mrs. Steffan earlier: Michelle was afraid of something. You might see if her husband has anything to add to that when you pick him up."

"I don't think Stan Steffan confides in chauffeur-level people."

"There's something else we got out of tonight too, of course. At least I did."

"Which was?"

"I got to spend it with you."

With a kiss even more tingly than the one on the back of the neck.

I doubted I'd have a chance to talk to Stan Steffan, let alone quiz him. He'd jump in the limo, slam the partition shut, and that would be that.

To my surprise, however, before I even had a chance to step out and open the limo door for him, he strode through the casino's double glass doors, sunglasses locked in place in spite of the late hour, and slid into the passenger's seat next to me. My nerves suddenly revved into high gear. I hadn't figured out a motive yet, but Stan Steffan was vying for top position on my tightrope of potential murderers. Did he know I was suspicious of him? And why was he sitting up here with me?

Chapter Nineteen

"I know who killed Michelle," he announced.

You looked in the mirror, and there he was?

But all I said was a wary, "You do?" as I eased the limo around the casino's circular driveway.

"I figured it out tonight. My subconscious is

always working when I'm at a blackjack table. That's where I get some of my best ideas."

Like the idea for that movie about the chainsaw-wielding vampire? Oh, yeah, great idea. Lots of artistic value. "One of the wedding guests?" I asked cautiously.

"Obviously the person was present at the wedding. That's a no-brainer. I'm seeing it like a script. In a good script, the murderer is never the obvious suspect. There's a twist, a hidden agenda, that the average person can't spot."

The implication being that he was much more clever than the average person.

"But in non-scripted real life, the murderer is often someone quite straightforward," I said. "The wife or the husband. The friend or neighbor or business partner."

He turned his head to look at me. I couldn't see any expression through the barrier of the sunglasses, but I got the distinct impression of Big Important Bug looking down on Tiny No-Brainer Bug. Squishing said bug being a strong possibility.

"So who do you say it is?" I asked hastily.

"I don't care to reveal a specific name yet, but I will when I have the proof to go with what I already know."

"You're turning detective?" I asked with as much dismay as Detective Molino no doubt felt about my sleuthing.

"These small-town cops will never figure it out. They couldn't find a candy thief leaving a trail of chocolate fingerprints. That's why Alice and I've stayed on. We want Michelle's killer brought to justice."

Detective Molino and I have our differences, but I didn't appreciate Stan Steffan's disdainful attitude toward the local authorities.

"Actually, Detective Molino is with the county sheriff's department, not the 'small-town cops.'"

He waved a hand to dismiss that as a trivial technicality. "Whatever."

"Do you intend to discuss your, umm, epiphany with Detective Molino?"

"I'll talk to someone higher up when the time comes."

No one but top brass for Stan Steffan. So why, I wondered, was he deigning to tell me all this? I flicked the turn signal and eased onto Hornsby Loop. "Are you considering the possibility that if the killer realizes you're onto him, or her, your own life might be in danger?"

"I can take care of myself."

The arrogant answer implied an invincible superiority. His superior intellect, no doubt. Maybe a black belt in karate, or a Colt .45 in his pocket? Or another obvious possibility: if he were the murderer, he had no reason to fear anyone else.

"Guy tried to carjack my Mercedes once. Bad choice for *him*."

He obviously expected me to ask why this was a bad choice for the carjacker, so I obliged. As he was telling me how he'd done the guy in by slamming the car into the side of a building, I figured out why he'd turned so chatty. Stan Steffan needed an audience, even if it was only a lone limo chauffeur. Praise. Applause. The kind of guy who, if he got away with murder, might turn it into a movie to parade his cleverness?

I failed to play my assigned part as breathless applauder, and we rode to the gate in silence. I slipped the remote control from the visor and touched the button. The gate opened, then closed behind us.

"Did you get a good look at the knife that was used to kill Michelle?" I asked.

"No. The body was covered by the time I saw it. Why?"

"I was thinking that if you'd seen the knife, perhaps you could identify it for the authorities."

"How could I identify it? It wasn't mine." Was that an undercurrent of alarm beneath the ever-present scorn? Identifying it as his wasn't what I'd meant, but it was interesting that he took it that way.

"Identify it in a general way, I mean. Since you're an expert on such matters."

"I collect Japanese swords of historic significance and value. I'm not knowledgeable about other types of knives." He added a wary-sounding question. "Did you see it?"

"Oh, yes."

"Could you describe it?"

"I don't think I can do that." With a certain superiority of my own I added, "Confidential information, you know."

Okay, so that implied I was working some insider role with the authorities, which wasn't exactly accurate, but I figured the fact that it was a butterfly knife *should* be confidential. Although the Stan Man here might already know exactly what kind of knife it was.

Yet the basic problem with that immediately jumped up to whack me again. What motive could he have for murdering Michelle? Her death ended any chance of his prying a sizable investment in his movie out of her.

I stopped the limo at the front steps. He opened the door, but before getting out he asked, "You were the first one to the body. I suppose you have some theory about who did it?"

"Solving murders is a matter for the authorities, not me."

"But someone said you helped catch the killer of some old boyfriend. Body in the trunk or something. A regular Murder-She-Wrote woman."

Any egotistical temptation I may have had to claim super-sleuth powers was doused by a feeling that knowing too much might not be healthy around Stan Steffan. So all I said was, "I'm a limousine chauffeur, not a detective."

After dropping him off at the steps, I parked in the graveled alleyway between the house and garage. I was circling the house to go in the back way when my cell phone rang. I glanced at the caller ID.

"Fitz?" I said, wondering why he'd call at this late hour.

"You're okay?"

"I'm fine. No problems."

"Good. I just wanted to make sure you got there okay." Fitz's concern felt more warming than a dip in the hot tub.

"You think Stan Steffan is a murderer?"

"Everybody's a suspect, remember? But even if he isn't a murderer, we know he's a woman chaser. And you're a very attractive woman."

I could have argued that Stan Steffan's taste ran to targets considerably younger and more shapely than yours truly, but I decided to bask in the compliment instead. "He told me he knows who killed Michelle. Though he doesn't intend to reveal who it is until he comes up with the evidence."

"What made him so talkative?"

"I was surprised too, but he's big on impressing people, and I guess I was the only one available at the moment."

"Stan Steffan playing detective sounds dangerous to me."

"Because there's nothing worse than an amateur bumbling around in murder?"

"Because maybe he isn't looking for evidence to incriminate someone. Maybe what he really wants is to grab any evidence that might incriminate *him*. And maybe he wouldn't be averse to eliminating someone who got in his way."

"You're a suspicious man, Keegan Fitzpatrick."

"That's the key to long life for a detective. Watch out for that guy, Andi. I'd feel a lot better if you moved back home."

"I will as soon as I can."

He paused, as if considering pushing for a more definite commitment, but finally said, "Okay. Talk to you tomorrow."

I woke with the peculiar feeling something had wakened me, but I lay there in the dark for several minutes without hearing anything. I turned on the lamp and checked the clock. 2:45. I lay there sleepless for another ten minutes, then got up and slipped a robe over my pajamas.

I padded barefoot down the hallway to Michelle's office. Pam had said I could "poke around" in there if I wanted. She probably hadn't expected me to do it in the middle of the night, but a couple of years ago, in one of my occasional self-improvement frenzies, I'd decided that whenever I couldn't sleep I'd get up and do something constructive with the time. On that theory I've finished my taxes, reorganized the medicine chest in the bathroom, and learned that a do-it-yourself haircut at two thirty A.M. is not a wise idea.

Except that someone else apparently had the same thought about not wasting sleepless hours. Faint light from the upper hallway shone down the stairs, dimly illuminating the closed door to the office, but glimmers of light also flickered unevenly under the door. Someone with a flashlight? Or could a computer screen make that jumpy light?

Who? Why?

I could yank the door open—

Yeah, right. And find myself facing a murderer. With more potent weaponry than what I had, which, after feeling around in the pockets of my robe, appeared to be two bobby pins and a paper clip.

Yet, even unarmed, I couldn't ignore the situation and slink silently back to my room. Knowing who was in there could be the key to identifying Michelle's killer. No convenient keyhole to peek through, however.

No problem! The guest closet was on the other side of the foyer. I'd just hide in there and have a sleuth's-eye view when the office door opened.

The catch on the closet door made only an infinitesimal click as I turned the knob. So far, so good. I'd just make myself comfortable in here—

But I almost panicked when I slipped inside. The closet wasn't empty! Someone large and hairy and long-armed—I stifled a shriek, then twisted and turned and flailed my fists in a frantic effort to escape the smothering presence.

And managed a triumphant victory over my ruthless opponent—a fur-collared jacket.

I had no idea how much noise this one-sided battle had caused, but I crouched there frozen, expecting the murderer to fling the door open at any moment. But after several minutes all that happened was that the fur made me sneeze, my back stiffened, and my left foot went to sleep. Carefully I straightened to a slightly less uncomfortable position leaning against the back wall.

Then I waited. And waited. My nose itched. My right leg cramped. My ears developed a peculiar ring. Who was in there? It had to be one of the people in residence at the house. Top guess: Stan Steffan. Although the search seemed rather quiet for someone of his bulk and impatience.

After what felt like hours, though was probably no more than fifteen minutes, I eased the door open a few inches to peer out. All I saw was

Phreddie sitting on the steps leading upstairs.

I was less certain now that what I'd seen—and could still see—was really light under the door. Maybe what appeared to be a flicker of flashlight or computer screen was some trick of moonlight through the office window. I might hide here stiff-kneed until daylight and no one would ever come out of that office.

Now what? The drapes on the windows in the office were probably closed, but if I sneaked out on the front porch I could at least tell if there was an actual light on in the room. With a lucky break, I might even be able to see who was in there.

Okay, lights, camera, action!

I squeezed out of the closet, tiptoed to the front door, turned the lock, and slipped outside. The deadbolt type lock was reassuring. Even if the night breeze coming off the inlet blew the door shut, the deadbolt wouldn't lock by itself and leave me stranded outside.

Right away I spotted the dim, jumpy light in the room. Yes, someone was definitely in there! Sliding along the wall, hands behind me, I inched closer to the window. If there was just a tiny gap between the drapes—

The room went dark just before I got there. Could the searcher somehow be aware I was out here? I stiffened against the wall. A moment later I heard the office door open and close softly.

Someone coming after me? Or getting away?

Recklessly I lunged back toward the door. If I could peek inside I might still see who it was—

In astonishment I saw the door swing shut before I reached it. Could the night breeze do that?

A moment later the distinct *snick* of the deadbolt told me this was no force of nature; this was human action. I stared at the knob, then jiggled it in dismay.

Just my luck. A neat-freak murderer, conscientiously tidying up so some nasty burglar couldn't get inside.

I tried to correlate that personality trait with the occupants of the house. Considering Stan Steffan's stated intention to find "evidence," he loomed as top suspect in this clandestine search of the office, but I couldn't see him conscientiously locking the door. Shirley'd do it, of course, but she could search the office whenever she wanted; she didn't have to sneak in at night. Also, except for an allegiance to Fitz's "everybody's a suspect" philosophy, I'd about 99 percent eliminated Shirley.

That left Mrs. Steffan and Sterling's parents. Phyllis Forsythe? A quiet, probably methodical woman. She'd close and lock doors. But she was scared even in her bed, so it didn't seem likely she'd be out sneaking around. Which left—

Oh, good one, Ms. Hotshot Sleuth, I interrupted

myself. I'm busily running a personality inventory on suspects while ignoring a crucial detail of the moment. Which is that I'm standing here in my pajamas and robe, with a damp breeze shivering my bare toes.

And I'm locked out of the house.

Chapter Twenty

I circled the house eying windows. At Shirley's, I tossed a chunk of gravel against the pane. No response. I tried the back door, hopefully thinking I may have left it unlocked when I came in that way. No, I'd locked it as conscientiously as the killer had locked the front door. I tried another pebble at Pam's attic window, but at that upward distance I may as well have been trying to hit a passing jet.

Inspiration! The limo. A great place to spend the night, secure and comfortable. Like a pajama party with an old friend. There was even a blanket in the trunk. I rushed back around the house, bare feet ouching on the gravel when I got off the grass. Only to find that I'd securely locked the limo too. I tended to be diligent about that ever since finding the old boyfriend's body in the trunk.

Nothing to do but wait it out. I circled back to

sit on the front porch, feet tucked under my robe, back against the wall. To my surprise, Phreddie joined me. He'd apparently sneaked out when the door was open. I rearranged my legs into a lap, and he climbed in. My friend Joella, whose baby had been born in my limo, had once told me stray moments were good for talking to the Lord, so I took advantage of this opportunity.

Dumb thing I did here, God, right? Do You look after people who make dumb mistakes? I hope so. Thanks for not letting whoever was in the office catch me. I could be sitting here not just cold and uncomfortable; I could be clunked on the head or have a knife in my back. Lord, it's kind of off the subject at the moment, but help me to be a better witness and example to Pam. Fitz too. Oh, and thanks for sending Phreddie to keep me company.

I was still cold and uncomfortable, but Phreddie made a purry bundle of warmth in my lap, and I must have drifted off to sleep.

Because I woke in the midst of a tangled dream about murderers and cats and Fitz.

"Andi, Andi, wake up! What are you doing out here? And Phreddie! Bad cat. You're not supposed to be outside at night."

Then it wasn't the dream I was tangled in, it was my robe twisted around my feet. Pam grabbed Phreddie when my struggles disturbed him, and I scrambled to my feet.

What *was* I doing out here on the porch in the middle of the night? It took me a moment to remember.

"Someone was in Michelle's office. I was trying to see who. I got locked out of the house. So did Phreddie. What are you doing out here?"

"I've been drinking coffee and talking to Mike."

"You're just getting home? It must be—what? Three or four o'clock in the morning!"

"You sound like a mother."

"I *am* a mother."

"We had a lot to talk about. Let's get you inside. You're cold as ice. What do you mean, someone was in Michelle's office?"

She unlocked the door, and I creaked inside. Hunched on a hard board floor in the damp night air makes mature joints feel like the rusting transmission of a '73 Pinto.

"Someone was prowling around in Michelle's office with a flashlight. Or maybe they had her computer on. Could you tell if anything's missing?"

"I doubt it. I haven't been in there since she was killed. But maybe we shouldn't touch anything in case there are fingerprints."

"I doubt Detective Molino is going to rush out here with fingerprint powder just because I thought someone was in the office. Fingerprints wouldn't prove anything anyway. Everybody's been in and out of the office."

"Yeah. I guess so." As if she couldn't think of any further reason not to enter the office, Pam turned the knob and flicked on the light.

We both looked around cautiously. I knew whoever had been in here was gone. I'd heard the prowler leave. Yet I couldn't escape a nervous apprehension of lurking danger. Like some kid peering under the bed looking for the resident monster, I leaned over and peered under the desk.

Nothing there but a plastic mat to protect the hardwood floor from the scootings of the office chair.

Phreddie squirmed, and Pam set him down. He shot away from the room as if some essence of Michelle remained. Pam looked as if she'd like to follow him.

"Are you okay?" I asked.

"This just feels so . . . creepy. As if Michelle might be watching. And not like us snooping around."

"No one's watching us," I assured her. Except maybe that glassy-eyed leopard. Irrelevantly, looking up at it, I asked, "Have you thought of taking that thing down?"

"I guess I could."

But I doubted she would. Her father may not have acquired the leopard as some personal trophy to his masculinity level, but he'd bought it, and maybe she considered that a trophy of sorts.

"How about if I fix you something hot to drink before you go back to bed?" she asked.

"Not so fast. We need to look around in here."

"Now? You're shivering. Oh, all right," she muttered. She slipped off her jacket and draped it around my cold shoulders.

I didn't protest. I clutched the jacket around me with one hand and pointed to the desk with the other. "There's Michelle's file about the wedding."

A few pages spilled out of the thick folder. A couple of legal looking agreements, lists, and lots of magazine clippings of floral arrangements and wedding cakes. From the amount of material in the file, going through it all would take considerable time.

With one finger, I pulled the top drawer of the desk open. It held neatly arranged office supplies: pens, tape, paper clips, rubber bands, staples, brass letter opener, computer paper in the back section. Nothing looked touched. But then, a particular size of rubber band probably wasn't what the intruder was searching for.

Pam turned to the filing cabinet. She seemed reluctant to touch it, so I pulled a drawer open.

I felt a tingle of excitement. Someone had been in here! Michelle would never have left the files in such sloppy condition, pages sticking out, some bent or crumpled when the drawer had been shoved shut. And a hair! A short, dark, curly hair caught on the edge of a manila folder. I carefully extracted it, got a sheet of white paper from the desk, and laid the hair on it.

Pam and I stared at it.

"Definitely not Michelle's," I said.

Pam touched the neckline of her own curly, dark hair. "I guess it could be mine," she said reluctantly.

"But you said you haven't been in here since Michelle was killed."

"I'd forgotten until now, but after I thought I saw Mike at the wedding I was wondering who Michelle had hired for the fog machine. So I came in and poked around."

"Why would you look in that drawer? The wedding file is on the top of the desk."

"I don't know. I'm not sure what I did. I was kind of . . . dazed, I guess."

I'd decided early on that Pam had nothing to do with Michelle's murder, and I still believed that, but this inconsistency about being in the office made me uneasy. She'd also been slow to tell me Mike had been at the wedding. What else was she holding back, intentionally or otherwise?

"Pam, I can't help you if you give me misinformation." I didn't make any effort *not* to sound severe. Although a moment later I guiltily realized she was under no obligation to tell me anything.

"I'm sorry. But until right now I honestly

didn't remember coming in here that one time. I was so afraid Mike could have killed her."

"They do DNA testing on hair, right?" I asked.

"Yes, but I think the root has to be attached. I looked up some information about it for my book. But it's expensive and takes time, and it's the same situation as the fingerprints."

Not something Detective Molino would leap on with glee. And, as with the fingerprints, even if the hair could be identified, anyone could come up with an innocent explanation for its being in here.

Even Pam.

Pam definitely wasn't the person who'd been prowling in here tonight, however. The hair, though interesting, probably wasn't of much value as a clue. Although all I had to go on was Pam saying she was just now getting home. . . .

Pam, much too observant, noted my mental waffling. "You're still wondering if I did it, aren't you?"

"No, I don't think you killed her. You can search the office any time you want. You don't have to do it in the middle of the night." And the hair wasn't really as curly as Pam's. I turned back to the filing cabinet.

Had the person found what he or she wanted? Or had the drawers been angrily shoved shut, crumpling some of the papers, because the sought-for paper wasn't found?

Neat labels identified the files. The top drawer covered house and property matters, records on the remodeling, bills and receipts, vehicle and health insurance. The next one, in which I'd found the hair, appeared to be health club files; the drawer below looked like mostly income tax returns and legal papers. I spotted one folder labeled *Pam's Trust Fund*, another *Gerald's Estate Tax Records*. The bottom drawer was about Michelle's movie career, with some old contracts and a lot of clippings.

Although it had been done fairly tidily, which went along with the neat-freak door locking, the office had definitely been searched. Again I wondered if the person had found what he or she was looking for. Or was this a general fishing expedition just to see what might turn up?

"I suppose I'll have to go through all this stuff sooner or later," Pam said reluctantly. She turned and looked at the dark screen of the monitor. "The computer too."

I reached over and touched the computer, but I couldn't tell if it had recently been used.

"Did Michelle leave a will naming heirs and an executor? If there's an executor, you can probably turn everything over to that person."

"I don't know. Probably. She was pretty well organized." Pam sounded hopeful about this possibility. "There's a safe in here somewhere, but I have no idea where it is." She turned in a tight circle, still not touching anything. "Maybe someone was looking for her jewelry."

That thought hadn't occurred to me. I'd assumed this search was connected with the murder, but maybe it was someone simply hoping to rip off the family valuables. Although murderer and jewel thief weren't mutually exclusive.

"Did she have expensive jewelry?"

"I know Dad gave her a diamond necklace and an emerald ring. Emerald earrings too. She didn't wear her engagement and wedding rings any more, so they're probably in the safe. Plenty of stuff worth stealing."

"What about the necklace and earrings she was wearing when she was killed?"

"Detective Molino said everything would be returned after the autopsy."

"Well, whatever they were after, we know the search was done by one of the five people here in the house. Sterling's parents, the Steffans, or Shirley."

"Seven."

"Seven? You're including you and me?"

"No, but a few minutes after you left last evening, Cindy called. She said something was wrong with the electrical system at the cottage, and they didn't have lights. It was too late to get an electrician, so I suggested they spend the night here in the Starlight Room. It's the one next to Michelle's bedroom."

"Has this ever happened before?"

"You mean an electrical problem at the cottage? Not that I know of."

So, there's an unusual electrical event. Uri and Cindy . . . afraid of the dark? . . . rush to the house for the night. Michelle's office is stealthily ransacked.

What does it take to create an electrical event? Hmmm.

"Maybe we should try to locate the safe," I suggested.

"Yeah, maybe."

She made no move to do so. I squeamishly lifted the edge of the leopard hide and looked behind it. Nothing. Also nothing behind the African masks or the painting of an African landscape.

"What's going on here?"

Pam and I both jumped.

Shirley stood in the open doorway, plaid bathrobe cinched over blue nightgown, three pink curlers in her hair, rolling pin clutched in her hands, fire blazing in her eyes.

She lowered the rolling pin and blinked. "I'm sorry. I thought it was, uh, someone who didn't have any business being in here."

Shirley, unlike yours truly, obviously didn't hide in a closet when she suspected strange activity. She came out armed for battle. I should be so prepared. Although a rolling pin isn't exactly the kind of weapon you conceal in your bra.

I didn't go through the whole long tale of someone being in the office and my getting locked out. Instead, without giving any reason for the unlikely hour, I just said, "We're looking for the safe."

She hesitated, then pointed under the desk to the area covered by the plastic mat. "It's down there, under the floor."

The hesitation, I suspected, was because she wasn't eager to admit she knew where the safe was located. Probably not part of a cook-housekeeper's job specifications.

I slid the mat aside, revealing the line of a square in the polished floor.

"Press on the top right corner."

I did, and the square of flooring popped up. A black metal safe lay underneath, only the door and the knob of a combination-type lock visible.

"I'll probably have to get a locksmith to open it." Pam sounded as if she still figured Michelle was watching disapprovingly.

"Maybe the numbers for the combination are in the desk," I suggested.

"I doubt Michelle would leave something like that lying around. Besides, she had an incredible memory. She knew lines from movies she'd been in years ago. She'd remember the combination without writing it down."

"Twelve, sixteen, seven, twenty-nine, nineteen," Shirley said.

"She told you the combination?" I asked, surprised.

"No. It's written on the underside of the center drawer. But it doesn't look like Michelle's writing. The seven is made that peculiar way, with a little line through it."

"That's how my dad made sevens." Pam knelt under the desk and scrunched her head around so she could see the bottom of the drawer. "Yeah, it's right here."

"I just happened to run across it one time when I was cleaning. I clean very thoroughly, you know," Shirley added, her tone defensive.

But what I was thinking was that her remembering the numbers also suggested a rather remarkable memory. No senior moments here.

"But maybe the numbers are something else entirely. I never tried them to see if they work."

I wouldn't vouch for the accuracy of that claim, but neither did I intend to question it. I thought sharing the numbers with us, rather than trying to protect herself with pretended ignorance, was generous of her. The thought occurred to me that if anyone knew anything about a knife collection tucked away somewhere, it would be Shirley.

Pam unwound herself from the awkward position staring up at the underside of the drawer. Then, as if she felt she were reaching into a snake pit, she turned the knob to the first number. Twelve. But a small commotion at the door startled us all, and Pam bumped her head on the underside of the knee hole as she hastily slammed the panel shut and scrambled out from under the desk.

Uri and Cindy stood there in matching blue-and-white shorts and T-shirts with the Change Your World logo blazoned across the back, both looking all bright-eyed and perky even at this hour. Uri was bareheaded, but Cindy wore a visored cap over her hair. I stared at her hair. Short. Dark. Curly.

A match for the hair taped to the paper.

But then, I rather tardily realized, that although Shirley's hair was mostly gray, there were still some dark strands in back, and they, too, were curly from a perm.

"What's this? A party we didn't know about?" Cindy asked.

I was certain she'd seen the hair displayed on the paper, but apparently she intended to ignore it.

Uri ran in place, like some racehorse chomping at the bit, but I saw his eyes dart to the knee hole of the desk, from which Pam had so hastily exited. Had they both been prowling around in here? Were they now mentally kicking themselves for not looking under the desk when they searched the room? Or had they been innocently sleeping in the Starlight Room, and this was just a generic curiosity about this peculiar little daybreak gathering?

Cindy'd be a door locker, I decided. Yet even if they had been in the office, the search wasn't necessarily related to the murder. The hair had been in the health-club drawer, and maybe they were just after something to do with the partnership. Although surely they could have chosen a less sneaky way to get it.

"You're going running now?" I asked.

"We like to go at sunrise," Uri said. "There's something almost spiritual about seeing the sun come up while you're running. It gets the day off to a right start."

Shirley, ever the conscientious food provider, asked, "Will you be here for breakfast?"

"We eat only whole grains at our morning meal," Cindy said. "No meat or eggs. And we prefer guava juice."

"I'm afraid we're fresh out of guavas." Shirley spoke blandly, though I suspected that, like me, she couldn't identify a guava if it squirted her in the eye.

"We'll probably just grab something at Heavenly Health, then, when we go up to the fitness center. Some exercise mats are supposed

260

to come in today. We'll pick up the things we left in the room later."

"I'll get an electrician over to the cottage as soon as I can," Pam said. "You can stay here again tonight if you need to."

Pam hadn't re-locked the front door behind us, so Cindy and Uri didn't have to turn the deadbolt to get out. I shoved the drapes aside and watched them jog toward the beach. Pam looked over my shoulder. They made a great looking pair, like some glossy ad extolling the beneficial marvels of the Uri-Blaster Extreme Body Builder. The rising sun enveloped them in a golden glow.

"The family that runs together stays together?" Pam murmured.

Maybe. Although a more ominous thought occurred to me. The family that murders together stays together?

Chapter Twenty-One

Pam knelt to open the panel under the desk again, but now we had another visitor. What was this, old home week?

Phyllis Forsythe peered in the door, demure in white shorts, pale blue blouse, and white sandals. Her hair, though limp as ever, was neatly brushed in place. "I heard voices and wondered if something was wrong?"

I resisted an urge to tell her to drop that whispery little voice and speak up. And maybe use some industrial strength mousse on that hair. Then I felt guilty. She was so nice, and I shouldn't be thinking unkind thoughts.

"Everything's fine. I'm sorry we disturbed you so early," Pam said.

"Oh, you didn't disturb us. I've been waking up early. We've been down in the hot tub—Joe's still there."

In spite of her immaculate outfit, she didn't look nearly as perky as Uri and Cindy. Her eyelids sagged, and her fingers worked nervously at a loose thread on the belt loop of her shorts. Of course, if she'd been up in the middle of the night pawing through Michelle's files . . .

Oh, c'mon, timid little Phyllis?

Timid little Phyllis who was ready to do battle with the deputies when she thought her son was threatened.

But what could she possibly want to find in Michelle's office?

I wasn't surprised when Pam decided the safe-opening would have to wait until later. She briskly herded everyone into the hallway and shut the door.

"Isn't it a beautiful morning?" she said.

Phyllis and Joe Forsythe, Pam, Shirley, and I all

ate an early breakfast in the kitchen. Bacon and eggs, biscuits and jam. Plain old orange juice, straight from the Minute Maid container. I wanted to ask Shirley about the possibility of a valuable knife collection around somewhere, but right after breakfast Mrs. Steffan showed up, and she and Shirley were deep into a biscuit discussion while Shirley prepared more breakfast for her.

Pam said she was going to call the lawyers who handled the trust fund and set up a meeting with them as soon as possible. I halfway expected her to ask me to accompany her, and I was pleased when she didn't. I hoped it meant she was moving into a take-charge mode. Maybe I could be out of here by tomorrow.

I decided to run over to my duplex and catch up on things there. I'd talk to Shirley later. On the way out the front door I stopped at the closet and put my fur-collared sparring partner back on a hanger.

My nosy neighbor, Tom Bolton, was clipping the hedge in his yard when I pulled into the driveway at the duplex. He came to the chain-link fence and motioned me over. He was wearing shorts, in one of his usual strange plaids, with the tail of a blue shirt hanging over his paunch.

"Your renters moved out. Looked like they took a lot of furniture with them."

"That's okay. Their rent was paid up, and it was their furniture."

"Oh." He sounded disappointed.

I wouldn't call Tom mean-hearted, but he'd rather give you bad news than good.

"One of the newspaper photos about the murder at the wedding showed the back end of your limo. All that murder stuff must be hard on business."

"There were a lot of photographers around. But business is fine, thank you."

"Pretty gruesome stuff, huh? Woman getting knifed right in the middle of a big wedding."

I ignored his fishing for juicy details. "Your yard is looking very nice."

"Some woman was here looking for you. I talked to her."

As if someone looking for me was any of his business, but I managed not to say that.

"She said she was interested in renting your place."

"Really? I haven't even advertised it yet."

"I think she saw those people moving out and thought it might be for rent. She was wearing one of those peculiar tent things. She didn't look like someone who'd have good references."

I wasn't sure what a "tent thing" was, but I didn't ask for a fashion explanation. "Young woman? Old?"

"Not young. But younger than you."

Good ol' Tom. Call 'em like he sees 'em.

"I asked if she wanted to leave a number where you could call her, but she said no."

"Maybe she'll come back when I advertise, then. I should be home within a few days."

"Your lawn needs work. It's getting scruffy looking. And you ought to do something about that dead limb out back. It's a hazard."

I gritted my teeth. The limb wasn't visible from Tom's yard. He'd have had to go around back of my house to see it. Too bad the limb hadn't fallen on him.

No, no. WWJD. People had talked at Bible study about using that What-would-Jesus-do question to guide your actions. What would Jesus do about a nosy troublemaker like Tom Bolton?

I knew Jesus wouldn't do what I felt like doing, which was grabbing the clippers in Tom's hand and whacking off his shirttail. So, summoning more sweetness than a triple-fudge brownie, I managed to smile and say, "Would you mind keeping an eye on the place for me till I get back? I'd really appreciate it." Since he was going to snoop anyway, he may as well do it officially. Or maybe, to be contrary, he *wouldn't* snoop.

To my surprise Tom straightened his heavy shoulders as if I'd assigned him the job of guarding the treasury.

"I'm busy," he said gruffly. "I have a new . . . lady friend. But I'll keep an eye out."

I didn't know what surprised me more. His unexpectedly cooperative attitude or the news about a "lady friend." Tom's wife had died several years ago, and I'd never known him to have any kind of social life. Had meeting this woman softened his grumpy outlook on life?

I wanted to know more. What kind of woman would be interested in Tom Bolton? Where had he met her? How serious was this? But, remembering my annoyance with his nosiness about my life, I held myself to thanking him.

"If I had your cell phone number, I could call if I notice anything you should know about."

This change in Tom made me uncomfortable, as if the world had taken a sudden tilt. Continents and glaciers were shifting. I gave him a business card with the cell number.

"You oughta do something about all those digger squirrels ripping up your yard," he growled after me as I headed back to my sidewalk. "First thing you know, they'll be moving in over here. You'll be liable if they do."

Tom also liked to sue, as a couple of other neighbors had found out.

So Tom, new lady friend or no, was still Tom. I felt safer. I gave him a friendly wave. "Have a nice day."

In the house, I checked my answering machine.

I returned calls, turned down limo appointments for this week but scheduled a couple for later. I called Sarah in Florida, reached her between college classes, and we caught up with what was going on in our lives. Granddaughter Rachel had a new boyfriend.

"And he has a *motorcycle*," Sarah wailed. I smiled. Things had come full circle.

I used my old Toyota to run to the post office and check my mailbox, then wrote checks to pay bills. I dropped the place cards from the wedding off at the sheriff's office for Detective Molino. They were looking well fingered by now. I was glad he wasn't there to ask what had taken me so long or what I'd been doing with them. I didn't leave any helpful list of suspects.

I called Fitz, and we met at the Sweet Breeze bakery, where Joella used to work, for lunch. I filled him in on the night's events. The *Miss Nora* was leaving on a three-day run that afternoon. He said he'd go over and mow my lawn before they left.

I was back at the house by 1:25. The crime-scene tape was gone and the tent had been removed, only an area of trampled grass showing where it had been. The sculpture still stood, but its sharp edges had softened and blurred, and now it was more ice blob than bridal sculpture. There seemed a certain symbolism in that.

Pam was sitting at Michelle's desk going

through the wedding file when I went inside the house. She motioned me into the office. The leopard was gone from the wall.

"I kept feeling as if he was sneaking up on me," she said by way of explanation. "I put him in an upstairs storage room."

"Good. Maybe he'll scare off the mice. Did you get to talk to the lawyer?"

"Oh yes. I got right in."

Which suggested the trust fund was big enough to make the law firm jump to attention, because my infrequent dealings with lawyers were usually on a-week-from-next-Tuesday basis.

"They've started the ball rolling to get the trust fund transferred to my control. Though I think it makes them nervous. Like they're afraid I'm going to spend it all on Soulja Boy and Yung Joc CDs."

"Maybe you should retain them in an, oh, advisory capacity in handling the money."

She surprised me by nodding agreement. "It's a lot of money."

I was curious how much, of course, but the fact that she didn't volunteer the information suggested that she was weaning herself from her brief dependence on me. Good. "What about this house?"

"Michelle's obligation was to provide a home for me until I turned twenty-three, graduated from college, or got married, and then it would be hers. None of those conditions were fulfilled, so the lawyer thinks it should be mine. Although there could be complications if her heirs want to contest that."

"Maybe you're her heir."

She dismissed that with a wry, "Yeah, right. And maybe Phreddie's in for a million bucks." She looked around the office thoughtfully. "I don't know that I'd bother arguing if the heirs do want the house. It doesn't mean that much to me, and I have enough money in the trust fund."

I found that attitude also admirably mature. Too many people never consider any amount of money "enough."

"Did you get an electrician for the cottage?"

"They're going to have to replace a lot of old wiring. Some wires shorted out—"

"Accidentally?"

"I guess so." She looked up sharply. "You're suggesting it was deliberate?"

"Don't you wonder? Uri and Cindy move in to the house, and the first thing that happens is the office is ransacked."

"It will take a day or two, maybe longer, to get the wiring replaced. So they'll be staying here. You think that's a . . . concern?"

"Lock up your guavas. Anything interesting in the wedding file?"

Pam glanced down at the open folder. "Just that I still owe a lot of money. Including for the fog machine, which seems kind of ironic, doesn't it? Though I can be grateful Michelle didn't go ahead with some of her ideas. She considered having doves fly out of the wedding cake."

The possible consequence of disoriented doves zooming around the wedding cake and guests was not pretty. Perhaps Michelle had realized that too. Pam and I smiled at each other.

"Do you still think she was planning to try to kill you at the wedding?"

"It seems kind of . . . far-fetched now." Although a certain reluctance in the admission suggested Pam wasn't yet willing to abandon that suspicion entirely.

I noted she'd taped the hair we'd found to the piece of paper. "Planning on framing that?"

"Just leaving it displayed. Maybe it will rattle someone's nerves." She propped the sheet of paper against the lamp on the desk where anyone looking in from the foyer would see it.

"Someone such as Cindy of the dark and curly hair?"

"Joe's hair is brown too. And short and curly."

That startled me. I hadn't even thought of Sterling's father in connection with the found hair. But what was left of his brown hair indeed had that unexpected hint of boyish curl.

"Anything from Detective Molino yet about the autopsy?"

"Not yet. But I've called a funeral home, and

they'll pick up the body when it's released. I found the name of Michelle's law firm in her files, and I have an appointment with them tomorrow. I'll talk with Phyllis about the funeral services. I suppose she should have some say since she is Michelle's cousin."

I was impressed at the way she was grabbing hold of the situation.

"So now all we have to do is open the safe," she added.

I noted the we. "You don't need me for that. Look at all you're accomplishing on your own!"

"I'm all false front. Like an inflatable bra. I may deflate any moment." She smiled. "C'mon, you're curious, you know you are."

"I guess I am," I admitted. "But remember that big deal about the 1930s safe being opened on TV? Big letdown. Maybe this one will be empty too."

Pam knelt by the desk, pulled the plastic mat aside, and pressed the corner of the concealing panel. She gave me a nervous little smile and blew on her fingertips like some safe-cracking expert.

"Here goes."

She clicked the numbers without having to crane her neck to look at the underside of the drawer. Her memory was good too.

Michelle's safe was not empty.

The first thing Pam pulled out was a white

velvet jewelry box. It was empty, but that probably only meant that it had held the necklace Michelle had worn to the wedding. Then emerald earrings and ring, a joined wedding and engagement ring set, a diamond tennis bracelet, the biggest diamond-stud earrings I'd ever seen, half a dozen gold chains, numerous other earrings, and a beautiful, old-fashioned looking strand of pearls in an alabaster box.

"These were my grandmother's!" Pam exclaimed. "I remember my mother wearing them when I was a little girl. What was Michelle doing with them? She didn't have any right to them!"

Papers filled the bottom of the safe. Lots of papers. She passed them up to me. Deeds, birth certificates, passports, legal papers on the Change Your World Fitness Center partnership, house insurance, a lot of other legal-looking stuff, a death certificate for Pam's father. She studied that for a long minute. Then she pulled out what I think we were both waiting for. A will.

Pam backed out of the knee hole still holding the stapled sheaf of crinkly legal papers in a blue cover. "Do I have any right to read it?" she asked as if her conscience had suddenly jolted her.

I peered at the last page. "This isn't the original. It's a copy, with the signature just typed in. Her lawyer probably has the original.

I think anyone can read it when it's probated."

Or, I wondered guiltily, was I using that to justify reading it now because I was so curious?

"It's dated, let's see, about a month after Dad died. So I guess it's okay."

Not that date had anything to do with it, but her rationalization sounded okay to me.

We stood over the desk together as we read. It started with the usual formalities about paying bills and taking care of final expenses. It named a lawyer in the legal firm as executor.

"Oh, good," Pam said. "I'll just give him everything. I don't even need to read any more."

But I'd spotted a name farther down on the page, a name that seemed totally out of place in Michelle's will.

"I think you'd better read it," I said.

Chapter Twenty-Two

There, buried in the legalese about the giving, bequeathing, and devising of all her worldly assets, was the name of Michelle's lone heir.

With the even bigger shocker of the two words before his name. *My son.*

Everything Michelle Gibson possessed in this world went to her son.

Sterling Forsythe.

"Sterling is Michelle's *son?*" Pam gasped. "How can that be?"

"He was adopted, obviously. You didn't know that?"

"He never mentioned it."

"Would he have told you if he knew?"

"I don't know. Not necessarily. We didn't talk a lot about personal stuff."

"Could he have known about this?" I tapped the crinkly paper that gave Sterling all Michelle's worldly possessions. Would that include Pam's grandmother's pearls? And how about Michelle's partnership in the health club? What would Uri and Cindy think of this development?

"I have no idea. I'm just . . . flabbergasted. Michelle wanted me to marry her *son.*"

"She must have had a very high opinion of you, then. She surely wanted a good wife for him."

Pam contemplated that for a moment, and then she slammed the will against the desk as if she wanted to smash it. "She didn't care anything about me as a person. She didn't want Sterling to marry me because I'd be a good wife. She wanted him to marry me for my trust fund!"

"Oh, Pam, that isn't necessarily so." But I probably didn't sound convincing, because what she said struck me as all too possible.

"Oh, yes, it's so! That's all Michelle cared about. Money! Sterling has all that prestige running the lab when he's so young, but the money—" She turned her thumb downward and made a scornful *pffft* sound. "It didn't matter to me, but I'm sure it did to Michelle."

Suddenly Michelle's bribing Mike's sister to sabotage Pam and Mike's relationship made sense. She had to get the guy Pam loved out of the way, so she could slip her son into his place. For the trust fund money.

"Money was everything to Michelle. She married my dad for it. She killed him for it!" The blaze of passion abruptly fizzled, and Pam slumped against the desk. "Compared to murder, what's the minor matter of arranging a marriage?" she asked in a voice as whispery as Phyllis's.

"But surely she wanted her son to be happy," I protested. "She wouldn't want him to marry you unless she thought it would make him happy."

"To Michelle, money and happiness were one and the same, inseparable. I could be a two-headed, cult-worshipping, shrieking maniac, and she wouldn't care. Just so long as I had the trust fund to bring to the marriage."

"But this proves one thing, doesn't it? Michelle wasn't planning to kill you to get the trust fund for herself. Why would she? She could get the benefits of the trust fund for her son through the marriage."

"Then she could kill me after her son got hold

of the trust fund, and they'd all live happily ever!"

That was pretty far out, but it was wildly possible, I had to admit. But it was also ferocious speculation, and I certainly didn't intend to encourage that thinking. "Pam, here you are ranting and raving—"

"I'm not 'ranting and raving'!" Then she looked down at her hands, and we both saw they were shaking. She managed a hint of sheepish smile. "Maybe a little rant."

"Aren't you even wondering *how* he's Michelle's son? Did she choose Joe and Phyllis to adopt him because she couldn't raise him herself? Or did they adopt him, not knowing he was Michelle's, and then she managed to find out who had him?"

Pam blinked, as if in her fury about the money and trust fund, all this had bypassed her. But finally she said, "It seems more likely they knew, doesn't it? Considering that Phyllis is Michelle's cousin."

"But what were the circumstances of his birth? Who's his father?"

The timing would have been right for Phyllis to appear in the door and dramatically proclaim the facts of Sterling's birth. But what happened was that Phreddie wandered in and coughed up a hair ball.

"I guess I'll just have to ask them," she said.

I saw undercurrents here, ominous possibilities. Motives. Maybe even dangers. I didn't like to mention them, yet where murder was concerned I didn't think we could shove anything under the table.

"If Sterling knew who he was, and also knew about this—" I tapped the crinkly page again and spelled it out even further, since Pam was looking at me so blankly. "And was ruthless enough to go after the inheritance . . ."

Pam paled as my ominous implication got through to her. "He could have murdered her for the inheritance." Almost as an afterthought, she added, "And then he wouldn't have to marry me."

Actually, that was exactly how the situation stood, I realized. Michelle was dead, Sterling inherited everything, and the wedding was off. Sterling's plan? Or someone else's? Or a coincidental side effect of some other unrelated plan?

"Do you think he could do that . . . murder?"

Sterling had struck me as self-centered and inconsiderate, totally focused on himself and his work, definitely not prime husband material. But murder? So much hinged on what Sterling knew. He'd certainly removed himself from the murder scene and rushed back to California with all possible speed. Although he might have done that even if the wedding had proceeded normally.

"I'm not sure what anyone is capable of," Pam said, sounding both bewildered and somber.

This, I realized, put a harsher spin on Sterling's mother's actions toward the deputies after the wedding. Was she so protective of her son because she thought . . . or *knew* . . . he'd killed Michelle?

"Or there's another unpleasant possibility," I added reluctantly.

Pam nodded. "Joe and Phyllis. They had a motive to murder Michelle too. Get her out of the way, and their son collects a big inheritance. Providing for him what they couldn't provide themselves."

"If they knew about the will."

Pam nodded.

"Except that simply marrying you gave him access to the assets of a hefty trust fund. They didn't have to kill Michelle to set their son up financially. Michelle had already done that by arranging the marriage to you."

"But maybe they had another reason for murdering her." Pam had jumped ahead of me here.

"Other than money? What other reason?"

"Maybe Sterling doesn't know Michelle is his mother. Maybe Joe and Phyllis were determined he not know. And maybe Michelle was planning to tell him." Pam's mouth twisted in a wry curve. "A special little wedding gift from Mommy."

"Surely something like that isn't important enough for *murder*. I mean, lots of adoptions are open. Birth mother and adopted parents know all about each other. They keep in touch. Adoption isn't the big secrecy thing it once was. Neither is being unmarried and pregnant."

"The operative words being *the way it once was*. Twenty-nine years ago things were different, weren't they?"

Yes. Twenty-nine years ago the movie magazines weren't full of articles and pictures about pregnant fiancées and star couples happily celebrating parenthood without being married. And adoption was seen by some people as a sign of failure, infertility a weakness, and everything was hush-hush. Phyllis and Joe, not sophisticated or worldly people, might be exactly the kind of people who'd keep adoption a secret. Even from the adoptee.

Pam suddenly bent her head and put her palms to her temples. She squeezed as if she wished she could squeeze all this out of her head. She stayed that way for several long minutes.

I didn't interrupt. I was busy fitting all that had happened into this startling new scenario.

Phyllis, determined that Michelle not have a chance to usurp her role as mother, willing to kill to keep that from happening? Joe, willing to do whatever it took to protect Phyllis? Or maybe it really was money, the two of them

279

wanting Michelle's inheritance for their son, figuring an inheritance was something that couldn't get away from him, unlike a wife's trust fund that she might pick up and walk off with someday.

I tried to take myself back to the scene of the wedding, to clear away the fogginess, and pinpoint details. Joe and Phyllis had been sitting up front. I could see the back of her limp blond hair, his inexpensive blue suit. The candles gave off a faint fragrance. Someone coughed. The pastor fingered his neck brace. How far away from Michelle were Joe and Phyllis? Had the processional yet reached them when the blast of fog erupted?

Neither Phyllis nor Joe seemed athletic or aggressive enough to leap up and attack with a knife. Yet there were stories of people under stress who'd done the seemingly impossible, everything from lifting a car to swimming a river.

"I'm going to go talk to Joe and Phyllis about this right now." Pam sounded decisive, but her tone went vulnerably fifteenish when she put a hand on my arm and added, "Come with me, Andi. Please."

I didn't argue that she should stand on her own. She put everything but the will back in the safe, and I followed her upstairs to the Nautical Room. She carried Phreddie, but set him down at the door and gave him a scoot to send him on his way. She knocked. No answer. Another knock, harder. Still only silence.

"Maybe they're down in the hot tub again," I suggested. "They seem quite fond of it."

We started down there, but on the way we ran into Mrs. Steffan, who said the Forsythes had called a taxi to go downtown. "Phyllis thought she needed to find something more appropriate to wear for the funeral. Has the time or place for that been decided?"

Pam managed a "Not yet," and Mrs. Steffan said, "If there's anything I can do to help, just let me know."

So the investigation with Phyllis and Joe fizzled for the moment. Pam went back to the office to look through more of Michelle's files, and I decided this was a good time to talk to Shirley. She was in the kitchen rubbing a cross-rib roast with some special seasoning mix for dinner. The kitchen smelled of a delightful blend of garlic and onion and some more subtle spice I couldn't identify.

"I have some raspberry-flavored tea made," she said.

"Great." I added a smidgen of sugar when she put the tall glass in front of me. I'd already decided I shouldn't mention the startling revelation in the will. "Everything going okay?"

"Well, I'm thinking I'm going to have to start

looking for a job. I can't imagine Pam keeping me on after everyone leaves."

"I'm sure she'll help you with a good recommendation." Okay, enough small talk. "Shirley, did the authorities ask you anything about the knife that killed Michelle?"

"Me? No. They mostly asked about the guests and my relationship with Michelle, how long I'd worked here, that kind of thing. I've wondered about the knife, but it must not have been a kitchen knife, or they'd have been digging around in here for sure."

"I saw it. I don't think I'm supposed to say anything about what it looked like, but it was, ummm, an unusual type of knife, very fancily decorated, and probably quite valuable. Pam said she remembered that at one time her father had a knife collection, so we're wondering if it could have come from there. Do you know anything about a knife collection?"

"A collection? I think maybe her father collected guns. There are enough of them up in the attic. But knives? No . . . although, come to think of it . . ." She tilted her head, then crooked a forefinger at me to follow her. "Let's take a look."

I followed her to Michelle's bedroom. I'd wondered why Detective Molino hadn't been in there with a search warrant, but with the crime scene outside perhaps they couldn't think of anything to search for in the house.

The first thing that hit me when Shirley opened the door to Michelle's room was the fragrance, the same delicately heady scent that had always followed her. Most of the room was as feminine as the fragrance. King-sized, canopied bed draped with lush layers of pale blue chiffon. A window also draped with chiffon. The window through which the killer bees were supposed to have come?

Shirley rushed over and flung the window open. "This place needs some *air*."

A flowery comforter and an acre of ruffled pillows covered the bed. Pillow heaven for Phreddie, although he'd undoubtedly never been allowed in here. Dressing table covered with lotions, perfumes, and cosmetics, the mirror with sides adjustable for views from all angles. Not what I'd personally want to confront first thing in the morning. One angle in a mirror at that time of day was bad enough. A TV hung from the ceiling so it could be viewed from the bed. A nightstand held a stack of DVDs.

Master bath with double sinks, jetted tub, double shower, marble counter with more powders and lotions. I peered through the open door of the walk-in closet loaded with clothes, everything from sequins to Spandex.

"I didn't come in here often," Shirley said. "Michelle just let me know when she wanted the room cleaned. I figured she thought I was going to snitch a spray of her Faberge perfume." She walked over to the dressing table and picked up a gracefully contoured bottle. "Though when you get up into the price range of this stuff it's no longer perfume, it's *parfum*. Here try it. Michelle isn't going to care now."

She held out the bottle to me, finger poised on the spray button, but I backed off. Unperturbed, Shirley sprayed and sniffed her own wrist. "What do you think? Two hundred bucks an ounce?"

I moved on to look at a wall covered with movie posters and professional glamour photos of Michelle. No Oscars on the curved table under the photos, but there were some other awards. It was an impressive display, and yet all it aroused in me was a feeling of squeamishness. Michelle's shrine to herself.

"Over here," Shirley said.

The corner she led me to wasn't exactly a shrine to Michelle's dead husband. It took up only a minimal amount of space in a corner at the end of a blue sofa. Perched atop a cherry wood cabinet, one formal photo of Gerald Gibson and another of their wedding. He was an ordinary looking guy with a longish face and receding hairline. I didn't see any resemblance to Pam. In the wedding photo, his gaze focused adoringly on Michelle. She had a hand on his shoulder, perhaps to display affection. Perhaps to display that impressive set of rings we'd seen in the safe. Her gaze focused on the camera.

A display case holding a collection of twenty or so arrowheads hung above the cabinet, labels indicating area of origin apparently meant to suggest Gerald had found them himself. Flanking it were plaques honoring Gerald from some builders' associations. Shirley swung the cabinet door open.

"Knives!" I said.

"It isn't really a collection," Shirley said. "There aren't that many. But maybe he had more and just kept the nicest ones. Or maybe Michelle got rid of most of them. They do look valuable."

There were eight knives in the display case, each one unique. The two on the bottom were hunting type knives, with blades of obsidian and handles of bone and carved ivory. The others were folding type pocketknives, but these knives had undoubtedly never seen anything as mundane as a pocket. The handles were of turquoise and silver, agate, gold, and coral, and the diamond-pattern on one was outlined with what I didn't doubt were real diamonds. The knives were fastened to the white velvet background with clear plastic fasteners that didn't intrude on the designs.

"But there isn't one missing," Shirley pointed out. "See, they're lined up evenly in pairs. There'd be an extra one left over if one had been taken."

There were also no butterfly knives. "May I take the case out of the cabinet?"

"Sure, help yourself."

I reached for the display case, then thought better of just grabbing it. Carefully, using tissues from my pocket and touching the frame only on the corners so as not to disturb fingerprints, I removed it from the cabinet.

I opened the latch and studied the area above the two rows of displayed knives. Two sets of tiny holes. I pointed them out to Shirley.

"There *was* another knife in here!"

"Actually," I said, "I think there were two more knives."

"What does that mean?"

"I suppose it could mean whoever took them thought two knives missing would be less noticeable than one, because taking just one would leave an obvious empty spot." That was the most benign of my thoughts.

"Or maybe the person thought he might need a second knife. A backup for the murder!"

Possible. Although knives didn't tend to jam, like guns. But a neat-freak murderer who locked doors might conceivably want a backup knife just to be prepared. "Could be," I agreed.

"Or maybe . . ." Shirley began uneasily, and I knew our minds had jumped to the same track here.

"Maybe the killer needs another knife—"

She finished the thought. "Because he has another victim in mind."

Shirley looked around nervously. So did I. The door was partly open, and we heard steps in the hallway outside. I rather wished she had her rolling pin with her. But the steps passed on by without pausing. Still holding the display case of knives, I crossed the large bedroom and closed the door.

"I think we'd better tell Detective Molino about this."

Shirley nodded.

"Who's been in here?" I asked.

"Recently? Or before Michelle was murdered?"

"Both. But before would be most important, because the knives were taken then. Assuming a knife that came out of this case is the murder weapon." And I was quite certain it was.

"Well, let's see. Cindy was in here any number of times, I'm sure."

Of course. Cindy the BFF. "Uri?" I asked.

She gave me a sharp glance, as if wondering exactly what I was suggesting, then a nod. "Yes, I think so. But once the guests arrived, any of them could have been in here. I know Michelle showed off her wall"—Shirley gestured toward the display of memorabilia—"to a few people."

"When they could also have spotted the display case of knives, and then come back to steal them later."

"Except that the knives wouldn't be seen unless the cabinet door happened to be open," Shirley pointed out.

True.

"Or anyone could have come in uninvited and snooped when Michelle wasn't around. There isn't a lock. They could have just accidentally run across the knives and decided to grab one. Two," she corrected herself.

"While looking for something else," I mused.

"Something else? What would that be?"

"I don't know. But someone searched the office last night, obviously looking for something. That's why Pam and I were in there so early this morning."

I thought Shirley might suddenly say she'd had enough of this weird job, weird house, weird people, and murders, but instead she looked around, expression thoughtful.

"I haven't cleaned in here for quite a while. I think the room definitely needs a good cleaning."

"Cleaning? I don't see anything that needs—" Then I caught her meaning. *Cleaning*. As in snooping. Looking for something the killer may have been looking for. I reversed my stand on the status of the room's level of cleanliness. "Oh, yes, indeed. This room definitely needs cleaning."

We smiled at each other.

Chapter Twenty-Three

Still careful not to contaminate the display case with my own fingerprints, I carried it to the office to show Pam and suggest she contact Detective Molino. I expected to find her deep in Michelle's files, but the office was empty.

A glance outside showed why. There was Pam, flying down the driveway on her skateboard. I eyed the file cabinet. I had an urge to dig around in there, and I knew Pam wouldn't object.

I also had an urge to go out and fling my aging body around on that skateboard. The deciding factor was that old saying, slightly modified for the occasion.

All work and no play makes Andi a dull sleuth.

Perhaps, as Pam claimed it did for her, skateboarding would clear my mind and make me think better too.

An extension of that old saying is that skateboarding makes Andi sore-bottomed, although I actually fell only twice, and neither was a real bone-crusher.

"You're doing great!" Pam called after my fourth run.

I swooped toward where she was watching me

from the gate. She was letting me start a ways up the hill now, and I was a little giddy with exhilaration. "Maybe I should buy my own board—"

The glamour of that swoop dimmed when I miscalculated and rammed into her with all the grace of a pirouetting pig.

She *oofed* and managed to keep us both from going down, then advised, "Maybe you shouldn't invest big bucks in one just yet."

I had to agree. But I was improving!

I was resting, sitting on the grass and letting Pam have a turn on the skateboard, when the gate opened to let a taxi in. Phyllis waved to me as it went by. Pam did a kickflip, then stood beside me to watch the Forsythes get out of the taxi at the front steps. They were loaded with packages. What was Phyllis planning, a triple change of costume mid funeral service?

"Are you going to talk to them now?"

Pam looked at her watch. "Shirley planned dinner for six o'clock, and it's almost that now. I guess I'll have to wait."

Phreddie's and my positions in the household had both been elevated. He had the run of the house now, and I was more guest than employee. I ate dinner with the others in the dining room. Uri and Cindy showed up too, reporting that there were still wires dangling all over the cottage. The dinner was superficially cheerful. . . . *Isn't the lasagna fantastic? What a great fall day. Wasn't that a pod of orcas swimming up the inlet?* But I sensed less cheery undercurrents.

I saw Pam looking at her might-have-been in-laws from a different perspective now. Had they kept the truth of Sterling's adoption from him? Had they killed Michelle in some misguided scheme to provide for him or hide the truth of his origins? Again I wondered why they'd stayed on. Michelle's funeral didn't really seem an important enough reason.

Uri Hubbard mentioned that they'd had car problems, and their car was in the shop. They had a loaner, which Cindy was not happy with.

"Will you be selling Michelle's BMW?" Cindy asked Pam. "We might be interested in buying it."

"I don't think it will be my decision," Pam said, which brought an exchange of glances between Cindy and Uri. "But I'll let you know."

This brief exchange surprised me. I'd thought there might be complications with the health club finances now that the main check writer was out of the picture, but this sounded as if the Hubbards' finances were fine. On impulse I asked, "Is the grand opening for Change Your World still on schedule?"

"Oh, yes," Cindy said. "We think Michelle would have wanted it that way."

I looked at Stan Steffan, wondering what he'd been up to today, and a bombshell of a thought exploded in my head.

Michelle and the Steffans went way back. She'd even lived with them. Mrs. Steffan was grateful that Michelle had never had an affair with her husband. But what if she was mistaken?

What if Stan Steffan was Sterling's father?

What if Michelle had planned to give Sterling the whole scoop on his family background after the wedding? What if Stan Steffan was afraid that his wife's tolerant attitude might not extend to cover this long-ago indiscretion, and he had to take desperate measures . . . murder! . . . to prevent the revelation? I thought back, trying to remember if he'd shown any particular interest, or wariness, about Sterling.

Or did Mrs. Steffan, in spite of what she'd told me about a non-affair between her husband and Michelle, know there had been one? And decide on a better-late-than-never *coup de grace*? Could she even have known Stan was the father, and Stan himself, because Michelle had never told him, not known? I figured that even though Mrs. Steffan might have a high tolerance for her husband's extra-curricular activities, not much got by her.

And maybe sleuthing wasn't my forte. Maybe I should be writing soap operas, because this was definitely a neat little soap-opera twist. Like a snake making a U-turn.

I must have been staring at Stan Steffan, looking for some resemblance between him and Sterling, because the dark glasses suddenly swiveled to me, and he snapped, "No, it's not a toupee. Would you like to give it a yank?"

I dropped my fork in astonishment. Phreddie pounced on it under the table, and I had to fight him for it. I came up flustered and embarrassed. "I-I wasn't thinking that at all!"

Yet what I was thinking would probably shock him even more, so all I said was a lame and irrelevant, "I was just wondering if you ever did cameo appearances in your own movies. Hitchcock did that, didn't he?"

"Hitchcock was overrated."

The phone rang, and Shirley popped her head in from the kitchen. "It's Detective Molino for you, Pam. Do you want to talk to him? Or call him back?"

Pam pushed her chair back. "I'll take it in the office."

"Maybe they've arrested the killer," Joe Forsythe said.

Could be. Although I doubted that. All *my* main suspects, except Sterling, were right here at this table, none of them under arrest. Was it one of these people whom Michelle had been afraid of?

Pam came back from the phone call and said,

as if it were an ordinary matter for dinner conversation, "Detective Molino said the autopsy showed Michelle's death was caused by the single knife wound. Lab tests aren't complete yet, but so far there's no indication of any unusual drugs in the body. They're checking out various leads."

We already knew one of those leads was Mike, because he'd told Pam he'd been questioned, long and hard. Pam and Mike were both afraid he might soon be arrested.

"The body's been released, then?" Phyllis asked.

"The funeral home has already picked it up. If you'll join me in the office after dinner, we'll discuss funeral arrangements. Detective Molino will be out in the morning to return Michelle's personal belongings. He asked that everyone be available so he can, as he put it, 'clear up a few details.'"

Joe and Phyllis got up from the table a few minutes later and headed for the office. Pam motioned for me to follow. In the office, Pam sat in the swivel chair at the desk. Joe and Phyllis sank onto the leather sofa. I perched on the arm.

Actually, the funeral discussion didn't take long. Pam had her hands firmly on the reins, and this meeting was more courtesy than mutual discussion.

"Michelle will be buried in the plot next to my father, of course," she said briskly. "The funeral home is offering several options. One is a big service using their facilities, with viewing of the body, enough seating for half of Hollywood, and full fanfare. Cremation is an alternative."

Joe and Phyllis exchanged glances. "We don't favor cremation," Joe said.

Pam nodded. "My thought is that we have a simple graveside service for family and close friends only."

One of whom, I thought uneasily, *was surely the murderer.*

"Michelle might have preferred something more elaborate," Phyllis suggested in her timid little voice, and I suspected she could be right. A woman planning the wedding of the century might prefer something more along the lines of the funeral of the century too.

"That's possible," Pam agreed. "However, her will"—like a magician pulling his rabbit from the hat, Pam smoothly pulled the blue-covered document from the desk drawer—"doesn't give any specific instructions, so we'll just have to do what seems best under the circumstances. The weather is good for a short outdoor service, and I personally would rather not have something that turns into a media event."

Neither Joe nor Phyllis offered any differing opinion. They were both staring at the will. I had the impression that at this point they probably wouldn't object if Pam announced she was stuffing Michelle in the egg-yolk VW and planting her in the backyard. Their attention was riveted on the will. Anticipation? Apprehension?

And I suddenly realized that *this* was the reason they'd stayed on. Why they were willing to put up with the awkwardness of accepting their son's ex-fiancee's hospitality. Was it to see if Sterling inherited anything, or to find out if the mother/son relationship was revealed?

"The big funeral would have to wait until at least Monday, but the funeral home can do a simple graveside service Thursday afternoon. So, unless you have objections, that's what we'll plan on. They'll supply a preacher-in-a-can to conduct the service." Pam picked up the will as if about to tuck it away.

Not certain exactly what a preacher-in-a-can was, although I assumed it was someone simply generic, I said, "I could talk to the pastor at my church and see if he could do it. He's a caring and compassionate sort of person. Not too wordy," I added, in case that mattered.

"Yes, thank you. I'd appreciate that," Pam said. She blinked, and I knew she wasn't as blasé about this as she was trying to pretend.

"I'll let you know what he says."

"Now, about the will," she added, as if she were relenting on a point.

Phyllis surreptitiously slipped her hand into her husband's.

Pam opened the blue cover carefully. She smoothed the crinkly pages. She traced a finger down the lines of print. She had, I realized, an unexpected flair for the dramatic. Then she dropped the zinger.

"It makes," she said, "a rather startling revelation."

Stan Steffan would have supplied a thunder of portentous music if this were one of his productions. Here, all that happened was that Joe's stomach growled . . . the lasagne at dinner? . . . and a fly buzzed at the window.

"Sterling doesn't know," Phyllis suddenly blurted. "We never told him."

The truth, or the tiger-mother still protecting her young? Was she saying that without knowledge of his origins, Sterling would have had no reason to murder Michelle? Or was she willing to go down for him and protect him by confessing to the murder? Or did she actually do it herself?

Joe apparently wasn't tied to this agenda, because he said, "But Michelle may have told him. We don't know."

"The will leaves everything to him. Everything," Pam emphasized. "And if Sterling knew that—" She tapped the blue cover with a stubby fingernail and didn't mince words. "Maybe he killed her because he wanted her money."

Phyllis jumped up. "No, no, no! Sterling would

never do that. He's talented and brilliant. He doesn't care about money."

"I know now that Michelle went to a great deal of trouble to break up my relationship with another man so I'd marry Sterling. Michelle's ethics may have been questionable, but in her own way, I don't doubt she loved her son. I want to know more."

Phyllis flopped back on the sofa. She folded her arms as if she intended to stonewall. Joe squirmed a little, but he started talking.

"It wasn't an unusual story. Young, unmarried girl gets pregnant—"

"Except that Michelle wasn't about to let an unexpected pregnancy interfere with her plans to be a big movie star!"

"And we should be grateful for that, or we'd never have had our son," Joe snapped with uncharacteristic sharpness. Then he gave his wife's knee a placating pat.

"Phyllis has a few distant relatives in the Midwest, but we'd never kept in touch with them. We don't even know how Michelle got our name back then, but she called us saying she'd won three beauty contests and was coming out to California to get in the movies. And could she stay with us for a while. We both figured the movie thing was some starry-eyed dream, but we said okay. We didn't want her wandering the streets on her own. But when she arrived—"

"How old was she then?" Pam interrupted.

Joe and Phyllis looked at each other. "Only eighteen, I guess."

I sneaked in a question. "Was her movie-star name her real name?"

"No," Joe said. "She was Miriam Peterson back then. She'd just graduated high school, and when she arrived we could certainly see why she'd won the contests."

"She was beautiful," Phyllis said flatly. "And she knew it."

"She'd also gotten some movie contacts through the beauty contests, apparently pretty good ones. We were surprised, but she right away got an agent and picked up parts as an extra, then she got a few speaking lines in a TV sitcom."

It all fit. Innocent young girl from Hicktown USA meets big producer with well-worn casting couch. Bingo!

"Then she found she was pregnant. She didn't want to delay her career by carrying the baby—"

"And she sure didn't want to be stuck raising a baby, which might put a real crimp in her career," Phyllis threw in.

"So she was going to get an abortion. But we talked her into having the baby—"

"*Money* talked with Michelle," Phyllis corrected. "We said we wouldn't pay for an abortion, but we would pay all her expenses to have the baby. We also promised to pay her living expenses for six months after the baby was born. Which we did, plus we gave her everything else we could scrape up. Which included every cent we had saved plus taking out a second mortgage on the house."

"But it was worth it, every penny," Joe said.

"Then you adopted Sterling when he was born?"

"Actually . . ." They looked at each other again, as if we'd reached a sticky point here, but finally Joe said, "Michelle went to a hospital in a different town from where we lived. She used Phyllis's name and identification. So we, Phyllis and I, show as birth parents on the birth certificate. No adoption."

"So he's always been ours," Phyllis said with more of that tiger-mama fierceness. "She had no right to tell—"

"We don't know that she told him anything," Joe repeated. "Or that she even intended to. Maybe she planned to let it remain a secret until she died, which she probably didn't intend to do for decades yet."

"So Michelle didn't keep in touch with you and Sterling over the years?" I asked.

"What she did was use the money we gave her to buy herself a fancy wardrobe and a jazzy little car, and then she was on her merry way to stardom," Phyllis said. Even though she obviously loved Sterling fiercely, she seemed more resentful than grateful to the birth mother who'd provided him.

"We didn't hear anything from her for several years, but then she started sending toys and money," Joe said. "We wouldn't let her spend time alone with Sterling, but she came to the house occasionally as Cousin Michelle. She paid for his education. On a bookkeeper's salary, we couldn't afford private school or a prestigious university—"

"He said he had scholarships," Pam cut in.

"He did have scholarships. Very good scholarships," Phyllis said. "Half a dozen universities wanted him."

"But Michelle also arranged for him to receive a considerable amount of other money that just looked like scholarships," Joe said.

"Did she want Sterling to know she was his mother?" I asked.

"She never mentioned it," Phyllis admitted. "Early on, there was no way she could prove it even if she wanted to, but with the DNA testing they can do now . . ."

"Are you going to tell him?" Pam asked.

Phyllis didn't answer, but Joe said, "If he's going to inherit everything, there's no way to keep him from knowing."

Phyllis glanced around the office, her expression suddenly brightening. Redecorating?

No one else seemed inclined to bring up the

subject, so I did. "The father, he was someone she, ummm, encountered in the movie industry?"

I waited expectantly for enough information to identify Stan Steffan as the father, or maybe even his name to drop, but Joe said, "No, she was pregnant before she came out to California, though she didn't know it. A graduation night party. Some high-school basketball player. A jerk, was how she described him."

"She was sure?"

"She told me once that she kept telling herself she just couldn't be pregnant and didn't even go to a doctor until she was past five months along," Phyllis said.

"Did she know the Steffans by then?" I asked, still not convinced about the hometown jerk.

Joe looked puzzled by the question, but he said, "No, it was a year or so later before she got a part in one of his productions. About the same time she got her name legally changed to Michelle DeShea."

Well, so much for my dramatic little soap-opera scenario. Which subtracted a couple of motives. Stan Steffan hadn't killed Michelle to hide some past indiscretion with her, and Mrs. Steffan wasn't wreaking late vengeance.

So did all this eliminate the Steffans? And Joe and Phyllis too?

It lowered their standing on my suspects' list. But it didn't eliminate them.

And there was still the matter of Stan Steffan wanting big bucks from Michelle before he'd give her a part in his movie. I felt there was a strong significance in that, though I couldn't figure out what it was.

It seemed doubtful now that Joe and Phyllis had known Michelle was leaving everything to Sterling, which eliminated that motive for murder. Although one of them might still have killed her to prevent Michelle from revealing the truth to Sterling. And whether Sterling did or didn't already know that truth direct from Michelle was another combustible question.

Phyllis stood up. "I'm going down to the hot tub."

"Good idea," Joe said.

They marched out, and Pam and I looked at each other, neither of us with anything decisive to say. Then I remembered the display case of knives I'd shoved under the desk. Still careful not to contaminate anything with fingerprints, I pulled the case out and set it on the desk.

"Where did this come from?"

"It was in Michelle's room. She had this little corner devoted to your father. Shirley knew about it."

Pam didn't ask what I was doing in Michelle's room. She just nodded as she looked at the exquisitely decorated knives, as if they touched some dim memory from the past. "I think there were more."

"Maybe they're stored away somewhere. Or maybe Michelle sold some. They look like collector's items. Anyway, it appears to me that two knives are missing from the case." I pointed out the tiny holes in the white velvet. "So I think you should show this to Detective Molino in the morning."

"I'll do that. Two knives," she mused uneasily, obviously seeing the same significance Shirley and I had found in that.

"And Pam . . . watch your back."

I thought I'd go to bed early, but once in my room my cell phone played the hard rock thing my granddaughter had programmed into it. Fitz, saying two of their guests had been delayed, so they wouldn't be sailing until morning.

I jumped out of bed eagerly. "Oh, good. I have a lot to tell you! I'll meet you . . . where?"

"How about if we go in something less conspicuous than the limo? I'll pick you up in, say, twenty minutes?"

"I'll meet you at the gate."

I didn't want the discomfort of being locked out of the house again, so I asked Shirley if there were an extra key I could borrow for the evening.

She readily supplied one, then added in a conspiratorial whisper, "I think I may be on to something. I'm going to do more 'cleaning' in Michelle's bedroom tonight."

I hesitated. I wanted to see Fitz, but I was tempted to join Shirley. But Fitz won, and I said, "Good. If it isn't too late, I'll talk to you when I get back."

"Doesn't matter how late. Just knock on my door."

I wasn't sneaking out. Yet there was something that seemed deliciously sneaky about grabbing the remote control from the limo so I could get back through the gate later, jumping into Fitz's car the minute it pulled up, and zooming back down the tree-lined lane.

Although what we did was decorously un-sneaky. We picked up cappuccinos at a stand and drove down to the city park that overlooked the bay. I told him about someone searching the office and my getting locked out, the discovery of the knife collection, with two knives missing, plus the surprise revelation in Michelle's will.

"You've been busy. That's almost as speedy as ol' Ed Montrose solving cases in a half hour on TV."

"Except that nothing is getting solved. There are just more twisty trails and questions."

"Especially," Fitz said thoughtfully, "what the killer plans to do with that second knife. Maybe you could talk Detective Molino into searching the house for it?"

"Because whoever has it would definitely have some explaining to do." Yes! Detective Molino wasn't particularly receptive to suggestions from amateur sleuths, but maybe he'd see value in this one. "Or if he doesn't want to do it . . ."

From Fitz's appalled look, I knew I shouldn't have been thinking out loud.

"No," Fitz said. "No, no, no. You go looking for that knife, and what you may find is the knife, all right. Firmly grasped in someone's hand and aimed at *you*."

"But—"

"I think your brain needs a rest from all this detective work," Fitz said firmly.

So we went to a movie. Where we ate popcorn and held hands and laughed at the delightfully brainless antics of a young woman falling off a boat, losing her memory, and being rescued by a hunk with a pet alligator on a desert island. Never mind that desert islands don't tend to come populated with alligators, it was all great fun.

I went back to the house feeling upbeat. And rather nicely kissed goodnight.

Yet a thought troubled me as I unlocked the front door, and it had nothing to do with knives or murderers. Fitz wasn't anti-God. He'd gone to church with me a few times. He enjoyed the music; he liked the way the pastor enlivened his sermons with funny anecdotes about his own foibles. But neither was he a part of what I'd heard called the "kingdom of believers."

I'd had a real encounter with God the night my friend Joella's baby was born in my limo. I was still stumbling and meandering in my faith, but it was definitely expanding, becoming a stronger and ever-larger part of my life. But when the pastor preached on Jesus saying, "I am the way and the truth and the life. No one comes to the Father except through me," Fitz had remarked that believing there was only one way to God seemed narrow-minded. He suggested we should be more broadminded and tolerant.

Tolerance was surely a virtue. I appreciated Fitz's easy acceptance of people and his tolerance of my shortcomings, including that bane of my life, these jiggly thighs. And yet, if there was only one way to God, through Jesus, then all the tolerance in the world wouldn't help someone with misguided beliefs make it into an eternal life with God. Was this difference in our thinking sooner or later going to become a barrier?

I put those thoughts out of my mind for later, and headed for Shirley's room. Detouring to peer at the digital clock on the kitchen range, I saw that it was almost one-thirty. She'd said anytime, but this was a little late for senior pajama partying, and I couldn't see any light under her door.

I tapped anyway, then again, harder, and got no response. If she was sleeping that soundly, I didn't want to wake her. So, disappointed, I just slipped into my own room and went to bed.

Chapter Twenty-Four

After being up so late, I slept later than usual in the morning. I thought, when I finally showered and dressed and went out to the kitchen, that I'd find everyone had already breakfasted.

Instead, people were milling around the kitchen and dining room, looking lost and disoriented. No scent of fresh coffee or baking biscuits. No glasses of juice or pitchers of hot syrup or stack of warmed plates.

Pam was trying to figure out the big coffeemaker. She'd apparently been out skate-boarding already, because the board was leaning by the door to the hallway.

Cindy muttered to Uri, "Michelle would never let an employee get away with something like this."

"I can make pancakes," Mrs. Steffan volunteered. "I haven't done it for years, but I'm sure I still know how."

Stan Steffan glanced at his wife as if she'd just suggested a platter of roadkill. "I say we all get in the limo and go out to the casino for their breakfast buffet." He looked at me as if his breakfast-less condition were somehow my fault, and I'd better get my limo around here and correct it.

I asked what seemed the obvious question. "Where's Shirley?"

"I don't know," Pam said. "I knocked several times and finally looked in her room. Her bed either wasn't slept in, or she got up early and made it."

My earlier thought that Shirley may have had her fill of spooky guests and murder bounced back. She'd also made that comment about looking for another job. Could she have just picked up and taken off?

A more ominous thought hit me. Could she have found something that frightened her into leaving? "Is her car here?"

"Shirley doesn't have a car," Pam said, a fact I hadn't realized. "Most of the groceries are delivered, although once in a while Michelle let her use the BMW. Sometimes she walks up to the main road and catches the County Transportation System bus."

"Could she have taken a walk on the beach or down the road? Did you see her when you went running this morning?" I asked Cindy.

Today she and Uri were in burgundy sweats with the inevitable logo of a world slashed with a lightning bolt on the back.

"We didn't go this morning. Uri stepped on a rock and bruised his foot yesterday." She turned to Pam. "You really ought to let that woman go. This is inexcusable, with a houseful of guests."

I had an uneasy feeling. Shirley had said she was going to do more "cleaning." I slipped away and ran up the stairs. Michelle's door was shut. I shoved it open, halfway expecting to see Shirley sprawled across the bed.

But the room looked exactly the same as it had yesterday. A hint of the delicately heady fragrance lingered in spite of the still open window. I peered warily in the bathroom and the walk-in closet. Empty. The cabinet door, from where I'd removed the display case of knives, was still open.

I went back to the kitchen. Phyllis hadn't exactly taken charge. She wasn't a take-charge kind of person. But she'd gotten out the toaster and bread, and was now cracking eggs into a bowl. Pam had given up on the coffeemaker, and I went over and got it started. How much coffee to put in? Plenty, I decided, and tossed in a couple of extra scoops. I figured we all needed a jolt of caffeine.

"Don't you think this is rather peculiar?" Joe said to Pam. "Maybe you should call that detective."

"The Case of the Vanishing Cook?" Cindy asked, her tone laden with sarcasm. "Right. Let's call out the FBI and CIA too. Maybe she absconded with all the pistachios and caviar. Personally, I'll bet she's tucked away in some hidey-hole, sleeping it off."

"Sleeping it off?" I repeated, puzzled.

Cindy gave me a what-planet-are-you-from glance.

Mrs. Steffan said, "Shirley *drinks?*" She sounded horrified, and I was startled.

"Michelle said once that wine vanished around here faster than donuts at a cop convention," Cindy replied.

That struck Stan Steffan as funny, and he guffawed like some overalls-clad hayseed on *Hee Haw*. It was a bit disconcerting, like seeing a circling shark suddenly start giggling.

Pam glanced at her watch. "Detective Molino said he'd be here about nine-thirty. If Shirley hasn't shown up by then, I'll mention it to him. Has anyone seen Phreddie?"

"You should keep him out of the kitchen," Cindy said. "Cats don't belong around food."

We ate, some standing, some sitting at the kitchen table, some gathered around the dining room table. Phyllis's scrambled eggs were nicely fluffy, the toast richly buttered. My coffee was strong enough to eat holes in bedrock, but it had a marvelous aroma. And enough caffeine to lift off a rocket. Stan Steffan wanted me to take him to the casino immediately, but Pam nixed that with the reminder that Detective Molino wanted everyone available for further interviewing.

"Maybe he'll bring a script from CSI so he'll

know how to do it," Stan muttered. "These small-town cops don't know—"

I "accidentally" slopped coffee on his arm. "Sorry," I said sweetly.

Cindy looked at the clock on the stove. "We need to get over to the health club. Something's wrong with the hot water system."

"I'm sorry, but you'll have to hang around until Detective Molino gets here."

Everyone, with various disgruntled noises, wandered away. I gathered plates and silverware from where they were scattered in both rooms. After Stan Steffan stumbled over Pam's skateboard in the doorway, she moved it out to the front closet.

"Did Shirley say anything to you about quitting?" Pam asked as I arranged plates in the dishwasher.

"She mentioned she might have to look for another job, but I didn't get the impression she was in any big rush."

"It just doesn't seem like Shirley to take off and leave us in a lurch like this. She's always been so dependable. I don't know how I'm going to feed all these people if she doesn't show up."

"Do what the Stan Man suggested. Haul 'em out to the casino and let 'em stampede the buffet. Or stop feeding them, and maybe they'll all go home."

"I should be so lucky," she muttered.

Though that scenario wasn't likely, I decided. The Hubbards would stay until the wiring at the cottage was fixed, and if they had some ulterior motive for being here I wouldn't put it past them to do some electrical sabotaging to extend their stay. The Forsythes weren't leaving until Sterling's grasp on the inheritance was secure. The Steffans—

I didn't get to the Steffans because a scream started from somewhere beyond the kitchen. A scream that rose to megablast proportions. Like a psycho locked in a cage, fourteen teenage girls watching a horror movie, a ghostophobic opera singer trapped in a cemetery.

I couldn't tell where it was coming from. Everywhere! Rising from the floor, spewing out of the woodwork, exploding from the light fixtures.

"What is that?" I cried.

Pam pinpointed the source and ran. "Downstairs!"

I pounded after her as she raced along the hall, then tore down the steps to the Fitness Room. I almost slammed into her when she stopped short at the door.

Phyllis was hunched on the floor by the hot tub, waif-like in a blue swimsuit with a demure little skirt. Her eyes were squeezed shut, her hands over her ears, and there was nothing whispery or timid about the howl emanating from her open mouth.

She was outshrieking even that girl at the wedding, and that took some doing.

Joe shoved us aside as he charged through the door and across the room to his wife. "Phyl, what is it? Are you hurt?"

She took one hand away from an ear and pointed at the rumbling hot tub. Pam and I ran to it. The water churned. Something rose and fell in it.

An amorphous blob. No . . . an arm. A leg. A face.

"Shirley!" I gasped.

The churning water gave the body an eerie semblance of life, as if Shirley were playfully enjoying some dolphin game, twisting and turning, flinging one body part forward and then another. Pam dashed around the tub and pounded the control to shut off the churning. As the water calmed, Shirley, in a fuchsia bathing suit, bobbed facedown in it.

Phyllis still shrieked. "I got in there with her! I didn't know, and I got *in with her!*"

Joe, kneeling, wrapped his arms around his wife and pulled her face against his shoulder, muffling but not stopping the amazing volume of sound coming from her.

I finally snapped out of my momentary paralysis. "We've got to get her out of there!" I climbed on the steps and leaned over the edge of the tub. "Maybe she's still alive!"

314

Pam and I were trying to pull Shirley out of the tub when stronger arms took over. Uri lifted her over the edge. I grabbed a towel Phyllis had dropped and spread it on the floor.

"Stand back," Uri said after he set her on the towel. "We know CPR."

I hoped they could help her. Her body had felt warm. Maybe that meant she was still alive. But as Uri and Cindy worked frantically to revive her, compressing her chest and pinching her nose and breathing into her mouth, the hope sank. The warmth I'd felt was only from the heat of the water, not a lingering flicker of life. Her body looked a little bloated, but the skin was wrinkled and blotchy.

Nausea roiled my stomach. Shirley hadn't been sleeping in her room when I tapped on her door at one-thirty this morning. I was certain of that now. Was there a knife wound in her back?

Oh, Shirley, Shirley . . . last night alive and curious and a bit mischievous with her "cleaning." And now . . .

The suddenness with which life could end dizzied me. We rush along, making our plans, complaining about this, worrying about that. And it all comes down to a moment like this. God time.

Stan Steffan didn't come close, but he actually lifted the dark glasses to peer at the body from a distance. "Someone better call 911."

We were all in the Fitness Room now, crowded together . . . except for Stan . . . as if for protection against some unseen danger, everyone looking concerned and bewildered and horrified.

Except that one of those concerned expressions was phony. One of these people had killed Shirley. Murder in the Hot Tub.

Another thought jolted me. If I hadn't gone to meet Fitz last night, if I'd stayed here to help Shirley, would I now be floating facedown in the hot tub too?

Pam went upstairs to call 911, but she returned only a couple of minutes later with Detective Molino. He couldn't have gotten in past the locked gate on his own, so apparently he'd buzzed the electronic signal and Pam had let him in.

Uri and Cindy stepped back. Detective Molino knelt by the body and put his fingers to Shirley's throat, then his ear to her chest. He rolled back an eyelid.

He didn't announce it, but the fact was obvious now. Dead.

"This is the housekeeper?" He looked at Pam. "Shirley—?"

"Shirley Berkhoff. Housekeeper and cook."

Uri wiped his hands on the legs of his wet sweatpants. Cindy's outfit showed big wet blotches too. She looked pale, even a little greenish. She was holding her stomach, as if she might have to run for the bathroom any minute.

They'd worked very hard trying to save Shirley.

Which didn't necessarily mean one or both of them hadn't earlier worked equally hard to kill her. A cynical thought, but what better camouflage for murder than this noble endeavor to save the victim?

"But I was talking to her just last night!" Mrs. Steffan protested, as if that meant there must be some mistake about Shirley being dead.

Detective Molino jumped on that. "You were the last one to see her?"

"Well, I-I don't know about that. It was about ten o'clock, I guess. I ran into her in the upstairs hall and asked if I could bother her for a cup of tea. Which she made for me. A nice tea called Sleepytime."

The upstairs hall. Because Shirley had been in Michelle's room?

"Did she say anything about coming down to the hot tub?" he asked Mrs. Steffan.

"Not that I recall."

"I'll have to get the medical examiner out here."

"For an accident?" Stan Steffan demanded.

Like spectators at a tennis match, every head swiveled toward his arrogant tone.

"Well, it's obvious. She came down for a late soak, slipped when she was getting in the hot tub, hit her head, and drowned."

It was a plausible scenario. Shirley had told me herself that she liked to come down for a solo, late-night soak. I didn't like to think it, but maybe she had overdone it on the wine. Alcohol and hot tubs are a notorious no-no, especially solo. Was that what had happened here? Not one of my scenarios of murder, but a simple situation of alcohol-impaired balance or judgment?

Yes, it could be a tragic accident. Just because there'd been one murder didn't mean this was another. Shirley wasn't young. Even sober, slips and falls were a danger at our age.

Yet wasn't the Stan Man pushing the accident explanation a little too much, like a used car salesman hyping an old Buick? Why the objection to the medical examiner?

And what had Shirley been doing before that soak? Had she found something in Michelle's room that incriminated one of these oh-so-concerned guests? Someone who followed her down here and stuck that missing knife in her back, or maybe just shoved her in the tub and held her head under?

Yet it *could* have been a simple accident, and Detective Molino's expression revealed nothing. Not even when he looked at me and said, "How come I'm not surprised to see you here?"

Detective Molino cleared everyone out of the Fitness Room and sent us all to the living room.

A newly arrived deputy put up yellow crime-scene tape that barred anyone from going farther back in the house than the living room. Which, as an interesting complication, also cut off the bathrooms. An assistant medical examiner and more deputies arrived. We couldn't see what was going on down in the Fitness Room, but people in various garb . . . uniformed, white-coated, and plainclothes . . . came and went. There were cameras, both digital and video, radios squawking outside, cell phones in use inside, evidence bags, latex gloves, tape measures, and various pieces of equipment I couldn't identify.

Pam stood at the yellow crime-scene tape and called for Phreddie several times, but he never showed up. I figured if he hadn't already been hiding somewhere, Phyllis's shriek and all this police activity had surely sent him into cat seclusion.

Nerves among the living room contingent escalated and clashed. Except for Phyllis, who, shrieking completed, now huddled in a corner of the love seat and appeared to be in an unblinking coma. The others bickered and squabbled. Cindy snapped at Uri about the health club showers. Mrs. Steffan jumped on Joe for not taking proper care of his wife, that he should be demanding medical attention for her. Someone turned on the TV and treated us to a game show in which several hyperactive women squealed about a vacation in Cancun.

Pam called Michelle's lawyer's office to cancel her appointment. Then she nervously knocked over an expensive crystal sculpture of an orca, which hit an abstract of welded iron, and crystal shrapnel exploded.

Stan Steffan prowled the room like a lion on No-Doze.

I, in no better frame of mind that anyone else, said to him, tartly I must admit, "How does Shirley's death fit in with your blackjack epiphany about Michelle's killer?"

"It's irrelevant. She slipped and fell." He glared at me as if I should go and do likewise.

Eventually a bathroom became top priority. Pam remembered one in the garage. Deputy Molino gave permission to use it. We were not, in fact, required to stay on the property, since no one was under arrest, but his tone suggested we'd better not run off. We took turns trooping out to the garage bathroom, but no one left. I wondered if we each figured we needed to keep a wary eye on everyone else.

Noon came, and Pam ordered sandwiches delivered from a sub shop in town. Phyllis wouldn't eat. Stan Steffan complained that the ham wasn't real ham, it was that "turkey stuff." Uri and Cindy discarded the bread and ate only the meat and vegetables. I felt like shoving everyone into the limo and dumping them out in the woods far from civilization.

The body was eventually removed in a body bag. I followed Deputy Molino out to the porch and touched his arm when he was returning from escorting the body to the van.

"Volunteering to be first in line for questioning?" he asked.

"The tape says crime scene. Is that what this is?"

"We don't have tape that says, 'This is none of your business, folks, just keep out.' Whether it's truly a crime scene depends on what the autopsy shows. Where's your sidekick, ol' Fitz? Shouldn't he be here sticking his nose into things too?"

"Fitz left on the *Miss Nora* this morning. Three-day trip."

"We should all be so lucky. I happened to catch a couple of reruns of his old TV detective show on satellite a few nights ago." Sounding a little grudging, he added, "It was kind of dated, like all those old shows, but not bad. Not a lot of unrealistic high-tech stuff like the current shows have, and real cops only wish they did. And Fitz was good."

"I'll tell him you said that. He'll be pleased."

Okay, enough of Mr. Chatty Nice Guy, Detective Molino apparently decided, because now he asked suspiciously, "How come you and the limo are still here?"

"Pam decided she needed my services a little longer. Will you be getting a search warrant for the house?"

"Maybe. You want me to keep an eye out for lost pantyhose or something for you?"

Oh, Detective Molino was in fine form today. I ignored the facetious question. "There's something you might add to your list of items for the search warrant." I knew from past experience that they couldn't just do a wholesale search in hopes of turning up something interesting; they had to name specific items before a judge would authorize a search warrant. "If you have time to look at something now in—" I started to say *Michelle's office,* but changed the wording. "In Pam's office?"

"We're public servants. At your service."

I led Detective Molino to the office. It was also blocked off with yellow tape, but he held up the tape and we both ducked under. I showed him the display case of knives and pointed to the tiny holes that suggested two were missing.

"I'm thinking the knife that killed Michelle may have come from this case. I saw it, you know. Not the same kind of knife as these, but also very fancily decorated, with jewels on the handles."

He looked up sharply. "Have you discussed this with anyone?"

"Only Fitz. He said my description, with the

double handles, sounded like a butterfly knife."

Detective Molino neither confirmed or denied the butterfly knife identification. "Where was this display case?"

"In Michelle's bedroom. I brought it here for safekeeping. I was careful about fingerprints, so you may want to dust it to see what's there."

He stuck his head out the office door and called to one of the deputies to bring a fingerprint kit.

The deputy brought it in a minute later, a flat black kit a little smaller than a fishing tackle box. Detective Molino carefully dusted fingerprint powder on the display case with a small brush that looked as if it would make a fine blush applicator. It didn't take any expert to see there wasn't even a smudge of fingerprints on the case.

"I thought there'd be something," I admitted, disappointed.

"Actually, this is something," Detective Molino said thoughtfully. "Ordinarily an object will have fingerprints of some kind simply from past use. Because there's nothing, not even a smudge here, I'd say the case has been wiped clean. Very carefully wiped clean."

"Same as the knife in Michelle's back?"

He waggled a finger at me. "Did you really think I'd fall for that and give you information?"

"Worth a try," I admitted.

"How did you happen to find this?" He indicated the display case.

"Shirley remembered seeing it in Michelle's bedroom. She showed it to me yesterday. Last evening she told me she thought she was on to something, and she intended to do some more looking. So now I'm wondering if she found something that somebody didn't want her to find."

"She was 'on to something' where?"

"In Michelle's bedroom, I suppose." Although I realized that wasn't necessarily true.

"Was Shirley a drinker?"

"She liked an occasional glass of wine," I said reluctantly.

"I'll see if I can hurry them into doing the autopsy yet this afternoon."

"To check on her blood alcohol content?"

"That's standard in a situation such as this."

"So you want to find out if she died by drowning, or if she was dead before she was put in the water?"

"Now, Mrs. McConnell, you know I can't discuss matters such as that with you," he chided, but I was reasonably certain the matter of speed on the autopsy meant murder was a strong possibility.

"Or she could still have been murdered even if she did drown," I speculated. "If someone pushed her in and held her under—"

"Accidents happen too. More often than murders," he pointed out.

True. "Anyway, what Pam and I were thinking is that perhaps the person who took the knives still has the second one hidden away somewhere. If it wasn't already used to kill Shirley?"

No comment from Detective Molino about whether there was a knife wound on the body.

"Finding who has the extra knife now might be pertinent," I suggested.

He slapped a hand against his forehead. "Brilliant! Thank you, Ms. McConnell, for pointing that out to me. I'm sure that thought would never have occurred to me otherwise."

I gave him an embarrassed smile, and to my surprise, in spite of the facetious sarcasm in his reply, he smiled back. "Maybe you should think about a job with the sheriff's department."

"Maybe I should. I make coffee that'll knock your socks off. There's still some in the kitchen if you need it."

"One thing, did the housekeeper have a friend who might have visited her last night?"

It took me a moment to realize what he was asking. "You mean a male friend she may have invited in?" I paused thoughtfully. "I don't think so. She never mentioned one. But I don't know for sure."

"Just checking."

"You do think this could be murder, don't you?"

He gave a theatrical sigh. "You never give up,

do you, Ms. M.?" Then he relented fractionally. "I've been in law enforcement a long time. I'm a suspicious man. And then there's your being here, of course, whose presence seems to attract murder like a dog does fleas."

I squeaked an indignant protest. Calling my limo a "magnet for murder," as he once had, was better than this comment about my presence attracting murder like a dog does fleas, but he didn't give me a chance to turn the protest into words.

"You can wait in the living room with the others. Everyone's going to be questioned."

Chapter Twenty-Five

I thought Detective Molino would have several deputies handle the questioning, but instead he took people one by one into the office and did it himself. This didn't necessarily signify murder, but neither did it seem routine procedure for an accident scene.

He called Mrs. Steffan in first. Meaningful? Or was Mrs. Steffan chosen first simply because she was standing closest to the office?

When she returned, we all looked at her like pilgrims staring at someone who's been to the mountaintop, but she said, a bit smugly I thought, "Detective Molino said we shouldn't discuss the case among ourselves."

"What does he mean, 'case'?" her husband growled. "This is a big waste of time over a simple, stupid accident. I'm going to call my lawyer."

"Then you'd better hurry, because he said to send you in next."

The Stan Man grumbled, but he went. Mrs. Steffan settled on the sofa and looked rather pleased with herself, as if she'd just aced a job interview. Phyllis and Joe huddled together on the smaller love seat. Pam and I crawled around on the far side of the big living room, still picking pieces of broken orca out of the carpet.

Mrs. Steffan came over and looked down at us. "Why don't you just use a vacuum cleaner?"

"Well, yeah, I guess we should," Pam said, and I had to wonder why neither of us had thought of this. Because we had other things on our minds, I suppose.

"Mrs. Steffan, did you see Phreddie last night when Shirley was fixing tea for you?" Pam asked.

"I don't remember seeing him, no. But he liked to prowl the house at night. I've seen him before. He's such a wonderful kitty, so sweet and friendly."

My first thought was, *what was she doing up prowling on other nights?* My second thought made me choke up. *Would the person who killed Shirley casually take a cat's life too, maybe because he got in the way or made a noise? Was poor Phreddie's body flung in a corner somewhere?*

I didn't mention that to Pam. She was worried enough that Phreddie had simply wandered off, and I didn't want to add cat murder to her fears. Mrs. Steffan returned to her sofa. I decided to look for the vacuum cleaner.

Pam was onto another worry now. "I need to notify Shirley's next of kin about her death, and I have no idea who that might be."

"Wouldn't Michelle have a job application in her files? Or surely there's an address book or letters or something in Shirley's room. I remember her mentioning a granddaughter."

A granddaughter she'd told me had to work part-time and squeeze in college classes when she could, with a snarky comment about how all Pam had to do was tap her trust fund.

"I guess I'll have to ask Detective Molino if he'll let me look for something," Pam said.

I started wondering if Detective Molino was playing psychological games with us, stretching this out to see if someone snapped when we got on each other's nerves.

I started after the vacuum cleaner, but now Cindy was on her way over, her stride purposeful. She and Uri had been whispering together for some time, but whatever was on their minds, Uri was apparently leaving it up to Cindy because he was just looking out the window now.

"Could I talk to you for a minute?" she asked Pam.

"Sure."

Cindy looked at me. Again, I took a step to leave, but Pam, still on the floor, grabbed my ankle. Cindy's eyebrows bunched together, as if she'd rather I went away, but she didn't actually balk. She got down beside Pam on the carpet and folded her legs into a neat cross-legged position.

Could I do that? Not as agilely as Cindy, no, but I managed it better than I figured. Only a couple of protesting joints creaked.

"Okay," Cindy began. "Well, umm, about that hair in the office. The one you taped to the paper?"

"Andi and I found it in a file drawer. We think someone was in the office going through things the other night."

"Well, it's probably mine. I guess I should explain. Then you won't have to mention to the detective that the office had been . . . looked at."

Looked at. Somehow a much less incriminating term than searched or ransacked.

"I'm not sure I understand," Pam said.

"If you tell the detective someone was in the office, he might think it had something to do with the murders. Which could cause unnecessary confusion, because it *didn't* have. Nothing whatsoever to do with murder."

I picked up a word buried back there. Murders. A meaningful slip?

Pam also caught the plural, because she asked, "So you think Shirley's death was also a murder?"

"No! Well . . . maybe. But not necessarily. The way that detective's acting, who knows? I get the impression he'd be delighted to run us all in and put us in thumbscrews or something."

Irrelevantly, at least to this moment, I wondered if the fact that Shirley's body had been in the churning water of that hot tub for some indefinite period would complicate determining time of death. If time of death was important.

"Okay, you were in the office, and you dropped a stray hair in the file cabinet. You alone, or Uri too?"

"Just me."

"And you were looking for—?"

"I wasn't doing anything terrible. Not snooping into things that are none of our business. Not stealing anything! We just needed to find something."

"Find something that *is* your business?"

"Yes! As you know, Uri invented the exercise machine we're featuring at Change Your World, the Uri-Blaster. It's a fantastic invention.

Everyone who's tried it gives it rave reviews."

"But?" I put in. Because a *but* obviously lurked in there somewhere, even though I remembered Mrs. Steffan praising the machine.

Cindy didn't concede a *but*. "Uri based his ideas . . . only *based* . . . on a design he brought over from Germany."

Pam immediately caught the bottom line buried in that slippery statement. "Someone else's design?"

"Well, partly. Uri worked for this old guy and helped him clarify his ideas, and contributed a lot of his own, too. The old guy is dead now, and he never actually built the machine. He just had this kind of . . . partial design of it. We had a prototype built before we ever met Michelle. So it really doesn't matter at all."

"You don't do a middle-of-the-night search for something that 'really doesn't matter at all,'" I pointed out.

Cindy ignored me. "The thing is, Michelle had a copy of that old design. And with her dead, we were afraid the design papers might somehow turn up and cause . . . complications."

Pam stated the obvious. "Because it might look as if Uri had stolen the design rather than invented it."

Cindy didn't confirm that, just said, "We thought it would be best simply to remove anything in her files about the design."

"And did you find it?"

"Yes."

"And?"

"We destroyed it. I hope this won't cause . . . complications."

"Even if Michelle's copy has been destroyed, couldn't there be more copies of the design elsewhere—which could be equally 'complicating' if they show up?" Pam asked.

"Uri said he didn't leave anything behind in Germany. The design wasn't of value to anyone else anyway. The old guy's heirs wouldn't know an exercise machine from a can opener."

"I see. Well, I don't suppose it will be necessary to bring any of this up to Detective Molino."

"Thanks, Pam. We really appreciate this. I hope I didn't, umm, disturb things too much in the office."

"You locked me out, you know," I said.

Cindy gave me a blank look. "Locked you out? Of the office?"

"No, the house. When the front door was open, and you locked it after you searched the office."

Another blank look until she said, "Oh, uh, that. I'd forgotten. I didn't know you were outside. I'm sorry."

"Something else I've wondered about," I said. "Uri said he turned off the fog machine at the wedding. But the fog machine operator says he turned it off himself."

"Uri did think he'd turned it off! The fog was so thick he could hardly see or breathe back there. But maybe he just . . . tightened the valve or something."

I thought her explanation was a little lame, but it was possible Uri wasn't deliberately lying. Maybe he really did think he'd turned the fog control off. Or it was also possible, as I'd originally thought, that he'd been murdering Michelle when he claimed to be back at the fog machine.

Cindy went back to her husband, whose back was still to us. She put an arm around his waist and reached up to whisper in his ear.

"So, what do you think?" Pam asked.

"I think Cindy doesn't know anything about a door, open or locked."

"I think so too. Which means . . . what? That someone else may also have been in the office that night, and that person locked you out?"

"That seems likely. Grand Central Station in there. Maybe you should install traffic lights."

"I don't see why Cindy didn't just ask me for what they wanted instead of sneaking around. And why did she pretend she'd shut and locked the door if she didn't?"

"I suppose she really could have forgotten she did it. Prowling in someone else's files may muddle your thinking." I spotted another sparkle of crystal and retrieved it. "Or maybe she figured if she didn't admit she'd done it, you'd start some big investigation about who had been in the office, and she'd wind up with everyone knowing about the design from Germany."

"But if she wasn't the one who locked you out, who was?"

"Good question."

"In any case, I can't see that this design thing has anything to do with Michelle's murder. Can you?"

"They didn't need to get rid of Michelle to keep her from exposing it. She was planning to cash in on it at the fitness center too. And it was certainly no reason for them to kill Shirley."

With a certain reluctance, I crossed Cindy and Uri off my list of suspects. Although I did it in mental pencil.

"I'm going to call Mike," Pam said. She pulled out her cell phone and headed outside. I saw that she stopped and grabbed her skateboard "thinking aid" out of the closet as she went.

Cindy was next to be questioned, then Uri. The Forsythes followed, Joe asking to go in with his wife because she was so distraught.

Distraught because she'd climbed into the hot tub with a dead body? Or because she hadn't counted on having to commit a second murder? Distraught because she was afraid Detective Molino was going to nail her?

I wasn't giving up my suspects easily. I still

figured Phyllis had been dead set—maybe literally—on Sterling not finding out Michelle was his birth mother. Though I had to admit I couldn't see why this would also require murdering Shirley.

Sleuthing is easier on TV, where every clue is Meaningful. And you have those clever writers figuring out everything. Me, I'm just muddling around on my own, strolling along tangents and jogging down dead ends.

Detective Molino didn't have a lot to ask me when my turn came, because we'd already talked earlier. While Pam was being questioned, I called the pastor, who said he'd be pleased to do a graveside service for Michelle. When Pam came out of the office, I gave her a number to contact the pastor.

She said Detective Molino had returned the jewels and watch Michelle had been wearing when she was killed, but not the gown, which they were keeping for evidence. She'd already put the jewels back in the safe. She'd also asked Detective Molino if she could take the other items in the safe, because she might need them to talk to the lawyers. After looking the papers over briefly, he'd let her have them. She had a thick, oversized envelope in her hand.

"So he's going to pick up and go home now?" I asked hopefully.

That hope crashed and burned when Detective

Molino appeared in the living room doorway, ominous legal-looking papers in hand.

"Search warrant," he said. "Deputy Hawks just came from the judge with it." He handed the papers to Pam to examine.

"Look for the part that tells what they're looking for," I whispered. Was the missing knife on the list?

"After the search, you'll be given a list of any items seized," Detective Molino said in that formal you've-just-been notified tone.

"And what are we supposed to do now?" Stan Steffan demanded. "Sit around here all evening twiddling our thumbs while you jokers pretend you know what you're doing?"

"This is a large house, and I anticipate the search will take most of the night. You may twiddle your thumbs as much and as long as you please," Detective Molino said.

"We can't go back to our room all night?" Mrs. Steffan looked at her husband, and for the first time I saw her taking on the role of big producer's wife, ready to throw her weight around. "Stan, really, this is not acceptable."

"I think we'll go back to the cottage," Cindy said. "We can manage without electricity for a night."

"I can go on home too," I said.

"No, no, everyone, calm down," Pam said, although she was the one who seemed most agitated. She handed the search warrant back to Detective Molino after giving it no more than a cursory glance. "We need to stick together. I'll call the Tschimikan Inn. They should have plenty of rooms on a week night. We'll all move out there for the night, or however long it takes Detective Molino and his men to search the house. Andi, you can take us, can't you?"

I wasn't in uniform, but I clicked my heels for my chauffeur's bow. "Your chariot awaits."

"Okay, it's settled then."

Detective Molino had a deputy take each of us separately to our rooms to collect necessities for the night, each item carefully examined to be sure it wasn't on the search warrant list. Pam went outside and called for Phreddie again, but we finally had to leave without him.

So there we were. Eight of us. Pam and me up front, three couples in the back of the limo. Seven innocent people, one murderer.

Unless this was a couple's conspiracy. Two murderous Hubbards. Two killer Forsythes. Two slayer Steffans.

The cell phones were running hot on the drive. Beside me, Pam had hers clamped to her ear. In the back, Stan Steffan barked into his. Cindy hunched down with hers, a hand shielding phone and mouth. Even Phyllis was in on the action.

We all clustered around the desk at the inn a

few minutes later. "Yes, four rooms, that's what I asked for when I called," Pam said to the clerk. "You don't mind sharing with me, do you, Andi?"

"Fine with me."

I was surprised to see Mike come in through the double doors. So at least I knew who Pam had been talking to. That alive glow momentarily lit up Pam's face when their eyes met, then, as if she'd drawn strength from the touch, she was briskly back to business.

"Are the rooms ready?"

"Actually," a little voice piped up on the other side of me, "we'll need one more room. There's another guest."

Chapter Twenty-Six

"Sterling is coming," Joe said. "We called him earlier. When Phyllis talked to him just now, he said he'd be getting in at Sea-Tac at 10:20 tonight."

"Did you tell him—" Pam broke off as she apparently realized she didn't want to ask in front of everyone whether Sterling knew about his relationship with Michelle.

"We just thought, under the circumstances, he should be here for the service." Considering her earlier near-hysteria, Phyllis spoke with surprising self-control. Her voice was back in the whispery range now.

"This means I should go pick him up?" I asked.

Pam started to say something, but Phyllis interrupted. "Could you? We wouldn't want him trying to find transportation on his own in the middle of the night."

"That's my job."

"We'll come along so you won't be driving alone," Phyllis added. "We want to meet him at the airport anyway."

Of course. Brilliant, talented, twenty-nine-year-old Sterling mustn't be left to wander all alone around the great big airport. Then I mentally whacked myself for such a disparaging attitude. I still worried about my daughter Sarah, and she was almost forty.

Pam turned back to the desk to arrange for another room, plus tickets to the dinner buffet for everyone. The rest of us trooped up to the rooms we'd been assigned. The group didn't plan to go en masse to the buffet, but I arranged to meet Phyllis and Joe in the lobby later for the drive to Sea-Tac.

In the room, before Pam arrived, I called Fitz on my cell. He was busy fixing spaghetti for dinner, but we talked while he worked, laughter and chatter from guests on the boat bubbling in the background. I'd eaten Fitz's great spaghetti. I could almost smell the garlic, and I knew about his secret ingredient, a smidgen of cinnamon. I wished I were there, not here knowing I must be rubbing elbows with a double-murderer. I told him about Shirley.

"I don't like this," Fitz said. "I'd rather you'd get out of there. Now."

"I don't think it's *officially* a murder yet—"

"Get out, Andi. Go home. I don't want anything happening to you."

"If there is a double murderer running around, maybe he or she would come after me at home. Although I can't see any reason I'd be a target."

Silence while Fitz gave that some thought and then reluctantly said, "I suppose you're as safe there at the inn as anywhere."

"Detective Molino isn't saying anything about whether there were any wounds on the body, but I don't think the killer used that extra knife. The hot tub was the murder weapon."

"A killer can always find a weapon of some kind. They make do with what's available."

"We're hoping Detective Molino finds that second knife in their search of the house. At least you don't have to be concerned that I'll be looking for it now."

"I'm grateful for small favors," he muttered.

We talked a little longer about doings on the boat, then said goodnight when Pam and Mike came in the room.

"I miss you," Fitz said before he hung up, as he usually does.

"I miss you too."

I wasn't sure if our exchanges would ever escalate to I-love-you's. Or whether I wanted such an escalation. But still there was something in *I miss you* that made warm fuzzies in my heart.

Watching Pam and Mike together, I wondered how she felt about the return of the her ex-fiancé, Sterling. Then I wondered about Sterling. Did he have in mind trying to patch things up with Pam? Or was this trip only about his inheritance? I couldn't see him getting all sentimental and rushing up here for Michelle's service even if he'd found out about their mother-son connection.

The buffet was fantastic, all the crack-it-yourself fresh crab you could eat. Messy but delicious. Getting away from the house where murder had happened encouraged the appetite, I realized a bit guiltily.

It was almost dark when I met Joe and Phyllis in the lobby for the trip to Sea-Tac. I thought they'd be friendly and chatty, but they closed the partition and I never heard a peep out of them. I couldn't tell if Sterling was on his cell phone during the drive from Sea-Tac to Vigland this time, but he had it in his hand when he got in the limo and it was still there when he got out.

When we were a few miles from the inn, I called Pam to let her know we were arriving. "In case you want to roll out the red carpet for Sterling," I told her.

"I would, but it's at the cleaner's."

I dropped my three passengers at the door and drove around back to park the limo for the night.

By the time I got back to the lobby, they'd all vanished. I thought Pam and Mike might still be talking, but when I got up to the room Pam was alone. She had papers that had come from the safe spread across both beds.

"Mike didn't stick around?"

"He'll be out for an early breakfast before work in the morning."

"Did he and Sterling meet?"

"Oh, yes."

"Big fireworks?"

"A duel over the fair maiden with drawn cell phones? Andi, you flatter me."

"You don't think Sterling has ideas about getting back together, then?"

"Whatever ideas Sterling has, they don't include me. Thankfully."

"Do you think Joe and Phyllis told him about the inheritance, and that's why he's here?"

"I don't know." And she didn't seem all that interested. She picked up a sheaf of papers covered with fine print. "Andi, could you look at this and tell me if it means what I think it means?"

A knock on the door interrupted. Pam dropped the papers back on the bed, looked through the peephole, then released the chain.

"Sterling," she said. She sounded neither pleased nor dismayed. Just surprised on a ho-hum level, as if it was the FedEx man and she was expecting UPS.

"I thought we should talk for a minute."

"Come on in. Andi is sharing the room." Pam motioned a hand toward me.

He came in but didn't take the chair I scooted toward him. Probably because he didn't even notice my existence. Were Joe and Phyllis *positive* their son wasn't related to Stan Steffan? The two certainly shared an arrogance gene.

"This information about the relationship between Michelle and me no doubt came as a considerable surprise to you," Sterling said.

"That's putting it mildly. But not a surprise to you?"

Which was my thought too, from his detached, unsurprised sounding statement.

"Michelle told me several years ago, although my parents didn't know that. I let them tell me on the phone without letting on I already knew."

Reluctantly I gave Sterling points for that smidgen of sensitivity.

"How do you feel about her?"

"I can't say it was any big surprise when she told me. My parents are good people, but we

343

have practically no characteristics in common, and she'd always seemed unusually interested in me. As for what I feel about her . . ." He shrugged.

"Did you ever ask her about your father?"

"Some jerk back in Kansas, she said."

Okay, so Stan Steffan was definitely not in the picture. I was still disappointed that my brilliant theorizing about a relationship there was totally off base.

"You also knew you stood to inherit everything?"

"No!" The denial was surprisingly vehement, given Sterling's usual demeanor, which had all the sparkle of a concrete block. "Michelle never told me that. So I had no reason to kill her, if that's what you're thinking."

"So why are you here now?" Pam asked bluntly.

"I need to talk to the lawyer. I'd like to know the approximate size of the estate, and how soon I can reasonably expect settlement. I want to leave the company and start my own research firm. This may, depending on the size of the estate, enable me to do that. So I need her lawyer's name and contact information."

One thing to be said for Sterling, he didn't try to manufacture emotion or sentimentality where none existed. Which, I realized reluctantly, pushed him way down on my suspect list. If he'd killed Michelle, I figured he'd have tried harder to sound all broken up about her death. Although his parents were still on my list.

Pam looked at one of the papers on the bed, scribbled the information about the lawyer on a scrap of paper, and handed it to him.

"I'd like a copy of the will too."

"I'm sorry, but I don't have an extra. But I'm sure the lawyer can provide that. He must have the original."

"You haven't talked to this lawyer yet yourself?" he asked.

"No. I had an appointment for this morning, but Shirley's death last night changed things. I don't know if you met her, but she was the housekeeper and cook at the house."

"Was her death connected with Michelle's murder?"

"The police aren't saying much yet, but it seems likely."

"That should erase whatever doubts you might have about me, then. Obviously, I couldn't have done it."

"Sterling, no one has accused you of anything. Although you have to admit, you are the one who benefits most from Michelle's death. That's always a strong motive for murder."

"Especially in those inane murder mysteries you find so fascinating." With that parting crack, Sterling departed. He had not, obviously, come to spread any charm around. Not that he had any to spare.

Pam stared after him for a moment, then shook her head. Probably bewildered by the fact that only a few days ago she'd been ready to marry this guy. She turned back to the paper she'd started to hand to me. I took it and struggled through the fine print.

And in two minutes I'd forgotten all about Sterling Forsythe's or his parents' possible connection to Michelle's murder. Because two other discarded suspects suddenly rocketed way ahead of all others.

Chapter Twenty-Seven

"It is what I think it is, isn't it?" Pam said when she saw my shock. "And there's more. Look at this."

I set the insurance papers aside and skimmed through the partnership agreement. I had no expertise in deciphering legalese, but buried within the *whereases* and *wherefores* were a couple of startling facts.

The partnership agreement was set up so that if something happened, such as the death or mental incapacity of one of the partners, full ownership went to those remaining.

Michelle's death meant that Uri and Cindy owned Change Your World.

Personal insurance was set up and paid for by the partnership—not an unusual situation for key persons in a corporation or partnership, but ominously meaningful in this instance. Each partner was insured for a million dollars, that amount to be paid to the partnership in event of death so as to insure smooth and continuous operation of the business.

Michelle's death meant Uri and Cindy collected a million bucks.

No wonder they weren't worried about the grand opening or keeping the fitness center going. And whatever it took to buy Michelle's BMW, and call it a business expense? A pittance.

And, unlike Sterling, who probably hadn't known in advance that he stood to inherit Michelle's estate, the Hubbards knew exactly how they'd benefit from her death.

Another thought hit me, maybe far out, maybe not. The partnership and insurance set-up seemed very generous on Michelle's part. Pam thought Michelle had murdered before. Did she have in mind doing it again, getting rid of troublesome wife Cindy and acquiring Uri, Change Your World, and a million bucks for herself?

But Cindy had beaten her to it?

"How does all this work with Michelle's will

leaving everything to Sterling?" Pam asked.

"I'm no lawyer, obviously, but I don't think the will has any effect on any of this. It's all outside the will."

Had Cindy also been searching for these papers in Michelle's office? Yet surely they had copies. Or did they think removing Michelle's copies, like getting rid of that incriminating original design for the exercise machine, would lessen chances for "complications"?

Because this spelled Motive for Murder in brighter lights than that lightning bolt sign at Change Your World. Had Uri wielded the knife? Or Cindy? Uri was bigger and stronger. He was also a thief, I was reasonably certain, on the exercise machine design. With Michelle's death, he came out ahead on fitness center ownership and insurance money. But could he cold-bloodedly kill a lover?

Cindy had one more motive than her husband. She not only got ownership of Change Your World and the million bucks, she got rid of a rival.

But why Shirley? Why did they need to get rid of her too?

As if I'd asked the question aloud, Pam answered it. "Shirley must have found something incriminating about them in Michelle's things. They were watching and knew she'd found it."

"But what?"

"I don't know, but Michelle liked to hoard information she thought might prove useful." Pam made a strange little sound, half rueful laugh, half choked gurgle. "Once when I was a kid she caught me cutting her out of a picture of Dad and her and me. I was so young and dumb. I guess I hoped cutting her out of the picture would cut her out of our lives too."

"Probably not an unnatural hope."

"She grabbed the pieces and said if I didn't stop making trouble for her she'd show them to my dad. And fix it so I'd never come home from school even on summers."

Nice lady, this Michelle. What had she tucked away about Uri and Cindy? Maybe something incriminating about Uri back in Germany? Or did Cindy have some ugly tidbit in her past?

"I'm thinking we should suggest to Detective Molino that he search the Hubbards' cottage as well as the house," I said. "The knife may be there."

"They've probably disposed of it."

"You never know. Criminals make mistakes."

I was vaguely aware when Pam slipped out of our room early for breakfast with Mike the next morning. It was at least an hour later when I crossed over to the buffet in the casino building. By then Fitz had already called, making sure I'd made it safely through the night and telling me if everyone moved back to the house today that I shouldn't go with them. His concern was sweet, but I wondered if it could become overbearing.

Pam and Mike were just leaving when I reached the buffet. Uri and Cindy came in wearing running shorts, their faces flushed with all-American glows of health and vitality. Mrs. Steffan breakfasted with Joe and Phyllis, neither Sterling or the Stan Man in sight. I dodged them all and ate alone.

Back upstairs I studied the insurance and partnership papers again. When Pam came in, I asked if she planned to see Michelle's lawyer today.

"No, I'll let Sterling get the ball rolling there. I need to go by the funeral home and finalize things for tomorrow. But first I want to go back to the house and look for Phreddie. I should have brought the Bug last night, but I didn't. Can you drive me?"

"Of course. What about the other guests?"

Pam wasn't feeling very hostess-y this morning. In a let-them-eat-cake tone, she muttered, "They can figure out their own transportation."

At the house, the electronic gate stood wide open. Crime-scene tape encircled the entire house now. One sheriff's department car was still on the scene, but I didn't know if it was Detective Molino's. Whoever belonged with it was apparently inside the house.

"Do you want to see if they'll let you look through the house for Phreddie?"

"With all the strange people and activity in there, I'm sure he's scared to death and has run off to hide by now. You look east of the house, and I'll go west, okay? And look up because he likes to climb trees."

I parked the limo in its usual place in the graveled lane leading around the house and started plowing through the underbrush. Hard going. Blackberry bushes, viney green stuff, other stickery stuff, drooping fir and cedar branches. Snakes? Spiders?

"Here, Phreddie, Phreddie," I called every few steps. Alternating with a more generic, "Here, kitty, kitty." I've never been convinced cats know their names no matter how positive their proud owners are.

A couple of times things rustled in the underbrush, but they weren't Phreddie. No Phreddie in the trees, either.

My half of the wooded acreage was a big territory to cover looking for one small kitty. I crisscrossed it several times. On what I'd decided was my last trip I came out at the cottage where Uri and Cindy were staying. You'd think there'd be a trail between cottage and big house, but I hadn't stumbled across one. I could see the gate for a separate entrance.

It was a cozy looking place. Rustic brown

siding, with a stone chimney rising above a weathered shake roof, and a yard landscaped with lush grass, rocks of impressive size, and rhododendron and holly bushes, plus a couple of fruit trees. Woodsy, back-to-nature looking. I didn't see any evidence of electrical people at work.

Impulsively I went to the door, covered my hand with a corner of my shirt, and tried the door. Locked. But around back a window was open. A trellis covered with climbing ivy under the window looked sturdy.

Not as sturdy as it looked, unfortunately, and a break skidded me downwards a couple of feet as I climbed, but I hung on and made it to the open window. Where I had to crawl out into the kitchen sink. Not easy with clenched fists so I wouldn't leave any fingerprints. Once on the tiled floor I grabbed the first thing I could find to cover my hands while I did a quick search.

The burglar with a dish towel.

But I wasn't really a burglar, I assured myself. This was merely advance scout work for Detective Molino.

I did a quick search of the kitchen drawers and cupboards, which didn't turn up a fancy knife but did turn up two large, unopened jars of guava juice, plus enough bottles of vitamins and minerals and various supplements I'd never heard of to energize most of Vigland. Upstairs, one corner of the only bedroom was set up as a small office with a desk and computer. I poked through a stack of invoices, including to-the-max bills on a half dozen charge cards. The Hubbards *needed* that million bucks of insurance money.

I looked under the bed, felt between mattress and springs, searched a chest of drawers and the closet. No knife. Which didn't mean anything, of course. There could be hidey-holes under the floor or up in the attic, or a zillion other places I hadn't time to investigate. And time was running short, I realized, when I heard a car engine, and a peek out the window revealed a white van with THREE BROTHERS ELECTRIC SERVICE on the side. I flew down the stairs and out the back door.

Dumb idea anyway, I acknowledged as I plunged into the thorny underbrush a few feet beyond the door. I'd rationalized my curiosity, but even if I'd found the knife I couldn't have done anything with it. Detective Molino needed to find it in a legal search.

My return slog through the woods brought me out at the rear of the main house. I circled around to the front and spotted Pam and four deputies just below the front steps. Her skateboard leaned against the curb beside her. Apparently she'd intended to take some time to "think" with it. A second sheriff's department car was parked behind the first one now. I hurried toward them. Maybe they'd found Phreddie.

Only to realize as I got closer that there was something peculiar about this little gathering. Pam's hands were behind her.

And she was wearing handcuffs.

Chapter Twenty-Eight

"What's going on?" I gasped.

"They have a warrant for my arrest," Pam said, disbelief in her voice even as her wrists squirmed in the reality of the handcuffs. "They read me my Miranda rights and they're arresting me."

"This is ridiculous!" I sputtered. "Did you tell them about the partnership agreement and insurance papers we found? Cindy and Uri, those are the people you should be arresting!" I blazed at Detective Molino.

"They found the knife," Pam said. "A butterfly knife, with rubies in the handles." She made a little hip jiggle, nodding toward some papers sticking out of the rear pocket of her jeans.

I grabbed them. A list of the items seized in the police search.

"Okay, so you found a butterfly knife," I conceded.

"It was in Miss Gibson's room," Detective Molino said.

I looked at Pam, and she lifted her shoulders in a gesture of helplessness. "I have no idea how it got there."

I turned to Detective Molino. "Somebody planted it! Can't you see that?" Maybe the Stan Man was right about small-town cops. "Were there fingerprints on it?"

"You're asking questions again," Detective Molino chided. But then he relented. "It's been wiped clean."

"You're saying that Pam was smart enough to wipe off fingerprints, but dumb enough to keep the knife in her room where you could find it?" I challenged.

"Killers aren't necessarily consistent. Fortunately for us, they make mistakes."

I looked at the list in my hand. Most of the items on it seemed irrelevant to me. A small cedar jewelry box, with a list of the items in it. Two notebooks. An opened bottle of Riesling. A can of—

"Bean sprouts?"

"The giant, thirty-two ounce size, if you'll notice. A fairly formidable weapon. With a few hairs and a trace of blood on it. Neither of which have been lab-tested yet, but which we're reasonably certain will prove to be the housekeeper's."

"So?"

"Shirley was hit on the back of the head," Pam said with a shaky rattle in her voice. "She may or may not have been unconscious when she was put in the hot tub. But the blow with the can of bean sprouts kept her from being uncooperative while she was drowned."

"That is speculation." Detective Molino scowled, but from the way he said it I figured Pam's speculation was correct.

And this proved what Fitz had said, a killer can always find a weapon. A can of bean sprouts. It might be a long time before I had an appetite for chow mein again.

"Andi, I need a lawyer," Pam said.

"I'll call that one in Olympia. What's his name?"

"Bloombarton. He's part of Jefferson, Bloombarton, and Wilmington, on Capitol Way. But they know trust funds and finance, not murderers."

"You're not a murderer!"

"I'm sure Miss Gibson appreciates your vote of confidence," Detective Molino said. He stuck out his hand for the papers I held, then tucked them into Pam's handcuffed hand. "I'll see that her attorney gets these. He'll need them." He put his hand on her upper arm and turned her toward the squad car.

"What about bail? Michelle's funeral service is tomorrow!"

"That'll be up to the judge. But I wouldn't expect it that soon."

A judge also might not be sympathetic to bail to allow the accused to attend the funeral of the victim.

"Talk to Phyllis and Joe," Pam said. "And Sterling, too. Maybe the service can be postponed for a few days."

"This knife in her room and a can of bean sprouts aren't enough to convict her!" I hurled at Detective Molino.

"We'll see," he said.

Pam looked so scared, so young and dazed. I squeezed her arm.

"It'll be okay," I said. "Just think how you'll be able to use all this in your next mystery. Great personal, firsthand research."

It was a weak attempt at comfort, and we both knew it.

"I'm not writing any more. I've had my fill of mysteries . . . and murder. I may never even *read* another mystery."

"Oh, Pam, I'm so sorry," I said as the deputy reached over and removed my hand from her arm—not rudely, but firmly. "I'll pray for you. This would be a good time for you to pray too."

"Why? God can't listen to everybody! He can't *care* about everybody. Not if there are a million voices all talking to Him at once."

"But He can," I said. "That's one of the

miracles of prayer. We each have our own lifeline to God. A Pam line. An Andi line. No waiting in line! It doesn't matter how many others are praying at the same time, because He cares about each of us. Use your prayer line, Pam. And I'll use mine."

I have to give Detective Molino credit on this point. He didn't interrupt our little personal conversation. Pam's last words, as he put a hand on her head and squished her into the squad car, were, "Call Mike!"

The car with Pam, Detective Molino, and another deputy pulled away. Two deputies remained. This all felt vaguely unreal, as if I'd stepped onto the set of one of Fitz's old shows.

One part of me couldn't believe it, the other part groaned *They're going to nail her.* Her skateboard lay on the grass like the fallen armor of a captured soldier.

"Can I go in the house?" I asked the deputies. "I need to get some names and phone numbers."

"Not yet."

"When?"

"Probably tomorrow morning. Possibly this evening."

Behind them, the amorphous ice sculpture was smaller than ever. I felt as if I were melting too, going all blobby and shapeless. But I determinedly pulled myself together. This was no time to melt.

I started to run for the limo, then turned back with another question. "Have you seen a cat? Kind of Siamese looking, with blue eyes, but some extra grayish blotches?"

"Yeah, come to think of it, I did see a cat skulking around the garage," one deputy said. "Though I didn't check out its eyes or blotches."

Cats obviously were not high on his list of priorities. I hesitated. Go after Phreddie? Or Mike and a lawyer?

I compromised and made a quick dash around the garage while alternately calling, "Phreddie! Phreddie!" and "Here, kitty, kitty." Nothing.

Then I jumped into the limo and sped to my duplex. No nosy Tom in the yard checking up on me. Maybe he was off somewhere with his lady friend. Inside, I got a number for Mike's landscape and yard maintenance service from the phone book. But before I could call, a battered pickup pulled into my driveway.

The woman who came to my door was tall and lanky. This must be the woman Tom had mentioned, because what she was wearing might be described as a "tent thing." More technically a muu-muu, long and shapeless, with a wild pattern of twining vines and orchids. Something that would no doubt set Mrs. Steffan's flower-loving heart to fluttering.

The tattoo of a rose showed on the woman's left arm, a butterfly on her right. A strip of leather pulled her coarse blond hair into a ponytail. More leather fringed a purse that looked as if it had been run over a few times. And beneath the muu-muu . . . could it be? Yes, motorcycle boots.

"Your neighbor thought your duplex might be for rent. I saw the other renters moving out."

I had no time for renters now. I doubted I'd ever have time for this particular renter. I gave myself a quick chastising for that rush judgment, but what I did not need was an aging biker babe and her cohorts squatting in my rental.

Tom's assessment that she was not young, but younger than I, was about right. Forty-five, or maybe not quite. But with what I'd guess was an ages-you-fast lifestyle behind her.

"I'm sorry," I said, "but I'm really busy right now. I just don't have time for rental business."

"That's okay. I can wait out in my pickup."

"No, please don't. I have to clean the place up yet and—and do things."

"I don't mind if it hasn't been cleaned. Maybe I could help you 'do things'?"

"It's about a murder. Two murders, actually." I figured that would end this conversation, but it didn't.

"I know how to use a gun," she said.

I blinked, but I didn't have time to analyze that mildly alarming statement. I just needed to get rid of her.

"There's only a bed and table in it. No real furniture. And I'm going to have to raise the rent." I named a monthly price $10 over what I'd been charging.

"That's fine."

"I just don't think—"

"Please? I'd really like to rent it." She turned and looked out across the yard and neighborhood. "It's such a wonderful place. With grass and trees. A nice neighborhood. So . . . normal looking."

Normal looking. As if *normal* were the most valuable commodity in the world. And, looking at her, I had to guess normal, at least by my standards, hadn't played a large part in her life.

Then she turned back to me, and I saw the look in her blue eyes. Not a pleading for help or pity or understanding. Just a yearning. For normal.

I guessed Tom was right. She probably didn't have an impressive list of references.

"What's your name?" I asked.

"India Beauregard."

"Really?" I asked doubtfully.

"Beauregard was my great-grandfather's last name. French aristocracy back there somewhere, he claimed. And I always wanted to be an India."

Chalk it up to being rattled about all that had happened and rushed by all the things I had to do. To worry about Pam and not wanting to waste time standing here with this unlikely person.

But mostly it was that yearning in her eyes.

Or—who knows? Maybe a nudge from God.

"Okay, India Beauregard, you can rent it. But we'll have to take care of the rental agreement later. I'll need first and last month's rent and a $400 deposit."

She opened the floppy purse, reached inside, and counted out the full amount in twenty-dollar bills. Whatever lifestyle she'd had, apparently it had not been un-lucrative. Which was also a bit disconcerting.

I stood there holding the money, strongly thinking about handing it back to her. Which she must have realized, because she adroitly stepped out of reach.

"You don't need to bother with a receipt. Is it okay if I move in now?"

"This is a one-person deal. You can't have anyone else move in with you," I warned. "No biker friends with motorcycles parking on the lawn. No drugs or wild parties, or anything . . . not normal."

"Sounds good to me." She crossed her heart with a tanned hand that looked surprisingly well cared for, considering her leathery face. "I promise."

We went over to the other side of the duplex and found the keys on the table. The previous renters had left the place clean, and a quick tour showed nothing broken. I'd have to get their security deposit back to them.

I tossed her the keys. "Okay, make yourself at home."

She looked around as if I'd given her the keys to the Taj Mahal. "Oh, I will."

I still had my doubts. But at least those tattoos were a rose and a butterfly, not daggers and demons.

I forgot my new renter and went back to the phone. I got hold of Mike at a landscaping job and shocked him with the news about Pam. He said he'd go to the sheriff's station immediately and see what he could do. Lawyer Bloombarton in Olympia was properly horrified when I gave him the news and said he'd contact a good criminal lawyer for Pam. I gave him my cell number to call me back. I tried to call Joe and Phyllis or Sterling at the inn, but they weren't in their rooms.

Now what? Find them, I decided. A little grimly I wondered if they were on another shopping spree. Everybody, it appeared, came out winners with Michelle's death. Except Pam.

Back at the inn, I knocked on both doors. No answer. But Stan Steffan went by while I was knocking, and I asked him if he'd seen them.

"They're over in the casino playing video poker. Sucker's game," he growled disapprovingly. "Just takes longer than slots to lose your money."

Since Stan was back at the room, I guessed that meant he'd been on the losing end already. I crossed the glass walkway over to the casino. The main floor of the casino wasn't crowded at midday on a weekday, but neither was it hurting for customers. The gambling area was divided for smooth traffic flow, sounds muted, no clink of coins since the slots now used a paper system. But the place made me vaguely uncomfortable. No windows. Soft lights that stayed the same day or night, so you had a feeling that time no longer existed. I also felt as if an earthquake or nuclear bomb destroyed everything outside, no one in here would even notice.

I found Joe and Phyllis at video poker machines, Sterling at a dice table nearby.

"I'd never realized this could be so much fun!" Phyllis enthused.

"Of course it's fun for her," Joe said. "She's five bucks ahead. I'm two behind."

They were, I saw, playing nickel machines. Not exactly high-stakes gambling, but I had the feeling jumping to higher stakes or even becoming addicted wouldn't be all that difficult for Phyllis. I saw Sterling lay down a twenty-dollar bill on the dice table.

"I need to talk to you," I said to Phyllis. "Could we go somewhere?"

"Can't it wait?" Phyllis said. "I think this machine is about to pay off big."

"No," I said flatly.

They reluctantly gave up their padded stools. Phyllis patted her poker machine as if it were an old friend. "I'll be back."

"Sterling too," I said.

The dealer had just grabbed Sterling's money. He scowled, but he came when Joe motioned him. I led the way out to a wide hallway.

"Pam has been arrested," I said. No one said anything, not even a squeak. "For murdering Michelle."

"What about Shirley?" Phyllis asked.

"Well, for murdering her too, I guess." Not so much as a peep out of any of them about Pam's welfare, I noted.

Joe and Phyllis looked at each other. Sterling looked at his watch, then felt for the cell phone clipped to his waist as if he needed reassurance it was still there.

"I guess I'm not surprised," Phyllis said. "I've been afraid of this all along. There was such *hostility* between them. And Pam was the person closest to Michelle in the wedding procession. She had the easiest access."

"But she didn't do it!" I cried, appalled at Phyllis's easy acceptance of Pam's guilt. "They've made a huge mistake."

"Is there anything we can do to help?" Joe asked.

He didn't sound ready to slay dragons, but at least he'd asked, which was more than the other two did.

"What needs to be done at the moment is contact the funeral home about the service that's scheduled for tomorrow. Pam thought perhaps it could be postponed for a few days."

There was a silence that unexpectedly felt ominous before Phyllis finally spoke.

"I don't think that would be . . . appropriate."

"You don't?"

"Think about it," Phyllis said. "How would it look, postponing the service just so the person who's accused of killing her can come? Sterling can be there, and that's what really matters. He's her *son*."

A relationship, now that Phyllis knew Michelle's estate went with it, she suddenly seemed eager to claim and display.

Sterling looked at his watch again. "I have an appointment with the attorney at three o'clock. I want to be able to get out of here right after the service tomorrow. I can't hang around for days."

I looked at Joe, the only one here who seemed inclined toward anything but total self-interest. But when it came to the bottom line, he flunked too, because he said, "I think the original plan is probably best."

I looked at them in mixed anger and dismay. Was I a hundred percent sure Uri and Cindy, and not this selfish, callous little triumvirate, were the killers?

Chapter Twenty-Nine

I didn't really know where I was going, but I headed out to the comforting, old-friend familiarity of the limo. Reluctantly I conceded that even though Forsythes & Son were greedy, self-centered jerks, they probably weren't murderers. It was Uri and Cindy I needed to concentrate on.

As I slid into the limo, my cell phone played its little hard rock tune. Fitz again, and now I had this ominous news about Pam to give him. I had to cut the call short, I told him, because I was expecting the call from the lawyer.

"Okay, but call me back as soon as you can."

As soon as that conversation ended, the phone played again, this time lawyer Bloombarton saying he'd arranged for a criminal lawyer named Dietz Dietrich to represent Pam. He thought Dietrich would be coming over to Vigland this afternoon.

"Is he good?"

"You remember the burglar they accused of

murdering the older couple in their house over in Bellingham? He got him down to a manslaughter charge."

"But Pam isn't guilty of anything!"

"I'm sure she isn't," he agreed soothingly, though I wasn't convinced he meant it. "Dietz will take good care of her."

Okay, now what? I'd looked over that list of seized items rather hurriedly, but I hadn't seen anything on it that would connect Uri and Cindy with either murder. Was whatever Shirley had found implicating them still in the house? No, surely they'd have grabbed and destroyed it after drowning her in the hot tub.

A discouraging thought. But a second possibility. If they hadn't had time or means to destroy it . . . lighting a bonfire in their room would have been a bit noticeable . . . and with no idea at that time that the house would be searched, perhaps they'd just hidden it somewhere.

Whatever "it" was.

So I needed to get into the house and do my own search, because the incriminating item was undoubtedly something Detective Molino and his deputies hadn't even been searching for. I drove back to the house, hoping the police were through early there, but the crime-scene tape still fluttered in the breeze. I parked just outside the gate and used the time to call Fitz back.

Three rings, and he said, "Fitz here. Available for romance, adventure, and fantastic food on the high seas. What's your choice?"

"Do you answer all your calls that way?"

"Only the ones from beautiful limousine drivers."

I appreciated his attempt to cheer me up with a bit of frivolity.

"I've got a lawyer for Pam, but I'm not sure what to do next. I'm almost certain Uri and Cindy killed Michelle for the partnership and the insurance money. I think they also killed Shirley because she came across something implicating them."

I prudently did not include my trellis-trip into their window. I couldn't remember Fitz climbing trellises back in his Ed Montrose days. He'd operated on a more intellectual and dignified level.

So now he surprised me by saying, "It sounds as if you need to do your own search in the house."

"But what do I look for? Michelle couldn't have tucked away proof that they killed *her*."

"All I can say is that you'll probably know it when you see it. It almost has to be something on paper, notes, or a document, something like that."

My thought too. "But I don't think I can ignore the crime-scene tape and go digging around in there."

He paused just long enough to make me wonder if he was going to suggest a devious sneak-in, but finally, with what sounded like a twinge of regret, he said, "No, you can't. Which means you'll just have to wait until they release the house. If we get back to the marina by then, I can help."

"The deputy said this evening or tomorrow before they release the house. I don't think it can wait longer than that."

"Then you have to make certain Uri and Cindy don't get back inside the house. Not before you search it, and especially not while you're searching it. If they killed Shirley because she found something—"

Right. What's a third murder when you're already down for two? "I'll be careful. Thanks, Fitz. I miss you."

"I miss you too."

With *keep Uri and Cindy out of the house* at the top of my priority list right now, I headed for the fitness center. The front door was locked, but I went around back and found a plumber's van and an unlocked door.

Inside, Uri, Cindy, and a guy in a khaki jumpsuit with DoneRight Plumbing stamped across the back were faced off by a treadmill. The plumber held some complicated looking piece of plumbing, Uri had another piece, and they all looked ready to start blows in the Great Plumbing Wars. Cindy spotted me and came over.

"Would you believe? This guy crossed some of the hot and cold water lines, and now he wants to charge extra to make them right."

Plumbing problems were not a priority with me. "I thought you should know. Pam has been arrested for murdering Michelle. And Shirley too, I guess."

"Pam killed Michelle?"

"No! They've just arrested her for it. She didn't do it."

"So why did they arrest her?"

"They found a knife similar to the one that killed Michelle in her room. And a . . . weapon that was used to hit Shirley with before she was drowned in the tub. That was in Pam's room too."

Which you undoubtedly knew, since you planted them there. I waited for her to inquire what the weapon used on Shirley was. Wouldn't an innocent person be curious? But she didn't ask.

"That's funny," Cindy said. "Oh, I don't mean that the way it sounded! Not *funny* funny. *Strange* funny. I was sure Stan Steffan did it."

"You were? Why? Did Michelle mention being afraid of him?" I asked, momentarily distracted.

"No, not afraid. She was just furious that he

tried to pressure her into investing in his new movie. She said it was just like blackmail, that if she'd invest, then he'd give her a part in the movie."

"Was she considering it? She really wanted to be in it, didn't she?"

"I guess she did, though I don't know why. Change Your World is going to be a big success."

But not enough if what you yearn for is bright-lights, big-screen success. And for the Hubbards, was there only enough success for two partners, not three?

"So why did you think he'd killed her?" I asked.

"Oh, I suppose it's unfair, but he's just kind of . . . creepy, you know? And Michelle and the Steffans went back a long way. Who knows what went on back then? But now to find out it was *Pam,* after all. I can't believe it. Or maybe I don't want to believe it." She shook her head. "Weird, peculiar little Pammi. After all Michelle did for her."

I wanted to yell *She didn't do it* again, but I realized there was no point in it. Because what I was getting here was an expert little acting job from Cindy. Maybe she should have been after a movie part too.

"I also wanted to let you know that we can't get back in the house for probably a couple of days yet. I was just out there, and deputies are still all over the place." Both of which were only tiny stretches of the truth. "So we'll all be staying at the inn again tonight. Pam had the charges fixed up to cover however long we need to stay. Okay?"

"Okay, fine. I'll tell Uri. What about Michelle's services?"

"Apparently they're still on for tomorrow afternoon. Will you be there?"

"Yes, of course. Michelle was my closest friend."

That old saying seemed appropriate here: With friends like this, who needs enemies? But I figured I'd done what I came for, which was to keep Cindy and Uri away from the house.

I went back out to the inn. A peek in the casino showed Phyllis was back at the video poker, although she'd moved to a different machine. Neither Joe nor Sterling was around.

I went up to my room and lay down. I felt as if I needed a nap, although I didn't think I could actually sleep. But I did and felt mildly refreshed when I woke. I went early to the buffet for dinner, partly because I wanted to avoid the others, partly because I had a plan. Or at least a hope.

Chapter Thirty

Yes! The search had finished up early. The crime-scene tape was gone, along with the sheriff's department vehicles. The gate stood wide open, although I found the door to the house locked. But I still had the key Shirley had given me. I let myself in, then locked the door behind me. I didn't want to be unpleasantly surprised to find myself not alone in the house.

Okay, where would Cindy and Uri have hidden "it," whatever it was, the item for which they'd killed Shirley? Down there in the Fitness Room? No, assuming they had planned to get "it" out of the house as quickly as possible, most likely in their own room.

I dropped my purse in the downstairs hallway and headed directly to their room. It wasn't in disarray, but I could tell from open drawers and awry mattress that the deputies had been in there. However, I'd already decided we weren't searching for the same thing, and I looked in and under and around everything. Undersides of drawers, back side of headboard, under lamps, inside the toilet tank. Nothing but some publicity-type photos of Uri in a body-building pose—leopard-print Spandex, muscles bulging.

Not a sight for *these* sore eyes, thank you.

Pam's room? No. They'd hidden the items they wanted to incriminate Pam there, but they wouldn't hide something that incriminated them in her room. I didn't waste time there.

I did peek in what appeared to be a catchall storage room on the attic floor. I couldn't tell if it was already a mess, or if the deputies had done a thorough search. What I did do was nearly jump out of my shoes when the leopard skin Pam had stuffed in there fell on me.

Between Uri in leopard-skin Spandex and a real leopard skin, I'd had enough of spotted creatures.

My hopes were running out. The logical action would have been to destroy the crucial evidence, and that was probably what the Hubbards had done. I almost skipped Shirley's room. Partly because I figured that if they'd killed Shirley for some piece of evidence, they'd surely have taken it, not left it in her room. And partly because poking around in her belongings made me feel queasy in a way that prowling in Michelle's things didn't.

But I stiffened my nerves and opened the door. Little snippets of Shirley cut at my heart: photo of her granddaughter and a recipe for "rosemary chicken" clipped from a magazine on her nightstand, her scuffed old slippers by the bed. After fifteen minutes or so of searching, I found, tucked in a drawer under her IRA records and some medical reports, a newspaper flier for carpet cleaning.

Odd, but probably something accidentally dropped in there, I thought at first. Then I turned the flier over and saw numbers scribbled on the backside.

Shirley's scribbling? No, it looked different from some other writing in the drawer. Some of the numbers had cryptic abbreviations beside them. *Hon.p-off. Dscvr. Mstrcrd. Dr.D.* And at the bottom of the page was an underlined, exclamation-pointed $1,000,000.

Then my pulse jumped. I went back over the numbers and expanded on the abbreviations. Hon. p-off. Uri and Cindy had a Honda sedan. The amount it would take to pay off the Honda? *Discvr.* Easy! Their Discover credit card, with a whopping balance. Same with *Mstrcrd.* Their Mastercard credit card. And *Dr.D.* must be some medical bill. A couple of other unidentified big figures I recognized from the bills I'd seen at the cottage.

This was Cindy and Uri's solution for getting out of their financial hole. Using the insurance money from Michelle's death!

Then I hesitated. This looked meaningful to me, and Shirley must also have considered it meaningful to hide it in here. She must have found it in their room. But would Detective

Molino see it as incriminating? Was it, in fact, strong enough evidence that Cindy and Uri would murder Shirley for it? And since they had murdered her, why hadn't they taken this? Or had they not found it, and might be coming back for it. . . .

I was suddenly aware that it was getting dark, and I was alone in the house. Would Cindy and Uri ignore my effort to keep them away? It was possible Michelle had given Cindy a house key at some time, which could make her considerably more dangerous than a dead leopard skin.

Okay, time to get out of here.

I folded the flier and tucked it into the back pocket of my jeans, grabbed my purse where I'd dropped it in the hallway, and stopped in my room to pick up my New Testament and the printed guidelines for the Bible study we were doing at church. I desperately needed some study and prayer time with God. Murder and hidden secrets were getting to me.

I was just locking the front door with the key when a car drove through the open gate and stopped at the curb below the steps. My own words came back to me: *What's a third murder when you're already down for two?*

But the occupant of the car wasn't Uri or Cindy.

"Mrs. Steffan," I said, surprised when the

headlights went off and she slid out of the car. Sweetly grandmotherly in a summery dress flowered with purple and pink daisies on a sunny yellow background, looking as if she'd just stepped off the pages of a vintage fashion magazine.

"We decided to rent a car so we wouldn't have to bother you for transportation all the time," she said.

"Do you need something from your room?"

"I was going to look for . . . earrings to match this dress. But if you've already locked up, it isn't important. You came to look for something yourself?" She spoke offhandedly, but she eyed the folded papers in my hand rather sharply.

"My Bible study lessons."

"You came all the way out here for Bible lessons?"

The skepticism in her question nibbled at my nerves. The sun had dropped behind the forested hillsides to the west of Vigland. The inlet lay in blue shadows, the water calm at that dead point between high and low tides. We were alone, just Mrs. Steffan and me, on ten acres of woods and grass.

I was almost positive Cindy and Uri had committed the murders. The numbers on the back of that flier put their motive in neon. But the back of my neck prickled as if it had a suspicion agenda of its own. Why was Mrs.

Steffan skeptical about my papers? And what was that odd hesitation before she came up with *earrings* as the reason she was here?

"They're very important Bible lessons." I thrust the pages under her nose so she could see. "We're studying Romans."

She gave the lessons a cursory glance. Her sharp gaze spotted something else. "What's that other paper, the one sticking out of your back pocket?"

My instinctive reaction was that this was none of her business. I decided to pretend I hadn't heard her. "I think I'll be getting back out to the inn now."

"May I see it, please?"

The blunt request surprised me, her outstretched hand like some teacher demanding you hand over that note you were passing to a girlfriend. The nibble on my nerves escalated to shark bites.

"Or maybe I'll go by and see if I can visit Pam for a minute. You know she's been arrested, don't you?"

"You have something to show her, perhaps? Her and her lawyer?"

"I've never met her lawyer." An irrelevant comment, but the best I could do at the moment, since I had no idea what she was referring to.

"Actually, I think you've already found what I came here for, haven't you?"

The menace in her voice startled me. I made some murmured denial and tried to edge around her on the steps, but with surprising quickness and strength she yanked me around, slammed me against the railing, and snatched the flier right out of my back pocket. I was astonished. It was like your friendly teddy bear suddenly turning into King Kong.

Before I could even yelp a protest, she said, "I knew that wicked woman kept the proof hidden away somewhere. I've looked and looked and haven't been able to find it, and now you—" She squinted at the flier, moving it back and forth for better focus in the dusky evening light.

I had another thought. Mrs. Steffan had "looked and looked." She was the one who had searched Michelle's office that night, the one who had inadvertently locked me outside.

"What is this?" She demanded indignantly, as if I'd cheated her. "It's just an advertisement."

"That's what I said it was."

She turned the sheet over, then sideways. "What are all these numbers? Some kind of code!"

"I think it's just scribbles."

She tossed the flier away. "Where is it? I know you must have it! That's why you're out here sneaking around."

She grabbed at my purse, and the strap over my shoulder yanked me forward. She did a quick twist of the purse, and there I was, trussed up in purse and strap, our faces just inches apart.

Too much purple-ish eye shadow for a daisy outfit, I noted. Although not particularly relevant at the moment. I gave a strangled *glug* as she yanked the strap across my throat with one hand and ripped the purse open with the other.

"In here, is that where you hid it?"

Still keeping the strap taut across my throat, she pawed through the purse, tossing items like confetti. Cell phone, address book, a handful of Andi's Limouzeen Service business cards, a safety pin, breath mints, a coupon for a free latte.

"You should be ashamed of this mess," she muttered, still tossing. Pennies. Paper clips. Crumpled receipt. Oh, so that's where the receipt for that hair coloring I wanted to return had gone. I'd decided Razzle-dazzle Blond was not for me.

"See?" I gurgled. "Nothing in there."

She turned the purse upside down and dumped the remainder of the contents at our feet. Charge cards, coin purse, two packets of Taco Bell sauce, nail file, checkbook, Band-Aids, used Kleenex. Under different circumstances I'd be embarrassed by the clutter, but at the moment my shortcomings in the area of purse management didn't seem of vital importance. Also, dumping the purse had loosened the stranglehold across my throat.

I tried again. "Mrs. Steffan, I don't know—"

"Of course you know. Michelle told you, didn't she? So now you're looking for it, so you can blackmail us too!"

"I was Michelle's limousine driver, not her confidante."

But the truth was roaring up on me like the tide sweeping up the inlet. Michelle had accused Stan Steffan of blackmail with his scheme to make her ante up a million dollars for a part in the movie. But there'd been more to that conversation Shirley had overheard, something that had slipped right by me until now. *If that was the game he wanted to play, she could play it too,* was what she'd said to him.

Michelle had information with which to blackmail the Steffans. She'd used it to bargain for a part in the movie. One of them had killed her to keep her quiet. Killed Shirley too? Oh yes. Because Shirley had been digging around, and she had either found something incriminating, or the Steffans thought she had.

And me? I didn't know the details of all this, but I knew way too much. Enough to put me on Mrs. Steffan's personal death row. Another *glug,* as that thought alone choked me.

But Mrs. Steffan, in spite of these highly peculiar actions, hadn't gone so far as to actually admit to murder, and if I could just convince her I was dumb as a pet rock . . .

I twisted my head, trying to get away from the

strap that was still a threat. "I thought—" No, no, rephrase that. "I think Uri and Cindy killed Michelle. I came out to look for something incriminating about them. I think that flier may be it."

"How could a page of scribbles mean anything?" she scoffed.

"Because they're a plan for using a big insurance payoff on Michelle's life to pay off their debts. It's a powerful motive for murder, and the proof's all there!" Not quite true, but in the ballpark.

"Really?" She picked up the flier again and studied it in the dim light. "We didn't know about an insurance payoff, but Stan and I have thought from the beginning that one of them did it."

But she looked at me, her gaze as appraising as an antique expert eying a phony Ming vase, and my heart plummeted. She knew that I knew. Cindy and Uri may have greedy plans, but she or Stan had killed Michelle and Shirley. The strap was loose enough now that I surreptitiously slipped it over my head and dropped the purse at my feet while I tried to think how to convince her I wasn't suspicious of her.

"So I'm really sorry about this little misunderstanding," I said brightly, as if I was all to blame.

"Oh, I am too!" She reached over and dusted the

dent the strap had left across my shoulder. "This is such an awkward situation. I got carried away there, I'm afraid. We all make misjudgments when we're under stress, don't you think?"

"Well, then, I'll just be running along. I can take these incriminating numbers about Uri and Cindy to Detective Molino."

"Perhaps we could talk for a moment first?"

I figured I wasn't fooling her. "Well, uh, okay." Sure, let's have a conversation. *What-da-ya think about them Seahawks?* Although I doubted that was what she had in mind.

"I like you, Andi. I liked you from the very first day you brought us in from that silly little airport they have here. You're smart and nice and so wonderfully unpretentious, unlike everyone else here. And very attractive too, in an, oh, marvelously inconspicuous kind of way."

Not the most memorable of compliments, but under the circumstances I'd take what I could get. "Thank you."

It also occurred to me that she was actually being shrewd, phrasing it that way, because she knew trying to make me believe I was a raving beauty would never work.

She laughed gaily, as if this were indeed just a friendly little chat. "Don't be upset. It can be a most useful asset in Hollywood. There are all kinds of character parts for an older, attractive but inconspicuous woman."

"You're talking about *me* . . . and Hollywood?"

"Oh, yes. There's no need for you to spend your days chauffeuring people around in that limo. I can get you a part in Stan's new movie, and with his help you can have a fantastic future in Hollywood. Wouldn't you like that?"

"And I wouldn't have to come up with a million bucks to invest to get the part?"

She apparently missed the sarcasm. "No, of course not. You just come down to Hollywood and start a whole new life."

It wasn't quite laid out like a road map, but the path was clear. Mrs. Steffan obviously believed anyone would do anything to be up there on the silver screen. All I had to do was forget the earlier part of this little confrontation, forget she or Stan had committed murder, and she'd make that new life in Hollywood come alive for me.

Of course I might find myself dead before that ever happened, but I wasn't supposed to suspect that.

Not that it mattered. I wouldn't ignore what the Steffans had done if she promised a full-body rejuvenation and a starring role as an overage vampire. It was on the tip of my tongue to tell her what she could do with her offer, but on second thought I had a better plan. Mrs. Steffan thought a chance to be in the movies would make anyone pant and drool. Okay, I'd pant and drool for her.

"Mrs. Steffan—"

"Call me Alice."

Oh, we were really getting chummy now.

"Alice, I don't know what to say. This is just so generous of you. Perhaps your husband could come up with a movie—or a whole TV series!—about a woman with a limousine, and I could even be a *star!*"

"Oh, yes, that's a fantastic idea! Stan will love it."

"I think we can work something out, then, about this . . . awkward situation."

"Marvelous! You can clue that detective in on what you know about Uri and Cindy's motives and show him those numbers. And it wouldn't hurt to, oh, you know, dramatize things a bit. Perhaps you remember now that you saw Uri running away from the body, into the fog?"

"Yes, I think I *do* remember that. Oh, this is so exciting! Me, in a movie!"

"Movies," Mrs. Steffan said, emphasizing the plural.

"I do want to get Pam out of this unpleasant situation as quickly as possible," I said as if it were an afterthought. "She shouldn't be in jail."

"Of course! Such a sweet girl."

Yeah, right. A sweet girl who was under arrest because Alice here had planted that incriminating evidence in her room. But we were going to sweep that detail under the rug. I went for a little further distraction.

"She's long thought Michelle murdered her father, you know."

Mrs. Steffan's eyebrows lifted. "No, I didn't know that. But it's quite possible. Exactly the kind of thing Michelle would do." She nodded as if this cleared up something she'd wondered about. "I've long known Michelle killed Pam's mother."

"Really? Oh, poor Pam. Michelle did it so she could grab Gerald?"

"And his money, of course. There was never any actual proof, but it was obvious to anyone who knew the situation as well as I did."

I started to say *You knew this but you never said a word to the authorities?* But at the moment keeping that thought to myself seemed prudent. "You're such an *aware* sort of person," I gushed instead.

"I always figured she got the idea from Stan's . . . problem," Mrs. Steffan added.

I knew Pam's mother had died in a hit-and-run situation. If Michelle had copied that from Stan, he must have been involved in one too. "His hit-and-run problem?" It was a guess, but I syruped it with all the sympathy I could manage.

"The situation was entirely different with Stan, of course. His was an unfortunate *accident.*"

But he'd gotten away with it, and Michelle had figured if she could make Pam's mother's death look like an accident, she could get away with it too. Except that she'd kept some kind of record or proof of Stan Steffan's "accident." As Pam had said, Michelle hoarded things like that in case they'd come in handy someday. And this one had. Except it had also gotten her murdered.

My mind galloped around the details I knew, leaping fences and hurtling tall buildings. I pounced on one detail.

"I see such wonderful, ironic justice in Michelle being killed by one of her husband's knives. Michelle killed *him,* and then one of his knives killed *her!* Did you do it that way for that reason?"

She beamed as if I'd just aced a test. "I didn't know when I found the knives in Michelle's room that she'd killed him, but now that you've told me I'm so glad I did it that way. It is, as you say, wonderfully ironic justice."

"But wouldn't there have been a problem if the stinky fog hadn't offered you such a wonderful opportunity?"

"I had a different plan originally, but the fog was a surprise blessing."

Blessing. I shuddered at Mrs. Steffan's use of the word, but I managed to keep looking brightly interested. I was, after all, supposedly on my way to a career in the movies, so she'd expect me to be flying high.

"But I'd have managed without it," she added. "I planned to get Michelle to step out back of the tent with me for a minute, where she'd be found much later. But when the wonderful fog engulfed everyone I just . . . what's that saying? . . . grabbed the bull by the horns and did it!"

"So you were the one, not your husband?"

"I'll bet you didn't think I could do it, did you?" She sounded almost coy.

"No, I guess not."

She stepped back, then astonished me by bending her right arm and flexing the muscle into an impressive bulge. "See what working out on those exercise machines can do? I'm thinking I'll see if Pam will sell me that machine down in the Fitness Room, the one Uri invented. It's really a fantastic machine. All my friends back home will be green with envy, and with Uri, well, *incapacitated,* there won't be any more available."

"You did this all for Stan? To keep anything from coming out about his . . . problem?"

"I've been really upset about Shirley. I liked her. Such marvelous biscuits! But under the circumstances . . ." She lifted her broad shoulders in a that's-the-way-it-is shrug.

"The circumstances?"

"She acted so strange when I asked for tea that night. I knew she'd been rummaging around in Michelle's things and must have found what Michelle had kept about Stan's accident."

"You saw what Michelle had?"

"No, but that wicked woman had it all written down. Date. Time. Circumstances. Somehow she'd even sneaked over and taken a *photo* of the damage to Stan's car before he got it fixed."

"I don't think you have anything to worry about," I said, forcing the cheerfulness again. "I'll do some more looking around in the house and get rid of anything that looks . . . troublesome. And that flier will nail Uri and Cindy. You did this all because of your love for Stan?" I repeated, injecting admiration into the question.

"Love?" She sounded surprised.

"You've been married a long time."

"Yes, we have. I've put up with a lot. Women, gambling, bad temper." She suddenly sounded furious. "No way was I going to let his stupid *accident* drag us down and destroy everything."

"If Michelle came out with what she knew, it would do that?"

"We'd sink like a cannonball in a duck pond. And no way could she be *in* that new movie, an aging has-been trying to play such a youthful part. We'd all be a laughingstock. I couldn't let that happen. And it would, if she got away with her blackmail."

"But scandal never ruined anyone in Hollywood," I protested. "I mean, scandal almost seems to be the name of the game."

"Not if you're trying to raise money. It may up

your visibility level and get you in the tabloids, which can sometimes be a good thing. But with some awful criminal charge hanging over him, Stan would never be able to raise the money for this next production. He might even have wound up in prison! You know how Hollywood is. They attack like barracudas if you're down."

"And if Stan went down . . . you went down with him."

"I couldn't let Michelle destroy my position as wife of one of Hollywood's important producers. You can see that, can't you?"

She peered at me in the growing darkness. She sounded righteous and a bit anxious, as if it were important that I understand. I even saw her point. If her husband lost his powerful position, she had no Hollywood standing of her own. No getting by with umbrella-to-the-derriere pranks. No invitations to A-list parties. No making some Hollywood underling accept her eyelash in his drink. No access to designer daisy outfits. The prestige and power for herself were why she'd put up with the Stan Man's infidelities over the years, why she'd protect him even if she had to murder twice to do it.

Three times, if I weren't careful. *Lord, help me now. Get me out of here!*

Chapter Thirty-One

I had Mrs. Steffan's confidence, however. She thought she'd bought me with a movie career.

"This accident of Stan's, how did Michelle know about it?" I asked. I knew I was pressing my luck asking for more information, but I needed to know more, and I figured I could outrun her to my limo if I had to.

"She was with him. Stan drank a bit in those days, which he was doing that night. Now he has ulcer problems and can't touch liquor." She sounded pleased, though whether it was because he had to stay away from liquor or simply because he had an ulcer, I wasn't certain.

"The person he hit was a stranger, someone standing along the road?"

"No, she was one of those little hussy starlets, and it was near the studio where they were filming *Big Storm Brewing*."

"When was this?"

"Oh, a year or so before Michelle married—" She broke off and eyed me suspiciously. "Why are you asking all these questions?"

"Just curious about Michelle." I tried to distance myself from the questions. "So, I'll talk to you again later about my future in Hollywood.

Thank you so much!" I took a step toward leaving.

"But you aren't asking about Michelle. You're asking about *Stan*."

I couldn't think of any quick response to that. She moved a step closer. "You have no intention of living up to our agreement, do you? You're just pumping me for information so you can turn us both in! I don't think I like you so much after all."

A low popularity rating with Mrs. Steffan had implications more dangerous than missing an A-list party.

Okay, I reasoned to calm myself, she's feeling murderous. But how can she do it? No knife or gun. Poison was too slow for the situation. I didn't see any canned vegetables she could clobber me with. We were on the bottom step of the front stairs now. I wasn't going to fall to my death if she pushed me. I'd just walk away. *Run away.*

But I'd forgotten Fitz's little axiom. *A killer can always find a weapon. They make do.*

Mrs. Steffan made do. She grabbed my fallen purse and snapped the long leather strap between her hands, a deadly gleam in her eyes. I shoved, about as effective as shoving a flowered refrigerator, but it momentarily tipped her off balance. I jerked away, stumbled, and went to my knees on the concrete. She was right behind me.

The leather strap hit my back as she tried to wrap it around my neck. I whammed my elbow backwards. I don't know what I hit, but it felt fleshy, and she gave an *oof.*

Lord, help me! I never had any ambitions toward being a lady wrestler!

We weren't even in the same weight class. If she got me down, I was a goner.

Then I spotted my means of escape. Pam's skateboard, abandoned when she was arrested, still leaning against the curb just a few feet away! I lunged and snatched up the skateboard, flung it to the concrete, and shoved off.

Away I went, hurtling down the sloped driveway. Yes! Beyond the gate, I'd hide in the heavy brush alongside the road. It was almost dark now. Mrs. Steffan would never find me.

I gained speed as I swooped down the hill away from her. Pam would be proud of me. Faster than I'd ever gone before. Such speed! Such grace! I could do ollies or kickflips or jump the inlet if I had to. The skateboard and I were one!

Not quite.

My mistake was not following Pam's instructions. I didn't keep my eyes to the front. I looked back to see where Mrs. Steffan was, if she was coming after me.

And *c-r-a-a-c-k!* I rammed the curb at the edge of the concrete driveway. My speed and grace collided with concrete and gravity. The skateboard momentarily stopped. I didn't. I hurtled over curb and grass. Flying, tumbling, seeing the world in a whirling kaleidoscope of grass and sky. Crashing! Skidding on damp grass, spinning, somersaulting, stopping only when I smashed into something hard and solid and unmoving. A final insult to my downfall from speed and grace came when I looked up just in time to see the skateboard following me like a guided missile and then—

Clunk.

I missed a few moments there, but a deluge of water brought me back. A cloudburst! A flood! I blinked and shook my head, dizzy and disoriented as I came up on my elbows. I had the peculiar feeling I'd been cheated, that I was entitled to at least a few minutes of unconsciousness here. Instead water rained down on me like a shower gone amok, a veritable tempest of it. I was already lying in a puddle.

Which was the least of my troubles, I realized, even as I identified the fountain of water as coming from the pipe below the water faucet stand I'd crashed into and broken.

Far bigger was the other problem. Which was Mrs. Steffan, roaring down the hill after me like a flowered tank.

Okay, I was halfway to the gate. I'd just get to my feet—

Except that my feet bones didn't seem connected to my leg bones, and I floundered in the grass. I wiped wet hair out of my eyes and peered up the hill again.

Mrs. Steffan was still coming, dragging my purse at the end of the now broken strap as if it were some recalcitrant pet.

I belly-scrambled sideways frantically looking for something with which to defend myself. *A killer can always find a weapon. . . .*

But I'm not a killer—

I grabbed the only item available as she bore down on me. I staggered to my feet. My motion when she arrived was neither pretty nor speedy, and graceful it was not. But it was effective.

The jolt shook my teeth and rattled my bones when the skateboard connected. But it did even more to Mrs. Steffan. She went down like a bag of bricks.

I stumbled toward her. I didn't want to kill her! "Mrs. Steffan? Mrs. Steffan, are you all right?" I shook her shoulder frantically, but she was rag-doll limp.

No response, but my fingers on her throat found a pulse. Unconscious but not dead.

Okay, this was a good situation.

I ran back up the hill and found my cell phone where she'd dumped it on the steps. Then, afraid she'd regain consciousness and come after me again, I ran back to her. I straddled her back and dialed 911. The woman said they'd send someone right away. I asked, if it was possible, to send Detective Molino.

"That isn't how we usually handle things—"

"Tell him I have a murderer for him."

But Mrs. Steffan was surely going to regain consciousness before anyone got here. What then? She'd buck me off like a rodeo bronc. Then she'd have a variety of weapons to choose from. The skateboard. The purse strap. Maybe just squashing me.

I used my teeth to start a tear at the hem of my blouse, then ripped a strip free. I pulled her arms around behind her and tied her wrists. Then, for good measure, I reversed my straddled position, tore off more strips of blouse, and tied her ankles.

She came to while I was doing that and started struggling. I felt as if she might buck me off even if she was hogtied. She paused, her body suddenly rigid.

"Andi, is that you sitting on my back?"

"I'm sorry, but I'm, uh, going to have to stay here until Detective Molino arrives."

Then, her voice a little muffled because she apparently had a mouthful of wet grass, she said, "This is all a terrible mistake."

My worse-for-wear purse lay near us. I grabbed it and put it under her head so her face wouldn't be in wet grass and mud. The broken pipe had stopped making like a fountain, but it still burbled with incongruous merriness.

"I don't think it's any mistake. It was *you* Michelle was afraid of all along, wasn't it?"

"Actually, I kind of . . . invented that afraid thing."

And I'd swallowed her whole diversionary tactic. "Your husband said you stayed on to help in the investigation. But it was really to try to find the evidence Michelle had against him, wasn't it? Does he know you killed her?"

"We never talked about it, but I suppose he does. At the beginning, he really thought Uri did it. Actually, we can still make that work, you know."

She sounded so calm, so rational, which in its way was just as scary as her earlier fury. Because it was in this calm, normal-appearing state that she had planned her murders.

"The movie career thing? Thank you, no. I'm really quite happy driving my limo."

I stared disbelievingly as a furry figure peeked out from behind the remnant of the ice sculpture. Phreddie!

"Here, kitty, kitty!" I called. He sat down by the ice blob and looked at me, only mildly interested. Okay, maybe some cats do know their names and don't like the generic approach. "Here, Phreddie, Phreddie!"

He trotted over and rubbed his head on my leg.

"What's happening?" Mrs. Steffan demanded. "Is it the cat? Oh, I'm glad. I was worried about him."

She's willing to strangle me, but she's worried about a missing cat. Psychotic? Unbalanced? Mental problems?

Whatever it was, Mrs. Steffan was a dangerous woman.

I scooped him up in my arms. "Pam has been so worried about you," I scolded.

Sirens blared in the distance. "Hold on, Phreddie." I squeezed him tighter. "We'll have Pam home shortly."

"I like the cat, but I wouldn't count on Pam coming back to him anytime soon."

Something in Mrs. Steffan's smug tone rattled my nerves. Someone who is flat on her belly and hogtied shouldn't feel *smug*.

"What do you mean?"

"It's your word against mine. I'll deny whatever you say and point out that you're just making a desperate, misguided attempt to make your little friend Pam look innocent. There's not a smidgen of actual evidence anywhere against me."

I set Phreddie on the ground, dismayed with the probable truth of that statement. "But when I tell them what I know, they'll find evidence." That had a hollow ring, even to my own ears.

"That detective will never believe you. And

you know what? I'm remembering now that it was *Pam* that Michelle said she was afraid of. No need to involve Uri and Cindy. Pam will do just fine. You'll wind up looking like a sentimental old lady making up ridiculous stories."

A police car barreled through the open gate. A deputy jumped out one side, Detective Molino the other.

Mrs. Steffan beat me to the punch. "Thank heaven you're here!" she called.

Detective Molino and the deputy ran to us, then stopped short when I yelled, "Hey, you're scaring Phreddie off again!"

Phreddie took off for the woods in rocket mode.

"I don't know what's wrong with this insane woman!" Mrs. Steffan struggled with my knotted shreds of blouse. "Get her away from me! First she tried to kill me with a monstrous slab of something, and then she tied me up! And now she keeps talking about a cat."

"Don't believe her. I hit her with the skateboard because she was trying to strangle me with my purse strap! She's dangerous!"

"Do I look dangerous?" Mrs. Steffan scoffed.

I had to admit she had a point there. A hogtied, daisy-clad, not-young lady lacks the element of danger obvious in, say, a deranged killer brandishing a broken beer bottle.

"That's the problem!" I argued. "She doesn't

look dangerous. But she is. She killed Michelle and Shirley too—"

"Andi, I know you're trying to protect Pam, and I admire that. But it isn't fair to try to blame me for what she did." Even with her face in my purse, Mrs. Steffan managed to sound both coherent and reproachful. "You were going to kill me, and then blame the murders on me too."

Had Alice Steffan been an actress in her younger years? Because she was doing a great job here. "Look, would I have called you if I were trying to kill her?" I asked Detective Molino. "She killed Michelle and Shirley!"

Detective Molino surveyed the scene as if he couldn't quite believe what he had here, which was two old ladies . . . one with belly button exposed below ragged end of blouse . . . accusing each other of murder and assault.

"Is anybody hurt here?" he finally asked.

I eased off the middle of Mrs. Steffan's back. "I guess I'm okay." A little worse for wear, but ambulatory.

"I'm not! I think I have a concussion where she hit me! My vision is going! I'm sick to my stomach!"

"I'll call an ambulance," Detective Molino said.

He untied Mrs. Steffan while we waited for the ambulance. He tried to untie her, that is. But even with the aid of the powerful beam of a police flashlight, my knots proved impenetrable.

The other deputy finally pulled out a pocketknife and slashed through the tangled strips of blouse.

The ambulance came and removed Mrs. Steffan, who groaned convincingly. Although I had to admit I'd whacked her pretty hard. Detective Molino told the EMTs he'd be at the hospital shortly.

"To arrest her?" I asked.

"Arrest *her!*" Mrs. Steffan yelled in parting. "She tried to kill me. Now she's trying to frame me!"

The ambulance zoomed away, although this apparently wasn't emergency enough to require siren or flashing lights.

"She did kill both Michelle and Shirley," I said, embarrassed that my voice sounded so quavery. "She admitted it to me."

"There's evidence to back this up?"

"No, but—" In a rush I explained about the Stan Man's hit-and-run and how Michelle had tried to blackmail her way into his movie with this information, so Mrs. Steffan killed both her and Shirley. "And then Mrs. Steffan was so desperate she tried to use a movie career to bribe me into framing Uri!"

"You didn't believe her?"

"Do I look like movie star material?"

Detective Molino was gentleman enough not to state the obvious answer to that question.

"And even if she could get me in the movies, I'd

never have gone along with her. She's a *murderer*."

Again he asked, "You have evidence of this?"

"No, but somewhere Michelle has evidence about the hit-and-run that she intended to use to blackmail Stan Steffan. Which is why Mrs. Steffan killed Michelle."

His expression was unconvinced, but he said, "Maybe I'll see if we can get another search warrant."

"Good. In the meantime, I'll just go find Phreddie again."

"No, in the meantime, Ms. McConnell, I'm afraid you're under arrest."

"Arrest?"

He nodded toward the skateboard. "For assault with a—" He eyed the skateboard as if undecided what to call it, since it wouldn't normally be described as a deadly weapon.

"It was self-defense!"

"We'll see."

Chapter Thirty-Two

I wouldn't recommend a night in jail. Hard bed, hard walls, hard floor. Bad smells, resident mouse, and anonymous snores from down the hall. But it had one thing going for it: plenty of time for prayer.

Also, because the county has limited space for women, only two cells to be exact, I wound up bunking with Pam.

"Andi!" she cried, when they put me in the cell. "They let you in to visit me? Did you find Phreddie?"

"I found him for a minute. He ran off again, but he's okay. We'll find him again."

The jail deputy locked the door behind me, and it got through to Pam then that we were in these chic matching outfits. "They make you wear one of these jumpsuits just to visit?"

"I'm here just like you. Incarcerated."

"They charged you with murder too?" she gasped.

"No. Just assault."

"Who did you assault?" She sounded bewildered.

"I didn't assault anyone," I said indignantly. "I was defending myself against Mrs. Steffan."

"What did she do? Attack you with a flowered earring?"

"Whose side are you on here?"

"Sorry." She patted my shoulder guiltily. "She just doesn't seem like the attacking type."

"She is. She's also the killing type. She killed Michelle and Shirley, and she was going to strangle me with my own purse strap."

"*Mrs. Steffan?* But I thought Uri and Cindy—"

"We were wrong."

"Mrs. Steffan confessed?"

404

"She admitted to me she'd done it, but then she denied everything to Detective Molino. She's in the hospital now."

"I feel as if I walked into the middle of a movie and can't figure out what's going on," Pam grumbled. "A very bad movie," she added.

"Mrs. Steffan also offered me a chance at a movie career."

"So you assaulted her?"

"I told you, it was self-defense!"

"So what did you self-defend her with?"

"Your skateboard."

"You were out joyriding on the skateboard and accidentally ran into her?"

"No. She came after me, so I picked it up and clobbered her."

"But that's a Zero American Punk board! The best one I've ever had! Is it okay?"

"It survived."

Then she realized what she'd said. "I'm sorry. That was awful, wasn't it? Asking about the board, instead of Mrs. Steffan. How is she?"

"She claims I gave her a concussion and ruined her vision. Probably gave her dandruff and dented her personality too, although she hasn't brought that up yet. I don't think she's really all that badly injured. Not from the way she was yelling when they hauled her away. She's a tough old bird."

Then it was lights-out time, so I had to whisper

405

in the semi-darkness to explain about Stan Steffan's hit-and-run, Michelle's blackmail scheme, Mrs. Steffan as a double murderer, and my short-lived chance at movie stardom.

"You'd think, if Michelle had something incriminating about Stan Steffan, that it would have been in the safe," I whispered.

"But it wasn't. Maybe she was bluffing and never really had anything."

"Mrs. Steffan was convinced she did."

Which didn't necessarily mean it would ever turn up. Which then meant Pam might . . . no, I didn't want to go there.

"I've been using my prayer line to God," Pam muttered. "Having you arrested was not what I was praying for."

Me, neither, come to think of it. All I could think of now was, "God works in mysterious ways."

"Which doesn't really explain anything," she said.

"But also explains everything."

That took a moment to sink in. She finally smiled slightly. "Yeah, I guess it does. And we're supposed to just keep praying, no matter what?"

"No matter what, just keep praying."

So that's what we did. Except sometimes we giggled too. Or shed a few tears. And sometimes did both at the same time.

It's a strange feeling, we who've been free all our lives, to realize that we are not free now, that we are actually *locked up*. Helpless. Once claustrophobia closed in on me. I felt the walls creeping in, the ceiling lowering and the floor rising to squash me between them. I felt rumbles of an earthquake trapping us under iron bars and crumbled concrete. I pictured a virus wiping out the population, sparing us, but leaving us here to molder alone and helpless.

Then I squeezed my eyes shut and opened that prayer line to God again, and He was there. It was a time like when the baby was born in my limo. God was with me, real and powerful and comforting. In control. Not saying He'd get me out of this, just verifying the eternal promise that He'd never leave me or abandon me. Pushing the walls and ceiling back, shutting off a coming shriek of panic, calming my terror.

I felt my soul floating free even if my body wasn't.

Thank You, Lord.

He also worked in a mysterious way that night, because Pam woke me up around 4:00 A.M. and whispered, "Something you said made me think of something."

"I didn't say anything," I muttered groggily. "I'm sleeping. Or at least I was."

"It was what you said earlier," Pam said. "That Michelle's evidence against Stan Steffan should have been in the safe, but it wasn't. I think there may be *another* safe."

• • •

Breakfast came early. Oatmeal or Superglue, I wasn't sure which. Afterward, I expected to be arraigned or whatever the legal procedure was that came next, but about ten-thirty the jail keeper and Detective Molino showed up at the cell door.

"You're free to go," Detective Molino said as the other deputy unlocked the door. "Mrs. Steffan says now that it was all a big misunderstanding. She says she realizes now that you weren't assaulting her, that you really thought you needed to defend yourself because you mistakenly believed she was trying to strangle you. She apologizes. We decided to drop the assault charge."

I was both puzzled and amazed. Grateful too, but a bit wary. What made her change her mind?

"Sorry about the night in jail," Detective Molino added.

"It's a strong deterrent, in case I was ever tempted to take up bank robbing or gun smuggling with the limo."

"Good."

"But what about Pam? Isn't she free too?" I asked in dismay as the door clanged shut behind me.

"The charges against Pam have nothing to do with Mrs. Steffan."

I looked back at Pam holding on to the iron

bars of the cell. In the orange jail outfit, she looked fifteen again. Scared and abandoned.

"Pam, I'm sorry. I—"

"I'll be okay. I'm using my special line to you-know-where." She managed a smile, but she was also blinking back tears.

"Should I bring the guests back to the house from the inn?"

"Whatever you think best. You're in charge."

Detective Molino took me back out to the house. The day was sunny and crisp. Boats zipped up and down the inlet. I wondered briefly if all those people appreciated their glorious freedom. I knew I'd never take mine for granted again. He pulled the cruiser up behind my limo at the house.

The reason behind Mrs. Steffan's generosity suddenly slammed me. "How long will Mrs. Steffan be in the hospital?"

"She'll be released later today."

"Not charged with anything?"

"No."

Mrs. Steffan had figured out that if I was locked up in jail, she couldn't get to me—and she had every intention of getting to me. Murder #3 was on the agenda. What creative weapon would she come up with this time?

"Are you interested in the possibility Michelle was killed because she was trying to blackmail the Steffans?"

"I might be."

I told him what Pam had said last night, that she remembered a safe and lock company van at the house one summer. She'd thought at the time they were doing something with the safe that was already in the office, but she thought now they may have been installing another one. Probably in Michelle's room.

"I can make a note of that when we get a search warrant."

"Pam put me in charge here. You heard her yourself. You don't need a search warrant. I can give you permission to search."

He looked momentarily undecided about that, but then nodded. So together we searched, and we indeed found another safe, hidden in the floor under the boxes stacked in Michelle's walk-in closet. A very securely locked safe, however, and no helpful Shirley to provide the combination.

I felt frustrated and let down. The safe might still provide information, but it would take time. Time while Pam languished in jail.

We were just leaving the house when a taxi drove up. Stan Steffan got out.

"My wife said the car we rented was still out here, so I came to get it."

"She gave us all the information we need about your hit-and-run, you know," I said impulsively. "That the victim was that starlet in *Big Storm*

Brewing, where it happened, what car you were driving, everything."

Mr. Steffan looked stunned, and I took a second wild stab. "Which is why you killed Michelle, because she was blackmailing you!"

"Ms. McConnell!" Detective Molino protested, horrified at my leap into conjecture. And into his legal domain.

"She's trying to pin Michelle's murder on me?" Stan Steffan growled. "No way!"

I started to protest that the conjecture about his being the murderer was mine, not what his wife had said, but he didn't give me a chance.

"*She* killed Michelle," he said. "And that housekeeper too!"

In spite of his shock with me, Detective Molino jumped on that. "You'll testify to that?"

Mr. Steffan hesitated. Sweat beaded his forehead. He wiped a hand on his pants leg. But then he shoved his sunglasses firmly back against his nose and backtracked. "You can't force me to testify against my wife."

"Okay, we'll get the details about your hit-and-run from Michelle's safe, and then we can file charges against you for that."

Mr. Steffan did not now look so scornful of the capabilities of "small-town cops."

"I want to see my lawyer," he growled, which seemed to be his normal manner of speaking.

"Mrs. Steffan's lawyer?" Detective Molino asked.

"No, *my* lawyer."

And the Hollywood Wars were on.

The Wars were still raging four days later when charges against Pam were dropped, and she was released. Accusations and counter accusations flew back and forth between the Steffans and their lawyers. By then the safe had been opened, and Detective Molino had the details about the hit-and-run that Michelle had so carefully preserved.

Joe and Phyllis Forsythe had at the last minute changed their minds about the graveside services, so Pam and I both attended when it was held a few days later. It was small and tasteful, and we both shed a few honest tears.

In spite of the accusations and counter accusations, the prosecutor charged Mrs. Steffan alone with the murders. A trial is scheduled for later in the year, at which I will apparently be a star witness.

Stan Steffan has his own problems down in California with charges against him on the hit-and-run death.

I was back home in my duplex now, the limo business doing nicely. I didn't know my new renter well yet. She still wore motorcycle boots under her muu-muus, but she liked weeding the daisy beds, mowing the lawn, and feeding the birds, so I really wouldn't care if she wore snowshoes and a bikini.

Change Your World opened with much fanfare, though the limo and I weren't included. Cindy and Uri posed with the Uri-Blaster for a photo that showed up in half a dozen newspapers. Both were photogenic in leopard-skin Spandex. They announced a free exercise program for children. I figured they were feeling a little guilty about the insurance money, even though they hadn't actually done anything dishonest or unethical to acquire it.

Detective Molino had notified Shirley's family of her death, and her body was shipped to Texas for burial. I sent her granddaughter a card and letter, telling her the good things I knew about Shirley.

Mike arranged Pam's luggage in the trunk, then we all climbed into the limo. Fitz in the passenger's seat beside me, Pam and Mike holding hands in back, Phreddie jumping back and forth through the open divider like a furry gymnast. He had his own special bed on the console between the front seats, probably the only cat in the world with a limousine bed consisting of half of a $24,000 wedding gown. The other half of the gown was his bed back at my duplex.

The late September sun shone gloriously

golden. Pam would be a few days late getting to the fall quarter at college, but they were letting her in anyway.

She had not changed her mind about being finished with mysteries. She'd be continuing her studies in math. That night in jail we'd talked about her parents' deaths, and we'd prayed about that too, and she'd put it behind her.

Today we were taking her to Sea-Tac for the flight back to Dartmouth. The Bug was at Mike's place. He'd whispered to me that this winter, when business was slow, he'd give it a new coat of paint. Pam and Mike's relationship was solid, but they'd wisely decided to give it more time before marrying.

Pam didn't look back as the electronic gate closed behind us. Some details of the will were still up in the air, including ownership of the house, but Pam and Sterling had agreed to sell it and split the proceeds.

Pam got her grandmother's pearls.

She'd had her eyebrows professionally plucked again. She looked great.

We were all rather quiet on the drive. At the airport, I let Mike and Pam out, with her luggage. Fitz and Phreddie and I would wait for him out in the parking area.

Pam gave me a final hug. "You've been a wonderful friend, Andi. A great limo driver. And a fantastic sleuth."

I gave her the same advice I'd give my own granddaughter. "You study hard. Be careful on that skateboard. And think about the 'God stuff.'"

"I don't think I'll ever come up with a mathematical equation that proves God exists. But I don't have to, because I'm pretty sure He does."

Step number one! *Guide her, Lord, help her to take that next step and come to know You personally.*

And me?

I have an intriguing new renter in my duplex. I have an affectionate new cat sharing my home. I have a great, also rather affectionate guy sharing my life. And I have a faith that's growing day by day.

God is good!

Center Point Publishing
600 Brooks Road ● PO Box 1
Thorndike ME 04986-0001 USA

(207) 568-3717

US & Canada:
1 800 929-9108
www.centerpointlargeprint.com